THE
OBSIDIAN
TOWER

Rooks and Ruin:
Book One

MELISSA CARUSO

www.orbitbooks.net

ORBIT

First published in Great Britain in 2020 by Orbit

13 5 7 9 10 8 6 4 2

Copyright © 2020 by Melissa Caruso

Map by Tim Paul

Excerpt from *There Will Come a Darkness* by Katy Rose Pool
Copyright © 2019 by Katy Pool

The moral right of the author has been asserted.

A CIP catalogue record for this book
is available from the British Library.

ISBN 978-0-356-51319-5

Printed and bound in Great Britain by Clays Ltd, Elcograf S.p.A.

Papers used by Orbit are from well-managed forests
and other responsible sources.

Orbit
An imprint of
Little, Brown Book Group
Carmelite House
50 Victoria Embankment
London EC4Y 0DZ

An Hachette UK Company
www.hachette.co.uk

www.orbitbooks.net

To my brother Dave
An excellent companion on many adventures
And a great teacher

Give no cunning voices heed
Make no bargains born of greed
Only this and nothing more:
Nothing must unseal the Door.

Blood endures through ages long
Build the castle high and strong
Keep your secret, guard your lore:
Nothing must unseal the Door.

Guard the tower, ward the stone
Find your answers writ in bone
Keep your trust through wits or war:
Nothing must unseal the Door.

ONE

There are two kinds of magic.

There is the kind that lifts you up and fills you with wonder, saving you when all is lost or opening doors to new worlds of possibility. And there is the kind that wrecks you, that shatters you, bitter in your mouth and jagged in your hand, breaking everything you touch.

Mine was the second kind.

My father's magic could revive blighted fields, turning them lush and green again, and coax apples from barren boughs in the dead of winter. Grass withered beneath my footsteps. My cousins kept the flocks in their villages healthy and strong, and turned the wolves away to hunt elsewhere; I couldn't enter the stables of my own castle without bringing mortal danger to the horses.

I should have been like the others. Ours was a line of royal vivomancers; life magic flowed in our veins, ancient as the rain that washed down from the hills and nurtured the green valleys of Morgrain. My grandmother was the immortal Witch Lord of Morgrain, the Lady of Owls herself, whose magic coursed so deep through her domain that she could feel the step of every rabbit and the fall of every leaf. And I was Exalted Ryxander, a royal atheling, inheritor of an echo of my grandmother's profound connection to the land and her magical power. Except that I was also Ryx, the family embarrassment, with magic so twisted it was unusably dangerous.

The rest of my family had their place in the cycle, weavers of a great pattern. I'd been born to snarl things up—or more like it, to break the loom and set the tapestry on fire, given my luck.

So I'd made my own place.

At the moment, that place was on the castle roof. One gloved hand clamped onto the delicate bone-carved railing of a nearby balcony for balance, to keep my boots from skidding on the sharply angled shale; the other held the wind-whipped tendrils of dark hair that had escaped my braid back from my face.

"This is a disaster," I muttered.

"I don't see any reason it needs to be, Exalted Warden." Odan, the castle steward—a compact and muscular old man with an extravagant mustache—stood with unruffled dignity on the balcony beside me. I'd clambered over its railing to make room for him, since I couldn't safely share a space that small. "We still have time to prepare guest quarters and make room in the stables."

"That's not the problem. No so-called diplomat arrives a full day early without warning unless they're up to trouble." I glared down at the puffs of dust rising from the northern trade road. Distance obscured the details, but I made out at least thirty riders accompanying the Alevaran envoy's carriage. "And that's too large an escort. They said they were bringing a dozen."

Odan's bristly gray brows descended the broad dome of his forehead. "It's true that I wouldn't expect an ambassador to take so much trouble to be rude."

"They wouldn't. Not if they were planning to negotiate in good faith." And that was what made this a far more serious issue than the mere inconvenience of an early guest. "The Shrike Lord of Alevar is playing games."

Odan blew a breath through his mustache. "Reckless of him, given the fleet of imperial warships sitting off his coast."

"Rather." I hunkered down close to the slate to get under the chill edge that had come into the wind in the past few days, heralding the end of summer. "I worked hard to set up these talks between Alevar and the Serene Empire. What in the Nine Hells is he trying to accomplish?"

The line of riders drew closer along the gray strip of road that wound between bright green farms and swaths of dark forest, approaching the grassy sun-mottled hill that lifted Gloamingard Castle toward a banner-blue sky. The sun winked off the silver-tipped antlers of six proud stags drawing the carriage, a clear announcement that the coach's occupant could bend wildlife to their will—displaying magic in the same way a dignitary of the Serene Empire of Raverra to the south might display wealth, as a sign of status and power.

Another gleam caught my eye, however: the metallic flash of sabers and muskets.

"Pox," I swore. "Those are all soldiers."

Odan scowled down at them. "I'm no diplomat like you, Warden, but it does seem odd to bring an armed platoon to sign a peace treaty."

I almost retorted that I wasn't a diplomat, either. But it was as good a word as any for the role I'd carved out for myself.

Diplomacy wasn't part of a Warden's job. Wardens were mages; it was their duty to use their magic to nurture and sustain life in the area they protected. But my broken magic couldn't nurture. It only destroyed. When my grandmother followed family tradition and named me the Warden of Gloamingard Castle—her own seat of power—on my sixteenth birthday, it had seemed like a cruel joke.

I'd found other ways. If I couldn't increase the bounty of the crops or the health of the flocks with life magic, I could use my Raverran mother's connections to the Serene Empire to enrich our domain with favorable trade agreements. If I couldn't protect Morgrain by rousing the land against bandits or invaders, I could cultivate good relations with Raverra, securing my domain a powerful ally. I'd spent the past five years building that relationship, despite muttering from traditionalists in the family about being too friendly with a nation we'd warred with countless times in centuries past.

I'd done such a good job, in fact, that the Serene Empire had agreed to accept our mediation of an incident with Alevar that threatened to escalate into war.

"I can't let them sabotage these negotiations before they've even started." It wasn't simply a matter of pride; Morgrain lay directly between Alevar and the Serene Empire. If the Shrike Lord wanted to attack the Empire, he'd have to go through us.

The disapproving gaze Odan dropped downhill at the Alevarans could have frozen a lake. "How should we greet them, Warden?"

My gloved fingers dug against the unyielding slate beneath me. "Form an honor guard from some of our nastiest-looking battle chimeras to welcome them. If they're going to make a show of force, we have to answer it." That was Vaskandran politics, all display and spectacle—a stark contrast to the subtle, hidden machinations of Raverrans.

Odan nodded. "Very good, Warden. Anything else?"

The Raverran envoy would arrive tomorrow with a double handful of clerks and advisers, prepared to sit down at a table and speak in a genteel fashion about peace, to find my castle already overrun with a bristling military presence of Alevaran soldiers. That would create a terrible first impression—especially since Alevar and Morgrain were both domains of the great nation of Vaskandar, the Empire's historical enemy. I bit my lip a moment, thinking.

"Quarter no more than a dozen of their escort in the castle," I said at last. "Put the rest in outbuildings or in the town. If the envoy raises a fuss, tell them it's because they arrived so early and increased their party size without warning."

A smile twitched the corners of Odan's mustache. "I like it. And what will you do, Exalted Warden?"

I rose, dusting roof grit from my fine embroidered vestcoat, and tugged my thin leather gloves into place. "I'll prepare to meet this envoy. I want to see if they're deliberately making trouble, or if they're just bad at their job."

Gloamingard was really several castles caught in the act of devouring each other. *Build the castle high and strong*, the Gloaming Lore said, and each successive ruler had taken that as license to impose their own architectural fancies upon the place. The Black Tower reared up stark and ominous at the center, more ancient than the country of Vaskandar itself; an old stone keep surrounded it, buried in fantastical additions woven of living trees and vines. The stark curving ribs of the Bone Palace clawed at the sky on one side, and the perpetual scent of woodsmoke bathed the sharp-peaked roofs of the Great Lodge on the other; my grandmother's predecessor had attempted to build a comfortable wood-paneled manor house smack in the front and center. Each new Witch Lord had run roughshod over the building plans of those who came before them, and the whole place was a glorious mess of hidden doors and dead-end staircases and windows opening onto blank walls.

This made the castle a confusing maze for visitors, but for me, it was perfect. I could navigate through the odd, leftover spaces and closed-off areas, keeping away from the main halls with their deadly risk of bumping into a sprinting page or distracted servant. I haunted my own castle like a ghost.

As I headed toward the Birch Gate to meet the Alevaran envoy, I opened a door in the back of a storage cabinet beneath a little-used stairway, hurried through a dim and dusty space between walls, and came out in a forgotten gallery under a latticework of artistically woven tree roots and stained glass. At the far end, a string of grinning animal faces adorned an arch of twisted wood; an unrolling scroll carved beneath them warned me to *Give No Cunning Voices Heed*. It was a bit of the Gloaming Lore, the old family wisdom passed down through the centuries in verse. Generations of mages had scribed pieces of it into every odd corner of Gloamingard.

I climbed through a window into the dusty old stone keep, which was half fallen to ruin. My grandmother had sealed the main door with thick thorny vines when she became the Witch Lord a hundred and forty years ago; sunbeams fell through holes in the roof onto damp, mossy walls. It still made for a good alternate route across the castle. I hurried down a dim, dust-choked hallway, taking advantage of the lack of people to move a little faster than I normally dared.

Yet I couldn't help slowing almost to a stop when I came to the Door.

It loomed all the way to the ceiling of its deep-set alcove, a flat shining rectangle of polished obsidian. Carved deep into its surface in smooth, precise lines was a circular seal, complex with runes and geometric patterns.

The air around it hung thick with power. The pressure of it made my pulse sound in my ears, a surging dull roar. A thrill of dread trickled down my spine, never mind that I'd passed it countless times.

It was the monster of my childhood stories, the haunt of my

nightmares, the ominous crux of all the Gloaming Lore. Carved through the castle again and again, above windows and under crests, set into floors and wound about pillars, the same words appeared over and over. It was the chorus of the rhyme we learned in the cradle, recited at our adulthood ceremonies, and whispered on our deathbeds: *Nothing must unseal the Door.*

No one knew what lay in the Black Tower, but this was its sole entrance. And every time I walked past it, despite the unsettling aura of power that hung about it like a long bass note too low to hear, despite the warnings drilled into me since birth and scribed all over Gloamingard, curiosity prickled awake in my mind.

I wanted to open it—anyone would. But I wasn't stupid. I kept going, a shiver skimming across my shoulders.

I climbed through another window and came out in the Hall of Chimes, a long corridor hung with swaying strands of white-bleached bones that clattered hollowly in a breeze channeled through cleverly placed windows. The Mantis Lord—my grandmother's grandmother's grandfather—had built the Bone Palace, and he'd apparently had rather morbid taste.

This wasn't some forgotten space entombed by newer construction; I might encounter other people here. I dropped my pace to a brisk walk and kept to the right. On the opposite side of the hall, a slim tendril of leafy vine ran along the floor, dotted irregularly with tiny pale purple flowers. It was a reminder to everyone besides me who lived or worked in the castle to stay to that side, the safe side—life to life. I strained my atheling's sense to its limit, aware of every spider nestled in a dusty corner, ready to slow down the second I detected anyone approaching. Bones clacked overhead as I strode through the hall; I wanted to get to the Birch Gate in time to make certain everything was in place to both welcome and warn the envoy.

I rounded a corner too fast and found myself staring into a pair of widening brown eyes. A dark-haired young woman hurried toward me with a tray of meat buns, nearly in arm's reach, on the wrong side of the corridor.

My side. Death's side.

Too close to stop before I ran into her.

TWO

I desperately flung myself away from the woman, obscenities spilling from my mouth in pure terror. Every piece of me was a deadly weapon I had to redirect: knees and feet and the arms that instinctively windmilled for balance. *No*, too near her face, *NO*—

My outflung hand hit her earthenware tray, knocking it from her grasp; it was the final push I needed to throw myself aside to the hard floor. The woman yelped, pottery crashed, and meat pies rained down all around me.

I hadn't touched her. She was alive.

Except that I couldn't sense her. I should have felt her heartbeat. This close, her life should have been a warm light in my mind. There was nothing.

"Oh! I'm so sorry! Let me help you—" She reached toward me, brows furrowing in concern.

I scrambled away on the floor, crabwise, my heart still thundering in my chest. "Don't!" I cried. "Stay back!"

She stood, hand still half-extended, meat pies scattered amid shards of pottery at her feet. "Are you all right?"

I lurched upright, stepping away to open more distance between us. A stray chunk of earthenware crunched under my heel. All I could think of was how close I'd come to killing her.

"Didn't anyone warn you? Why were you on the wrong side?" Her brow creased; I wasn't making any sense, every nerve still jangling. The fear that should have harrowed her face was missing. How could she not know about me?

Unless... "You're not from Morgrain."

That was why I hadn't sensed her before I saw her. My inherited link to the land let me feel the presence of Morgrain-born lives close by, but I had no magical connection to outsiders. And while she looked Vaskandran, the wide bands of colorfully embroidered trim on her crimson vestcoat, along with her golden-brown skin and thick black hair, suggested the lowland domains rather than the gray, pale hill folk of Morgrain.

I'd relied too much on my magical perceptions, allowed myself to get distracted and lazy, and almost killed someone. Again.

My legs trembled beneath me, threatening to dump me on the floor.

The woman smoothed the confusion from her face and dipped a quick bow. "Yes. I'm Kessa, with the troupe of traveling players who arrived this morning. The Foxglove Theater Company; finest in Vaskandar, if I do say so myself. I was trying to bring these from the kitchens for the other players"—she made a grand, tragic gesture toward the fallen meat pies—"and, well, it's easy to get lost in this place."

"I'm so sorry I almost ran into you," I said, which seemed like an appalling understatement given what had nearly happened. "You should stick close to the vines with the purple flowers when you're walking around Gloamingard."

"Yes, someone mentioned that. They were terribly dramatic about it, in fact, but I thought—" Her bright brown eyes came into sharper focus on mine then, and she broke off. I knew what she was seeing: lightning-blue rings around my pupils. Realization broke over her face like a cold wave. Who knew what rumors she'd heard—and if she miraculously hadn't heard any, the staff would have been eager to warn her the moment she crossed the threshold.

Whatever you do, don't go near the Warden. If you touch her, you'll die.

She killed a man when she was four years old. They say she's cursed.

Just last summer a stable boy bumped into her, and his heart stopped for half a minute. He didn't wake up for days, and he may never be the same.

"Oh!" Kessa's eyes widened. I braced myself for the inevitable flick of fingers out from her chest in the warding sign.

But it didn't come. Instead, she dropped to her knees in one fluid movement, head bowed. "Forgive me, Exalted Atheling. I didn't notice your mage mark."

My fingertips flew up self-consciously toward my eyes. "You don't need to kneel. We don't do that here."

Kessa rose, dusting her skirts off, and flashed me a smile. "Better safe than sorry, Exalted. We travel all over Vaskandar, and every domain is different. We just came from Alevar, and if I didn't kneel to a marked mage there, they might have decorated a tree with my head."

"This isn't Alevar." Now that I knew she was safe, I was eager for her to get out of my path so I could head to the Birch Gate. "Please be careful. I don't know what you've heard, but my magic is flawed. If I touch you, you'll die."

Her eyebrows flew up. "I heard that, but I thought they were exaggerating," she admitted. "That's got to be awkward. And the gloves don't help?" She nodded toward my hands.

Sympathetic curiosity wasn't the response I was used to. The only other people outside my family who'd reacted to my power without fear or aversion were a Raverran boy I knew and Rillim, the girl I'd once had mad dreams of courting. A flush crept up my cheeks, and I found myself inexplicably staring at the way dark strands of Kessa's hair lay against her neck as she tilted her head, waiting.

I couldn't get distracted; I had too much to do.

"Through the gloves, a quick touch might not kill you out-right," I said. "Skin to skin, it's instant. Now, if you'll excuse me... Wait a minute." A few things fitted belatedly together in my mind, and I frowned. "We're not anywhere near the kitchens *or* the Old Great Hall where the players are rehearsing. You're more than a little lost."

She let out a rich, warm laugh, but something flickered in her eyes. "More lost than I thought, apparently, *and* I ruined the meat pies. My friends will never let me hear the end of it."

"There's nothing in this part of Gloamingard but the old stone keep." And the Door, with all its compelling mystery and power. "You said you came from Alevar. Did you have any deal-ings with the Shrike Lord, perchance?"

"No, Exalted." She gave a convincing little shudder. "I've heard he doesn't have much of a sense of humor—a rather grave charac-ter failing, and one often coupled with a lack of appreciation for theater."

I couldn't help the smile that tugged at my mouth. I wanted to like her—she had lovely sparkling eyes to match her wit, and an easy grin that welcomed me in on the joke. But she'd been too quick with her explanation for being here, as if she'd pre-pared it in advance. Not to mention that much as I appreciated her relaxed and friendly manner, it didn't fit for a commoner used to domains where you had to kneel to avoid a mage's ire.

If she'd been poking around near the Black Tower, it didn't matter whether I liked her. The Gloaming Lore was quite clear on our duty: *Guard the tower, ward the stone.* The magical protec-tions on the Door were powerful, but that only made tampering with it all the more dangerous.

"Did you see anything interesting, while you were wander-ing lost?" I asked, deliberately casual.

Kessa hesitated only a fraction of a second. "With respect,

Exalted, every inch of this place ranges from interesting to out-right bizarre."

A new voice spoke, low and rough as the rumble of an approaching avalanche:

"She's asking because she thinks you're a spy."

My grandmother rounded the corner, her power gathered palpably around her like a cloak of thunder.

It was always her eyes that caught me first. Blazing orange rings circled each pupil, her mage mark standing out fierce and wild from her dark irises. Everything else fell into place around them: her white crest of hair, her strong jaw and hollow cheeks, the dagger-thin length of her body honed sharp as a weapon. A pale mantle of rust-barred owl feathers cascaded in layers from her shoulders, coming to a point at the small of her back like folded wings. She was ageless and ancient, a hundred and seventy years not so much weighing on her lightly as burned to fuel some secret inner fire. The sheer force of her power made the air around her tremble.

Kessa paled and stepped back, nearly slipping on a meat pie.

"Ryx," my grandmother greeted me, "I must commend you. Your instinct for finding trouble remains flawless."

"Better to find it by spotting it than by stepping in it." I didn't add *For a change*, but it hung unspoken between us nonetheless. "Grandmother, this is Kessa. She claims she's one of the traveling players visiting the castle."

"Is she, now." My grandmother paced toward Kessa with the deadly prowl of a predator, the sheer force of her presence oppressive in the narrow corridor. "You were clever, slipping into my castle while I was distracted by another visitor. But nothing escapes an owl's notice."

She swept past me like a cold winter wind. Kessa held her ground, still and silent—though by the strain in her eyes and the trembling in the hands she laced together behind her back, she knew very well the danger she was in.

My grandmother stopped in front of her, her voice nonetheless powerful as she dropped it to a whisper. "Nothing. Not even a rook."

The full implication of what she'd said sank in. "You're not spying for Alevar," I breathed. "You're spying for the Rookery."

I didn't know much about the Rookery, only a tangle of stories and rumors probably no more accurate than the ones about me. A mysterious group with the backing of both Vaskandar and the Serene Empire, they dealt with strange and dangerous magic when it became a problem others couldn't handle. Which was all well and good, but our strange and dangerous magic was *private*.

Kessa rallied enough for a you-caught-me grimace and a graceful bow. "I'm sorry for the deception." The regret in her voice seemed genuine, her brown eyes shadowed as they met mine. She turned to my grandmother. "We weren't certain you'd receive us if we announced ourselves properly, Most Exalted."

"For good reason," my grandmother growled. "I keep my secrets close, rook. I don't allow others to come poking around in them."

"It *is* our job to investigate and deal with magical threats." Kessa ducked her head in respect, her tone calm, reasonable, soothing. "We have a responsibility to the Conclave of Witch Lords to look into rumors of dangerous artifacts, and we heard that you might have one here in Gloamingard. All we wanted to do was determine whether it poses any kind of—"

"It does not," my grandmother cut her off, sharp as a knife slash. "Your investigation is over. You and your friends may go. Pack up your things and leave Gloamingard at once."

"Most Exalted—"

"*You may go*, little rook. Do not tempt me to rescind that permission."

My grandmother's words cracked like a whip. She wasn't

angry—I'd never seen her truly angry, and I never wanted to. I didn't have nearly such good control, myself; my hands still trembled from my near miss, and it felt like a personal betrayal that the one stranger who'd been warm and friendly to me despite knowing who I was turned out to be a spy.

Kessa was apparently smart enough not to want to see my grandmother angry, either. She bowed again, so deeply the tips of her shining black hair swept the ground. "Yes, Most Exalted."

She didn't wait to be dismissed again, but she managed to not quite flee, either. She cast me one last glance, a sort of shrug and grimace mixed with a roguish smile—the kind of look that might mean *Sorry, we'll have to finish our talk later.*

I doubted I'd have much more to say to a spy. I caught half a smile on my face and twisted it into a frown at once.

My grandmother turned to me, the lines of her face softening, the aura of power around her dampening.

"Ryx," she said, her voice rich and deep, full of layered meaning as if she could comprise everything I was in that one syllable. "I actually came here to find you. Something's come up."

My stomach tightened instinctively, bracing for a blow. Enough had gone wrong with these negotiations already, and the envoy hadn't even arrived. "What is it?"

She raked a hand through the bristling white crest of her hair in a rare frustrated gesture. "A rogue chimera has crossed into Morgrain from the Alevaran border, too powerful for the local Warden to deal with. He can barely keep it at bay. I'll need to dispose of it personally."

"From Alevar? Hells, I thought the Shrike Lord would at least wait until his envoy arrived to start a war."

"I've received a message claiming the chimera isn't his and he has no control over it." Enough irony edged my grandmother's voice to forge a sword. "I'm afraid it gets worse. Care to venture a guess as to who his envoy is?"

At this point, I had to assume it would be the absolute worst possible person—and there was no doubt who that would be. "Please don't say Exalted Lamiel."

My grandmother's chuckle held no more humor than teeth grinding on bone. "He is, apparently, exactly that audacious."

The Shrike Lord's betrothed, who had set off the very incident with the Serene Empire that we were trying to mediate. Lamiel had ambitions of becoming a Witch Lord—in which her betrothed encouraged her, presumably so that she could gain the immortality he already enjoyed. But making a Witch Lord required a domain; it was from the land, and all the countless living things populating it, that Witch Lords drew their near-limitless power. This need had driven endless petty wars in Vaskandar.

Lamiel had taken the unconventional approach of attempting to covertly lay a magical claim on Windhome Island, an imperial territory off the Alevaran coast. The Serene Empire had caught her in the act and been upset enough to dispatch a fleet of warships. Only Morgrain's intervention—*my* intervention—had stopped the situation from escalating into bloodshed.

This was who the Shrike Lord sent to represent him.

"She's not even a diplomat. The only reason to send her is to give deliberate insult to the Empire." I yanked at my braid in frustration. "Why is he sending an envoy at all if he's bent on sabotaging the negotiations?"

"Love is making the Shrike Lord reckless." My grandmother's lips twisted in contempt. "He needs to accept that he'll have to watch his loved ones age and die. The rest of us have."

I shook my head. "Reckless doesn't cover it. He's got to know he can't win a fight with the Serene Empire." They were too vast, and wielded devastating magic of their own.

"Not without allies," my grandmother agreed.

Oh. I let out a soft curse. "That's it. He's trying to provoke either Morgrain or the Empire into attacking first, so he can call on allied domains for help and paint us as the villain to the Conclave."

My grandmother snorted. "All we have to do is not start the fight, then, and I can collect a powerful list of grievances from him." Her eyes darkened to unfathomable pools, grave and deep. "Still, I don't like the timing. The Rookery must have heard something that prompted their investigation; clearly some kind of rumor about Gloamingard is making the rounds. And now Lamiel is drawing me conveniently out of the castle."

"You think they're after the Door, too." I kicked at a meat pie. "Should you leave the chimera to the local Wardens?"

"It's old and powerful, and it's holed up in a rocky cave where their magic has nothing to work with." She shook her head. "I'll deal with it as quickly as I can. You'll have to welcome the envoy and host Lamiel yourself tonight, but you're well capable of that. I'll be back before dawn."

It was awkward to play host from across the room, but I'd done it before when my grandmother was absent from Gloamingard. Never when the stakes were this high, but I'd spent the past week intensively preparing for these negotiations. I nodded. "I'll handle Lamiel in the meantime, and keep a watch on her to make sure she doesn't go near the Door."

"Thank you." My grandmother clapped me affectionately on the shoulder.

My heart lurched with the sheer, starving joy of a dog receiving a pat from its master. I tried not to show it on my face. She was one of the very few people who could touch me safely, and I'd sooner swallow a hot coal than let her know how much it meant to me. Better to keep things natural between us, without weighing down every interaction with a heavy burden of need and longing.

"*Guard the tower, ward the stone,*" she said softly.

"*Find your answers writ in bone,*" I finished. "*Keep your trust through wits or war: nothing must unseal the Door.* I won't take my eyes off her, Grandmother."

Nutty wood paneling sheathed the Round Room's walls, reaching up to a ceiling of living branches twenty feet overhead. Golden afternoon sunlight sifted down through the leaves, and a bird called sweetly from above. It was a warm and private room, perfect for welcoming an envoy; it encouraged confidences. *You can speak freely here*, it seemed to say. *This place is safe.*

It didn't feel safe now. Even sitting at the far end of a long table from Lamiel, she felt about as harmless as a shard of broken glass.

"The mysterious Exalted Ryxander." Lamiel's lips curled into a smile above her teacup; she cradled it in both hands, drinking in the almond-scented steam. "I'm honored and frankly a bit surprised to meet you in the flesh. I half thought you were a myth."

Shining pale hair fell loose about her like a mantle, and the mage mark stood out bright silver from her hungry eyes. She wore a gray vestcoat of the softest leather, cut in the close-fitting, almost military style popular in Alevar but trimmed with an asymmetric trail of dark leaves and delicate white flowers rather than mere embroidery. A subtle note of polished condescension in her tone set my teeth on edge.

"As you can see," I said, "I'm entirely real."

"One hears so many strange things, though." She sipped her tea. "That you're a ghost. That you're a crazed murderer stalking the halls of Gloamingard." She paused, gauging the impact of her words, cheeks dimpled with amusement.

"You can't believe everything you hear." I returned her smile through my teeth.

Her lashes dipped, half veiling her eyes. "Why, I've even heard that you're a Skinwitch."

The teacup in my hand cracked, a hairline fracture spiking down from the rim. I set it down on its saucer, struggling with limited success to keep the anger from my face.

"This is my house, Exalted Lamiel," I said, biting off each word. "I am your *host*. Will you truly insult me at my own table?"

Her laugh rang out like little bells. "Oh, I don't *believe* those rumors. How could they be true? After all, no Skinwitch in line to inherit a domain may be allowed to live, by order of the Conclave. To be able to use life magic on humans you have to be a soulless monster with no sense of kinship to humanity." She gestured to me with one elegant hand, a motion like twisting a knife. "Given that you're an atheling and you're alive, well, you *surely* can't be a Skinwitch."

I couldn't tell whether she truly believed I was lying or if this was simply another attempt to provoke me. Either way, this boiling rage that strove to burst out of me in scalding words would do me no good.

"Is there some point you're trying to make?" I asked, my tone frosty.

Lamiel shrugged. "It's curious, that's all," she said. "I'd heard that you killed a man with a touch when you were four years old. Only a Skinwitch can do that."

Those cursed rumors again. No matter how hard I tried to patiently correct people, to spread the truth, someone would always do their own mental addition and start whispering *Skinwitch*. I could hardly blame them; it made sense.

"I'm no more a Skinwitch than you are," I said. *Keep smiling*. "My magic is flawed."

"If you say so." Lamiel winked, as if we shared a secret.

I curled my hand into a fist under the table, tight enough the leather of my glove creaked. "It's the truth."

"I suppose your father should have expected something to go wrong, marrying a woman without any magic in her bloodline." She lifted her lip in genteel disdain. "It was quite the scandal, as I recall. The Lady of Owls' own middle son, an Exalted Atheling in the direct line of succession, marrying some utterly powerless Raverran diplomat! Such a waste."

I pushed my chair back from the table and stood. "I can see what you're trying to do," I said, forcing my voice to be viciously pleasant. "I'm sorry to inform you that I'm not so easy to provoke. If I were, I'd leave a wake of corpses behind me." I gestured toward the door, precise and polite. "Now, I'm sure you're weary from the road. Why don't I call my steward to show you to your guest rooms for some much needed rest?"

Lamiel stared at me a long moment, her face guarded and calculating. Then she slapped the table and burst out into a merry peal of laughter. "I *like* you, Ryx! May I call you Ryx?"

"No."

"The Lady of Owls has been hiding a gem all this time. We'll be great friends, you and I." She flashed me a too-brilliant smile.

I gave her a level stare and didn't bother trying to hide my loathing.

"I rather doubt it."

I warned Odan and the housekeeper, Gaven, that Lamiel might be up to trouble, and that we had to keep her away from the Black Tower in particular. Odan frowned at this news, his bristling gray brows descending like thunderclouds over his deep-set, intelligent eyes.

Gaven, twenty years younger and far more prone to whimsy, broke out in an eager grin. "Ooh, so you want us to spy on her, Exalted Warden?"

He bobbed into half a bow on his toes, his fingers flicking out almost absently from his chest in the casting-off motion of the warding sign. *Avert misfortune.* For the staff who'd lived in the castle for years, it had become almost a friendly greeting, like a wave; it was a rote gesture worn smooth with use, with no real fear in it anymore. When I was small it had bothered me that they did that, but now I barely noticed.

"Not spy," I corrected him, glancing around. We stood ten feet apart beneath the cavernous timbers of the Old Great Hall, and lowering our voices wasn't an option. "The Alevaran delegation are our guests. Just keep an eye out in case they try anything foolish, that's all."

"You realize," Odan said gravely, "that if Exalted Lamiel *does* try to approach the Black Tower, none of the rest of us have the authority to stop her. You're the only mage-marked in the castle, with the lady gone."

"That's true." I twisted the end of my braid, considering the implications. If Lamiel's goal was to provoke a grievance between Alevar and Morgrain, she might be looking for a chance to take issue with the castle staff. "Tell everyone to see to her needs, but to keep out of her sight as much as possible. If any problems arise, alert me, and I'll come at once."

"We should still spy on her, yes?" Gaven sounded so hopeful.

"From a distance," I conceded. "But Odan's right. If she tries anything dangerous, you won't be able to stop her. I'll have to watch her myself."

It was easy enough at first. No one knew the secret corners and hidden passageways of Gloamingard like I did. Lamiel played the part of a guest weary from the road, withdrawing to her rooms; I watched from the ivy-masked windows of an old turret as messenger birds came and went from her balcony all afternoon, alighting on her pale hand. After dark I moved to an empty guest chamber across the hall from hers, the better to intercept her if she tried to sneak around at night once the castle went to bed.

Which was all well and good, except for the part where I needed sleep, myself.

Midnight came and went, and still Lamiel showed no sign of stirring. I didn't dare abandon my post, but as the hours of peering beneath my door to watch hers wore on, the floor became far too comfortable.

It didn't help that every time I came close to dozing off, vivid bits of unpleasant memory rose like bubbles from the depths of a murky swamp, stirred up by Lamiel's prodding.

Scarlet peach juice running down a boy's chin as he stood with eyes closed in forbidden delight, the snow-white stolen fruit trembling in his hand. Rage blazing on a bearded face, and the horrible thud of a fist against breaking bone.

The boy's terrified cries for mercy. The guilty peach forgotten on the ground, smeared in blood and dirt.

I'd known what would happen when I grabbed that man's arm to stop him from hitting my friend again—Hells, I couldn't even remember the boy's name. Afterward, my father told everyone that I didn't understand; I was only four years old.

I knew. In that moment, I didn't care. I was too angry, too desperate.

The terrible feeling of life turning to death under my hand, of flesh hardening and something precious departing. The dull glassy stare of eyes with no soul left in them. The ponderous, ground-shaking thud of his empty shell falling to the hard earth.

That was when people stopped looking at me. Instead of waving hello, they made the warding sign, fingers flicking out from their chests: *avert.*

My father had explained, the grass-green rings of his mage

mark glistening with tears, that I'd have to go foster with my grandmother. She was a Witch Lord, stronger than the mountain, more cunning than the river, ancient as a tree. She could handle me. She would keep me safe, and keep me out of trouble.

And she had, more or less. For seventeen years, I'd barely left the castle, washing down my yearning to visit other places with a bitter draft of *It's safer for everyone this way.*

After all that caution, trouble had come here to find me, wearing flowers and silver-ringed eyes.

My head jerked up from the cool wooden boards of the floor, and I blinked grit from my eyes. I *had* to stay awake. Lamiel hadn't arrived here a day early just to sit in her room; it was only a matter of time until she made her move.

A voice spoke behind me, soft as silk sliding across my palm.

"It'll be easier to kill her if you leave the door ajar."

THREE

I barely stopped myself from leaping up and screaming. Instead I made a muffled choking noise and twisted around to face the lean, elegant creature who sat in the window, tail curled around his paws, backlit by the moon behind him.

"Hello, Whisper," I said. "Thank you for your rather morbid advice, but I'm not currently planning on killing anyone."

"Suit yourself." His tone suggested that I was being foolish, but he was too polite to point it out. "How will you stop her if she tries to enter the Black Tower?"

"Don't you have anything better to do than sneak up behind people and ask them ominous questions?"

"No." He leaped down and prowled closer on silent paws. "And that's not an answer."

Whisper was a chimera, created by one of my Witch Lord ancestors long ago. He had the splendid tail and pointed face of a fox, the nimble grace and sharp hidden claws of a cat, and the sinuous lethality of a weasel. His fur was so black he seemed to vanish into two dimensions, a slip of mislaid shadow, except for the burning yellow glare of his eyes.

No one knew who had created him or what centuries-old

purpose he served. He'd already been slinking about the rooftops and windowsills when my grandmother was a girl, making short work of any small, sly creatures other mages might send to spy on the castle. He obeyed no one's orders, kept his motives secret, and followed his own rules. The rest of my family treated him like something between an ill-omened haunt and a household pest.

He was one of the only friends I had.

"If words aren't enough, I don't know how I'll stop her," I admitted. "Grandmother's hunch aside, I don't have much reason to think she'll try to open the Door. I'm more worried about her stirring up political trouble."

"Then your priorities are wrong." Whisper slipped past me, his fur brushing my arm, soft as a night breeze. I flinched instinctively, despite knowing that whatever magic extended his life also fortified it enough that my touch didn't harm him.

"Is what's in the Black Tower so dangerous?" I asked. I had no doubt it was—I only had to walk past it to know that—but I'd take any chance to tease out more of a glimpse into Whisper's own secret priorities.

"Dangerous enough." Whisper's bushy tail flicked, like a knife cut across the air. "Dangerous for you. Stay away from it, Ryx."

"I know the Gloaming Lore." I paused, eyeing him. "You've lived here longer than anyone. Do *you* know what's in there?"

He settled on his haunches, fixing his gleaming yellow eyes on me for a long moment in silence.

"Something best forgotten," he said at last, his voice soft as falling snow.

Well, *that* was unsettling. "Care to explain?"

"No." He lifted his head, and his ears pricked and swiveled toward the door.

On the far side came a creak of hinges. Quiet footfalls sounded in the hallway.

"You'd better see to that," Whisper said.

I muttered a curse and pulled on my gloves. Lamiel was on the move.

Gloamingard lay dark and empty, with nothing else awake but shadows and moonlight. Lamiel crept through the castle with guilty care; I watched her from crawl spaces and balconies, behind curtains and fantastical sculptures, trailing her or guessing her route and scampering ahead. The latter was made more difficult by Lamiel's lack of knowledge of Gloamingard's twisting halls; more than once she peered out a window, muttered a soft curse, and doubled back the way she came.

I'd known she was up to no good. The only question that remained to be seen was precisely what kind of mayhem she was planning.

She passed into the Green Palace, and I had to stop, watching her shining pale hair disappear behind a curtain of swaying moon-silvered fronds. It was a section of Gloamingard hollowed by magic from the hearts of massive living trees, carpeted with moss and flowers—all grown and sculpted five hundred years ago by the Sycamore Lord himself, one of the Eldest, the first Witch Lord in our family line. I'd never set foot in there; I might kill the trees and bring whole sections of the castle tumbling down.

I didn't need to follow Lamiel to know where she was going now. On the far side of the Green Palace lay nothing but the old stone keep, the looming spire of the Black Tower, and the Door.

I hesitated for one frozen second, dozens of thoughts flashing through my mind in the space between heartbeats. I could run around the long way to meet her at the Door and confront her, or I could go get reinforcements—wake Odan or call for the battle chimeras. But if I went for help, Lamiel would get to the Door first and have at least several minutes with it completely undisturbed. The tower wards should keep her out, but they also might seriously injure her if she trifled with them, and that was the last thing I needed. Besides, only a fool believed any ward to be impenetrable.

If I were a proper mage, I could touch the tree tower and seal her inside it, or send one of the birds or mice who nested around the castle as a messenger to fetch help. All I had was my own voice and legs and hands, curse it, and I could only be in one place at a time.

I couldn't risk it.

I swerved down a side corridor; if I hurried, I might be able to beat her there. I couldn't quite bring myself to sprint through the Bone Palace—not after I'd almost killed Kessa earlier today—but I walked as swiftly as I dared through its stark bone-lined chambers, past friezes formed from magically twisted ribs and scapulae, and through the Hall of Chimes. I all but leaped through the window into the old stone keep, bursting into a run at last as I breathed in the musty scent of its abandoned halls.

As I approached the Black Tower at its center, magic resonated in the air, rich and deep as a bow scraping a long, shuddering note from a bass violin. I slowed, trying to quiet my breath, straining my ears for intruding footsteps.

A pale light flickered awake down the hall, illuminating a slim figure with trailing hair. Lamiel stood before the Door's shadowed alcove, leaning forward on her toes to peer into the darkness, a light burning in her hand.

It was a luminary crystal, no doubt imported from the Serene Empire, where such things were far more common. It cast a cool white radiance across her face and sent her shadow lunging down the corridor as she slowly turned to meet me.

"Oh, hello," she said, with false cheer. "Couldn't you sleep?"

"You shouldn't be here," I said coldly. "It's dangerous."

Lamiel laughed, the sound ringing echoes from the bare stone walls. "I'm certain it is. It's always the dangerous things that are most interesting. Why do you think I'm courting a Witch Lord?"

I stepped closer, carefully narrowing the distance between us. Power pulsed electric in my blood, a pressure in the air, a sound too deep for hearing. I could never tell whether it came from the Door itself, or from the tower beyond.

Either way, Lamiel was far too close to it.

"That's between you and him," I said. "But the Black Tower isn't for you."

"My dear, everything is for whoever reaches out and takes it." Lamiel turned to face the alcove and lifted her light higher, until its pale radiance fell upon the Door. It caught the gleam of obsidian, the thin black shadows of lines etched into the stone.

She sucked in a breath through her teeth. "An artifice seal. I didn't anticipate that."

"It's there to keep reckless fools with no respect for their host's privacy from getting killed." I made my voice stern, pulling it up from the deepest chambers of my chest. "Now go back to your rooms and stay there until morning."

"Oh, Ryx," she said, almost fondly. "I can hardly go back and meekly wait for the Lady of Owls *now*, when I worked so hard to create a diversion that would keep her away from the castle."

My stomach dropped. So it *had* been a distraction.

"Morgrain will not forgive this," I warned, forcing myself to take another step forward. Every instinct cried out that I shouldn't approach so close, but I had to stop her somehow.

"And what will you do?" Lamiel spread her arms, the luminary crystal in her hand throwing giddy shadows against the flat black plane of the door. "Kill me? Perhaps you could, but if you murder an Exalted guest with your Skinwitch magic, every Witch Lord in Vaskandar will turn against you."

She might well be right, even if I could convince the Conclave that I wasn't a Skinwitch. I tried another tactic. "What do you think you can accomplish here?" I gestured to the Door. "You're no artificer. You can't unlock that seal with your magic, and if you try, the wards will strike you down."

Lamiel shook her luminary to brighten its fading light, holding it to shine upon the runes on the obsidian door. "You're right," she muttered. "The runes of the seal dictate that the Door shall open only to the blood of the guardians."

Her words prickled a warning in my mind. "Step away from there," I said sharply.

"Of course." She moved back from the alcove, bowing in mocking acquiescence.

Suddenly she spun, her hair flying in a wide circle around her, the silver rings of her mage mark blazing with intensity. She thrust the luminary at my face, and I threw up my arms to block the sudden light.

I didn't see the knife until it slashed across my forearm.

I yelped and staggered back, grabbing my arm, shocked at the blood blooming on my sliced sleeve, and the queasy feeling of flesh not quite matching up anymore. "*Pox!* You lunatic—Hells take you!"

Lamiel grinned at me as if she hadn't just cut my arm open— as if we shared a secret, or were about to have a lovely forbidden adventure together. She held up the red-streaked knife.

"Let's find out if your family are the guardians." She whirled back to the Door.

"No! *Stop!*" I lunged toward the alcove, still clutching my bleeding arm, furious and desperate.

I was too late. Lamiel pressed the bloody knife blade flat against the center of the seal.

Glaring red light blazed from every carved rune and line, painting the corridor scarlet. A shuddering sound like the scream of a rusty metal gate dragging against granite reverberated inside my skull. A sense of terrible loss pierced me, as if something that had kept me safe and warm all my life was suddenly torn away.

Stone ground against stone, and the obsidian slab began to move. A blast of heat and a scent like the air after a storm escaped through the widening crack at its edge.

The Door was opening.

Everything I'd learned in my twenty-one years of life, every instinct, every scrap of common sense I possessed all screamed out to stop it from opening completely. But Lamiel stood between it and me, and if I tried to push past her I'd kill her.

"Looks like you're a guardian," Lamiel said brightly. "Congratulations."

"Close that Door at once, or I'll show you how I can guard it." I trembled on the edge of grabbing her, and to the Nine Hells with the consequences.

"There are other things I'd rather find out." With a last flash of teeth, she slipped through the widening opening into the tower beyond.

My instincts recoiled, a wild ragged fear straining to bolt and run. More red light poured through the gap, and the oppressive flood of sheer magical power forced me back a step. Dread built in my chest, along with a strange recognition, as if this were a recurring nightmare made real.

I had to stop her. I could try to close the Door, to seal her in there and wait for my grandmother to return, but I had no idea what lay within. It might be a weapon Lamiel could use, a power she could claim, a sleeping nightmare creature she could awaken; I couldn't leave her in there alone with whatever the Door was meant to keep sensible people away from.

Red light glared in my eyes as the door swung wider. The last thing I wanted to do in all the world was to step across that threshold, but precious seconds were slipping past. I couldn't let fear stop me, no matter how frantically it clawed at my chest, tearing the breath to ribbons in my lungs. I was a guardian, and the Warden of Gloamingard. I had a duty to protect everyone in this castle from whatever horrors she might unleash.

I plunged through after Lamiel into the Black Tower.

FOUR

The chamber soared impossibly high above me. The entire lower half of the tower must be hollow, forming this one room. The ceiling would have vanished into darkness if it weren't for the trails of artifice sigils that blazed red all the way up the walls, meeting in a great circular seal of astonishing complexity far, far above. The inky black walls absorbed the scarlet glow, leaving the place somehow both impossibly dim and awash with crimson light.

At the center of the chamber stood a dark rectangle of an obelisk. More glowing runes encircled it, forming another artifice ward on the glossy black floor. The stone itself reflected no light, as if someone had cut a hole in the world looking out to a starless sky.

Before it, hands on hips, stood Lamiel.

Guard the tower, ward the stone. This was it. Whatever that obelisk was, this was what my bloodline existed to protect. A great tide of certainty swelled up in me: I couldn't let her touch it.

I moved toward her, but it was like pushing my way through deep snow. Palpable horror radiated from that flat black stone, which loomed twice Lamiel's height. I had the unnerving sense that it was alive, and hungry, and watching me.

That it *knew* me.

"Get away from that thing!" I shouted, my voice raw with fear and anger.

Lamiel's eyes fixed on the obelisk with reverence. "So much power," she whispered. "To think you've been hiding this all these years."

She lifted a hand toward it. Sparks flew from her fingertips when they reached the edge of the circle inscribed on the floor, and she snatched them back.

"Another seal." Her fingers twitched as if they yearned to touch the black stone. "And there's one more on the artifact itself. What were they so eager to lock away, I wonder?"

Now that I'd forced my way closer, without the backlighting blinding me to details, I could see she was right. Precisely carved symbols and a perfect circle seal marked the center of the obelisk, laid down over a deep groove that bisected it top to bottom. Despite the unnatural warmth baking my skin, a chill shivered up my spine. There were potent magical seals all around this thing, and still it let off this much heat, this much raw power, radiating around and through me with sickening, crushing strength.

My resolve hardened like forming crystal. Lamiel had less caution than a dog trying to snatch meat off the table before its master came home. I couldn't let concerns about her safety hold me back anymore.

I raced across the room and threw myself between her and the rune-marked circle, spreading my arms wide. Turning my back on that stone felt no safer than if it were a ravening battle chimera—and Lamiel was far too close, with not even two feet separating our chests.

"Leave or die," I growled.

To my horror, the scalding waves of power coming off that rock resonated in my voice, a deep bass rumble in my belly.

It flowed through me as if I were nothing, not even a leaf in a stream, carrying my words with it like some paltry wisp of smoke dissipating into the air.

Lamiel stepped back, eyes widening. Then she glanced down at my feet, and her lips curled in a satisfied smile. "You can cross *this* barrier too, I see. Perfect."

I couldn't help it. I looked down.

The heel of my right boot crossed the glowing circle that protected the obelisk, obscuring one of the runes. Red light poured up around my foot, and my leg tingled with the touch of magic, but I hadn't even noticed it in the overwhelming press of energy coming from the stone.

"Pox," I breathed.

In my moment of distraction, Lamiel struck.

She lunged at me, seizing both my arms above the elbow. Her fingers dug iron-hard through my thin shirtsleeves, her mage mark shining with determination. She shoved me through the now flickering ward—and plunged through the barrier with me.

"No!" I tried to catch my balance as I staggered backward, desperate to pull away from her. "Don't touch me, you'll—"

She'd hit me with too much force. My heels skidded out from under me.

The moment slowed, terrible and clear, each detail burned into my senses.

Lamiel's face as her eyes widened with the first sense that something was wrong. The warm rush of magic in my arms, where her fingers clutched at me. The giddy swoop of falling, and the soaring panic of knowing what was behind me, waiting, hungry and awful as death itself.

My fingers tangled in Lamiel's hair as I grabbed desperately for balance; life magic surged into me through my reaching hand. But it was too late. I'd passed the tipping point, and I was going down.

Searing hot stone slammed against my head and shoulders as I toppled into the obelisk. Pain flashed through my skull, and the breath whooshed out of my lungs.

A blinding light erupted all around me.

Horrible crawling pain ripped through my body, as if worms of lightning danced through my veins. The whole vast chamber vibrated with an unheard sound, and the heat of a furnace seared the air. Sheer panic shrieked along my nerves. *No, no, good Graces no—not this, not this—*

White radiance blazed from the stone at my back, stripping every shadow from Lamiel's face as her mouth shaped a silent scream. It hollowed her cheeks even as her eyes went dull and glassy.

I shoved her off me, desperate; a thrill of magic coursed up my gloved fingertips. She tumbled to the floor, loose and limp, the pale threads of her hair spreading around her.

Ash and ruin. She looked dead. *Please don't let her be dead.*

Power still blasted through me; I would shatter into pieces any moment from the force of it. I wrenched myself away from the stone with a cry.

It was impossibly difficult, the obelisk pulling at me like iron draws a magnet; the line down the center shone blindingly bright, as if the rock might crack open from the magic unleashed within it. With all the frenzied force of terror fueling me, I broke free, stumbling over Lamiel's body.

The dazzling white brilliance began, ever so slowly, to fade.

Everything hurt. My whole body shook uncontrollably, and tears leaked from my eyes. A wild uneven strength coursed through me, and I didn't know if it was Lamiel's life energy or sheer panic or both.

Blood of the Eldest, I'd made a mess of this. I was stunned, numb, waiting for the full horror to hit. The Door open, Lamiel probably dead—this was a nightmare. No, my nightmares were never this bad.

I dropped to my knees beside Lamiel, unsure what to do. Curse it, she had the mage mark; if she'd anchored herself against my magic before touching me, like bracing for a tug-of-war, she'd be fine—but she hadn't believed me about not being a Skinwitch, hadn't listened to my warnings, and I'd yanked her life from her like rope from slack hands. Now she lay utterly still. She didn't seem to be breathing.

If she wasn't dead yet, my touch could kill her. But I couldn't leave her here, with light still pouring from that cursed stone and dread building in the air like the sky's own wrath.

"I'd get out of that circle if I were you."

Whisper stood in the doorway, his tail a dark bristling cloud, his yellow eyes fever-bright. Strain roughened his usually silk-smooth voice.

"Is she—" My throat was dry to crackling with fear. "Did I—"

"Dead," Whisper said. "A clean kill, though you might have done it sooner and prevented this madness. Now get out of there!"

No. Ashes, no. I couldn't have killed her. He was only a chimera; he had to be wrong.

I grabbed fistfuls of Lamiel's vestcoat, trying not to touch her, and hauled her out of the circle along the shining black floor. Something about the heft of her told me I was dragging a thing, not a person.

He was right. She was gone.

"I didn't mean to." My entire chest seemed to seize up, as if something was trying to fight its way out from inside me and I had to stop it. "Whisper, I swear, it was an accident."

"That's the least of our worries," he hissed, glaring at the obelisk that still shone with a terrible, eye-searing brilliance. "Let's get out of here—bring the carcass, to be safe—and seal the Door."

I dragged a sleeve across my eyes, nodded grimly, and picked up Lamiel's booted ankles, ignoring the throbbing of my wounded arm. I tried to wipe my mind blank as I hauled her across the floor, her long hair trailing behind her, stained red as blood by the light of the wards. But I couldn't stop thinking, no matter how much I wanted to.

Whatever else I had let loose here, I'd unleashed war.

I hauled Lamiel's empty husk out into the dusty stone alcove and turned to face the lurid glow pouring from the open Door to the Black Tower, my breath coming high and fast. Whisper, who'd skittered through to safety ahead of me, backed away down the corridor with his tail puffed and his eyes glowing.

I scrabbled at the heavy stone Door, searching desperately for any kind of handle or purchase. At my touch, it began to move under my fingers, grinding slowly shut. The line down the center of the great black obelisk still blazed with terrible light; even at a glance, it stabbed into my mind like a diamond blade. I could only pray to the Graces that whatever I'd triggered would fade without doing any harm.

The Door clunked into place. The runes flared one last time and went out, plunging everything into darkness.

My breathing scraped harshly in the shadows, and my pulse surged loud and reckless in my ears. I groped for a wall and found rough, gritty stone.

Solid. *Real.* I could almost persuade myself this had all been a nightmare—the Door opening, the red chamber, the obelisk, Lamiel's life pouring into me. That only this rock was real, and the comforting darkness that protected my eyes from any more awful sights, and the rest was some mad hallucination.

But my eyes slowly started pulling details out of the shadows, adjusting to the dim light: the faint red aurora that marked the outline of the massive Door, the lingering gleam that remained in Lamiel's expended luminary. Whisper pacing with restless agitation, and Lamiel's sprawled form twisted in empty discomfort on the hard stone floor.

And approaching down the corridor, the burning orange

circles of my grandmother's mage mark, glowing in the dark like a cat's eyes.

"Ryxander." Her voice fell on me like a mountain. "What have you done?"

I clutched my bleeding arm against my chest, words collapsing to dust in my mouth. "I'm sorry," I managed, my voice a breathless rasp. "I couldn't stop her."

My grandmother seized my shoulders with both hands, her face blazing with intensity even in the darkness. "Are you all right? Ryx, look at me."

"I'm fine, but Lamiel—"

She gave me a sharp shake. "*Look at me.*"

I *was* looking at her, as much as I was looking at anything, but the red lines of the Black Tower wards still burned into my vision. I swallowed and forced myself to focus on my grandmother's face and truly meet her eyes despite the jittery pounding of my heart and the nerve-scalding energy still pouring into my limbs.

My grandmother's gaze roved across my face, scanning it as if she could read words there.

"You're safe," she breathed at last, and her hands dropped from my shoulders.

"The Door." I tried to pull the chaos of my thoughts into order. That was the most important thing—even more important than the Shrike Lord's betrothed dead at my feet. I had no idea what that surge of energy meant, or what danger it might pose to everyone in the castle. "Lamiel used my blood to get into the Black Tower, and she...I tried to get in her way, but she wouldn't listen, and she knocked me into the stone." My throat burned, cracking my voice.

"Seasons have mercy." My grandmother's blazing eyes flicked past me, then down to settle on Whisper. "Is this *your* doing?"

"Hardly." Acid infused the chimera's tone. "If I'd wanted to open the Door, I wouldn't have involved some visiting human fool."

"How long was it open?" she demanded, something disturbingly like fear in her voice.

I had never, not even once, known my grandmother to be afraid.

"Only briefly," Whisper said, his fur still bristling along his spine. "But that may have been enough."

She turned from me to face the closed Door, the shadows on her jaw flexing in the dim light. "I have to deal with this now. It can't wait."

"Let me help you." The words burst out of me on a hot surge of guilt. "This is my fault. And Gloamingard is my responsibility."

"No," she said harshly. "You can't go near that thing again. I'll handle it."

"Wait." I grabbed the edge of her feathery mantle in desperation. "At least tell me what's going on. I killed someone tonight, and I want to know why."

She closed her eyes. The dim red light seeping around the Door played across her lids.

Without warning, she spun and clasped me in a fierce, bony hug.

"Listen to me, Ryx," she whispered, low and close to my ear. My skin prickled as my flawed magic strove to draw her life into me, but the Lady of Owls was more than powerful enough to resist that pull. "I don't know what's going to happen. I'm going to go in there and find out what we're facing. Most likely the danger is past, the only casualty is Lamiel, and the Shrike Lord's wrath is the worst we'll have to deal with." She held me out at arm's length, her eyes grave. "In case it isn't, I need you to do something. To help protect Gloamingard and all of Morgrain."

"Anything," I said, trembling with the need to undo whatever unspoken damage I'd done.

My grandmother drew in a long breath. "Go get the Rookery."

"What?" I stared at her, stunned. They might be experts at dealing with magical accidents, but bringing outsiders into this went against the Gloaming Lore.

Whisper seemed to share my skepticism. "Are you sure?"

My grandmother ignored him, keeping her eyes locked on mine. "They took the southern road toward the Serene Empire. They're camped at a traveler's shelter a few hours from here; you can catch up to them tonight if you hurry. Tell them we have a magical emergency and I'm requesting immediate assistance."

My stomach dropped even further. "What magical emergency? Ashes, tell me, what did I do?"

A shadow lay within my grandmother's eyes. "Hopefully nothing," she said. "Just in case, I'm sending messenger birds to the rest of the family, warning them to stay away from Gloamingard. And I want you to go after the Rookery and bring them back here."

"Then send the Rookery a bird, too," I urged her. "I can't leave Gloamingard now. I'm the Warden. If that artifact poses a danger to the people in the castle, I have to help neutralize it or get them out. Not to mention that the Raverran envoy arrives tomorrow morning, seasons have mercy, and I need to be here."

"The best way you can help protect your people is to get the Rookery as quickly as possible," my grandmother said grimly. "A bird could be misunderstood, intercepted, or ignored. I need them here immediately—no delays, detours, or refusals. I trust you to accomplish that."

She wanted me gone. The knowledge cut deeper and more unexpected than the slash in my arm. I had no doubt everything she said was true, but I was no fool; I could think of half a dozen trustworthy staff I could send in my place. For whatever reason—to keep me from making things worse, or for my own safety—she wanted me out of Gloamingard.

But she was the Witch Lord, and an emergency was no time to argue. I nodded reluctantly. "All right. I'll do it."

"Good." She paused, as if a thought struck her. "One more thing—don't tell anyone what really happened to Lamiel. So far as anyone else is concerned, she tampered with things she shouldn't have and the wards killed her. Do you understand?"

"But what about—"

"Tell *no one*. I'm going to have enough trouble placating the Shrike Lord as it is. Our chances of keeping this between Alevar and Morgrain are much better if he can't call in allies with a cry of murder."

"It wasn't murder!" The protest tore from me before I could stop it. "*She* grabbed *me*. After attacking me with a knife, no less."

"I know. But if it comes out that your magic killed her, they'll cry Skinwitch, and we'll have Nine Hells of a time convincing anyone otherwise." She planted one swift, forceful kiss on the top of my head; it left a spot of warmth on my scalp. "Go now, and move quickly. Speed is crucial. I love you."

"I love you, too." The words bunched in my throat.

"Go. Run." My grandmother faced the black Door, her expression grim. "I've got my own work to do."

Her power began unfolding invisibly around her, swelling vast as a mountain's shadow at sunset. I didn't stay to find out if the pressure of it fully unleashed would crush the breath from my lungs. She'd given me a task, and by all Nine Graces, I'd do it.

I ran through Gloamingard's twisting halls and out into the wild night.

My feet ached from the pebbly road, and the chill of the early autumn night had worked its way through my vestcoat. The bandage I'd improvised for my wounded arm had stopped the bleeding but didn't keep it from throbbing with sharp insistence. I forced myself to keep going at as brisk a pace as I could manage, pushing pain and weariness down deep inside with the fear and the guilt and everything else I couldn't afford to give in to right now. Until I knew everyone in Gloamingard was safe from whatever I'd unleashed in the Black Tower, there could be no rest.

I needed to figure out some solution for the diplomatic disaster, too. Holy Graces, this was bad. I couldn't see a path that led to peace. The wheels of my mind were stuck, too shocked to turn, and I couldn't think.

It was the time of night my mother called the demon's hour, when all the world lay asleep. No lights shone through the shuttered windows in the huddled gray villages I passed through, though the scents of livestock and woodsmoke thickened the night air. As an atheling of Morgrain, if I knocked on any door, the inhabitants would rouse and give me whatever aid I asked for: food, a horse cart, anything, their fingers flicking out from their chests and their eyes averted.

Outside of Gloamingard, however, no one was practiced in staying away from me; to interact with the townsfolk would be to put them in danger. All it would take was one unexpected movement, one misjudged reach or stumble. A hobbyhorse leaned by one weathered cottage door, its mane carefully crafted from horsetail clippings; a child's enthusiastically messy brushstrokes had painted flowers on another. These were my people, secure in their beds with the knowledge that my family watched over them. I wouldn't risk their lives for my comfort or convenience.

The stars gleamed hard as chips of broken glass in the sky above, watching, judging. Fields of silvery windswept grass and leaning lichen-scarred rune stones gave way to a black patchwork of forest shadows. Reaching pines swallowed the sky, leaving only a ragged ribbon of stars above the road for me to follow.

I was safe enough from any perils others might fear in the wild inky night; this was my grandmother's domain, and every living thing here knew me and would defend me from harm. But it was too easy for my mind to fill the darkness with blazing red lines of light and a single vertical slash of terrible white radiance, and Lamiel's eyes going dull and flat.

The Shrike Lord would know she was dead by now. She was part of his domain, and he'd have felt her die. He wasn't the sort of man to let such a terrible grievance pass unanswered; the question was what form his retribution would take. I could only hope we wouldn't be at war by the time the imperial envoy arrived tomorrow morning.

I wasn't looking forward to explaining that the ambassador they'd come to negotiate with was dead.

Hell of Discord. Everything I'd worked for, everything I wanted to preserve, was falling apart around me. No, not falling—I'd smashed it to pieces with my own hands. I had to get back to Gloamingard with the Rookery as soon as possible.

Finally, the warm light of a campfire flickered between the trees in distant glimpses, promising a normal sort of warmth and comfort. A traveler's shelter, like my grandmother had said. Hope pricked up its tired ears within me. *Graces, please let this be the Rookery's fire.*

I picked my way along the narrow side path that led to the shelter, straining toward the cheery light. The campfire ruined my night vision and robbed the forest around me of depth, turning the tree trunks into flat black bands of shadow and making the darkness around me impenetrable. Even with the blood connection to my grandmother's land that gave me an instinctive feel for the terrain, it took concentration not to trip over rocks and roots with every other step.

I hesitated a few paces before the edge of the clearing, peering in through the trees. A brightly painted wagon stood by the crude wooden shelter; several horses dozed nearby. One big gray lifted his head at my approach and pricked black-tipped ears in my direction. A dark-haired young woman sat on a sawed-off stump before the fire, poking it with a stick. *Kessa.*

"I've come to the right place," I breathed aloud.

"I wouldn't be so sure of that," said a shadow.

Steel scraped against leather, and the firelight caught the edge of a sword leveled straight at me.

FIVE

I backed away, my hands lifted empty before me. "I'm not your enemy. And you don't want to point that at me."

"Oh, but I think I do." The swordswoman advanced a step to match me. With the light behind her I couldn't make out any details, but she was whipcord wiry and couldn't be much more than five feet tall. "No one up to any good stays out past dark in the woods of Vaskandar."

I couldn't really argue with that. Many Witch Lords let all the fiercest wild denizens of their domains hunt freely at night—natural predators and mage-made chimeras alike—on the assumption that anyone with honest business would be indoors. "Well, I'm here to talk, so you can put your sword away."

"Talk fast. You can start by telling me what you're doing sneaking around our camp." The angle of her sword changed, flashing firelight; a reflected gleam caught at the corner of her eye.

The tree branches shivered. My awareness of the pines around us sharpened, as if they were coming suddenly awake. The land sensed a threat, and it was responding.

The last thing I needed was to kill someone else today, all because the trees were feeling overprotective.

"I'm not sneaking around," I objected. "I have an urgent message."

"That's what all the assassins say." The girl shifted her stance in the darkness, and the trees came wide awake, their attention focusing on her as their branches quivered. Everything balanced a hairsbreadth from blood and violence.

"*Asheva!* Are you threatening random passersby again?" called a familiar voice.

Kessa stood at the edge of the clearing, peering down the dark path at us, her hands on her hips.

"Nothing random about it," the swordswoman—Asheva—said. "She was skulking around alone in the darkness."

"This is a traveler's shelter, dimwit. People come here to be safe. I'm so sorry." She addressed this last to me, her voice softening. "Please disregard my overly suspicious friend, and come join us by our fire."

She clearly hadn't recognized me in the darkness. As I hesitated, she turned to the swordswoman. "Ashe—Rule Four. Back off, and let her come into the light."

"You're no fun, Kessa. Besides, this one's dangerous." Asheva let the tip of her blade drop to a more relaxed guard, however, and slipped out of the covering shadows into the firelight.

With ice-blue eyes and spiky tufts of near-white hair to match her pale skin, she could have come from Morgrain or any of the mountain domains of Vaskandar. She was older than her size had led me to believe at first—around my age—and wore breeches tucked into boots beneath her short, fur-trimmed vestcoat, along with an air of barely leashed violence.

"Now, what would make you think that?" Kessa sounded amused, but she paused in the act of beckoning me forward.

"Because she's out alone after dark, just had a sword pulled on her, and she's not afraid."

She was wrong. I was desperately afraid—just not of her.

"I don't care if you trust me, so long as you listen." I stepped out into the light, careful to maintain a safe distance between us. "I have a message from the Lady of Owls."

Kessa's welcoming smile froze, and a more guarded, calculating look entered her sparkling brown eyes. She bowed, with more courtly grace than she'd shown when she was pretending to be a simple traveling player. "Exalted Atheling. Please forgive our poor reception of such an august visitor."

"Call me Ryx. There's no time for niceties. We have a magical emergency at Gloamingard."

Kessa whistled. "An emergency indeed. I've never known a Witch Lord to ask for help."

"I know." My grandmother never had before today. She'd never needed it. I swallowed to wet my raw throat. "Please hurry. I don't know what's happening at the castle."

Kessa and Ashe exchanged a meaningful look. Without another word, Ashe rolled her neck, slammed her sword into its sheath, and moved with quick springy grace toward the horses.

"I'll wake the others," Kessa said grimly. "We'd better go at once."

The Rookery clearly were no strangers to late-night emergencies. Kessa and Ashe worked as a reassuringly swift and competent team to harness the horses, while a gangly, sleepy-eyed man in a burgundy jacket packed up their belongings from the shelter and tossed them in the back of the brightly painted wagon with equal speed. They left me no doubt they were taking this seriously and moving as quickly as possible, so I squashed down my urge to tell them to hurry.

The fourth member of the Rookery, an elegant gentleman in an exquisitely tailored dove-gray frock coat, approached me with the wary grace of a big hunting cat. He paused a safe distance away and gestured to a ring of sawed-off stumps surrounding the fire.

"Sit down, my lady. Let's talk."

His use of *my lady* rather than *Exalted Atheling* marked him as Raverran, sure as his clothes and accent did; his deep brown skin and eyes like dark honey suggested ancestors from the imperial client state of Osta. Beneath his open coat, a belt with dozens of small pouches rode his hips, with a flintlock pistol slung on one side and a dagger on the other.

"There's no time," I objected. The last thing I wanted to do right now was sit, despite my aching feet.

"Unless you want to walk back to Gloamingard carrying all our equipment, we're not going anywhere until the wagon is ready. You're weary, and there are things that should be clear between us. Please, have a seat."

His voice remained smooth and calm, but there was iron in it. I sank onto a stump, cradling my wounded arm in my lap, still stiff with tension.

He settled onto another stump just out of lunging range, poised as if the smoke-scented clearing were some fine Raverran salon. "You can call me Foxglove. I'm the leader of this Rookery field team."

I jerked my head in a nod.

"Now. What kind of magical accident are we talking about? Alchemical leak? Escaped chimera? Explosion? And how long ago did it happen?"

"A few hours, and I don't know."

Foxglove regarded me a moment, the firelight drawing fingers of light and shadow across his face.

"My lady," he said, "I possess many skills, but mind reading isn't one of them. I can't help you without information."

"Fair enough." The Gloaming Lore said *Keep your secret, guard your lore*. Still, my grandmother had sent me to the Rookery; she couldn't mean for me to keep them ignorant of the situation. "There's an ancient artifact in Gloamingard, sealed and locked away. It's...been activated. By mistake."

One eyebrow lifted, but there was no real surprise in it. "An artifact, you say. The one we were trying to investigate?"

I grimaced. "Yes."

Foxglove rubbed his forehead. "I'm about to be blunt, my lady. You do realize that if the Lady of Owls hadn't ejected us from her castle this afternoon, we might have been on hand to deal with— or even prevent—this magical catastrophe in the first place?"

"The irony hasn't escaped me," I assured him.

"Then let me make something clear." He leaned his elbows on his knees. "If you invoke our aid, you can't change your mind. We'll help you on our own terms. No trying to stop us from doing our work because we're getting too close to family secrets or uncomfortable truths." The weary undercurrent in his voice suggested this was a common issue. "I'm well past the point in my career where I've got any patience for people who tell me to ignore the skeletons in the well or to not ask questions about the howling in the attic."

"I have every intention of letting you do your work," I said, "but I can't make promises on behalf of my grandmother."

"The Lady of Owls should understand what it means to call on us for help. Once you bring us in to clean up a mess, we'll finish the job. Whether you want us to or not."

His gaze held mine, steady and sharp. It was unnerving. No one looked me straight in the eyes besides my immediate family.

I nodded slowly. "Fine. But *you* should understand that if I think you're about to do something that could pose a risk to the inhabitants of the castle, I'll stop you. I'll explain, but I'm not going to let my people get hurt."

"I wouldn't want it any other way." Foxglove dusted his hands together as if that were that. "Let's get going. You can explain the rest as we travel."

Morgrain was restless.

Tension ran through the earth. Leaves stirred without a breeze to shake them. Unnerving calls split the silence of the night at odd intervals from birds that should have been asleep: the scream of a jay, the mournful cry of a dove. It surged in my blood, too, and I leaned forward on the wagon bench as if I could somehow urge it to move faster as it rattled along the night-empty road toward Gloamingard.

I'd never felt anything like this through my link to the land before. Whatever was happening back at the castle, it was bad enough that my grandmother's agitation had infected the entire domain. Terrible possibilities chased each other through my head: the Shrike Lord could have already declared war over Lamiel's death, or the obelisk I'd activated in the Black Tower could have unleashed some wave of deadly power upon Gloamingard. I kept imagining people I knew sprawled dead on the castle floor: Odan protecting his young nephew Kip, both of them inexplicably in pools of blood; Gaven lying in a twisted heap, ungraceful for once at the end. *Seasons have mercy.*

"So, tell me about this artifact."

I almost jumped. It was the gangly man in the high-collared burgundy jacket. He leaned forward with a charcoal pencil poised over a leather-bound notebook, his liquid brown eyes riveted on my face.

He sat on a costume trunk in the back of the wagon; Foxglove drove, and Ashe rode alongside. They'd given me a seat on the bench next to Kessa, who'd laid out an offering of bread, apples, and cider as a barrier between us, making hospitality out of necessity. The hard knot in my stomach wouldn't let me more than nibble any of it.

"This is Bastian," Kessa said, gesturing to the young man with a teasing flourish. "I'm sure he's very pleased to meet you. You'll have to forgive his lack of manners; he thinks an introduction is the thing you find at the beginning of a book."

Bastian winced. "Sorry. My mentor at the University of Raverra was very, ah, results-focused, and sometimes my social graces can be lacking."

"That's all right." I couldn't stand the thought of wasting time with pleasantries right now. I tugged at my bloodstained gloves as if I could somehow draw them on even further. "Ask me your questions. I want to get this... *thing* safely locked up again as quickly as possible."

"What is it?" Bastian's pencil hovered eagerly over his notebook. His long, graceful fingers contrasted with the roughness of his olive skin, as if those elegant hands had seen hard use. "A vivomantic artifact, I assume, like a domain boundary stone?"

It was a reasonable assumption. In Vaskandar, nearly all mages were vivomancers, unlike in the Empire, where magical bloodlines held more variety due to their long history of trade. But while I had little familiarity with the other kinds of magic—my knowledge didn't go much further than that alchemists made potions, artificers made wirework devices and enchantment circles, and warlocks left trails of destruction through fire or storm—my home and family were drenched in life magic. And this wasn't that.

"No, not vivomancy." I shuddered at the memory of the terrible power that had ripped through me in a great tide. "Something else. The wards on the Black Tower are all artifice seals, hundreds or thousands of years old. Maybe the stone was an artifice device, too; I don't know."

Bastian scribbled in his notebook. "So you have family stories about this artifact? What do you know about it?"

"That it's too dangerous to let anyone pry around it," I said stiffly.

"Mages," Ashe snorted, from the back of her horse. "You keep everyone else away from your bad-idea death traps because you don't want to share power, and then you set them off yourselves. And call *us* in to clean up after you."

"My family knows better than to meddle with the Black Tower," I retorted angrily. "It was Exalted Lamiel who opened the Door."

"Exalted, you say. Which means mage-marked," Ashe pointed out, in an I-told-you-so voice.

"Yes, but—" I stopped myself. Arguing with the Rookery would do no good. And besides, she had a point. "What bothers me is that Lamiel shouldn't have known about it. *You* shouldn't have known about it, for that matter. How did you find out?"

Kessa exchanged a long glance with Foxglove. "You can't have a giant, sinister, sealed-off obsidian tower at the heart of your castle and not leave people wondering about it. I'm sure there must be all sorts of rumors. Most likely Exalted Lamiel was reacting to the same ones we were."

Her evasiveness reminded me all too sharply of how she'd acted so friendly when I'd nearly run into her in the corridors of Gloamingard—too sympathetic, and with such gentle questions about how my magic worked. I kept wanting to trust her because of her lovely face and warm smiles, but I needed to be more wary.

Questions about my magic, indeed.

"You didn't come to Gloamingard to investigate rumors of some ancient artifact," I realized. "There are ancient artifacts all over the continent of Eruvia, and ours wasn't causing any problems. You came to Gloamingard to investigate *me*."

Bastian buried his face in his notebook, color creeping onto his cheeks.

Kessa let out a long sigh. "Well, this is awkward, but you're right," she said. "We did hope to sneak a look at the artifact while we were in the castle—though you caught me before I could get close—but we were primarily there for you."

"Because you heard I was a Skinwitch." My stomach turned over, and I clenched my hands tightly enough in my lap that my gloves nearly popped a stitch.

"We know you're not, though," Kessa said. "A Skinwitch wouldn't kill people by accident; all those safety vines and such wouldn't make any sense. So it's all right."

"What would you have done if I *were*?" I demanded. None of them met my eyes, and the sick feeling twisted deeper in my gut. "Grace of Mercy. You would have killed me."

"Never," Kessa protested, even as Ashe chuckled, "Maybe."

"My lady," Foxglove said, "they would hardly give us authority to operate in every country in Eruvia if we went about murdering the local royalty."

That wasn't exactly reassuring. They might not have done me in personally, but they'd have passed on information to their superiors that they knew would get me killed. The hard wagon seat became twice as uncomfortable knowing I shared it with people who'd infiltrated my home to determine whether their governments should allow me to live.

But none of that mattered if they could keep my castle safe from whatever lay behind the Door.

"Actually," Bastian said in a small voice, peering out from behind his notebook, "I was wondering if you'd ever considered getting a jess."

A jess. I let out a long sigh. "Of course I've considered it."

They were the bracelets the Serene Empire used to seal and control the powers of the mage-marked. In Vaskandar, magic conferred the right to rule and the duty to protect, and the power of the Witch Lords was absolute; in the Empire, they'd found a way to level the field. Every mage powerful enough to bear the mark in their eyes was given a jess as soon as their magic appeared, and a linked Falconer who could seal their power at any time with a single word. The practice had started as a means to seize control of the magic in each new client state Raverra gained through treaty or conquest, but over time it had changed to become a mere preventative measure, at least in theory. A way to give those without magic recourse against mages who abused their power—or lost control of it.

"And what did you decide?" Bastian asked curiously.

When I'd first heard of the jesses as a child, I'd asked my mother if I could get one, with tears in my eyes. *So I can hug you*, I'd said.

She'd crouched down and looked me in the eyes, her own going soft and misty. *Oh, honey. You're royalty here in Vaskandar. You can't give control of your magic to a foreign power.*

But I'm Raverran, too! I'd protested. *Like you!*

She'd pulled the scarf from her shoulders that she kept there just to gather her warmth for me. I drew it close around me in place of a hug and breathed in its scent, trying not to cry.

If you give them your power, they will try to use you, she'd said gravely. *They'll turn you into a weapon. An assassin.* She had flashed me a bright smile. *And if when you grow up, you decide that's what you want, well, we can—*

My father had given her one of his Looks, and she'd broken off with a laugh. I'd laughed, too, without knowing why. The memory put a bittersweet tang in my throat.

"It doesn't much matter," I said, my voice thick. "I'm Vaskandran. I can't get a jess."

"There *is* a precedent," Bastian offered hesitantly, exchanging a glance with Foxglove. "As the Rookery archivist, I can tell you that there have been a few instances where special exceptions were made when the Rookery was called to deal with a Vaskandran mage whose powers were in some way dangerous or uncontrolled." He grimaced with apparent distaste. "They even gave a jess to a Skinwitch, once, as an alternative to killing them."

"I'm certain the Serene Empire is all too happy for a chance to acquire control over a Vaskandran mage's power," I said, not bothering to hide the irony in my voice.

Foxglove laughed, with something of a bitter edge. "I see you know my country well."

"My mother is a former Raverran diplomat."

Ashe shook her head. "Could have told you she wouldn't be interested, Bastian. No Vaskandran mage would ever give up their power."

That shouldn't have bothered me—after all, Ashe might well come from one of the domains where mages ruled as cruel tyrants—but it did. Lamiel's death was too fresh, and my repugnance at my own magic too gut-churningly strong.

"Of *course* I'd give it up if I could," I snapped. "Do you think I *like* killing people?"

An awkward silence fell, as if no one had really asked themselves how I knew that my touch was fatal. By the widening of Bastian's eyes and the sudden guardedness in Kessa's face, I could see them doing the math now, wondering how many times over I was an unintentional murderer.

A trembling started in my shoulders and traveled in shuddering waves down my chest. *Don't think of her eyes. Don't think of her dead eyes, for Graces' sake.*

I turned to stare out at the star-scattered sky and the open moon-soaked pastures around us, pretending to admire the view to hide my face. A faint gray-golden light bathed the east, above the black rising swell of the hills.

Dawn was coming. The light would reach the tips of Gloamingard's towers first, then slide down the walls, warming them with golden light.

An image sprang unbidden to my mind of my castle twisted and broken, blasted open and smoking. *No.* I wouldn't let that happen, no matter how great the Shrike Lord's wrath, no matter how terrible the consequences of opening the Door.

I couldn't chase the image away.

The sun had come full up by the time Gloamingard appeared atop the emerald sweep of its hill, mismatched spires scratching at the blue sky. Relief poured through me to find it standing as it always had, its window-riddled living trees interspersed with sharp spires of bone, blocky stone and log towers standing among them like the bass line that carried a wild melody. At the center, the Black Tower reared up highest of all, windowless and ominous even in the bright daylight.

Whether the people inside were all intact as well remained to be seen. Surely my grandmother would have sent a bird to let me know if anything terrible had happened. Most likely she'd just sealed the Door and was waiting for the Rookery while attempting to mitigate the political consequences of Lamiel's death. I gripped the wagon's edge to bleed off some of my white-knuckled need to be there helping her.

The town at the base of the hill certainly didn't seem disturbed by any signs of disaster. It was still all cheery whitewashed buildings crossed with dark log beams; wreaths of grain and late-summer flowers hung over the windows in anticipation of the upcoming equinox festival, and the first gold leaves of autumn lay scattered on the doorsteps for good fortune.

I huddled down in my seat as we rolled into town, hoping to avoid recognition. But people were up and out about their business, and there was exactly one half-Raverran with a lightning-blue mage mark in all of Morgrain. Occasionally someone we passed would look at me a second time and bow hastily, or lower their eyes in fear. And always, their fingers flicked out from their chests. *Avert.*

Bastian frowned. "What's that they keep doing?"

Kessa glanced at me, then warningly at Bastian. "Oh, just the warding sign. It's to cast off ill fortune."

"A common superstition in Vaskandar," Foxglove said, his voice dry with cynicism. "People make it when talking about anything from demons to bad weather. In domains with cruel rulers, they make the sign whenever they speak the Witch Lord's name."

"Then why—oh." Bastian glanced at me and grimaced an apology. "Never mind. Sorry."

"My grandmother isn't cruel," I said shortly. "They don't do this when *she* passes them. Only for me."

Ashe, who rode ahead of the wagon, suddenly lifted her head. "Something's coming," she told Foxglove, dropping back.

"What is it?" Foxglove straightened in the driver's seat, his hand straying toward the pistol on his hip.

"A carriage. With outriders making everyone clear a path. Some mage, probably." Ashe grinned. "Want to start a fight over right of way?"

"Rule Four, Ashe," Kessa said sternly.

"Rule Four?" I asked. She'd said something similar earlier.

"Don't use violence when words will suffice," Kessa supplied, at the same time that Ashe said, "Talking before stabbing."

Kessa laughed. "You get the idea. We made some rules for Ashe because she previously worked for an organization that's less, ah, diplomatically inclined. There have been certain adjustments necessary since she joined the Rookery."

"Forgive me for not feeling diplomatic toward someone who thinks I should scramble out of their way just because they've got fancy circles in their eyes," Ashe muttered.

I shifted uncomfortably on the bench. She was right, plain and simple; she shouldn't have to. All the street traffic uphill drew to the side, people pressing up against the buildings to make room; some frowned with annoyance or shook their heads, and others moved with dull routine acceptance. It hadn't even occurred to me before that this wasn't simply something done for *all* carts and carriages, and that a merchant's wagon wouldn't get the same treatment—but it should have. I resolved to ask the town council to come up with new right of way rules based on practicality rather than rank.

Foxglove sighed. "I suppose we'd better move over, too."

There was something odd about the sound of the approaching hooves. A suspicion settled on my chest like a pile of stones.

Sure enough, the riders who passed us moments later coming down from the hill wore gray and black and white, their faces set and serious, escorting a carriage with a shrike emblazoned on the doors and drawn by wild-eyed stags. The guards wore twists of briars around their arms to display the suffering of mourning, and someone had draped the carriage in trailing streams of gray moss and hung a bird skull over the door.

The Alevaran delegation was leaving. Hell of Nightmares. The negotiations I'd worked so hard to arrange—our best hope to extinguish the spark of war—had fallen apart before they began.

Foxglove frowned. "That's the Alevaran envoy's carriage. I saw it when we were leaving yesterday." He turned to me, brows lifting. "Did the envoy *die*?"

I couldn't help it; I flinched. "She ... ah ... yes." They stared at me, expecting more.

Hells. My grandmother had made it very clear that I shouldn't tell them I'd killed her—but I had to tell them *something*. Lamiel's empty shell lay in that carriage, in stiff and silent accusation, going home to her betrothed with all the solemn circumstance accorded to the dead.

I swallowed and tried again. "She was the one who tampered with the Black Tower. The protections killed her." It was technically true, if you counted my family among the tower's protections, but I couldn't quite meet their eyes. "I have to hope Alevar will send a replacement envoy to the negotiations, but ... they may not."

Kessa let out a low whistle. Foxglove tapped his fingers on the seat beside him. "That complicates things. We've got a diplomatic role as well as a magical one; half our job is smoothing over disputes about magic. It's why we're an international organization. If we're walking into a political midden fire, we've got to be ready."

"The Shrike Lord isn't known for being the type of sweet, forgiving soul who'd overlook the death of his beloved for the sake of international harmony," Kessa said, grimacing.

I rubbed my temples, using it as an excuse to hide behind my hands. "He certainly isn't. I'm sure my grandmother is busy sending birds back and forth, trying to avert a war." One that was at least partially my fault, and could claim thousands of innocent lives if we couldn't find a way to head it off.

"Let's get up to the castle," Foxglove said grimly, lifting the reins once more.

Gloamingard didn't feel right.

It looked the same as always, its jumble of towers looming

above me and casting cool shadows across the hillside. But where I'd expected it to pulse with the bright core of the restless anger that animated the land, there was instead a brittle emptiness, like a blown-out milkweed pod. Something vital was missing, leaving a silence, as if the castle's heart had frozen between beats.

I leaped out of the wagon seat before the horses had clattered to a halt in front of the Birch Gate, vaulting over the side.

"Odan!" I called. He was already hurrying toward the wagon, his face grim as old stone. "What's happened? Is everything all right?"

His sharp eyes raked across the Rookery, taking in their presence, before returning to my face. He offered me a perfunctory bow, fingers barely sketching the warding sign in his urgency. "Warden. Thank the seasons you've returned. Is there word from our lady?"

I stared at him blankly, only dimly aware of the bustle behind me as the Rookery clambered down from the wagon. "What do you mean? Odan, is the castle safe? Is everyone well?"

He hesitated. "You may not have heard—Exalted Lamiel—"

"Ryxander!" A new voice roared. I froze where I stood.

An all too familiar figure stormed through the Birch Gate with the inevitable force of an avalanche. "What in the Nine Hells is going on here, Ryx?"

Pox. Not her, not now. I had enough to deal with already.

My aunt Karrigan strode past Odan to meet me, a fur mantle bristling on her shoulders, bloodred mage mark blazing in her eyes. The fists she planted on her hips bore half gloves mounted with bear claws; more claws woven into the iron-and-gold braids coiled on her head formed a spikey crown. She was the youngest of my grandmother's three children, and had terrified me when I was small. I wouldn't swear an oath she didn't terrify me now.

My pulse jumped in my throat as I raised my chin to greet

her. "Hello, Aunt Karrigan. I didn't realize you were visiting. Where's Grandmother?"

Karrigan glared as if my words offended her. "I was about to ask you that."

"What?" I glanced at Odan, but he nodded, grave lines creasing his face.

"No one's seen her since last night, Exalted Warden," he confirmed. "She's disappeared."

SIX

I stared at my aunt, uncomprehending. Odan turned to the Rookery and, ever efficient, spoke quietly with them about lodging as stablehands swarmed around the wagon. The grass withered beneath my feet, curling in on itself, dry and brown.

"She's gone?" I asked, stunned.

"I got a bird from her last night with a message saying to stay away, so of course I came at once." Karrigan swept an arm back toward the looming jumble of Gloamingard behind her. "And what do I find? A dead Alevaran atheling, and my mother missing. You're supposed to be the Warden of Gloamingard; explain this."

Witch Lords didn't disappear. You couldn't lose a Witch Lord under the bed, or wandering in the forest. It would be like losing a mountain, or the sky itself. It made no sense that my grandmother was gone—especially now.

"The Door," I said suddenly, a cold and nameless dread gripping me. "What about the Door?"

Karrigan went still. "What about it? Blood of the Eldest, Ryx, what happened?"

"I'll tell you later." I started toward the castle gate. "We need to get to the Door."

My aunt stepped in front of me, stopping me with a hard

hand to my shoulder. The touch shocked me more than hurt; I flinched back instinctively, even knowing she was powerful enough to resist the deadly pull of my magic.

"You're going nowhere until you give me a full explanation," she said.

I drew myself up, angry words forming on my tongue. Before I could loose them, Foxglove stepped up beside me, carefully beyond arm's reach.

"Exalted Atheling." He bowed deeply to my aunt. "The Exalted Warden is right. We need to see this artifact at once. It may be unstable."

The idea put a cold lump of ice in my stomach. If something urgent had called my grandmother away from the Door before she could fully deal with it, and that obelisk had been leaking some unknown power into the castle the entire time...I didn't know enough to imagine the consequences, but it twisted my heart to think I hadn't been here. Never mind that I wasn't sure what I could have done without functioning magic of my own; I'd have found a way, as always. Protecting the castle was my duty.

Karrigan turned to face Foxglove with menacing slowness. "And who," she asked, "are you?"

He bowed again, with fluid grace. "The leader of the Rookery eastern field team. The Lady of Owls has called on us, via the Warden, to help with a magical accident. If you'll please step aside, my lady, we have work to do."

"Such arrogance," Karrigan growled. "You expect me to believe that my mother invited *you*, a Raverran, to meddle in our most carefully guarded secrets?" She didn't move, but her magical presence swelled like an eventide shadow, pressing at the senses.

"It's true." I straightened, striving to project some fraction of the strength my aunt did so effortlessly. She was everything an atheling should be: wild and terrible and strange, overflowing with power. Everything I wasn't. "We can argue about it later if you want, but we don't have time now. We have to get to the Door."

Some emotion flickered in Karrigan's eyes; it could have been anything from sympathy to contempt. She had never deigned to interact with me much on her visits to Gloamingard, and her shifting moods had always been hard to read.

"Very well," she said at last. "Show me what madness you've unleashed at the Black Tower."

The moment our feet stirred the dust in the corridors of the old stone keep, echoes of distant magic began crawling across my skin. We weren't even near the Black Tower yet.

"Oh, that's ominous," Kessa murmured, rubbing her arms.

"You have no idea," I replied, dread building in my gut.

We rounded the corner into the hallway that ran past the Door. A wave of power hit me in the face, a sluggish pulse of energy thick as raw honey and infinitely more smothering. I gasped at the force of it. Heat filled the corridor, and a scent like lightning.

The red light falling on the floor from its alcove and the sheer power hanging in the air left me with no doubt: the Door was open.

"Blood of the Eldest," my aunt whispered hoarsely. She broke into a run.

Karrigan stopped before the open Door, staring into its scarlet glow. The Rookery followed more cautiously, fanning out behind her; I lagged behind to give them space, my pulse ragged with fear.

My grandmother would never have left it like that. But she was gone, and the Black Tower stood open, its secrets laid bare. The implications were far too terrifying to contemplate.

I braced myself for outrage and reprimand from my aunt,

for accusations that I had failed in my most important duty as Warden.

Karrigan's eyes narrowed and she breathed, "*That's* what she was hiding all these years."

And without another moment of hesitation, she strode into the Black Tower.

"Wait!" I protested, hurrying forward to face the bone-humming power pouring forth from the open Door. The Rookery gave way before me, exchanging worried glances as they made ample room for me to pass. "Have you forgotten the Gloaming Lore? *Nothing must unseal the Door.*"

"Well, something did, and I'm taking my cursed chance to have a look." She stopped a few paces in and gazed around her.

"My lady," Foxglove said quietly, too close to me for comfort. I stepped out of arm's reach, my heart quickening. "Much as I hate to say it, we need to go in there."

The last thing I wanted to do was cross that threshold again. But I was Warden of this as well.

"All right." I took a deep, ozone-scented breath and stepped into the Black Tower once more.

The vast circular room stretched above and around me, the lines and patterns and runes glaring with scarlet light. Karrigan stood gazing around with her face made hard and impassive to hide whatever she might be feeling at her first sight of the chamber we'd been guarding all our lives. The Rookery spread into a loose arc; by the soft gasps and low exclamations, I wasn't the only one overwhelmed by the barrage on my senses.

I had eyes only for the black obelisk that stood, stark and final, at the center of the tower.

No line of white light split its center. It stood as it had when

Lamiel first opened the Door, blank and flat and silent, the seal engraved upon it hidden by the harsh red light behind it. Only remnants of its searing power remained, like a lingering scent in the air, but those were enough to set me shuddering.

Ashe's fingers flicked out from her chest in the warding sign. Bastian started drifting toward the artifact, his eyes alight with fascination, but Kessa took a firm hold of his wrist and held him back.

"Not so fast," she said. "Remember what happened that time in Callamorne."

"Not so fast, indeed." My aunt turned to face them, arms crossed on her chest. "Invitation or not, you're intruders here. Give me one good reason I shouldn't cast you from this chamber."

I bristled. *I* was the Warden of Gloamingard, not Karrigan; it was up to me to decide whether to throw them out. I was about to tell her as much, but Foxglove stepped forward first and bowed.

"Because you have no idea what any of these runes and patterns mean," he said. "We do. Without us you'll never understand this tower's dangers, let alone counteract them."

Karrigan grunted. I could almost see the calculations passing across her face: the truth of Foxglove's words, the Rookery's reputation for untangling the most difficult magical knots, the ancient weight of the Gloaming Lore. Her gaze swept the room—the countless glowing lines and runes intersecting in patterns of dizzying complexity, the magical energy palpable in the air—and came to rest on the black obelisk at the center.

"I can't believe she was hiding something this powerful from us," she said. "She *must* have known about it, but she never told us a cursed thing. What does it *do*?"

"Let's find out," Foxglove said, seizing the opening. He turned to Bastian with as much confidence as if she'd told him to go ahead. "What do you think?"

Bastian gaped around the room, pausing occasionally to scribble and sketch in his notebook. "I've never even *heard* of an enchantment of this scope. The Sun Pillar in Osta is the closest thing I can think of, and you could fit five of those in this room. And look at all this obsidian!" He shook his head in awe. "Obsidian is one of the best sources of magical power. A chunk the size of my fist could hold enough to blow up a house. This much..." He gestured around at the massive obelisk and the obsidian-sheathed walls looming far over our heads. A chill shivered across my shoulders.

My aunt listened, eyes gleaming with guarded interest.

"It concerns me that the patterns are all wards," Foxglove said. "Whoever built this tower *really* wanted to contain something."

Nothing must unseal the Door. I swallowed and hoped to the Nine Graces that whatever it was, it was still contained.

Bastian's pencil scratched furiously, grating at my nerves. "It's definitely Ancient Ostan in origin. I can tell by the style. I'd say this tower is at least three thousand years old."

It didn't look old. The polished obsidian walls, the precise lines of the wards—everything was clean and sharp-edged as if it had just been finished. And the power humming underneath my skin, making my bones itch, was fresh and deadly strong.

"Are the seals intact?" I asked hopefully. "Can we just close the Door and walk away and not worry about it?"

"No," Foxglove said quietly. "Can't you feel it? They're leaking."

Karrigan's breath hissed through her teeth, and my heart curdled. That couldn't be good.

"Do I need to evacuate the castle?" I asked.

Foxglove exchanged a long look with Bastian. At last, he shook his head. "I wouldn't let anyone into this chamber, but not much seems to be making it past the tower door. The rest of the castle should be safe for now. As for in here—well, let me know if anyone starts feeling nauseous, has strange compulsions, begins melting, that sort of thing."

I let out a nervous laugh, though I doubted he was joking.

"The seals are working, but something compromised them," Foxglove continued. "We need to make sure they won't break open again—and figure out what will happen if they do." He turned to me, the red light tracing shadows on his face, and uttered the words I'd been dreading. "Ryx. Tell us what happened here."

Expectant stares fell on me from every direction. I couldn't lie to them—there was too much at stake—but I didn't want to tell the full truth, either.

"The Lady of Owls commanded me to secrecy on certain details of the circumstances," I said slowly, "but I can tell you everything that pertains directly to the artifact." Ashes, I'd have to step carefully here. "When it was touched, a line of white light appeared in that groove down the middle, and a wave of immense magical power came from it."

"Who touched it?" Foxglove asked sharply. "Was it Lady Lamiel? Is that how she died?"

Her hair spread on the floor, limbs tangled in the senseless sprawl of the dead. I'd been trying not to look at the spot where she'd fallen, or to think about dragging her corpse across the rune-marked floor.

"I touched it." My voice came out ragged and raw. "I was trying to keep Lamiel away from it."

"There's an astoundingly complex seal on the obelisk," Bastian announced. He stood at the edge of the final ward circle, which glowed in vivid scarlet on the floor. "Between the door, the tower, the circle, and the stone, that's a lot of nested barriers. I've seen similar layered wards in workrooms at the Mews, for when they're using dangerous magic. Whoever created this wanted to be able to release the artifact's power but contain its effects."

"So with the layered wards in place, it's probably safe to activate," Foxglove mused.

Something between hunger and outrage leaped in my aunt's face. "No one is activating that stone but an atheling of Morgrain," she declared. I had a suspicion which atheling she was thinking of.

Bastian bent closer to the circle on the floor. "Well, if I read these runes right, only a member of your family could pass this ward in the first place, so that seems to be a given. As for whether it would be safe, I suppose it should be, so long as you didn't disturb the warding circle around it."

"No one should activate it at all," I said. "It's too dangerous."

"Nothing happened when it was activated before?" Foxglove pressed. "A wave of power, but no other effects you could see?"

Kessa raised a skeptical eyebrow. "It did kill Exalted Lamiel. That's hardly nothing."

Now they were making assumptions about all this dangerous magic based on the half-truth I'd told them. I didn't want my deception to get someone killed.

"Not directly," I said carefully. Grace of Wisdom, help me tread the narrow path between telling them too much, and too little. "It was the protections that killed her, not the activation of the obelisk itself."

My aunt stared at the stone, a hungry light in her eyes that I didn't like. "You still haven't told me what it does."

Bastian flipped through pages in his notebook. "Given all the obsidian, it's possible the artifact is just a power source. Vast amounts of magical energy stored here in case the family ever needed it."

"One of my family could use this power?" Karrigan asked, too eagerly.

My spine stiffened. "This thing was sealed away for a reason."

"I suppose you could." Bastian scratched his head with the tip of his pencil. "I'm not certain how you'd harness it without some sort of intermediary device, though."

My aunt rubbed her hands. "Well, then. Will it help your investigation if I give it a quick touch, so we can see what happens?"

"*Are you mad?*" The words burst out of me. "The Gloaming Lore—"

"Says to keep the Door sealed," my aunt finished. "But it's too late for that. Mother has left us with this puzzle, for reasons she declined to share with us. If she wanted us to simply seal it away again, she wouldn't have called in the Rookery." She turned to face Foxglove. "Well? Can you understand it well enough to do your duty *without* seeing it activated?"

Bastian and Foxglove exchanged a long look.

"Perhaps, given time and reference materials..." Bastian began dubiously.

Ashe snorted. "It's your castle, Atheling. Up to you if you want to risk destroying it."

It wasn't Aunt Karrigan's castle. It was mine. My one and only charge, while my cousins were all Wardens of several castles and villages and towns each.

"If it would actually risk destroying the castle, I can't allow it," I said.

"Oh, I don't think it should." Bastian gave Ashe a dubious sideways glance that suggested she was not the expert on magical sciences in the group. "Any danger should be confined to this room."

"Shall I, then?" Aunt Karrigan asked.

I opened my mouth to protest.

It was as if an invisible finger laid itself on my lips: *Shh*.

I felt her presence, in the walls themselves and the land beneath me and the pulse of my own blood through my veins. *My grandmother*. She was *here*, her focus entirely upon us, stronger even than the oppressive magic that hung in the air.

My heart leaped despite the gravity of the situation. Wherever my grandmother had gone, whatever had happened, she was at least well enough to spare some attention for what was happening here.

If anyone else noticed, they showed no sign of it. Foxglove spread his hands. "It's your risk to take, my lady. We'd certainly learn something. I'd keep it to a quick touch, though; I can't guarantee it's safe."

Ashe gave him a skeptical look, but she didn't say anything. Bastian pulled out great round rune-marked spectacles ringed in artifice wire and settled them on the bridge of his nose.

Karrigan stared at Foxglove, and then at the obelisk. Beads of sweat formed on her brow. What she was about to do went against centuries of lore, and she knew it.

My stomach clenched so tight I almost couldn't breathe. Even my grandmother's presence couldn't reassure me. Karrigan wanted this too much.

"Don't," I whispered.

My aunt never did listen to me.

Without another word to any of us, she crossed to stand just outside the final circle. She stood a moment, regarding the obelisk with grim resolve. Then she reached across the barrier and laid the tips of two fingers against its glossy black surface.

I swallowed a cry of alarm, my chest tight with fear, bracing myself for a blast of eye-scouring light.

Nothing happened.

"See," Bastian said into the silence, nodding, "That's the thing I don't understand. There's nothing in the runes telling it to activate if you touch it."

Foxglove's brow creased. He turned to look at me. "You said it did something when *you* touched it."

I nodded reluctantly.

My aunt stepped back from the obelisk, her face guarded, rubbing her fingers against her thumb as if some residue clung to them. A wild, deep darkness haunted her eyes beneath the careful crease of her frown. I wasn't so certain that nothing had happened.

Fear. I'd never seen it on her face before, but that was fear. And something more, as well. Loss? Yearning?

Her gaze flicked to me, almost accusatory. "There's no reason it would work for Ryx and not for me."

Foxglove beckoned me forward, his expression mild. "It can't hurt to try, then, can it?"

All I could think of was that sickening blast of blinding white light and the crawling intensity of the power that had flowed from the gate—and the dulling of Lamiel's eyes, the life fleeing her body. Had I conflated the two too much? Was I overreacting under the pressure of that violent memory, and the weight of power in the air, and the ominous red light that bathed us all in blood?

No, this *had* to be a genuinely terrible idea.

"With all respect," I said, "I know you're the expert, but I'm not certain we know that it can't."

Ashe snorted. "Good instincts, for a mage. You're right. But we've dealt with dozens of these sorts of things, and there always comes a point where you have to poke it. Sometimes you regret it, but you have to poke it, or else give up and go home. You've got no other way forward."

Kessa laughed ruefully. "She's not wrong."

Ashe grinned. "I never am."

My aunt jerked her head toward the stone, jaw tight, eyes calculating. "Do it."

"Please," Foxglove added, with a little bow.

I could say no. I wanted to say no. The word formed in my throat.

Do it, said my grandmother.

Her voice came not from the air around me, but from the blood that connected us, the land that bound us, the magic that wove between us. It was more a feeling than words—a pressure, an urge—but it was her familiar, watching presence that pushed the impulse into my mind.

Do it, Ryx.

I had no idea why she would want me to activate the artifact.

It went against my every instinct. But if there was one person in the world I trusted absolutely, it was my grandmother.

I pushed down my fear and forced myself to walk to the edge of the glowing ward circle. The black obelisk loomed before me, filling half my vision. Its power pulled at me, like a sucking wind, resonating through me until all I could hear and feel was its deep, humming pulse.

Graces protect me.

I pulled off one glove, tucked it in my belt, and reached through the barrier. The magic tingled across my fingertips, my arm, all the way to my shoulder as I strained toward the stone.

There was something old and horribly familiar about the seal carved into its heart, crossing that deep cut of a vertical line. Like the face of someone I'd met a long time ago, in a bad dream.

I braced myself and brushed the tip of one finger against its center.

The world split open in a dazzling, burning flood of white light.

SEVEN

A gony ripped through me, the foaming crest on a wave of vast and terrible power. The room shuddered with it. Searing radiance blazed from the groove down the center of the black stone, and heat blasted me as if I'd opened an oven door. I was barely aware of a great commotion in the room, of voices crying out in shock and fear.

Someone grabbed my arm, fingers digging into my flesh, and yanked me back.

I let out a yelp of anguish—*No, not again, I don't want anyone else to die*—but it was Aunt Karrigan who squeezed my arm painfully tight and then let go, face pale with shock and very much alive. The white glare from the obelisk immediately began to fade.

"That's quite enough," Karrigan said roughly. She rubbed her hand as if it ached.

I shuddered, my whole body still buzzing with residual power. Bastian knelt on the floor, spectacles off and hands over his eyes, muttering, "Ow, ow, ow." Kessa bent over him, a concerned hand on his shoulder; Ashe glared at the obelisk through a squint, her sword eased half an inch from its sheath.

"Right," I gasped. "You've seen it. Now let's get out of here and close the Door."

"Good idea," Foxglove agreed, his usually smooth voice gone rough.

I turned toward the Door, swaying on my feet, eager to get out of this accursed place and seal it behind me.

An iron-haired woman in a sumptuous sapphire-blue gown stood just beyond the threshold in the alcove, dark eyes wide, staring in at us as scarlet light flooded her shocked face. A cluster of others hovered uncertainly behind her, all dressed in the Raverran fashion, with corseted gowns and frock coats. Odan's nephew Kip, a bright-eyed boy of about eight and a castle page, hopped up and down beside them; he appeared to have been frantically attempting to signal me.

The envoy from the Serene Empire had arrived.

"We seem to have arrived at an unfortunate time," the envoy said, her voice smooth and controlled even though strain showed around her eyes.

I stood blocking the open Door, red light bathing my back. With the Raverran delegation clustered just beyond the alcove, I was trapped, and the Rookery couldn't leave the tower without coming far too close to me. My bones throbbed with the unsettling heat radiating from the stone, and every muscle still ached. All I wanted was to get everyone out of here and close the Door. It was madness that I had to be polite and political now, but I forced the lines of my face into a smile.

"Not to worry, Lady...ah..." Curse it, I knew her; she'd visited Morgrain as a diplomat before. I'd helped her and my grandmother draft an agreement allowing imperial trade ships to dock in more of our harbors. "Lady Celia. Welcome to Gloamingard. I have, ah, matters to attend to now, but if you'd like to—"

My aunt strode through the Door, her fur mantle brushing

my shoulder as she swept past me. "You're trespassing," she told the envoy, her voice cold as a granite slab. "This part of the castle is forbidden."

Lady Celia stiffened.

Lovely. Karrigan had all the grace of a charging boar. I stepped up beside her before she could further insult the envoy. "Which you couldn't possibly have known, so that's all right," I inserted, before Celia could reply. I attempted a disarming smile, with questionable success.

"I told her, Exalted Warden," Kip piped up unhelpfully. "I told her we weren't allowed in here, but she said she had to see you at once, and Uncle Odan was off getting the Rookery's special gear settled, and—"

"Yes, thank you, Kip, that's enough," I cut him off, my cheeks burning. "Lady Celia, I must profoundly apologize for our lack of proper welcome at the gate. We've had some, ah, unexpected circumstances."

"So I gather." Irony dripped from Celia's voice. "I'm told the Lady of Owls is absent and the envoy from Alevar is *dead*, which is rather awkward given that I've come hundreds of miles to negotiate with her."

"The Shrike Lord is sending a new envoy." Karrigan flicked aside her concerns with a lazy hand. "I got a bird from Alevar. They should be here tonight."

Relief flooded me at this news, mingled with bitterness that Karrigan had known before I did, both there and gone in an instant. The new envoy was more likely to be carrying a declaration of war than a mission of peace. There was no way they would sit meekly at the negotiation table without some kind of reckoning over Lamiel's death.

"I'm glad to hear it," Lady Celia said, "but forgive me if this reception doesn't inspire me with confidence. I'm placing my trust and the Serene Empire's in Morgrain to be a fair mediator and keep us safe despite the history of war between us. So far the survival rate for envoys in your care is far from reassuring."

Karrigan snorted. "Exalted Lamiel died because she went prying in places she didn't belong. It was her own cursed fault."

"What my aunt means," I said, wishing a plague on Karrigan's throat to shut her up, "is that this chamber is dangerous, and it was an unfortunate disregard of warnings about that danger that led to Exalted Lamiel's tragic death in a magical accident." Couldn't the Raverrans feel the raw pressure of power scraping across my nerves and see what a bad idea it was to linger here?

Lady Celia's eyes strayed past me toward the glimpse of glowing red lines and runes of power beyond, an avid gleam kindling in her eyes. "Truly. We certainly saw an impressive release of power a moment ago."

She looked far too interested. I desperately wished she hadn't seen the inside of the Black Tower; no matter how much the Serene Empire might have gentled over the years, its thirst for magical power remained unquenchable. Foxglove stirred behind me, no doubt wanting to step up and smooth things over, but there was no room for him to get past me safely and no dignified way for him to interject from several feet behind us.

A new voice spoke up from the others clustered behind Lady Celia: an unexpectedly familiar male tenor. "Speaking as your adviser on magical matters, my lady, it *does* look highly dangerous. I have no desire to wind up blasted by some oversensitive ward or malfunctioning magical device. Perhaps we'd best retire to those rooms the kind page offered us for now."

My eyes flicked sharply to a young man in the scarlet-and-gold uniform of the Falconers. Good Graces, it *was* him—Aurelio Berelli, the protégé of one of my mother's colleagues and perhaps the closest thing I had to an old friend. His small, neatly trimmed beard was new since I'd last seen him some three years ago, as was the uniform. The fall of auburn hair over one eye was the same, however, and the sharp, lean lines of his face, and the deep, thoughtful eyes. It was surreal seeing him now, when the solid anchors of my life were being ripped up one by one, as if he came from a past that only existed in stories.

He hadn't shown any sign that he knew me. I'd only met him some four or five times, when his mentor visited my mother and brought him along, but I was *sure* it was him, beard or no. Wasn't it?

As I hesitated, he dropped one lid in a slow, subtle wink. A bright, heady warmth rushed up through my core. He remembered. We were still friends.

"That would be safest," I agreed, grateful. "I promise I'll welcome you properly to Gloamingard and offer you hospitality and explanations shortly. But first, by the Nine Graces, let me close this Door."

This time, no one disagreed.

It took everything I had to maintain both polite conversation and a safe distance as I escorted Lady Celia and the Raverran delegation to their rooms, trying not to stare at Aurelio to make sure that yes, it really was him.

"So unfortunate that the Lady of Owls should be away now," Lady Celia said, with a hooded glance in my direction. "Whatever could keep her from Gloamingard at a time like this?"

"She had to deal with a chimera that crossed our border from Alevar." It wasn't even a lie.

"Alevar seems to be causing all manner of trouble for their neighbors." Lady Celia's voice took on a certain acidity. "Do you think they'll still be willing to accept Morgrain as a mediator, between this and Lady Lamiel's death?"

She asked the questions I most wished I had answers to myself.

"I hope so. I assure you that I'll do what it takes to bring Alevar to the table."

Lady Celia made a noncommittal noise. I supposed the Empire had the least to lose, since its fleet could assault the Alevaran coast without needing to so much as set boots on land. *We* were the ones sitting directly in the path of any potential Alevaran offensive, and I'd probably just removed any hesitancy the Shrike Lord might have about invading Morgrain to get to the Empire.

"Does it even make sense for me to remain here, with the Lady of Owls gone and the Alevaran envoy dead?" Lady Celia asked.

"Of course!" The last thing I needed was for the Raverrans to give up and go home. "As you've heard, a new envoy from Alevar is on the way, and I'm sure the Lady of Owls will return soon." I could be sure of no such thing, with no idea where she'd gone. "And if she's not, it doesn't matter; I'm fully prepared and empowered to act as mediator."

"In all honesty, I'm almost more comfortable with you mediating alone," Lady Celia said, dropping her voice. "I know you and respect your work, and your mother served Raverra well for many years. I have confidence that you'll be fair to the Serene Empire."

Unexpected warmth bloomed in my chest at the novel sensation of having my Raverran blood appreciated rather than looked at askance. I smiled. "I'll do my best, my lady."

Gaven had set aside an entire hallway in the New Manor for our Raverran guests; we'd discussed little touches to make them feel at home, from imperial-vinted wine waiting in their rooms to scented baths ready for them on request. Lady Celia seemed quite pleased. It was a relief to see something, at least, going right.

I showed Aurelio his room last. Once we were alone in the wood-paneled hallway of the New Manor—still called that at a hundred and seventy years old—I turned to him and let my disbelief show at last.

"Aurelio!"

"Lady Ryx." He dipped a bow, smiling warmly. "I hoped you might remember me."

"Of course I remember you." I clamped my mouth shut before I could say *How could I forget?* By Aurelio's standards, I was probably a mere acquaintance, one of hundreds.

I'd met him on a few occasions scattered over several years, when he traveled with his mentor to Vaskandar on diplomatic visits. Aurelio had been the first stranger who'd been intrigued rather than afraid or disdainful when he learned of my power, showing a rather Raverran interest in all things magical. The last time I'd seen him, we'd spent an afternoon sitting on Gloaming-ard's western terrace with a good safe stretch of space between us and talking—him with a bottle of wine and me with a pot of rosehip tea, since I couldn't risk impairing my judgment or reflexes—waiting for the sun to go down over the hills.

There had come a moment when I knew that if it weren't for my broken magic, I would have sidled closer and maybe tried to kiss him. But the moment had passed, leaving a dull ache in my chest like a shard of glass healed into a wound. His mentor's diplomatic visit ended, and he went back to Raverra, and that was the last I'd seen of him for three years.

I doubted it meant as much to him as it had to me. But he'd remembered me.

"I'm so glad you're here," I said fervently. "Everything's gone to the Nine Hells, and it's good to see a familiar face."

His expression sobered. "I can imagine. What in the Graces' names has been going on here? You must be at your wit's end, with dead envoys and mysterious artifacts—"

"It's been twelve hours of complete madness. Hells, I'm not sure it's even been twelve hours." I passed a shaking hand across my brow.

Aurelio's eyes widened, and he stopped himself in the act of reaching toward me. "Grace of Mercy, your sleeve is all slashed and bloody! I didn't notice in the red light earlier. Are you all right?"

His concern fell on me like summer sunlight. No one in Gloamingard besides my grandmother so much as acknowledged it if I was hurt; perhaps because I was a mage, or perhaps because I was cursed, but either way they seemed to assume that pain and injury were meaningless to me.

"Oh, I'm fine." I tucked my arm self-consciously behind my back. It still hurt, but it had stopped bleeding long ago, and the wound seemed to be closed beneath my improvised bandages. "It'll be nearly gone by tomorrow. You know how quickly vivomancers heal."

"Still, you should have that looked at." He shook his head. I didn't point out the obvious—that no physician could treat me, and I'd always had to tend to my wounds myself. "Let me know if there's anything I can do to help."

"Since you mention it..." I hesitated, unsure how much I could presume. "I want to hold these negotiations together, no matter what it takes. Is there anything I should be aware of on the Raverran side, to help make this work?"

"Lady Celia herself is fairly committed to peace," he said, stroking his beard in a self-conscious way that made me wonder how long he'd had it. "Her main concern is making certain no Vaskandran would-be Witch Lord tries anything like this again on imperial soil."

"You say Lady Celia *herself*," I observed. "Are there others who might influence the negotiations who feel differently?" I'd learned from my mother that while the Serene Empire usually presented a united front to outsiders, the quiet political struggles beneath that surface could be fierce and sometimes bloody.

Aurelio hesitated. "Well, it's no secret that the Council of Nine is divided on Vaskandran foreign policy. Right now the majority still favor cordial relations, but there's a significant faction that believes war is inevitable. If not now, over this Windhome Island incident, then soon."

"We've kept the peace for a hundred and fifty years," I protested.

"More or less. There have still been diplomatic incidents like this every few years, and little border skirmishes. The Vaskandrans can't seem to stop making grabs for imperial land." He gave a sort of *those barbarians* grimace that made it clear he didn't consider me Vaskandran; uncomfortable feelings tumbled one after another into my stomach. "The difference in the past hundred and fifty years has been that there's an active and concerted effort to work together to resolve those issues. But there've been more and more clashes over the past decade or two; the border is heating up. It's only a matter of time. Or so this faction believes."

"So do they *want* war? Will they try to sabotage the negotiations?" The last thing I needed was people working against me on both sides.

"No, no." Aurelio waved the idea off. "They're not working toward war; they've just given up on sustaining peace. Their goal is to make sure Raverra has the edge when the conflict comes, so they're focused on gathering up all the powerful magic they can find. They may not try to interfere in the negotiations—but I can tell you they'll be more than a little interested in that artifact in your tower if they hear of it."

"Thanks for the context," I said wearily. "I appreciate it." This was exactly what I needed: more problems and complications, and more reasons why it was vital not to let these peace talks fail.

Most likely they already had. Alevar might be sending a new envoy, but getting them to the table would be a feat likely beyond my diplomatic skills. And it sounded as if at least some in the Empire were dubious that we could succeed.

Everything was sliding straight into the Hell of Nightmares, and I had no idea how to stop it.

I met with the senior castle staff next, asking them to prepare for the new Alevaran envoy's arrival, keep everyone away from the Black Tower, and let me know at once if they discovered any clues as to where my grandmother might have gone.

"What does it mean, that the lady is missing?" Gaven asked, his face pale and his usually cheerful voice unsteady. He had every reason to be concerned; no matter what a Vaskandran's opinion might be about their own Witch Lord, they were the only thing keeping their people safe from neighboring ones. Many of my grandmother's peers wouldn't hesitate to strike if they thought Morgrain undefended.

"She's alive," I assured him.

"The Lady of Owls has had unexplained absences before," Odan added, projecting calm assurance. "She doesn't need to keep us informed of her business. She'll return soon."

I turned to Jannah, the minor Furwitch who handled Gloamingard's messenger birds—and sometimes its feathery spies as well. "Can you pass me any messages meant for my grandmother until she returns, just as we normally would if she were traveling?"

Jannah, a bright-eyed and stylish woman in her forties, cocked an eyebrow. "Of course, Exalted Warden. And what do you want me to do if Exalted Karrigan asks for them?"

I let out a long breath. I still had to reckon with Aunt Karrigan. It was no accident that she'd come running when everything went wrong. My grandmother had three living children: my Uncle Tarn, the eldest, serious and cautious; my father, the middle child, warm-hearted and devoted; and Karrigan, the youngest, full of fire and ambition. My father had no interest in the succession. My grandmother had let it be known she favored Tarn as her heir, but Karrigan never lost an opportunity to attempt to convince her otherwise. Of course Tarn would stay away, obeying my grandmother's command, the dutiful son, while Karrigan rushed in to seize control, save the day, and prove her worth.

Right in the middle of my complex and delicate negotiations.

"My esteemed aunt is not the Warden of Gloamingard," I said at last.

Jannah's eyes twinkled. "Then she shouldn't read its correspondence without your permission."

"I should send messages to my father and uncle and fill them in on what's happening here." I ran the smooth bumps of my braid through nervous fingers. I wasn't looking forward to confessing how fouled up things had gotten on my watch.

"I'll have my fastest birds ready to carry them," Jannah assured me. "And let me know if you'd like any help writing them, Exalted. I'll be trying out my latest set of Raverran alchemical inks tonight anyway, writing letters to my daughters."

"Thank you, but I should probably handle these myself." I hesitated, almost dreading what I had to ask next. "Speaking of birds...I assume you've sent some to try to contact my grandmother?"

Jannah, nodded, her lips pressed together. Her silence told me all I needed to know about the lack of reply.

Usually the birds of Morgrain could find my grandmother instinctively, through her link to them and all living things in the domain. If even her birds couldn't find her, something was very wrong indeed.

I wanted more than anything to crawl into my room and collapse facedown on my bed until dinner. But there was one more person I had to talk to, if I could find him. I set out searching the shadowy corners and high places of Gloamingard for Whisper.

He could vanish like smoke in the wind when he wanted to. Sometimes I didn't see him for weeks; other times I couldn't turn around without finding him watching me through narrow yellow eyes, tail wrapped neatly around his paws. He'd seemed to take a particular interest in the Black Tower, however, and I suspected his secret purpose touched on it. Perhaps he was some guardian of the Gloaming Lore, or a piece of it himself. I'd seen his face carved out of bone and shaped from wood in odd corners of the castle, his distant stare as ambiguous in art as in life. I was gambling that he'd let me find him, this time.

Sure enough, I soon discovered him poised on the broad log railing of the second floor balcony that overlooked the Old Great Hall, watching Gaven direct the spreading of fine tablecloths and positioning of oil lamps in preparation for our noble guests. His tail swished thoughtfully back and forth below the railing, like the pendulum of a clock.

"Hello, Whisper," I ventured.

"One thing I will never understand about humans is how bent you seem to be upon your own destruction." He didn't bother turning to face me. "Why did you touch the stone a second time?"

That was a good question, and one I'd asked myself more than once this afternoon. I sighed and sank down to sit cross-legged on the balcony. "Because Grandmother told me to."

He flicked an ear back to point toward me, as if this answer caught his attention. After a moment, he stretched, flexing his claws on the railing, bushy tail lifted for balance.

"Do you always do what she tells you?"

"Well, she *is* the Witch Lord of Morgrain." I thought about it. "But no. Not always."

"Then you touched it because you wanted to."

"I need to learn more about the obelisk. Touching the stone was the only way we could think of to do that." I tugged my gloves off and ran the soft leather through my hands. "*You* know something about that stone. Don't you?"

"I know many things," he said, with great gravity.

"Do you know where my grandmother is?" I asked, unable to keep my voice from roughening. "Have you talked to her?"

His tail swished. "We're in communication."

My heart quickened with hope. "Is she all right?"

He stared at me a long moment from his vantage on the railing. I couldn't tell if he was considering the question, consulting magically with my grandmother over what to tell me, or just thinking about his dinner, curse him.

"She's as well as you or I," he said at last.

"Then why did she vanish?" I demanded, my frustration bursting out. "Why isn't she here at Gloamingard?"

"For the simplest reason of all," he said. "Because she doesn't want to be found."

"This is a crisis!" I threw down my gloves. "It makes no *sense* for her to disappear now. What in the names of the Eldest is she *doing*?"

Whisper's tail swished behind him, writing his restless thoughts on the air. For a moment, I thought he wouldn't answer. Finally, he spoke, his voice soft and surprisingly deep.

"Ryx. I'm going to tell you something, as a favor."

My skin prickled. He shouldn't be able to strike dread into me with such simple words.

"Yes?" I asked cautiously.

"Leave this alone."

I blinked. "What?"

"Don't dig any deeper. Patch up your human political problems, seal the Door, chase out the rooks, and forget any of this happened."

He caught me in the intensity of his stare, no longer aloof but layered with meaning I couldn't begin to read.

"I can't," I protested. "You know I can't."

"As your friend," he said, with careful precision, "I am asking you this. Leave it alone."

Your friend. Hells. He'd sunk his claws in my soft spot.

"I wish I could," I said quietly. "I wish things could go back to the way they were before Lamiel came, before the Door opened, before I touched that awful stone. But I need to know what I unleashed, Whisper."

"Why?" He glanced away when he asked it, as if he didn't care.

Which meant that it was an important question. I turned it over in my mind with the serious attention it deserved.

"Because if I caused any harm, I need to do what I can to fix it," I said at last. "I can't just walk away from a mess I created."

Whisper tilted his head. "Is that truly what you want?"

"Yes." I forced conviction into my voice.

He stared at me for a long moment. Then he rose and stretched, with deliberate languor. "I'm sorry. I can't help you."

"What?!"

"Not with this." He leaped down from the railing, landing lightly on the balcony. "I'm afraid we're at cross purposes. I may be your friend, Ryx, but I have never pretended to be your ally."

"Friends *are* allies," I protested. "If you know something, tell me!"

His yellow gaze slid away from me. "In all my life, I've only ever made one promise. I'm not going to break it now."

This was news to me. Whisper never talked about himself—his

purpose, his origin, any of it. I wasn't sure even my grandmother knew much about him.

"What promise?" I breathed.

"If I told you that," he said, "I'd have already broken it."

And he slipped away like a wisp of smoke from an extinguished fire.

EIGHT

Do you have any idea what sort of promise Whisper might have made?"

I'd finally gathered the resolve to talk to Aunt Karrigan, drawing her aside before we entered the Old Great Hall for dinner. My first question to her was tactical: she wouldn't be expecting this one, so maybe it'd throw her off and we could have this conversation on my terms.

"What, that cursed spook of a chimera?" Karrigan frowned. "No. You're not bringing *him* into this mess, are you?"

So much for escaping her disapproval. "I'm pursuing any leads I can to find out where Grandmother is. Have you heard from her?"

"No." She scowled. "And neither has Tarn or your father. She didn't talk to anyone in the family before she pulled this disappearing trick."

I dropped my voice low enough to make certain the sharpest ears couldn't overhear us. "There's no chance she's...in trouble, is there?"

"What sort of trouble could bother a Witch Lord in her own domain?" Karrigan shook her head. "I know the land was agitated earlier—even you must have felt it—but I don't sense anything like that from her now. She's fine. This is some gambit of hers." Anger colored her voice.

"What are the rest of the family doing?" I hated to have to ask, but even my own father was more likely to talk to Karrigan about important matters of domain security. Everyone in a Witch Lord's family had a place and a role, based on how much magic they had—everyone except me, who had magic but couldn't use it. And since I wouldn't fit in to the hierarchies of Vaskandran society, it was easier to ignore me altogether.

Karrigan grunted. "They're following my mother's orders like good little children, and staying away. But you can bet they're watching our every move to see what happens."

She started for the wide doors to the Old Great Hall, finished with our conversation. As I followed beside her, however, she leaned in close to me, coming much nearer than anyone would dare who couldn't counteract my power. "I'm about to sit down at this table to host an imperial noble, and I barely know why she's here. I have no patience for Raverran duplicity. What do I need to know?"

I swallowed a complex and bitter cocktail of possible responses. *You need to know that I'm the host here, not you. You need to know weeks of strategizing and preparation. You need to stay the Hells out of this and be polite.*

I couldn't say any of that without starting a fight. It would be easier to let Karrigan have her glory—to step back and allow her to be the face of Morgrain. As long as she was willing to listen to my advice, she could be my mask and gloves, the safe and acceptable face I presented in public while I guided matters from a few steps back.

I had only a moment before we took our places at the table and our guests started arriving, so I kept my explanation short.

"Whatever you do, don't insult her, because we want the Empire to ally with Morgrain if the Shrike Lord decides to attack us." Karrigan's brows lowered as if she might argue, so I pressed on. "The most important thing we need to do now is make sure Alevar and the Empire sit down at the table together and come to an agreement over Windhome Island. We can't let them walk away, or we get a war."

Karrigan grunted. "If either of them go to war with us, they'll regret it."

Maybe, but so would we. "Let's not give them the opportunity to make that mistake." She looked unconvinced. "Please, Aunt Karrigan. I know you don't follow politics outside of Morgrain, but believe me that this is important. The Alevaran envoy is going to show up soon, and they're going to be furious, and we have to do whatever it takes to get them to calm down and talk to us and to the Empire."

"Fine." Karrigan didn't look happy about it, but she wasn't a fool, either. She dragged out the host's chair at the center of the high table and dropped into it with the arrogant confidence of one born to rule.

I settled in my place near the end of the table, with several chairs removed between me and the next seats to create a buffer, misgivings multiplying in my heart.

The Old Great Hall began to fill, castle staff and guests trickling in to take their seats for dinner. The Rookery arrived at one of the lower tables, talking animatedly; Kessa spared me a grin and a wave. They had the look of people excited at an idea, rather than stumped or worried, which seemed like a good sign. I'd have to talk to them after dinner. They drew their chairs close together, smiling and nudging one another and generally acting like friends having a good time. A twinge of envy pricked my chest at their closeness, and all those casual touches.

I'd touched a friend once. Her name was Rillim, and I was in love.

She had the mage mark, so she could resist the fatal pull of my power if she was ready for it. She'd stayed at Gloamingard one summer when we were both fifteen; she had a smile full of wry humor, bottomless brown eyes, and graceful hands. I'd held one of those hands, her fingers warm and soft in mine, a thrill of glorious discovery coursing through me.

When I'd confessed to my grandmother that I was thinking of asking to court her, she'd sent Rillim home. I never saw her again.

I'm sorry, Ryx, my grandmother had said. *You can't ever be that close to someone. There's too much at risk.*

I'd been furious, but she had a point. No one could be braced and ready *all* the time. I stifled the ache of longing in my chest and turned my gaze away from the Rookery.

Lady Celia and Aurelio arrived at the high table. Tension rode up my spine and settled in my shoulders as my aunt and I greeted them. Now the game was on again, and everything I did had to convince them that diplomacy could advance, if not smoothly, at least effectively.

Aurelio came around the end of the table to say a more personal hello, which made my heart leap more than it should have.

"Feeling better?" he asked, with a nod at my arm.

"Mostly." I flexed it, feeling only a slight twinge of pain.

"Excellent." He grinned. "I'm sorry the circumstances are somewhat dire, but it's good to see you again, Ryx."

"And you." My face warmed.

Raverran custom demanded I make polite talk about inconsequential things, but I had almost no practice with this sort of casual conversation.

I blurted out the first thing that came to mind. "I didn't expect to see you in uniform."

"Ah, yes, do you like it?" He adjusted his collar self-consciously. "My mentor—Lord Urso, you remember him, he worked with your mother—managed to arrange an officer's commission for me. I'm very grateful. I'm only an ensign, but it's still unusual for those who aren't of patrician birth to start their military careers as officers."

That was one of the things my mother was most proud of about her home country—that unlike in Vaskandar, where your entire future was determined by the degree of magic in your blood, in Raverra you could rise through the ranks on merit. "And is your family proud of you?"

Aurelio rubbed the back of his head, reddening a little. "I've never seen my father smile so widely as when I came home in the uniform."

"That must be nice," I said, a bit wistfully.

Aurelio shook his head. "Your family should be proud of you, too. I still can't believe they look *down* on you for having unique magic. If you lived in the Empire, we wouldn't scorn your power. We'd use it."

I couldn't think of a polite way to point out to Aurelio that given that my magic seemed to only be good for killing and destruction, I'd rather people *didn't* see it as useful. It was a rare and wonderful thing to have a friend speak up for me; I wasn't going to ruin it by arguing with him.

"What are you doing on a diplomatic mission?" I asked instead. "Don't you have a Falcon to attend to?"

"Not yet. I'm an officer without a Falcon—which makes me perfect to act as an adviser for negotiations centering around magical military matters, like this incident with Windhome Island."

"An adviser already! Well done." I gave him a knowing smile. "Of course, I'm sure your presence in that uniform will also remind Alevar that if they make this a fight, the Serene Empire has considerable magical power to bring to bear, too."

He laughed. "See, this is how I know you're Raverran. You understand how we think."

There was nothing particular to Raverra about displaying

magical power as an unspoken threat, but I smiled back. "Vaskandar learned our lesson about Raverran magical might in the War of Ashes," I agreed. "I'm hopeful that Alevar will be willing to settle the Windhome Island dispute peaceably."

"Good." Aurelio's brows drew together. "But what about you and Morgrain? From what I've heard about the Shrike Lord, he doesn't seem the type to forgive and forget the death of his betrothed—but he's still sending an envoy. That's a good sign, right?"

"Not really." I hesitated over how much to tell him. But he'd been honest with me about the Raverran factions, and my fears were all rooted in matters that were common knowledge in Vaskandar. "Since Witch Lords can't effectively settle their disputes through violence, in Vaskandar we rely on a system of favors and grievances."

"Ah." Aurelio grimaced. "The death of his betrothed sounds like a pretty serious grievance."

"It is. We'd have to offer up a fairly dramatic favor in return to have any chance of the Shrike Lord declaring himself satisfied. Which we may not be willing to do, since her death was an accident." Those last words went stiff in my mouth; Lamiel's death might not have been murder, but it lacked the innocence of an accident.

Aurelio frowned. "So what happens if he won't accept a favor?"

"Then it all comes due at the next Conclave." The gathering of Witch Lords existed to resolve disputes, among other things, but the death of his betrothed was a sufficiently dramatic grievance that the Shrike Lord might be able to get enough allied domains on his side that he *could* invade us. Or worse, win the support of one of the Eldest. I suppressed a shudder at the thought. "Suffice to say it would be far better if we could find a way to pay back the grievance."

"But her death wasn't a murder," Aurelio protested. "She tried to get past a lethal ward and it killed her. Right?"

I hesitated a second too long. Graces help me, I'd never liked lying, and I had no practice at it.

Aurelio was no Vaskandran atheling, used to having his word treated as divine edict in a land directly dependent on his magic for bounty and protection. All his life he'd had to read people for the slightest chance at advantage. He didn't miss the flinch I couldn't keep from my face.

"Grace of Mercy," he whispered, his eyes widening. He barely mouthed his next word: *"You?"*

I shook my head frantically. Not to deny it, but because there were too many people in the room. No one was close, no one seemed to be listening, but by the Eldest, I couldn't risk anyone overhearing this.

He stared at me, mouth still slightly open, the truth slowly spreading to every corner of his face. I braced myself for him to jump up and denounce me. Or possibly worse, to recoil in horror, shutters closing forever between us in his eyes.

Instead of drawing back like I expected, he leaned forward, his face serious.

"I won't tell anyone," he whispered.

Gratitude shook me like a wind through dry leaves. I managed a faint smile. This must be what friends did; they kept quiet about the people you killed.

Lady Celia called Aurelio over to her side then, and we all sat down for dinner. Between the empty space around me and the vacant places for the Alevaran envoy and their second, it was a sparse and unbalanced table. My spine locked ramrod-stiff, but Lady Celia sipped a glass of the red wine I'd had brought out for our Raverran guests, relaxed as if there were nothing strained about the circumstances.

"I do hope the Shrike Lord won't become too distracted to

seal our agreement," she said. "It would be rather awkward to leave half a fleet sitting off the coast of Alevar indefinitely while he processes his grief."

I swallowed. "I can see why that might be inconvenient."

"Mind you, we can spare the ships." Lady Celia chuckled, somewhat ominously. "I'm more concerned that certain Raverran factions who favor an aggressive exercise of our magical might will succeed in their push for a retaliatory strike while we wait."

Karrigan grunted. "So long as your navigators know where the coast of Alevar stops and the coast of Morgrain begins."

"Hopefully it won't come to that," I said, wishing I could kick my aunt under the table.

Lady Celia swished her wine around in her cup. "Alas, there are those in my government who consider it low risk to bombard the coast of Alevar with hurricanes and magically augmented cannon fire, since so long as we don't set boots on the shore the Shrike Lord would have no way to retaliate—or at least, not without coming through Morgrain." She lifted her glass. "Something I'm certain everyone at this table wishes to avoid."

"That *is* why we're mediating this negotiation," I interjected, before my aunt could voice whatever stronger reply I could feel building like a storm around her.

"Of course." Lady Celia smiled wryly. "Hopefully the negotiation can proceed despite this unfortunate incident with Lady Lamiel. One does feel a bit like the Grace of Majesty in the Dark Days, wrangling all the petty kings to agree to band together against the Nine Demons while the Demon of Discord kept them fighting over trivialities."

Aunt Karrigan relaxed back into her chair with an appreciative grunt, the prickle of her gathered power fading from the air. "We have that story, too. Except in Vaskandar, we say it was a great mage who got everyone to work together, not your Grace of Majesty."

A commotion sounded outside the Old Great Hall, on the far side of the stout oak doors that sealed its entrance archway woven of delicately curving antlers. Karrigan frowned and lifted her head, and I knew she was thinking the same thing I was: if our grandmother were here, she would have known what approached, and whether it was a cause for alarm. Without her, we were blind.

The doors burst open. Odan stood there, out of breath, clearly having run to arrive ahead of the boots that echoed at a determined pace up the corridor.

"Announcing the Exalted Atheling Severin of Alevar," he called hoarsely. "The Shrike Lord's brother and heir."

Then he staggered as a middle-aged man with a pointed beard swept him aside with a polished bone staff. "Make way for the Exalted Atheling!" he called, his voice ringing harshly through the hall.

"That will do, Voreth," said a lazy voice behind him. And Severin of Alevar strode into the room.

NINE

Exalted Severin had a presence with edges so sharp he seemed to cut the air around him and leave it in glittering pieces. His shining black hair fell in a sleek tail almost to his waist, with two loose locks framing a fine-boned, golden-brown face. His mage mark gleamed stormy gray in dark eyes hooded with apparent disdain. He still wore black leather riding clothes from the road, and a narrow cape edged with elaborate knotted thorn designs floated from one shoulder. Every eye in the hall fixed on him at once—mine included, whether I liked it or not.

I rose to welcome him, though my aunt stayed seated, her mage mark smoldering crimson. Severin stopped in the middle of the hall; Voreth, his second with the bone staff, hovered at his shoulder, chin lifted. Voreth's eyes bore no mark, but he must be a mage to carry himself with such arrogance.

Severin raised an arm to command attention he already held captive. He did not bow.

"My brother offers you no greetings, Exalted Athelings of Morgrain," he called, and his smooth tenor voice chased echoes from the rafters. "He did not send me here to bandy niceties and sip beer in your halls. The Shrike Lord cares for one thing only: vengeance."

Well, at least he'd gotten straight to the point. Lady Celia's eyes widened, shocked at a directness no Raverran diplomat would dream of.

Karrigan pushed back her chair, the legs scraping against the floor like blunt claws, and rose. If she were my grandmother, the room would have darkened with her anger, and the castle would have shuddered awake at the young atheling's temerity. While she was no Witch Lord, the cold stare she gave Severin carried force behind it nonetheless.

"You are here in this house because we invited you to speak of peace. And yet you stand there with war on your tongue."

"Exalted Lamiel came in peace," Severin declared. Which was a dubious claim, but I still felt a pang of guilt. "And now she lies dead, after trusting herself to your hospitality. You have destroyed my brother's peace. You must make amends before he can respect yours."

Unease fluttered in my belly. Lamiel might have brought her own death upon herself, but it had still been my magic that ended her life. And the Shrike Lord's wrath might be unreasonable, but that made his grief no less real.

"Do not tell me what I must do here in my family's castle," Aunt Karrigan growled, her voice deep and dangerous.

I straightened my spine and let my own voice ring out to fill the hall. "We respect the Shrike Lord's grievance, though Exalted Lamiel violated our hospitality." Severin's gaze swiveled to lock onto mine; I nearly faltered as his intense gray-ringed stare struck me. I had to hope he wouldn't think too closely about the difference between respecting the Shrike Lord's grievance and acknowledging it. "If you've come to claim that grievance, we can discuss it while you're here for the negotiations. If you've come to reject repayment and declare war..." Eloquence fled my tongue in the face of such a dire prospect.

"Then your timing is awkward," Lady Celia inserted dryly.

"Because the Serene Empire sent me to discuss peace, and it will be terribly unfortunate for everyone if the subject of conversation turns to war instead."

For a moment, Severin's lips twitched, and I could have sworn he was on the brink of a wry smile. If so, he suppressed it quickly. "Alevar has no grievance against the Serene Empire, my lady, and I do hope to keep it that way."

Then he turned back to my aunt and me, his expression hardening. "Fortunately, my brother in his mercy has allowed me to offer you a peaceful resolution." Was that a rich undertone of irony on the word *mercy*, or had I imagined it? "If you will accept this condition, I am to stay and participate in the negotiations as his envoy. If you deny his generous offer, I am to return to Alevar at once to help my brother prepare for war."

Dread locked every muscle in my body tight and twisted the key. I could read the same suspense on the faces of my aunt and Aurelio, in Lady Celia's deceptively relaxed posture, in the wary stillness of the staff and the Rookery at the lower tables. No one wanted to plunge back into the near-constant conflict that had plagued the region before the War of Ashes, but we balanced on a knife's edge above an abyss of blood.

"And what is this condition?" I asked. My aunt rolled the claws of her half gloves in a clicking cascade on the table.

"It's simple." Severin spread his arms. "To appease his grievance, the Shrike Lord demands that Exalted Lamiel's murderer be handed over to him for justice."

Hell of Nightmares. I might as well have swallowed a bucket of ice. From what I'd heard, the Shrike Lord's justice most often involved impalement.

"Exalted Lamiel died in a magical accident, to be generous to the dead," my aunt objected. "That's hardly murder."

"No." Severin's voice rang sharp and clear to the rafters. "She was a part of my brother's domain, and echoes of her dying moments resonated in his mind. We don't know the identity of the killer, but he is quite certain she was murdered."

"Your brother is wrong," Karrigan replied flatly.

The air between the two mages crackled with unseen power, a pressure building around them as they glared at each other. My evasions were about to escalate out of control here and now. I pressed my palms flat against the table, the truth straining for release behind my teeth.

Lady Celia lifted a casual hand, like a delicate knife slid between braided layers of conflict. "If I may offer a solution, Exalted Athelings? Would it be fair to say that *if*, upon investigation, it turns out that Lady Lamiel's death was in fact a murder, Morgrain will turn over the culprit to the Shrike Lord for justice?"

"Certainly." My aunt folded her arms across her chest. "*If* it was a murder, the killer is yours to do with as you see fit."

My fingernails bit into my legs beneath the table. Ash and ruin, she might have just condemned me to death.

If it got Alevar to the table and secured peace, that might be worth it.

Foxglove rose from his seat and bowed deeply to both Severin and Aunt Karrigan. "We of the Rookery are expert investigators already looking into the magical accident in question," he said. "We would consider it an honor—and, indeed, part of our task here—to investigate this matter and attempt to discover the identity of the murderer."

Now my family *and* the Rookery had promised my head to our enemy. Still, I had to hope it would work. Thank the Graces no one was watching me, because I was certain my distress was written clearly on my face.

No, someone *was* looking at me—Aurelio, his eyes wide with concern. He glanced away with a grimace, clearly trying not to draw attention to me. I'd have to hope that he truly was the friend I thought him, and that I could trust his discretion.

"Very well." Severin gave a slight bow at last, his glorious fall of hair rippling with the motion; my aunt returned the belated courtesy with equal restraint. "The domain of Alevar accepts your offers. And I may now accept your hospitality."

A dizzying mix of sickness and relief washed over me. "Welcome to Gloamingard then, Exalted Severin."

I knocked at the Rookery guest suite feeling as if the weight of half of Eruvia pressed down on my shoulders. Severin might have agreed to negotiate, but my grandmother was still missing, the Shrike Lord still bent on vengeance, and the Black Tower still breached and probably dangerous. I hadn't slept since before Lamiel's fateful visit, and my legs trembled with exhaustion.

Kessa flung open the door. She didn't recoil in alarm on seeing me so close, as one of my own people would have; her fingers didn't flick in the warding sign. I pressed back against the smooth-worn log wall behind me, wishing the hall were wider.

"Ah, Exalted—that is, Ryx! The seasons smile on us! We were just about to send someone to ask if you could join us."

I had no business feeling this soft warmth at Kessa's smile. She wanted me here for practical reasons, not personal ones; her lack of fear was dangerous, not endearing. The sparkle in her eyes must be for whatever she was thinking about before I knocked on the door, not for me.

"Have you figured out what the artifact does?" I asked, trying to sound businesslike.

Bastian crowded behind Kessa in the doorway; every time I saw him, his hair was more tousled. "No, not quite yet. We may have made another important discovery, though."

"Oh?"

"I have a theory about why the artifact responded to you the way it did, and we were hoping you might let us test it." Bastian's brow creased as if his own words worried him. "We may have figured out how your magic works."

I stared at him in shock. No one had ever satisfactorily explained my broken magic, not in all my twenty-one years.

If you understood why something was broken, maybe—just maybe—you could fix it.

"Why don't you come in," he said gravely.

The Rookery settled themselves around the sitting room of their guest suite with the casual grace of a Raverran noblewoman's discarded accessories, distributed on furniture and windowsills along with an impressive spread of open books, scattered papers, and a few strange artifice devices coiled with gleaming wire. They'd set me up in a place of safe and splendid isolation by the fire, moving furniture to create a space around me. That had taken some doing, since Odan had put them in the Great Lodge, with its woodsmoke-scented homey comfort; all the chairs were built of massive logs and vein-poppingly heavy.

"We never did properly introduce ourselves, what with the death and politics and magical explosions," Foxglove said with a graceful bow. "How much do you know about the Rookery?"

"Not much," I admitted, trying to settle myself comfortably despite the racing of my pulse, which had spiked to a near hum at Bastian's announcement and refused to calm down.

"We solve magic problems," Ashe said. "Foxglove will give you a big boring lecture about international politics, but that's all you need to know."

"I'm, uh, interested in that part," I apologized.

Ashe grunted with disgust.

Foxglove ignored her. "After the War of Ashes, everyone

wanted some way to prevent future magical catastrophes. The Rookery was the creation of certain powers seeking more cooperation between Vaskandar and the Empire, and it's been around in one form or another ever since." He flicked imaginary dust off his cuffs. "There are, after all, a surprising number of ways magic can go wrong, and someone has to deal with it when it does."

"Sadly, not all of those ways can be fixed with stabbing," Ashe sighed.

Kessa shot her an affectionate glance. "Yes, well, much to Ashe's dismay, sometimes we clean up diplomatic messes left by magic, too. Settling disagreements over who gets to keep a powerful old artifice device dug up on a border, conducting discreet investigations when a public figure is suspected of unethical magical experiments, that sort of thing. All talking, with no stabbing at all."

"Or this investigation into the Black Tower," I concluded. "What have you learned so far?" Much as I burned to know what they might have guessed about my magic, the tower had to be my first priority.

"Well," Bastian said, "the sheer quantity of magical power in that obelisk is frankly terrifying." He had his little notebook out, running his long fingers down its leather cover as if for comfort. "And I suppose if it's been sitting there collecting energy for thousands of years, that's reasonable, but I'm a bit nervous about even a quick pulse of it being released without any idea where it's going or to what purpose it might be channeled." He fluttered his fingers in a gesture that could equally have indicated mystery or explosions.

"Me too," I agreed, rolling my shoulders uncomfortably at the memory of that power raging through me.

"We hope to unravel the Black Tower's mysteries soon," Foxglove said, "but part of that mystery is why the obelisk reacted only to you. And Bastian has a theory that we need your help to test."

"Only if you're willing," Bastian added, with a glance at Foxglove. "The tests are completely safe, but it's your choice."

I nodded my assent, trying to keep my face smooth so no one would guess at the pounding of my heart.

"Excellent. Thank you." Bastian beamed as if I'd given him a present. "Now, before we get started, for safety purposes, tell me—does anything block your power? Does it travel through cloth, glass, metal? Is it safe to hand you things if we don't touch you?"

"I wouldn't chance it." I held up a gloved hand. "Some things can muffle my power a bit, slow it down—like my gloves—but nothing stops it."

"Even air?" Foxglove asked curiously.

"Even air." I shifted uneasily in my chair, warding off bad memories. "When I was a child, I used to wither flowers if I bent close to smell them, but I've trained enough at holding it in that the effects don't reach much past my skin now. You might feel something from a near miss, but it's not fatal."

I expected them to make the warding sign, or at least lean away from me. They were the Rookery, however, and I supposed they'd seen far worse. They just looked interested, as if I were something new and intriguing rather than frightening or shameful. I swallowed a sudden tightness in my throat.

"Right, then! Let's see." Bastian rummaged in a great lumpy satchel by his feet and procured the same strange spectacles he'd donned in the Black Tower. Artifice runes marked the frames, and twists and swirls of beaded wire ringed the lenses, one of which was green and the other red.

"They call these Verdi's Glasses," he explained, settling them reverently over his eyes. "There are only about a dozen pairs in existence, because they require an exceptionally skilled artificer to create. They let you perceive certain flows of magical power."

"I see." I couldn't hide the nerves that wound my fingers

tight together. I might be on the cusp of some kind of definitive answers about my faulty magic at last.

Bastian fished around in his bag some more and produced a wire-wrapped pocket luminary. He shook it vigorously until it glowed, then held it out toward me.

"Take it," he urged, his face behind the glasses excited as if he expected something marvelous to happen.

I stared at him across the empty space the Rookery had so carefully set up between us. "Bastian," I reminded him, "I can't take that from you."

"Oh? Oh!" His brows flew up. "Right." He rose and set it on the mantel, within my reach.

I pulled off my glove, then carefully picked it up, the glass and beaded wire warm against my skin.

My fingers tingled, and the light winked out.

Anxious disappointment twisted my stomach. "Did I break it?"

"No, no," Bastian said, seeming delighted. "That's perfect. Amazing!"

"Like you thought," Foxglove said, with satisfaction.

"If it's all right with you, I'd like to try something else," Bastian said to me, his careful diffidence barely covering his eagerness.

I found myself glancing at Kessa, as the most familiar face in the room; she winked. "All right."

Bastian took a candle in a silver holder from the corner of a desk and lit it with a spark from another small artifice device, then set it on the mantel as well.

"Try putting your finger as close as you can to the flame," he suggested. "Without burning yourself, of course."

Foxglove leaned forward as I took up the candle, watching me avidly. Even Ashe kept an eye on me sidelong as she pretended to stare out the window.

Once the flame steadied, I held a finger near the candle, stopping when I felt its heat. This time, no strange miracle occurred.

"I'm not certain what this is supposed to prove," I said.

"Try closer," Foxglove urged.

"Fine." I moved my finger a little farther toward the flame, wary of pain. Bastian let out a nervous hiss.

When the fire was close enough that the heat seared my skin and I was sure I'd be pulling my finger away with a burn, the candle suddenly guttered as if in a draft. The flame bent toward my finger, dwindled to a blue nub, and went out entirely. A thin trail of pale smoke rose from a tiny red ember at the tip of the candlewick.

I hadn't pinched it, hadn't breathed on it, hadn't quite touched it.

"Ha!" Foxglove crowed. "You were right, Bastian."

"I don't understand." I tried to keep my voice even.

"Tell me, Ryx," Bastian asked, his voice unexpectedly gentle, "do you break things often?"

"I—yes." Hells. His theory was that I literally ruined everything. My face heated. "What does that have to do with the obelisk? And why did the flame go out?"

"It's nothing to worry about. It just proves my theory." Bastian removed his glasses and caught my eyes with his earnest brown ones. "Ryx . . ." He drew a deep breath. "You aren't a vivomancer."

That wasn't what I'd expected. "Of course I'm a vivomancer. My father is a vivomancer. My grandmother is a vivomancer. My aunt and uncle and cousins are vivomancers. I come from a long line of vivomancers, all the way back to the Sycamore Lord at the founding of Vaskandar."

"And you probably were born a vivomancer," he said. "Something must have happened to damage your magic. When did it start behaving strangely?"

"It was always this way." That sounded stubborn even to me. I softened my tone and explained once more; at least no one thought I was a Skinwitch this time. "I was very sick as a baby, just as my mage mark was forming. My parents say I nearly died.

After that I never could control my power, no matter how they tried to teach me."

"A serious illness right as your powers were manifesting—yes, that might do it." Bastian's hands fluttered as if he shaped the idea with his fingers. "You see, magical energy is just that—energy. And the right circumstances can transform one kind of energy to another, like how a fire breaks down the life energy stored in wood and turns it to heat, or an artificer creates a device that transforms the volcanic energy stored in obsidian into binding magic—somewhat like a magnetic field—to seal a door."

"You're saying I don't just destroy life." I forced the words out through a tight throat. "I destroy *everything*."

"Not *everything*," he said, seeming eager to reassure me. "And not really *destroy*—it's dreadfully hard to truly destroy anything. More perhaps unravel, or disrupt. Or maybe—"

"Focus, Bastian," Foxglove said dryly.

Bastian jumped. "Right! Yes. Normally a mage can only manipulate energy in one way. An artificer directs energy through patterns, an alchemist transforms and reshapes magical energy through combining various substances, and a vivomancer directly manipulates the already complex energy of life. They're all imposing new order on a particular type of energy through a specific method, and one step in creating that new order is often to unravel the old one."

"But all I can do is unravel," I said, feeling sick.

"Yes." Bastian gave me a tentative sort of smile, as if he believed this might be good news but wasn't sure how I'd take it. "Your illness must have cut off the development of your magic before it could become refined and controlled, and so you simply disrupt the energy of everything you touch, breaking down its order, sometimes to the point of dissolution." He made a sort of dispersing motion that was disturbingly similar to the warding sign, fingers flicking outward. "And you draw some of that energy into yourself. Life is just a very complex, fragile structure, so it breaks down most easily."

"Lovely." I pushed loose tendrils of hair back from my face as an excuse to rub my eyes. I knew the man was a scholar, but why did he have to look so *pleased* about this? "The list of things I shouldn't touch is longer than I realized."

"The list of things your power is useful for may also be longer than you realized," Foxglove put in, his dark amber eyes gleaming.

"Oh?" I arched an eyebrow. "Like draining the power from ancient seals and unleashing Graces know what upon us all?"

"Well, we do think that's what happened in the Black Tower, yes," Bastian agreed with an apologetic grimace.

Foxglove ignored him, keeping his attention locked on me. "Like neutralizing dangerous enchantments. Taking down traps and wards. Disarming magical weapons." He paused, and I hardly breathed, pinned by his glittering gaze. "Saving lives."

"I would love to save lives, instead of ending them." I couldn't look away from Foxglove's face. I knew full well he was selling me something; he was too intent, too charismatic, too Raverran. It was hard to care.

He spread his hands wide. "Consider what the Rookery does. A great deal of our job is dealing with the relics of old wars. You've grown up in the borderlands; you must have some idea how many of those odd lumps and hummocks farmers plow around are buried artifice weapons that could wipe out a village, or jars full of alchemical poison that could get into the drinking water, or tombs built to contain sleeping war chimeras until their masters need them again."

I could see where he was going with this, hum along to the song he was playing. By all Nine Hells, it was too cruel.

For almost my entire life, Gloamingard had been my world. I almost never left the castle grounds, and I'd dedicated myself wholly to my duty as its Warden. Every time a restless longing had risen in me to see my mother's country, or to visit other domains—even to travel to other parts of Morgrain, the land bound to my very blood—I'd ruthlessly yanked it out, like pulling up a weed. Every time I yearned to make friends, to be part of a group, I'd throttled those feelings, too. But like weeds, they kept coming back, day after day, year after year. Foxglove was pouring water and sunlight on them, bringing them to full, aching bloom.

"I do know this," I said carefully, trying not to show how my heart had quickened at his words. "And yes, I can see where being able to simply drain the magical energy out of such things could prove helpful."

"*Incredibly* helpful," Kessa put in, with a firm nod. "On half the missions we've done, your power could have spared us anything from severe burns to blister pox, and I can think of at least one or two cases where it would have saved lives. Our job would be much less dangerous if we had you along."

"*Less* dangerous? With someone whose slightest touch could kill you?" I snorted. "You're not thinking this through. I can't travel, go to cities, so much as step into a crowded tavern—Hells, I'm a hazard even in Gloamingard, where everyone knows to stay away from me."

"That's why we'd give you a jess," Foxglove agreed, a shrewd spark in his eye.

A jess. I gripped the armrests of my chair, doing everything I could to keep my face neutral. No matter how tempting the bait was, a jess was still a trap. I couldn't hand over control of my magic to the Serene Empire.

"You could at least give us a try," Bastian said, with a hopeful smile. "Maybe as a temporary auxiliary member? It's only a job, not a holy order; it's not as if you'd be signing your life away."

Part of me yearned to jump at their offer, like a child grabbing at a proffered sweet for fear it would be taken away. It was everything I wanted: a way to use my magic to *help* instead of wrecking everything. People who valued me, or at least valued what I could do. Most of all, an end to the constant fear of accidental murder—and the ability to feel life beneath my fingertips without it ending. To never have to stand over a body again, flooded with guilt and terror, wondering if this time I'd killed them or just stopped their heart for a moment.

To ride a horse, go into town, pet a dog, travel the world. Everything I'd never dared to think I could do, for fear it would hurt too much when I couldn't.

Hug my mother. Touch a friend. Kiss a lover.

I thought of the sweet curve of Rillim's lips, and the warmth of her hand in mine. A flush crept up my neck, and I became all too aware of Kessa's eyes on me.

But it wasn't that simple.

"I have other duties." I forced the words out. "I'm the Warden of Gloamingard, and an atheling of Morgrain."

Kessa stepped halfway across the room and crouched down to stare me in the eyes; I shrank back instinctively, trying to keep more distance between us. Ashe hovered behind her, clearly ready to snatch her back out of reach if needed, but Kessa seemed not to notice.

"Ryx," she said, her warm brown eyes gone soft. "I'm a vivomancer, like your family. A minor Greenwitch, not strong enough for the mage mark."

I blinked in surprise. Magical bloodlines were rare. Even without the mark, if she lived in Morgrain, she would be Warden of a village or town, protecting and sustaining it with her magic.

"I know Vaskandar," Kessa continued. "I may not be an

atheling, but I know the duties of a Vaskandran mage. And for-give me—I'm sure this is painful—but you must know you can't perform them."

Her gentle words struck me like a punch to the stomach, hit-ting all the harder because they were true. I couldn't ensure a bountiful harvest or make crops grow out of season. I couldn't grant livestock healthy, long lives or make them understand complex commands. I couldn't rouse the land to defend my people from enemies. All the normal duties of a Warden were impossible for me. I couldn't even seal a marriage alliance with another mage family, like athelings born without magic tradi-tionally did.

I tore my eyes away from hers and busied myself with pulling my gloves back on.

"Maybe not," I said, my voice rough. "But I'm not only a Vaskandran mage; I'm also Raverran. And Raverrans know you don't need working magic to help rule a country."

Ashe made an appreciative grunt—a *Hey, maybe you're less stu-pid than I thought* sort of noise. I found it far more gratifying than it had any right to be.

"Of course." Foxglove tipped his head in a gracious nod, almost a bow. "No one doubts your capability, or denies that you're needed here."

That only twisted the knife Kessa's words had stuck between my ribs. Most of my family would doubt and deny both of these things. If I were being completely honest, I wasn't so sure of them myself.

"I'm certain you could join us for a few days on certain field missions without abandoning your role as Warden," Foxglove continued. I stirred, and he raised a hand. "You don't have to answer us now, of course. Just think about it."

Oh, I'd think about it. I'd think about it every time I flattened myself against the wall, heart racing, to give a servant room to pass me with averted eyes and flicking fingers. I'd think about it when I woke from nightmares of Lamiel's dying eyes, or that stable boy lying cold and pale in bed, or the tutor I'd never seen again after we accidentally grabbed the same book when I was nine years old. My grandmother had never told me whether she survived, and I'd been afraid to ask.

"I'll think about it," I promised. *You have no idea.*

TEN

I slept restlessly that night, sure that I'd wake up any minute to find my grandmother had returned. In my dreams, she came to me with a wry smile and a cup of lavender tea, like she did when I couldn't sleep. Her presence enfolded me like an owl's wings, warm and powerful.

But when morning arrived gritty-eyed and pale to peer in my window, my grandmother was still gone. I dragged myself out of bed, filled the hollow in my stomach with strong black tea, and got to work.

First I tried to catch up on all the messages pertaining to my more regular duties as Warden, shoved aside for the negotiations and the series of emergencies we'd faced: approving Odan's leave to take Kip to visit his grandmother in a few weeks (assuming we weren't at war), selecting a location for the upcoming harvest festival (assuming we weren't at war), settling a dispute over grazing rights (not that it would matter if war broke out). I replied to a few messages from family, reassuring my father that I was all right and promising one of Aunt Karrigan's children that I'd keep her informed (because her mother never told her *anything*). Uncle Tarn hadn't bothered to reply to my letter about the situation with the Door, which wasn't a surprise. He generally preferred to pretend I didn't exist.

Hell of Despair, but my morning business was more depressing than usual. I rose, restless, and headed for the Aspen Hall to check on preparations for the diplomatic reception that afternoon.

A diplomatic reception meant very different things in Vaskandar and Raverra. Vaskandrans couched their diplomacy in ceremony and ritual; Raverrans dressed it up in festivity, preferring to keep the wine flowing and the food coming. I'd decided to merge the two, combining Vaskandran opening ceremonies with a Raverran-style ball. The Gloamingard staff had never hosted the latter before, and I'd helped plan it for weeks, picking out wines and consulting with the chef about Raverran dishes. I'd arranged for musicians from Loreice, the imperial client state across the border, who promised me they knew all the music most fashionable in the Serene City that year.

All of it knowing I couldn't go, because a room full of people mingling and dancing and drinking would be far too dangerous. With the Lady of Owls gone, it would be up to Karrigan to play host—never mind that while my aunt was terrifyingly good at many things, diplomacy wasn't one of them.

An aching anger built beneath my ribs. Whatever my grandmother was doing must be important, but she should be here. We were supposed to be doing this *together*.

As I ducked beneath an archway that dripped strands of trumpet-shaped white flowers, Aurelio came striding toward me down an intersecting hall.

"Ryx!" he called, sounding genuinely delighted to see me. "Ah, there you are!"

"Aurelio." I instinctively stepped back through the archway to give him space as he approached. My shoulder brushed a hanging tendril of flowers; it withered almost at once, petals falling brown and crisp at my feet. "Is everything all right?"

"Of course." He stopped out of arm's reach, offering me a hesitant smile through the frame of dangling flowers. "Is it true that you're thinking of getting a jess?"

I froze. "Where did you hear that?"

"Foxglove. He asked me if I had one with me. I do; it's standard for officers in the Falconers, in case of a magical emergency." He rose up onto his toes, barely restraining his eagerness. "So? Are you going to do it?"

I'd been trying not to think about Foxglove's offer. It was far too tempting, and I had too much to do: I had the reception this afternoon to prepare for, a second round in the Black Tower with the Rookery after that, and then meetings with the envoys this evening.

All of which would be safer and easier to accomplish with a jess, curse it.

"I'm not sure," I said. "It's a difficult decision."

His auburn brows flew up. "Difficult? I thought you'd jump at the chance! I remember when you told me how lonely you are, not being able to get close to people."

My face burned. When had I told him that? It must have been after my grandmother sent Rillim away. Old shame flooded me, seeping into familiar cracks and corners. "My family wouldn't be pleased. They consider the jesses a tool for the oppression of mages in the Empire."

"The oppression of mages?" Aurelio snorted. "Is that what they call it when mages have anything less than absolute power in a society?"

"Yes, well, their perspective may be a bit skewed." I couldn't help remembering my mother's response when my father had likened a jess to a dog collar.

Without the jesses, the Serene Empire wouldn't be a republic, she'd said, as if that settled the matter. *We'd be ruled by mages, like you are here in Vaskandar.*

Would that be so bad? my father had asked.

My mother had condensed volumes of warning into one word: *Yes.* And my father had been smart enough to drop the subject.

Aurelio must have read something in my face. His expression softened into uncertainty, and he leaned a shoulder against the wall, hands stuffed in his uniform pockets. "You have to understand what it's like," he said quietly. "Knowing someone has this unanswerable power over you, and you have no defense against it. No recourse if you're wronged. You can't have true justice if there's a power imbalance that profound between the rulers and the people."

I wished I could tell him he was wrong. But I'd seen it too many times in the way some mage-marked guests treated my mother and my staff, after glancing once in their eyes—the dismissive condescension, the casual certainty that nothing they could contribute would matter, and that no abuse the mages cared to heap on them would have consequences. I could tell myself it was different in Morgrain, and point to people like Odan in high positions despite their lack of magic—but the very fact that I was still here, free and unpunished and in a position of power, after the deaths and harm I'd caused throughout my life proved Aurelio's point.

"I suppose you're right." I spread my hands, feeling helpless. "The Witch Lord system isn't something we can put down and step away from easily, though. Any domain temporarily without a Witch Lord gets gobbled up at once by its neighbors. When this power exists, you have to be able to defend against it—so you need it, too."

I expected Aurelio to argue, but to my surprise, he nodded vigorously. "Yes! You *do* understand. That's the entire principle behind the Falcons; they exist so that we can have that defense without letting mages rule us. This is why we're so afraid of

Vaskandar in the Serene Empire, Ryx. Because it always seeks to expand, raising up new Witch Lords as it seizes land to create new domains—and once it claims land, we can't ever get it back. Before the War of Ashes, we had to fight off a major invasion every generation or two, and we know it's only a matter of time before that begins again. It's why we can't let the Windhome Island incident slide." He reached out a hand toward me; I stepped back, flowery tendrils swaying between us. "That's the wonderful thing about taking a jess. No one has to be afraid anymore. Not you, and not the people around you."

"I sometimes wish I'd been born on the Raverran side of the border," I admitted, dropping my voice almost to a whisper as if my Vaskandran family could somehow hear me. "Then I could have a jess without all this political baggage attached." I would have grown up with one—able to play with friends, cuddle animals, go to fairs and dances and marketplaces. I'd probably be courting some bright-eyed Raverran girl, attending balls in the evening and holding hands in a long-prowed boat as an oarsman rowed us through the twisting canals. My empty hand tingled within its glove at the thought, as if something precious had slipped from my fingers.

To my surprise, Aurelio grinned. "Well. The idea that birth doesn't control our fates happens to be very important to me. After all, my father and I were both born in the slums, living in poverty, and plenty of people told us that was all we'd ever be. My father saved enough to get some schooling, though, and Lord Urso noticed him—and now my father is his secretary, and I'm an officer in the Falconers, and we're doing very well for ourselves." He dropped his hand, but not in defeat—more as if he'd caught what he was reaching for, and now he put it safely in his pocket. "You're Raverran, too. If my father and I can be as rich and well connected as minor gentry, surely you can get a jess and live a normal life."

A normal life. The words resonated through me like the tone of a great bell. I laughed, startled into it. "I don't even know what that would look like."

"Well," Aurelio said, "maybe you should find out."

Odan's nephew Kip told me that his uncle was with Gaven in the kitchens, discussing the buffet for the reception with the cook. I couldn't go into the kitchens—too much bustle, too much fire, too many breakable and spillable things—so I had Kip bring Odan and Gaven to meet me in the broad, empty, log-framed space of the nearby Old Great Hall. I pretended not to notice Kip stealing sweets intended for the buffet from a table by the open doors as we discussed preparations for the reception.

We were well into a debate about Raverran dancing etiquette when a sudden commotion rose up from the far end of the hall.

"Well? Answer me!" an angry voice demanded. Odan's eyes flicked past me to the doors, and he let out a half-smothered exclamation.

I spun to see Voreth, the Alevaran envoy's second, looming over Kip as the boy backed away, shaking his head.

"I don't know. Honest!"

"You will address me as Honored Voreth, brat." Voreth drew back his hand and slapped Kip across the face, the sound cracking across the Old Great Hall.

A tremor raced up my spine at the memory of a bearded face mottled with rage, and a small peach thief curled bloody and broken on the ground. The man I'd killed seventeen years ago had been a Greenwitch without the mark; it had been the conviction in his eyes that he was doing no wrong, that the magic in his blood gave him the right to hurt a little boy, that had sparked so much anger in me even then.

I was halfway across the hall before the echoes of the slap faded, my blood surging hot in my veins. Floorboards cracked beneath my steps with a sharp splintering sound, one after another.

"*Voreth!*" I roared. "How *dare* you!"

Voreth turned to face me, scowling. Kip's face went white as new snow, and he fled.

He was afraid. Of me. That hit me like a bucket of ice water, cooling my rage to something cold and hard, like forged steel.

"Exalted Ryxander," Voreth said, indignation lifting his voice, "that boy failed to offer me my proper title or the respect due a mage."

I clenched my hands so tight my leather gloves creaked. "Count yourself lucky that I don't hit you back," I said.

He'd been warned about my power; he understood the threat. Anger flashed in Voreth's eyes, and he lifted his chin. "I have seen no signs of any investigation into Exalted Lamiel's death. This morning, I've taken it on myself to question your staff. Thus far, they have proven remarkably insolent and uncooperative."

I advanced another step and stopped, not trusting myself within lunging range of him right now. "You mean they've proven *loyal*," I said, my voice coming up from where my rage burned deep in my chest. "If you lay one hand on any of my staff again, you'll have ten minutes to leave this castle before I set the chimeras on you. Is that clear?"

"This is outrageous," he protested.

"Is it *clear*?" I held his gaze, not bothering to hide my contempt for him.

He met my stare for a moment. No mage mark appeared in his black eyes to match the lightning-blue circles in mine, however, and finally he glanced down at the floor.

"It is, Exalted Atheling."

"Good." I took a deep breath to settle myself. "I will overlook this grievance for now, for the sake of the negotiations. But I do not forget it."

I turned on my heel and marched back toward Odan and Gaven, dismissing Voreth without a word. He could hold himself insulted for all I cared; I was done with him. I'd taken only a few steps when a door slammed behind me, announcing Voreth's departure from the hall.

Odan stood tight-lipped. He'd come halfway across the hall behind me, stopping a safe distance from the confrontation once he'd seen Kip was all right. I had no doubt he wished he could have dressed down Voreth himself, and it pained him to have to leave that to me. There was no sign of Kip, but I had the vague sense of his life somewhere in the hall; probably hiding. I couldn't blame him.

Gaven hurried over to stand beside Odan, bursting into applause with a vigor that suggested he'd rather be applying those slapping palms to Voreth's face. "You tell him, Warden."

"Are you sure that was wise, Exalted?" Odan asked.

"Yes," I said, lingering anger roughening my voice.

"Perhaps, but we—" A scuffle sounded, and Odan's eyes flicked behind me, widening. "Kip! *No!*"

The bright warmth of a small life lurched at me. I spun, breath freezing in my chest, as Kip burst blindly out from under the tablecloth where he'd been hiding, about to stagger into me as he flung himself toward his uncle for comfort.

Odan lunged toward him, crying out in alarm. Hell of Nightmares, I'd be caught between them.

I hurled myself to the side, heart exploding into a panicked gallop in my chest. Kip's hand brushed the edge of my vestcoat, a mere inch from my leg, before Odan tackled him to the floor.

"Are you all right?" I demanded, scurrying backward. "Grace of Mercy! Are you both well?"

Odan rolled Kip into his arms, a stream of blistering curses coming from beneath his gray mustache.

"Ow," the boy yelped, shaking out his hand. "It's cold! *So* cold! Am I dying?"

My shoulders sagged with relief. If he could talk, he'd be fine.

"No, you're not dying, idiot," Odan growled, still holding the boy close. "Look where you're going next time. Your mother will have my head on a pike if I let you get killed. You *knew* the Warden was in the room. What were you *thinking*?"

He smoothed the hair back from Kip's face with a gentle hand. Gaven knelt down beside them both, clucking his tongue. "Let's see your face, and that hand, Kip. Ah, you're all right, but we should have a physician take a quick look at you."

"I'm sorry," I said, my voice unsteady. "Thank the seasons you were quick, Odan. I'm so sorry."

Odan's jaw flexed, and he gave a short nod, but he didn't speak or look at me. All his attention was locked on Kip. As it should be, but Gaven avoided my eyes as well, and his fingers flicked out from his chest.

"Avert," he whispered.

There was nothing I could say to help; Kip stared at me in terror past his uncle's shoulder, and my presence was only making things worse. I let my shaky legs carry me out of the hall.

My breath came high and fast, as if I'd sprinted up a hill. I'd almost killed a child. One of my own people, who I was bound to protect. An inch to the side, and Kip would be dead now.

It was only a matter of time until it happened again. Until I wasn't fast enough, and someone else died. No amount of family pride or political independence was worth that. I squeezed my eyes shut, but Kip's terrified face remained burned into my mind.

To Hells with politics. I wanted a jess.

ELEVEN

Warm sunlight sifted down through the branches in the Round Room ceiling. Foxglove and Aurelio settled at the far end of the table, making appreciative noises at the service of tea and coffee I'd had set out for them. A lick of pride stirred in my chest at this small thing; I could be a good host, even with everything threatening to come apart all around me.

A restless guilt kept me from getting comfortable myself. I didn't have time for this; the reception was coming up at noon, and I'd put off a meeting with Odan about increased security for the Black Tower and left Aunt Karrigan to play host to the envoys. Still, the chance to prevent more needless deaths had to come first.

"So," I said, "the deal you're offering is that if I join the Rookery, I get a jess."

Foxglove stirred honey into his tea, the spoon clinking. "Essentially. I'd love to get you a jess without any strings attached, but when Raverra does a favor, they always seem to want something in return."

I turned my own teacup in my hands, breathing in citrus-scented steam. "And that's the problem. They *can't* have me in return. I belong to Morgrain."

Foxglove acknowledged this difficulty with a nod. "I understand that you can't place yourself under Raverran authority. I've clarified with my superiors that you could join us in an auxiliary role—you'd officially be an independent adviser. You could bow out of any mission if you felt there was a conflict with your duties as a noble of Vaskandar. And for that matter, you could quit and leave the Rookery at any time."

"The Rookery isn't truly under Raverran control anyway," Aurelio put in. He poured himself coffee from its silver pitcher with the air of a man getting down to business—whether with me or his cup, I couldn't be certain. "They take their political neutrality very seriously. Sometimes to the Serene Empire's regret." He grinned slyly at Foxglove, who shrugged.

"Who *does* the Rookery report to, exactly?" I asked.

"We operate under the authority of both the full Conclave of Vaskandran Witch Lords and the Raverran doge and Council of Nine." Foxglove sipped his tea, his lids lowering with satisfaction. "Specifically, we report to the Crow Lord and the current holder of the Cornaro Council seat. They tend to allow us a lot of discretion so long as we don't make them regret it."

At least he hadn't said the Shrike Lord. *That* would have been a problem. I took a cautious sip of tea, the citrus bright on my tongue against the underlying bitterness. "There's one more problem. I can't leave Gloamingard often. I'm not willing to relinquish my duties as Warden."

Foxglove sighed and spread his hands. "Frankly, my lady, I'll take what I can get. If we can call on you to help when we truly need your abilities, that's enough for me."

There was a carelessness to his tone that I didn't trust; he wasn't worried. I'd bet he thought that once I went on one or two missions—once I tasted what it was like to travel and use my powers to do meaningful things, and got to know the Rookery well enough to have real, actual *friends*—I'd be eager to do more. Hells, he probably wasn't wrong. But if he thought that would get me to abandon my duties in Gloamingard and traipse about the world with the Rookery as if I really *were* running off with a traveling theater company—well, he didn't know me.

If it would get me through the next several days of negotiations without having to worry about killing anyone, it was worth a try.

I let out a long breath, setting the steam above my tea to dancing. "All right, how does this work? We hear a lot of dark rumors about the jesses in Vaskandar, though my mother tells me most of them are dead wrong."

Aurelio flashed me a quick grin at my implicit acceptance. "Well, some of those rumors might have been true centuries ago. Mages were conscripted against their will, and the jesses would kill you if your Falconer died and you didn't get a new one. It hasn't been like that for a hundred and fifty years, though."

"That's within my grandmother's memory," I pointed out. "Vaskandar doesn't forget easily."

"I assure you, it's different now! There were a lot of reforms around the time of the War of Ashes." Aurelio took a relishing gulp of coffee. "These days, imperial law only mandates that every mage with the mark receive a jess and a Falconer. After a bit of training, the Falconer usually leaves the mage's power unsealed by default. Under normal circumstances, that's the end of it, unless you choose to join the Falcons. The jess is there in case you use your magic to take up a life of crime or attempt to overthrow the government, and otherwise you're free to go about your business. Since your power is so dangerous, however, the situation is a bit different."

I gripped my teacup with both hands, the warmth seeping through the fine bone china into my fingertips. "I wouldn't want to leave my power unsealed."

"Indeed," Foxglove said. "And since we're hoping to use your unique talents on Rookery missions, Aurelio—or whatever

Falconer you find acceptable—will have to come with us on such occasions, so he can release your power when it's needed."

"Is that what you want?" I asked Aurelio, anxious. "I can't imagine this was what you had in mind when you joined the Falconers."

Aurelio shook his head. "You're right. It's even better."

I blinked. "Following me around? Are you sure?"

He leaned his elbows on the table, face serious. "This is why I joined the Falconers in the first place, Ryx. Because the best way to protect Raverra, the most powerful way to make a difference in the world, is through magic. And the Rookery is even better positioned to do that than the Falcons are. They deal with the most dangerous magic, on an international scale. *This* is how I can serve my country and make a difference." His eyes shone. "Lord Urso will be proud."

I tried not to show my relief. I knew no other Falconers, so if Aurelio had said no, I'd have had to contemplate giving control of my magic to a complete stranger. He was a friend, at least; I certainly wouldn't mind spending more time in his company. Warmth flushed through me at the thought.

"And...you don't mind being stuck with me?" I asked, trying an awkward smile.

"Are you kidding?" He seemed genuinely surprised. "I like you, Ryx. I'll be honored to be your Falconer, and to see you get to put your magic to good use at last."

I was more than a little wary of tying myself to so many new people and responsibilities. Aurelio and I would be magically linked, and while he was pretty to look at and one of the few friends I had, I'd be fooling myself if I pretended I truly *knew* him. And the Rookery...I'd seen the bonds between them. The closeness, the teasing, the way they worked as a group and relied on each other. I wanted that for myself—yearned after it with a pull relentless as the tide—but it was frightening, too.

Not as frightening as the idea of killing a child under my protection. It kept coming back to this: I couldn't risk harm to my own people anymore.

I still didn't know if I could trust the Rookery, but all I'd be giving them and Aurelio was the ability to stop me from using my magic. Given that I'd never actually *wanted* to use my magic in my twenty-one years of life, it seemed like an easy choice after all.

"All right, this could work." Excitement grew in my chest like an expanding bubble. This was really happening. "As my Falconer, you'll be able to seal and release my power?"

Aurelio nodded. "Anywhere I am in the world, if I say *Exsolvo*, your power is released, and if I say *Revincio*, your power is sealed. That's all it takes."

Revincio. One word, and my life would be changed. My pulse fluttered like a moth's wings.

A horrifying thought occurred to me. "How can we be certain the jess will work on me, though? Won't I drain the power from it?"

"It *should* be all right," Aurelio said. "The precise function of the jesses is a secret, but my understanding is that they turn a mage's attachment points or receptors for magic back inward onto each other to create the seal—like sticking magnets together. Instead of reaching out to grab and manipulate magical energy, you wind up essentially shaking your own hand. That way it doesn't matter how powerful the mage is; they can't overwhelm the jess by force, because all that force is simply directed back at itself in a circle." He drew a ring in the air with his finger, then flashed an apologetic smile. "Or at least, that's what they taught me in Falconer training."

Foxglove cocked his head. "What about if you unseal the jess, though? If you say the release word, her powers become active again. Would she drain it then?"

Aurelio blinked. "I have no idea. That's a good question. Jesses can replenish their own power, so I'd think that after a while out of contact with Ryx it'd restore itself, but I can't be sure."

"I'd be careful about when you unleash your magic." Foxglove rubbed his chin. "It might be days or weeks before you could seal it again."

"I don't have any desire to unleash it until we absolutely need to," I said, with feeling.

"So." Aurelio reached carefully into an inner pocket of his uniform jacket and pulled out a slender, gleaming strip of gold. "Still sure you want to do this?"

He laid the jess on the dark wood between us: a bracelet of intricately woven gold wire, its branches and loops and coils forming a secret magical language, dotted with crimson beads like drops of blood. This pretty little piece of jewelry had the power to seal my broken magic, like a bandage on an open wound.

"I think so." My fingers curled against my palms, nails biting into the soft leather tips of my gloves. In Vaskandar, many saw jesses as an abomination; placing control over a mage's power in the hands of someone without magic upset the natural order. To voluntarily accept such degradation was inconceivable. My mother had given me another perspective, and I'd never had any reason to love my own magic, but I couldn't help a certain gut-deep aversion to the idea of sealing off my power, even if my rational mind embraced it eagerly.

My family would be appalled when they found out. My grandmother might well forbid me to do this if she were here—but for better or worse, she wasn't. And I was already a shame to my family. I might as well stop being a lethal hazard, too.

"Yes," I said, with more conviction. "Let's do this."

Foxglove gave a slow nod, his amber eyes intent on me. "All it takes is for Aurelio to put the jess on your wrist."

I pulled off my glove and held out my hand, my nerves singing with tension. "Please be very, very careful," I said. "If you touch me before it's active..."

Aurelio paled. "Good Graces. I hadn't thought of that."

He lifted the jess and expanded the shining loop of braided wire as wide as it would go, so that no loose end dangled beneath the bracelet. The sun set the red beads to sparkling.

"Can you slide your hand through there without touching me?" His mouth sounded dry. Graces knew mine was.

I nodded. "I think so. Keep very still."

He held it out at arm's length. The light on the beads winked as the jess trembled.

I held my breath, tucked in my thumb to make my hand as small as possible, and reached for the golden circle.

Don't kill him. Don't kill him. He's the only person outside your family who's not afraid of your power. Except the Rookery, and it was their actual job, so they didn't count. *Grace of Mercy, don't let me kill him.*

My stomach knotted so tight it felt like a knife was twisting in it. I kept my hand steady through sheer will.

My fingers slipped through the shimmering ring of the jess, and all at once everything subtly changed. It was like stepping indoors: the sounds muted, the air stuffier, the world smaller and more comforting. Slightly colder, too, as if I'd taken off a light jacket.

It wasn't a *bad* sensation, but I wasn't certain it was good, either.

The jess settled, shining, over my wrist. Aurelio snatched his fingers back and rubbed them, eyes wide.

"Are you all right?" I asked anxiously.

"I'm fine," he said, watching me with an all too familiar wariness. "I just—cold was pouring off you like you were made of ice. It hurt. And I couldn't breathe, for a second."

I grimaced. "Sorry."

"No, it's all right. I was just startled." His grin returned, though it didn't quite light up his eyes the way it had before. "Should we try an experiment, to see if it's working?"

"I'm not going to poke you and see if you die, if that's what you mean." I tried to keep my voice light, almost teasing, as if I weren't shaking at how close I'd come to touching him.

Foxglove cleared his throat. "I'm certain we can come up with a less extreme solution. Come, let's go to the garden."

I crouched at the edge of a pebbled path in one of the inner kitchen gardens, the sunlight warming my back as it peeked over the mismatched roofs surrounding the little courtyard. A line of scraggly green weeds and a scrabble of grass poked up at the edge of the path, before the beds of neatly divided herbs began, a sign that the minor Greenwitch in charge of the castle gardens didn't care how this one looked so long as the cooks had everything they needed. I fixed my gaze on one weed, a scrawny thing with a half-withered shell-pink ball of a flower nodding from a thin stem.

It didn't deserve to die. It was doing its best.

Try it with the gloves, now. These ones are lined with silk. I remembered my father's face, his deep-set eyes and the lowering line of his brows giving away his concern even though he wore an encouraging smile.

I'd touched one gloved finger to the dandelion's sunny face, holding my breath with hope and fear, and counted silently. *One*... Still alive. Hope had begun rising in my chest, bright and sudden, with too many edges. *Two, three*...

But the dandelion had withered and died, like all the others. My parents had been excited because it had taken a few seconds, but I'd burst into tears, grieving for the bright spot of cheery yellow I'd destroyed with my touch.

"Well?" Aurelio urged, shifting nervously from foot to foot behind me.

I reached out toward the ragged little weed. The golden jess dangled from my bare wrist—a claim I'd let the Empire put on me, no matter how much they might try to assure me otherwise.

My fingers lit on the tough woody stem, the small round leaves. *So delicate.* A knot wound tighter in the back of my throat.

One, two, three. No tingling prickled my fingertips and ran up my arm. The leaves stayed green and soft. *Four, five, six...* Nothing was happening. The weed bent slightly beneath my trembling hand, but it lived obliviously on. *Seven, eight, nine, ten.*

Blood of the Eldest. It worked.

TWELVE

I t's not dying," I whispered. My eyes stung fiercely; I took my hand from the plant to rub at them.

"It seems completely fine," Aurelio agreed, crouching down beside me with a broad, triumphant smile. "Your power is sealed."

"I can't believe it." I shook my head. "For my whole life..." I couldn't finish. Too many words piled up and tangled together on my tongue, unspoken.

Aurelio caught my eyes and slowly, deliberately held out his hand. I stared at him, fear squeezing my chest.

"My father's from Callamorne," he said. "To say hello, or to seal a deal, or to form a partnership, they clasp hands."

"I can't." I leaned instinctively away from him. "It's too dangerous. What if the jess isn't strong enough? I could kill you."

"I'll be ready to pull my hand back quick as lightning if I feel the faintest lick of magic," he promised. "You have to try this on a human sometime, right?"

He kept his hand out, steady as a rock, waiting for mine. Biting my lip with dread, I reached toward him.

It went against every drilled-in instinct I possessed. I'd spent my entire life avoiding human touch as if people were made of fire. My mage-marked family could brace themselves in advance against the unraveling pull of my magic; my grandmother, as an immortal Witch Lord with all the power of a domain behind her, could safely ignore it. Anyone else I had to treat as fragile and precious, their lives too delicate for my rough, clumsy hands.

The jess had worked for the weed. There was no reason it shouldn't work for Aurelio.

I tapped his hand, a quick flicking eyeblink of contact, to be safe.

Nothing. No surge of power, no cry of alarm from Aurelio. Just the brief lingering warmth of his skin on my fingertip.

His hand didn't move, though his shoulders relaxed a bit. "No icy cold, this time. No pain. I think it's safe."

I reached out again, this time clasping his hand.

So warm. Like soft leather, but fluid, restless, *alive*. His pulse beat against my palm, subtle but present.

Such a strange magic. It was all I could do not to trace the veins showing through his skin, to lift his hand to my cheek. Instead I let him shake my hand once, firmly, as my face burned. I had to force myself to let go.

"Whew!" Aurelio laughed, shaking his auburn hair back from his eyes with a toss of his head. "Still alive."

"Yes." I swallowed, but it didn't clear the hard lump in my throat. "I guess now I don't have to worry anymore about accidentally starting a war."

"Oh, we can be more ambitious than that." Aurelio grinned. "Now that your power is under control, maybe someday you can *end* one."

I wanted to touch everything.

The rough, flaky bark of an apple tree. The slick ribbon of a blade of grass growing between the pebbles of the path. The tickling legs of a beetle I coaxed onto my hand. Each time I had to overcome an instinctive fear that set my pulse to pounding painfully hard and fast; but everything remained quick with life beneath my touch, vibrant, healthy, *alive*.

I could still feel the life around me through my link to the land—that wasn't dependent on my own magic, so the jess didn't take it from me—but now I could feel it with my fingertips, too. There were so many new sensations, as if I'd woken up from a dream into a different world.

I should go. Aurelio had already left, smiling and wishing me well, to get ready for the reception. I had a lot to do; I couldn't afford to waste time mucking about poking things in the garden. But a joy fluttered in my chest like nothing I'd felt in ages, and I didn't want to let it go.

I realized I was still clutching my gloves in one hand. I stared at them a moment—they were a second skin to me, broken in and worn with use. My hands felt naked without them.

"Hey. Mage lady." Ashe's unmistakable voice came from behind me.

I stuffed the gloves in my vestcoat pocket. The jess slid down my wrist, red gems winking. "Hello. Do you need something?"

Ashe gave me a strange, assessing look, her pale eyes traveling over me as if thinking about where she'd stab me to take me down quickly. "I hear you're going to be joining the Rookery," she said, without any particular relish.

"Sort of." I tried a tentative smile. "I've got my duties as Warden of Gloamingard, but I'll help out when you need my magic."

"Another mage is the last thing we need," Ashe said bluntly. "Especially some arrogant atheling with the mage mark."

I blinked, taken aback. "Well, I'll try not to get in your way."

She paced toward me with the smooth, menacing gait of a hunting cat. "You'd better not lord it over us. On missions, no one is going to bow and scrape to you. You'll be our most junior member—the one messing things up because she doesn't know what she's doing."

I laughed ruefully. "I've got a lot of experience in that role, so I should take to it naturally."

Ashe stopped in front of me, her ice-blue eyes locked on mine. Then her mouth quirked, and a half-suppressed laugh burst through her lips. As I stared at her in confusion, the laugh spread to shake her whole slim body like a reed in the wind. Without warning, she smacked my shoulder, too fast to dodge; I yelped and jumped back, smarting, and that only made her laugh harder.

"Oh, I think I might like you." She wrestled the laugh back down to a chuckle, wiping her eyes. "You'll do all right, I suppose. Had to make sure you weren't one of those insufferable bastards who thinks an extra ring in their eyes makes them the seasons' gift to the earth."

"Right," I said uncertainly, rubbing my shoulder. No one had ever slapped me before. I couldn't begin to untangle how I felt about it.

"Anyway, Kessa sent me to ask you if you wanted to get ready for the reception with us." Ashe waved a hand as if brushing away everything else she'd said. "You know, lace up each other's corsets and do your hair, that kind of thing. We've decided to go with Raverran-style gowns, since there'll be imperial dancing, and those big skirts twirl better than vestcoats." She flashed me a toothy grin.

I stared at her as the full implications of being able to attend the reception tumbled down on me. Parties and crowds and dancing all sounded wonderful, but also terrifying.

"Hells. I always assumed I wouldn't be going," I said. "I should wear a mix of Raverran and Vaskandran styles, to make it clear I'm not favoring one side over the other. But I don't have any Raverran clothes." I had a couple of formal vestcoats I used for ceremonies, floor length and stiff with embroidery, but they were extremely Vaskandran. My mother had once offered to bring me back lovely silk and brocade gowns from the Serene Empire, but with nowhere to wear them, it was another thing I couldn't afford to yearn for.

Ashe snorted. "Nothing on the seasons' sweet earth would make Kessa happier than helping you put something together. Half the reason our cover is a theater company is so that we can bring along all the clothes we need to blend in anywhere from palaces to back alleyways. We've got trunks full of stuff."

I hesitated. "I don't want to intrude ..."

"Don't say no," Ashe warned, steel coming back into her eyes. "It would break Kessa's heart."

"Well, we can't have that. Of course I'll come."

I smiled tentatively, but I couldn't help wondering what in the Nine Hells I'd gotten myself into.

"Oh, this is going to be fun," Kessa said, her eyes bright. "And welcome to the Rookery, by the way! We've never had an atheling before."

Behind her, Ashe rummaged through a trunk in a business-like fashion, tossing brocade bodices and great billowing puffs of silk skirts over her shoulder onto her bed in the Rookery guest quarters.

"Watch out, or she'll hug you," she grunted, without looking up.

A hug from Kessa sounded both wonderful and terrifying, like my cousin's description of riding a bear. I took an instinctive step back.

"Oh, hush." Kessa elbowed Ashe without looking. "Now, I'm sure you must have questions about us. The Rookery does have a terribly mysterious reputation, after all." She waggled her dark, graceful eyebrows.

I'd had dozens, but of course they all fled my mind the moment she asked. "Ah..." I stared into Kessa's sparkling dark eyes. "You said you're a vivomancer. If the Rookery cleans up magical messes, are you all mages?"

None of them had the mark, but less than one in a hundred mages possessed sufficient power for that. Most villages of a decent size in Vaskandar had their own minor Greenwitch or Furwitch, but there were only a handful of mage-marked outside my own family in all of Morgrain.

Ashe let out a bark of a laugh. "Not all."

"Foxglove is our artificer." Kessa held up a scarlet bodice in my general direction and narrowed her eyes critically. She gave a minute shake of her head and laid it back on the bed. "Bastian is an alchemist. We each have other roles, too. Foxglove is the leader, I'm a diplomat, Bastian is our scholar of magical sciences, and Ashe...Ashe is a woman of certain talents."

"I kill things," Ashe clarified.

Kessa shook her head. "You do more than that, Ashe."

"I also wound them," she amended.

Kessa picked up a sapphire-blue bodice and held it up to me, making a pleased noise. "Oh, this will bring out your mage mark nicely. Can't hurt to remind those Alevarans of your rank, yes?" I nodded, with a burst of warm relief; she *understood*. "I'm thinking a Raverran gown with an open Vaskandran vestcoat over. Do you have one that will match this?"

"I think so." Half my vestcoats had blue embroidery.

"Oh, good. Anyway, don't let Ashe fool you into underestimating her. She was a Fury before she joined us."

I whistled. I'd heard of the Furies; they were an elite order dedicated to hunting down the most dangerous rogue chimeras, able to single-handedly take out creatures that could lay waste to dozens of trained soldiers. "Impressive. I thought they only took mages."

Kessa grimaced as if I'd said something awkward. But Ashe only grinned. "I'm no mage."

"How..." I glanced at Kessa, who shook her head minutely, but I couldn't overcome my curiosity. "How did you become a Fury, then?"

Ashe's smile went dagger-sharp. "When I was small, I saw how mages lorded it over everyone else, and I didn't like it. So I started picking fights with mages, for fun." I stared at her, frozen in the act of picking up a matching petticoat. "I got pretty good at it. One day, I beat up one of the Furies' new trainees."

"How are you still alive?" I asked, amazed.

"The trainer decided this was a good way to teach recruits humility." Ashe scooped up the scarlet bodice Kessa had rejected, giving it a satisfied nod. "The Furies took me on to beat all their spoiled mage brat recruits at a certain point in their training— me, a tiny girl with no magic—so they'd learn not to underestimate their foes. They never meant to make me a full Fury, but I did all the training and passed all the tests, and they had no choice."

I could appreciate shoving your competence down the throats of people who thought you couldn't do your job without functioning magic. The grin I returned Ashe was as sharp as her own.

"There." Kessa set an overflowing armload of skirts, petticoats, stays, and stockings down on a chair beside me with an encouraging nod. "That should do it for your Raverran layers. Let me know if you need any help figuring it all out; I swear, Raverrans seem to feel that getting dressed should be like tying up a prisoner."

Ashe had found skirts to match the scarlet bodice and began stripping without ceremony, her wiry limbs pale in the warm afternoon sunlight. I struggled not to blush, but Kessa seemed cheerfully oblivious.

I'd never changed in company before. Raverrans helped each

other get dressed all the time, with their complex clothes and form-fitting lacing, though I gathered there were calculations of family and gender and friendship involved in knowing where to draw the lines of propriety. In Morgrain, we could get into our clothes just fine by ourselves, and it was too cold for much of the year to want to draw the process out; dressing was not a social event.

Besides, who would be mad enough to disrobe in the same room as the cursed atheling with the deadly touch? But the two of them seemed to accept my presence here as if it were perfectly normal, an everyday thing—as if I were just another regular person who got ready for parties with friends all the time.

As if we *were* friends.

Hells. I wasn't sure I was ready for this. Being able to get close to people opened up a whole world of subtleties and rules I'd never learned, but everyone else knew: when to touch, how close to get, what to say to someone who might actually not despise your company.

I grabbed a stocking with as much determination as if I were going into battle. "I think I can manage. My mother *is* Raverran, after all. I've seen all this before."

"Good for you if you can make sense of this madness," Ashe grunted. She slipped a long, wicked-looking dagger into her boot, then dropped her bloodred skirts back over it. I noticed they only fell to ankle length, rather than sweeping the floor like Kessa's did. "At least it's not Loreice, where they wear pox-cursed *panniers*. Can't strap a sword on over those, and I'm sure as death not leaving Answer behind."

"Answer?" I asked, curious.

Ashe grinned and scooped up her sheathed sword from the bed. "I got tired of everyone telling me I had one answer for everything."

I hadn't gotten a good look at her sword before, and now

stared at it in amazement. It was a slim swept-hilt rapier, but artifice wire wove through the guard in gorgeous, intricate patterns, shaping some enchantment with its language of twists and swirls. A polished sphere of obsidian formed the pommel, wrapped around with more artifice wire accented by glinting crystals. I'd never seen anything like it.

Kessa shook her head. "You can take the girl out of the Furies, but you can't take the Fury out of the girl, I guess."

She reached out to ruffle Ashe's spiky white-blond hair. And Grace of Love, Ashe's cheeks went pink. She was *blushing*.

An odd twinge of jealousy pinched my middle. Which was ridiculous, because Kessa wasn't mine, and didn't seem to notice Ashe's reaction anyway. I turned my attention to my pile of clothes with a certain muddled heat in my own face, as well.

I managed to get dressed mostly on my own. My only struggle was with the corset lacing; my mother had always made it look so easy.

"Here, let me help," Kessa said gently, approaching close, *too* close, reaching toward me. My grandmother's voice echoed in my memory: *I'm sorry, Ryx. You can't ever be that close to someone. There's too much at risk.*

I jerked away, and Kessa stopped, her gaze clouding.

"Do you trust me?" she asked quietly.

That was one Hell of a question. She'd spied on me, and I'd only known her for a couple of days. I hardly knew anything about her. Kessa's warm brown eyes waited, layers of sadness and joy laid bare and vulnerable within them.

"Yes." I forced myself to smile and tried not to look as if my heart were pounding. "I'd love your help. Thank you."

I flinched when her deft fingers brushed my back, a confused mix of warmth and terror coursing through me as her business-like touch worked up and down my spine, drawing the cage of boning tighter around my middle.

"Thank you," she murmured, so softly I almost didn't hear it. "I know it's hard to trust a spy."

I shrugged, uncomfortable. "No harder than it is to trust an atheling."

Ashe flashed me a smile at that.

Kessa did my hair next. Every muscle in my body locked rigid as her graceful fingers unraveled my braid and slid nimbly through my hair, twisting and pinning. Electric shivers ran down between my shoulders each time her warm hands brushed the back of my neck.

"Like riding a bear," I muttered.

"What?"

"Never mind."

At last she was done, and stepped back with a look of great satisfaction. "There," she said. "I'm no Raverran lady's maid, but that should do. Take a look!"

She gestured grandly toward an oval mirror standing in the corner. The woman in it was a strange creature: a fine Raverran lady in a sapphire-blue gown with a silver-and-blue brocade stomacher and petticoat, jewels sparkling in her dark hair. Acres of skirts fluffed out around me, and I felt inexplicably important in the middle of all this rustling, gorgeous fabric, like a jewel proudly displayed on a silk pillow. She'd done my hair up in a hybrid style, coiling several Vaskandran braids up on my head with elegant Raverran tendrils cascading around my face. The lady in the mirror appeared poised and regal, and far more confident than I felt. The jess gleamed on my wrist, a promise of a freedom I'd never known.

"With a vestcoat over everything, you should look less Raverran and more of a mix," Kessa said, tapping her lips and eyeing my reflection critically. "What do you think, Ryx?"

I touched my hair; parts of it were stiff with potion. "I don't look like myself," I laughed. That was the point of Raverran clothes, I supposed—to shape you into some artistic creation of the one who designed them. "It's lovely. Thank you."

Ashe snorted. "Tell me about it. Do you know how long it took me to get used to these things?" She twirled, and her red skirts flew out around her. Her eyes slid to Kessa, to see if she was watching. "But they're not bad to fight in, if you avoid low lunges. I can hope a war breaks out at the party, I suppose."

Kessa poked her shoulder. "You're incorrigible, Ashe."

The light, floaty bubble that had risen in my chest popped. War was a very real danger right now. It had been easy to forget, getting ready for the reception, that I was going into one of the most important battles of my life.

This was my chance to impose normalcy back on the negotiations. To show the envoys that even with my grandmother mysteriously absent, even with violent death and unexplained magic marring the proceedings, we could still have orderly and civil relations with each other. That peace could prevail between us.

"Right," I said, my voice steady and strong as if I weren't the slightest bit afraid, "let's go."

THIRTEEN

Afternoon light streamed breathtakingly golden down through the glass ceiling of the Aspen Hall, filtered into molten radiance by the leaves of the living aspen trees that gave the grand room its name. The Witch Lord's power kept the coin-shaped leaves perpetually autumn gold; the stark white trunks formed a double line of slender columns flanking the hall. Intricate leaf patterns of inlaid woods in varying shades covered a floor almost too lovely to walk on. If the visiting diplomats weren't impressed by the beauty of the space, there was something wrong with their souls.

It certainly possessed sufficient grandeur for the Vaskandran ceremony to open the negotiations. The envoys, Aunt Karrigan, and I stood in a loose circle around a great bowl of lustrous magic-shaped wood, abstract shapes swirling in eye-pleasing patterns in the varied shades of its grain. The rest of the assembled reception guests watched as Voreth and Aurelio poured earth from their respective countries into the bowl from clay jars, and then Severin and Celia stepped forward to plant seeds from Alevar and the Empire side by side in the fresh earth. Lady Celia moved with a confidence that made me suspect she'd rehearsed this strange custom in advance. Severin's swaggering grace was no less than I'd expected. Hells, that man could make planting a seed look like he was giving the Graces' gift to the earth.

The next part should have been mine. But it was Karrigan who stepped forward and held her hand above the bowl, coaxing green shoots up from the seeds the envoys had planted. It was her magic that wound the shoots together as they grew, shaking damp green leaves from tender buds, until two young saplings stood proudly twined in the center of the bowl.

"Let us meet in harmony and leave with accord," I announced, my voice ringing out in a room full of whispers. "I welcome you all to Gloamingard."

At that cue, soft strains of string music filled the air, and the formal ceremony ended. Servants hurried out to uncover the dishes waiting on the buffet tables; the guests broke up into fluid bunches, a murmur of conversation rising to the ceiling.

Right. Time to *mingle*, then. However that worked.

I pushed my jess up my arm, the cold metal unfamiliar against my skin. I hadn't told my aunt about joining the Rookery or getting the jess yet, and I doubted she'd be happy about it. And of course the sleeves of this cursed Raverran gown ended just above the elbow in a fountain of dripping lace cuff, which fell back to expose my wrists if I lifted my arms at all.

Nearly a hundred people circulated through the room, between the full delegations from Alevar and Raverra, the Rookery, and various officials, mages, and courtiers from Morgrain. All of them gave me a wide berth, as they'd been warned to do; I caught some alarmed sidelong glances in my direction, and Vaskandrans flicked the warding sign at me.

I should wander about, listen, talk to people and try to nudge them to think and do what I wanted—but I balked at the crowd. The air felt raw on my bare hands. Every instinct urged me to get out of here before something terrible happened.

Ashe sauntered up to me with a grin stretching her face, resplendent in her red gown, Answer gleaming wickedly on her hip.

"Relax," she said. "You look like you've never been to a party before."

"I haven't," I admitted, forcing myself to hold my ground and not open up more space between us even as my muscles tensed at how near she'd come. "This is my first one."

Ashe's brows flew up. "What, did they stick you in a box for your whole life?"

"No, no. Gatherings like this are just too dangerous." I waved a hand around the crowded Aspen Hall. "It was necessary."

"Maybe." Ashe didn't sound convinced. "It was still cruel."

"No one did this to me," I objected. "No one forced me. It's just common sense."

Ashe snorted. "You think you can't be cruel to yourself?"

I couldn't think what to say to that. Suddenly my life seemed gray and small, and I could only stare at her, too aware of the cold clasp of the jess around my wrist.

Ashe's eyes slipped past me, and she frowned. "Whoops, I have to go rescue Kessa from a boring conversation. She just gave me our secret signal. See you after the ball. Can't wait to take another look at that cursed black rock of yours."

"See you then," I said, still feeling a bit numb. Ashe was already gone.

I barely had time to shake my head and push my jess back up my arm before Lady Celia swept up to me, neatly as an intercepting warship, resplendent in a gown of Raverran ocean blue and gold. She held two glasses of red wine, and offered me one.

"I'm delighted to find a decent wine offered up in Vaskandar, and I suspect I have you to thank," she greeted me, her eyes sparkling.

I stared at the extended wine cup for a second too long. She'd come so close—but she must know about my jess, since Aurelio was part of her delegation. Still, there was no sense in letting my habits get sloppy, so I avoided her fingers as I took the glass and inhaled the fruity sting of its scent.

It was my turn to say something. Damnation. I was still new at this casual conversation business.

"Mmm," I ventured.

"Your domain is full of surprises," Celia said, half a smile crooking the corner of her mouth. "That stone in your tower chief among them, of course."

"I assure you, I was surprised, too." The words fell out of my mouth before I could consider whether it was a good idea to take her bait. "I've lived here since I was four years old, but I've never seen the inside of the Black Tower before."

"And yet from what I glimpsed as I arrived, you seemed to activate it easily enough," Celia observed, her gaze knife-sharp and analytical. "Do you think you could command its magic?"

"That's a rather bold question." I had to get better at controlling my face; I dragged my eyebrows back down to a more neutral position. "Why do you ask?"

"Consider this. That artifact undeniably represents a great deal of power." She swirled the wine in her glass. "From the Serene Empire's perspective, it's power in the hands of a domain with which we currently enjoy cordial relations, but which historically has been our enemy. If you can't control it, it's a potential threat. If you can—well then, it's also a potential threat, but of a different sort."

"Given that my family has guarded this artifact for thousands of years and never used it in Morgrain's various conflicts with the Empire, I think you don't have anything to worry about," I said.

Celia lifted an elegant gray brow. "Come now, Lady Ryxander.

Surely you're not so simple as to believe that a power having gone unused will stop people from coveting it or fearing it."

"You're referring to this Raverran faction that's collecting magic for a supposedly inevitable war," I guessed. I should ask Jannah to gather what information we had on them for me; they sounded likely to become a problem.

"Ah, the Zenith Society. Yes, but not only them." Lady Celia took a sip of wine, analyzing me over the rim of her glass; I filed the name away in my memory. "Surely you must have noticed that the vultures are starting to gather at your borders."

Hells. Morgrain, like most Vaskandran domains, usually depended on its Witch Lord's connection to the land for intelligence, while the Serene Empire had a vast spy network and lightning-quick communications. We were effectively blind without my grandmother, even to what was happening on our own borders; Lady Celia might well know something I didn't.

I couldn't let her see that. Showing weakness could be fatal right now.

I gave her a gracious nod of acknowledgment. "My lady, this is Vaskandar. The Witch Lords are *always* circling each other, looking for weaknesses."

"Precisely." Celia tilted her head, locks of gray hair swinging free by her jaw. "And what exactly is the succession situation here in Morgrain? I'm told that Witch Lords usually have only one heir, to prevent complications in the passing of magical dominion—but your family seems not to follow that rule."

My fingertips whitened on my untasted wineglass. "That's true. We believe that a larger family better sustains our domain, with more powerful mages to protect our people and more political marriages to keep our alliances strong." All to help guard the Black Tower: *Blood endures through ages long*, the Gloaming Lore advised us.

Of course, there was more to the current size of our family than that. But I was hardly about to explain to Lady Celia the horrifying implications of what my broken magic would do if I gained magical power over every living thing in Morgrain, or that my aunt and uncle had taken it upon themselves to have more children just to ensure I wouldn't somehow inherit the domain and unintentionally turn the place into a desolate lifeless wasteland.

"That's hardly relevant, though," I concluded, unable to keep an edge from my voice, "since the Lady of Owls is alive and well."

"Naturally, naturally." Celia waved a jeweled hand. "But perhaps some of your neighbors might entertain hopes to the contrary. Please forgive me if I'm curious about what *they* might expect to happen with the succession if they were not in fact doomed to disappointment."

It was a fine and unsettling point. Our neighbors would likely expect my father and aunt and uncle to fall upon each other contesting for immortality and dominion over the land—which many would take as a signal to invade during our moment of weakness and seize our precious land for themselves.

The Empire apparently knew it. Everyone saw Morgrain as undefended, and they were preparing to pounce. Wonderful.

"Our succession is clear," I said, trying to sound firm enough to close any perceived door of opportunity. "My grandmother has decreed that her eldest, Tarn, will inherit the domain, and the whole family is in agreement. No one will try to stop him from establishing his sole magical claim."

"Oh, good," Celia said. "I'm glad to hear the succession is uncontested." Her gaze slid pointedly to where Karrigan stood talking to Severin, standing with all the bold confidence of a Witch Lord in her own domain.

Odan appeared at my elbow, a few feet back for safety. His

posture remained rigidly correct and controlled as always, but urgency flattened his mouth behind his bushy gray mustache.

"Might I have a word, Exalted Warden?"

"Of course. If you'll excuse me a moment, Lady Celia."

Celia nodded graciously and withdrew—not quite far enough that she wouldn't have a chance to overhear, of course. *Raverrans*. I moved off a little farther and turned my back to her in the hopes of better blocking whatever news had Odan looking troubled on an already trying day.

"What new disaster are we facing this time?" I asked.

"I'd say not a disaster, but at this point I'm making no assumptions, Warden." Odan dropped his voice. "The Honored Atheling Ardith of Kar has arrived at Gloamingard. They'll be here any minute, but I wanted to give you some warning."

"Ardith!" I glanced around the Aspen Hall in a panic. Ardith was a child of the Fox Lord of Kar himself; they delighted in shaking things up as if the world were a jar of fireflies. "Why *now*, of all times? Wait, of course they're coming now. Hells take it." I sighed. "You'd better show them in."

Ardith, however, was not the type to wait for an introduction. They sauntered into the hall at that very moment, sporting a cheery grin and a buttery soft leather vestcoat with cutouts of swirling autumn leaves showing flashes of vermilion silk beneath. Their blaze of red hair fell loose to their shoulders, and a jeweled rapier hung at a dashing angle on their hip.

I was standing near the door, so their eyes fell on me at once. No colored ring interrupted their wickedly gleaming hazel irises. Born with magic too weak for the mage mark, Ardith was out of the line of succession, but a royal atheling of Kar and a force to be reckoned with nonetheless.

"Hello, Ryx," they greeted me. "Nice dress."

"Thanks, Ardith." I'd met them several times in the course of diplomatic relations with Kar and rather liked them, but they were invariably trouble. "Not that I'm not happy to see you, but why are you here?"

Odan shook his head at my blunt and casual language as he withdrew, but Ardith tipped back their head and laughed.

"What, you don't believe I'm just here for the free food? I can sense a buffet a hundred miles away." They started drifting inexorably in that direction; I followed, keeping a wary distance between us as if they were a prowling wolf.

"I won't deny that might be your ulterior motive," I said, "but you can't expect me to believe you can't get a good dinner in Kar."

"Maybe I have other reasons." They flashed a sharp grin. "Maybe I heard strange rumors, and I'm curious."

Lovely, there were rumors spreading already. "What rumors?"

Ardith made a dramatic gesture. "The Black Tower open at last! A mysterious artifact of great power discovered within it! Naturally, I'm dying of curiosity. Though not so literally as Exalted Lamiel, I hope."

I stopped in midstride, cold running down my sides like corset boning. "How do you know all that?"

"Oh, a bird told me." They cocked their head. "I'd guessed it must be from the Lady of Owls, but now I hear she's on some unannounced leave of absence, which frankly sounds rather ominous. You've been busy here, haven't you?"

"Rather unfortunately so, yes." I stopped myself halfway through reaching up to fidget with my hair as my lace cuff started to slide back from my wrist. "You have no idea who sent this bird?" It had to have been someone at the castle. Who in the Nine Hells would think it was a good idea to drag the Fox Lord into this? He was a significant force in Vaskandar, two centuries old and deviously cunning, with powerful allies. Maybe he was whom Lady Celia had been referring to with that talk of vultures gathering at our border.

Ardith shrugged. "Not really. Could have been one of our spies, I suppose."

"Spies!"

"Oh, come on, you have them, too." With effortless grace, they grabbed a glass of golden Morgrain ale from the tray of a server passing by on their way to restock the buffet. "Anyway, it's not as if any of this is secret. The news is all over the castle and in town, and it's spreading from there. I was close enough that I thought I'd pop in to see what was going on, but I'm sure others will come soon enough. Everyone always wants to stop and stare at an overturned carriage."

My fingertips whitened on my wineglass. I'd never wished I dared drink so much in my life, but even with the jess, I didn't want to risk impairing my judgment. "The last thing we need right now is a flock of curious athelings descending on Gloamingard in the middle of a delicate negotiation."

"Well, I might be able to help." Ardith took a long swig of ale. They let out a satisfied sigh and wiped their mouth. "Do you remember when I came to visit a few months ago? We were having a lovely time in one of the gardens—"

"I caught you turning all our apples blue."

"Yes, yes." A fond mistiness entered Ardith's eyes. "I asked you why I'd seen no less than twelve carvings around the castle imploring me not to open some door. And you gave me such unsatisfying answers that of *course* I had to know more."

"I seem to recall you trying to bribe me to open it with a box of Loreician sweets you'd pilfered from our own stores," I said acidly.

"I couldn't talk you into it," they sighed. "I was forced to eat the whole box myself. Still, I *had* to know what you were hiding behind that door. You know how it is—it's the thing you can't have that you want most. So I, ah, may have tried to encourage people to help me find out."

A sinking certainty settled on me. "You spread rumors about the Black Tower, didn't you? You're the reason Lamiel and the Rookery both came poking around it all of a sudden. *You* set off all this trouble."

"To be fair, I didn't mean to start rumors that would get to someone like the Shrike Lord—I was just speculating with friends—and I had no idea what you had in there was so dangerous. I do feel bad about it. Not really about Lamiel, she was an absolute stingroach, but about putting Alevar at odds with Morgrain. Luckily, I'm here to make things right." Ardith lifted their glass to me. "Or at least more interesting."

"Luckily." I let irony drip from my voice. "And how do you propose to do that?"

Their gaze flicked around us. We stood in isolation, since everyone had been warned not to come near me on their arrival at the castle, and I hadn't spread the word about my jess. Ardith stepped closer, warily narrowing the distance between us to a few feet; a vivomancer without the mark wouldn't be strong enough to be safe from my power, but they could at least slow and mitigate its effects somewhat, so a brief brush might not be fatal.

"I'm not here just to satisfy my own admittedly boundless curiosity," they said, their voice low. "I'm here as my father's eyes and ears. I'm watching the situation for him and his allies. So long as I think you've got this situation under control, probably no one will feel the need to call a Conclave."

"A Conclave!" That would be terrible. If the nineteen Witch Lords convened specially to discuss what to do about Lamiel's death and the Black Tower, with everyone's interests and alliances in play, the chances of it ending well for Morgrain dwindled dramatically.

"Right. No one wants that. Too much drama." Ardith nodded

as if we were in complete agreement. "Honestly, your safest bet is to tell me all about this artifact now, so I can allay the concerns of the other Witch Lords and we can all relax."

I narrowed my eyes. "You're threatening me."

"Am I?" Ardith seemed genuinely surprised. They considered it through another sip of ale. "I suppose you could see it that way. Perhaps I am."

"The Rookery is investigating the artifact," I reminded them. "When they've drawn their conclusions and made their report, I'm certain the rest of the Witch Lords will be told anything they need to know."

"Of course I do trust the Rookery to do their job." Ardith made a sort of grimace, as if acknowledging this pained them. "Advance insider secret information is so much more exciting and satisfying than some dry final report, though."

"It wouldn't be insider secret information if half the athelings in Vaskandar come nosing around here," I pointed out. "If that's what you want, you'd best do what you can to keep the other Witch Lords away."

Ardith sighed. "I suppose you're right." They finished their ale in one long, head-tipping draft and broke out in a broad grin. "See, Ryx? Aren't you glad I have your back?"

Before I could even begin to frame a reply to this extraordinary statement, someone behind me said, "Why, there you are, Exalted Ryxander."

I tensed. I knew that voice. I turned, struggling to compose my face.

Severin watched me, his mage mark gleaming storm-cloud gray between narrowed dark lashes. Elegant gold embroidery of thorns and birds snaked diagonally across his slim-cut black vestcoat; loose locks of black hair brought out his sharp cheekbones. He might be my enemy, but seasons witness he was pretty.

I offered him a shallow bow, my back stiff in my corset. "Exalted Severin."

"I was just observing to Voreth here what a beautiful hall you have." He nodded to his second, who hovered scowling at his side. "I suggested we should try to recreate something like it back in Alevar, but he was of the opinion that it would be far better to take possession of the original here in Morgrain. What do you think?"

I forced a false smile onto my face. "I think my grandmother would be disinclined to part with it."

"Oh?" He arched a brow. "Do you know where she is, then?"

I tried for a knowing smile. "That would be telling. Suffice to say we're in contact—she's given me instructions." Which was close enough to true, if I hadn't imagined her presence urging me to touch the obelisk yesterday.

"Is that so?" Voreth asked, his tone skeptical. "Forgive me, but I had the distinct impression that no one at Gloamingard Castle had heard from her for two days."

"And I was under the impression you were an outsider here and have no idea what you're talking about," I retorted.

Ardith turned their glass in their hand, catching the afternoon light; I had a feeling they were savoring Voreth's seething. "Witch Lords don't simply vanish, Honored Voreth, and there's more than one kind of communication. As a fellow neighbor of Morgrain, I'm more inclined to wonder what she's up to than to make assumptions about why she's not here."

I wished to the Nine Graces I knew what she was up to, myself. I tried to keep my mysterious smile fixed on my face.

Voreth's lip curled. "Witch Lords may not vanish, but there are plenty of ways they can become incapacitated, Honored Ardith, especially when they meddle with powers best left to a surer hand."

"A hand like yours?" Ardith snorted. "I wouldn't trust you

or your Shrike Lord to tie my boots, let alone wield the sort of power I've heard came off that artifact."

Ardith knew far too much. The Fox Lord was renowned for having good information, but this was ridiculous. The only people who'd seen me activate the stone were the Rookery, the Raverran delegation, and Kip; it was hard to imagine any of them sending a message to Ardith, so I had to assume someone had been telling the story to anyone who'd listen. Seasons spare me, I needed to ask Odan to have a stern talk with his nephew.

Severin smirked as if this exchange of barbs amused him, even though it teetered on the brink of offering a true grievance. "It's a good thing no one in Alevar has much interest in tying your boots, then," he put in, cutting off whatever angry comments were marshaling on Voreth's lips.

The first strains of a waltz slid like punctuation across the end of his sentence, reverberating through the hall. Exclamations of delight rose up from the crowd, and there was a general movement toward the dance floor—especially among the Vaskandrans, to whom a waltz was more familiar than the Raverran or Loreician court dances with their intricate steps.

Severin extended a slim, elegant hand toward me.

"Perhaps we could continue this conversation on the dance floor?" he asked. "My brother is not much for throwing festivities, and I rarely get the chance."

I stared at his hand as if it were a weapon.

I knew hidden places to watch from in every hall in Gloamingard that could host a dance. I'd looked down on bright twirling figures from balconies, listened to the music through windows, and lain on my belly in forgotten crawl spaces to watch the intricate movement of dancers' feet. Sometimes I'd let myself imagine what it might be like if I gained enough control over my power to become one of those dancers, twirling in a skirt made of living blossoms or a vestcoat of fine Loreician silk.

Never once had I thought my first dance would be with a man who wanted me dead.

But he surely couldn't know that I was the one whose life he'd demanded last night. This was an opportunity, and the Grace of Luck shunned those who let opportunities pass by.

I reached out, with all the care of a woman sticking her hand into a vat of poison, and took his offered fingers.

FOURTEEN

It had been strange enough taking Aurelio's hand in friendship. Now the life that pulsed against mine, palm to palm,
was that of an enemy.

Severin's hand was cool and dry, with restrained strength in
his long fingers. A strange urge came over me to crush his hand
in mine, some idiot impulse of domination, but I resisted it. His
grip remained firm but gentle, and I read tension and an inexplicable urgency in the line of his shoulders as we headed for the
dance floor.

This was really happening. Hell of Madness.

"I should warn you that I've never danced before in my life,"
I felt obliged to say.

He flashed me an unexpected smile. "That's unfortunate. I
wasn't joking about my own lack of experience in the ballroom.
Hopefully we can at least fake a waltz well enough not to fall over."

His whole demeanor changed. The icy control was gone, and
a reckless eagerness had taken its place. I stared at him suspiciously as we claimed an uncrowded corner of the dance floor
and faced each other.

He glanced at the other couples and grimaced. "All right, let's
do this."

Everyone else was stepping close to their partner, almost into an embrace. Panic flared up in my chest—I'd known this was coming, but I hadn't thought it through. I'd only been able to touch people for a few hours; I wasn't ready.

It was too late to back out. Carefully, gently, Severin laid his free hand on my back. My corset held the warmth of his touch off my skin like armor, thank the Graces.

After a moment of awkward hovering, I copied the others and laid my free hand on his upper arm. The space between us had almost vanished, and I found myself staring directly into his eyes at unnervingly short range. Beneath the mage mark, they were an even darker brown than mine, almost black.

I'd never been this close to someone who wasn't family. Holy Hells.

"Here we go," he murmured, and we swung into motion.

At first it was all I could do not to trip on my own skirts. I had plenty of experience being aware of other people's motions, but my instincts screamed to move away, not to move in concert. Fortunately, Severin seemed more interested in *looking* like we were dancing than in actually dancing, and it didn't take long to accomplish a credible sort of rocking turn that likely was entirely wrong.

"I asked you to dance so we could speak privately," Severin murmured.

"Well, this is certainly private." We were close enough that my skirts swished against him as we moved, and I could feel the heat coming off him.

"We don't have long, so let's skip the niceties." He dropped his voice even lower. "I know the truth about Lamiel's death."

It was all I could do not to freeze on the spot.

"Really?" I managed.

"I know she tried to seize the power your family has been hiding in Gloamingard." His mouth twisted wryly. "And my brother didn't exactly try to stop her. He used to be sensible, but I'm afraid he's turned more than a little reckless where Lamiel's involved."

"Reckless. Is that what you call it?" I seized on outrage, the better to hide my fear. Let him think I was rigid in his arms from anger, and not from dread that his next words would be a murder accusation. He could be trying to startle information out of me; I had to keep my thoughts off my face.

"Oh, there are plenty of other words you could use." Severin's voice dripped irony. "I assure you, none of this was my idea. I gather that my dear would-be sister Lamiel met the reception one would expect when attempting to steal power from a Witch Lord."

If he knew I was the one who'd killed her, he certainly was calm about dancing with a murderer. Maybe he was luring me into a clever verbal trap. Maybe he had been jealous of Lamiel, and this was part of some Alevaran power play. Maybe he was merely hoping to rattle me.

If so, it was working. His touch shook me enough even without the dangerous conversation. I had to stay focused on deflecting any admission of guilt away from Morgrain.

"Exalted Lamiel certainly transgressed against our hospitality," I said coldly. "What is your point, Exalted Atheling?"

He winced, as if either my tone or his title pained him. "My brother let Lamiel try her gambit for a reason. He wanted that relic of yours before he had cause for vengeance," he said. "And his interest in it hasn't lessened, even if he now wants Lamiel's killer more."

Ah. So that was what he was after. "And you think I can grant you access to its power."

"I frankly don't care. My brother would have broken a mountain in half for Lamiel, but I assure you he'll share no power with me."

Severin spun me, my skirts swirling. A strange, fierce lightness came into my chest. He didn't know I'd killed Lamiel; he was playing games. By the Eldest, I could play, too.

"Then why are we having this conversation?" I asked, boldness singing in my blood and seizing my tongue.

"Because I know your aunt can't turn over Lamiel's murderer to my brother." He whispered it almost in my ear, close enough that his breath stirred my hair. "The killer *must* have been someone in your family, or at least acting on your orders."

Hells, he was good at this. "If you think my aunt's promise was empty, why did you accept it?"

"To allow you to buy time to consider other options if you want to keep my brother from declaring war."

I glared at him. "I see. You're using this demand for Lamiel's killer to put pressure on us to surrender the obelisk instead, which is what your brother truly wanted all along."

"That does appear to be my brother's strategy," Severin said, that edge of almost self-mocking irony coming into his voice again. "Though I assure you, he truly would be even happier to get his hands on the murderer."

I marshaled a reply carefully on my tongue. I couldn't reject the idea of giving him the obelisk as laughable, much as I wanted to; it might provoke him into action. I had to find some way to draw him out further.

The half-formed words coalescing in my brain shattered as a shadow fell across us, blocking the autumnal light. A harsh grip closed on my forearm, ripping it from Severin's grasp.

My aunt glared down at me with the fury of an earthquake gathered in the lines of her face. She yanked my captured arm up between us.

The jess gleamed golden on my wrist, red crystals winking in the light like beads of fresh blood.

Karrigan shook my arm at me like a weapon, the jess dangling from my wrist.

"How could you *do* this?" she hissed. "Have you no shame?"

Severin's eyes widened, going from my jess to Karrigan to the fury I could feel glowing in my face.

"I can see this is a bad time, Exalted Atheling." He grimaced, but I couldn't tell whether it was in contempt or sympathy. "Far be it from Alevar to become involved in a family quarrel. We can continue our conversation later."

He bowed and retreated, but I could feel his eyes still on me, no doubt calculating what it meant that I was now wearing a jess.

My cheeks burned. "You're embarrassing me in front of our guests, Aunt Karrigan."

"*I* am embarrassing *you*? You've sold yourself to the Empire and disgraced our family!"

Heads turned in our direction. Lady Celia snapped open a fan in front of her mouth. Ashe rolled her neck and started our way, but Kessa dropped a hand on her shoulder, shaking her head. My aunt hadn't raised her voice yet, but her aggressive stance was enough; she was on the verge of making a scene.

"I've taken steps to ensure the safety of our guests," I said through my teeth. "Now let go of me. They're watching us."

She released me, leaving a white handprint on my arm, but she still stood rigid and glaring with anger.

"It was bad enough that your father married a Raverran woman without a drop of magic in her veins," she said. "Now you've gone and given what dregs of power you *do* have to our historical enemies. I never thought that even you would stoop so low."

That was it. I'd had enough. Anger flared up in me like sudden fire; the jess grew hot on my wrist. "It's not your place to chastise me for my choices," I snapped. "When Grandmother returns, if she chooses to reprimand me, so be it. I'll give the jess back if she orders it. In the meantime, I'm an atheling of Morgrain—equal in rank to you, whether you like it or not." I struggled to bring my rising voice back under control, smoothing the fury out of it, even as Karrigan's eyes widened in surprise, then narrowed calculatingly. "We shouldn't argue in public. I shouldn't have to tell you Morgrain needs to look united and strong now. Our neighbors are circling us *and* that stone like carrion birds."

Karrigan stared at me a long time, her expression unreadable, her brows lowered.

"Fair enough," she growled at last. "But there will be a reckoning for what you have done."

"Of that," I said, "I have no doubt."

It took a while to shake off my anger at Karrigan, and my shame at having my jess exposed in front of the entire reception like that. I was used to stares and whispers, but that didn't mean I liked them. I supposed I should have Odan spread the word to the staff and our guests about my jess now, to get ahead of the inevitable rumors; it could never have been a secret, but seasons witness I'd have liked to announce it in a different way.

Still, by the time I trailed back to my room in a cloud of silk and straggling hair and a faint sheen of perspiration, I had to admit that the reception had gone well. My aunt's reaction to the jess had been predictable, if maddening; but the ceremony had gone smoothly, the food and music had been good, everyone had mingled politely enough, and there'd been no diplomatic disasters.

And then there was Severin, who seemed willing to speak critically of his brother in private, which was something—even if I still had no idea what he was up to. The memory of his hand on my back set a flush in my face that had no business being there. The man had *demanded my death*, for Graces' sake.

I shook the thought from my head, cheeks burning. I had to focus on holding the negotiations together. I had separate meetings with each side scheduled tonight and hoped to wrangle them to an agreement tomorrow morning. If nothing went wrong, we might have the Raverran warships sent home by sunset tomorrow. After that I'd just need to find some way to appease the Shrike Lord's grievance that didn't involve my grisly death.

I opened the door to my room, ready to kick off my boots and begin changing into regular clothes to go meet with the Rookery for another look at the obelisk—from a safer distance, this time.

Yellow eyes gleamed at me from the long afternoon shadows. Whisper sat on my bed, waiting for me. *Sweet Graces.*

"Hello," I said cautiously.

"You're going back to the tower," he said. It wasn't a question.

"Yes." I crossed the room and sank down beside him in a puff of skirts. I started pulling off my shoes as if I didn't care what he wanted and no flame of curious dread burned inside me.

His bushy tail lashed across the covers. "Don't touch the stone again."

"Do I look like an idiot?"

"You're a human." He licked a paw and let me chew on that. "What do your Rookery friends plan to do with the obelisk?"

"Study it." I considered my answer carefully. If Whisper's purpose pertained to the Black Tower, what I said next might determine whether he helped us or hindered us. "Figure out whether it did any harm when I triggered it. If the seals need any repair or reinforcement, see to it. That's my understanding, anyway."

His eyes narrowed. "You should send them away before they can decipher what it does. That stone is more dangerous than they can imagine."

Given that I'd heard stories about the Rookery handling everything from ancient artifice weapons that could destroy a city to war chimeras created to take on small armies, this was unnerving to hear—and more so from Whisper, who I'd never known to fear anything.

"I don't have the power to send them away. They're backed by the Conclave and the Council of Nine." I took a deep breath. "And I wouldn't send them away if I could. Grandmother's *disappeared*, Whisper. Something strange and terrible happened that night. I need to understand what it was so that I can protect Gloamingard."

"You always were a sentimental fool," he muttered, and began pacing a sleek figure eight on the bed, his tail swishing in curt strokes behind him. "I could kill them, I suppose."

I froze, one stocking dangling from my hand, a chill blooming in my stomach. I couldn't tell how serious he was. For all I knew, he could do it; as a chimera he might be poisonous, or spit fire, or have claws that cut through stone.

"Please don't," I said. "They're Grandmother's invited guests, and my friends." I wasn't completely certain of that last—it was still a new concept, not yet broken in—but close enough.

Whisper's ears flicked a dismissal. "I suppose they'd only send more investigators if the first batch turned up dead." He gave me an unreadable glance. "You're not making this easy, Ryx."

"Sorry," I said softly, feeling an inexplicable pang of guilt. "I'd help you if I could. But I don't know what you're trying to do. Can't you tell me, Whisper?"

"I'm trying to protect you. And your precious Gloamingard, for that matter. I can't say any more than that without breaking my promise." He settled on his haunches with an air of complete disgust. "Ugh. If I can't keep you all away from the stone entirely, I suppose it's better to get this over with. The longer you spend poking at it, the greater the chance of catastrophe. I'll help you make this terrible mistake, if it'll get everyone to leave the obelisk alone as quickly as possible."

"Thank you." I barely dared to breathe for fear he'd change his mind.

"When you go to the Black Tower," Whisper said, "consider the Gloaming Lore. Your ancestors did create it to give you the answers you need, after all." His tail tip twitched. "Whether they did a competent job or not, I will leave to your discretion."

I turned that over in my mind. The answers we needed, eh?

"*Guard the tower, ward the stone; find your answers writ in bone,*" I murmured. I'd always assumed that line referred to the pieces of Gloaming Lore carved all over the castle, including the Bone Palace. But that line had to be older than the Bone Palace, if our family legends were to be believed—and Whisper had said to consider the lore in the tower itself.

"There's no bone in the Black Tower," I observed.

Whisper tilted his head, pointed ears cupped to catch some secret sound. "Isn't there?"

"Maybe I should look closer," I said. "Thanks, Whisper."

I reached out casually toward him. He sniffed my offered fingers with great dignity, then shoved his head into my hand. I scratched behind his ears until he sighed with contentment.

"Don't thank me yet," he warned me, his eyes half closing. "You'll be wishing you'd never heard of the Black Tower before the night is through."

"Blood of the Eldest, it feels wrong to be idling about in a room with that thing," Ashe grumbled. The harsh light of the Black Tower wards turned her pale hair scarlet and gleamed at the corners of her eyes. "All my instincts say to fight or run."

"Mine too." I shuddered and rubbed my arms. Even with

the seal back to what Bastian and Foxglove assured me was full strength, power crawled under my skin and throbbed in the air around me like a dull ache.

It didn't feel like a room a human could live in for long.

Kessa seemed to share my opinion. She crouched on the floor and put her head in her hands. "This place is making me sicker than the day after a night of bad choices. We should leave."

Ashe crossed to Kessa's side at once and laid a hand on her shoulder. "Go," she said, surprisingly gently. "This is Foxglove and Bastian's show. You don't need to be here."

Kessa shook her head and rose to her feet, but she squeezed Ashe's hand. "If I leave, who'll keep you all from doing regrettable things?"

Ashe snorted. "What makes you think you can stop us?"

I felt an inexplicable pang at the closeness between them. But I'd never had a chance with Kessa, even now that I had the jess. If I dared to court someone—a thrill raced along my nerves at the exciting, terrifying prospect—it would have to be a mage with the mark, or perhaps an unmarked atheling from a royal family, to seal or strengthen an alliance. Someone like Rillim—or Severin.

Memories teased my senses of Kessa's fingers sliding through my hair, and Severin's lean body clasped close to mine as we danced. I shook them away with difficulty. *Bones.* I was supposed to be looking for bones.

No matter how I scanned the chamber, all I saw was shining black obsidian and glowing scarlet wards.

Foxglove paced the room, his hands clasped behind his back. "This isn't anything so benign as a power storage device," he said. "It's something more dangerous, with all these wards. Perhaps a weapon—or a prison."

Ashe stroked the hilt of her sword, as if soothing it. "I have to admit even I wouldn't want to fight something that's leaking power like *this.*"

"I keep hearing this sound," Bastian said nervously. "A hissing, or a scratching. Almost like voices."

"You're going mad," Ashe suggested. "I don't hear anything."

"No, I can hear it, too," Kessa said, her voice strained. "Ugh, that's creepy. Close your eyes and listen."

I did, torn between curiosity and dread. A sound scratched at the edges of hearing—almost a whisper, but not in any human language I could understand. It was more like the scuttle of insect legs, or the hiss of the wind. The moment I tried to focus on the noise, it fell silent. I shuddered.

Kessa had the right idea. With my eyes closed, the stark visual impact of the Black Tower no longer assaulted my vision, overwhelming my perceptions. As the green afterimage of runes and patterns danced on the inside of my lids, I tried to open my other senses.

I caught a scent like the eerie freshness after a lightning storm in the air. The voices of the Rookery echoed oddly around me, bouncing off the tower walls. And the press of magic became even more overbearing, nearly crushing the breath from my lungs.

But there was something else, beneath the pall of power hanging thick in the room. Something that tugged at my blood connection to Morgrain. All through the walls, reaching up to the roof of the tower and down beneath the floor, stretched a delicate tracery of life.

No. Not quite life. The magical energy of life, imbued into a thin filigree of bone within the chamber walls.

The Black Tower itself was a chimera.

"Holy Hells," I breathed.

Bone chimeras were forbidden by laws more ancient than Vaskandar itself, but the Black Tower long predated such rules. It didn't seem aware, thank the Graces—not truly alive, not even to the degree that an insect was alive—but someone, long ago, had imbued it with power and given it bones.

And those bones, hidden within the walls, spelled a message. The intricate patterns and thin spiraling traceries all came together on the far wall, behind and above the obelisk, to spell out words taller than a man, bold and urgent, an ancient warning hidden so that only one bound to the life of Morgrain could see it.

THE GATE MUST REMAIN CLOSED.

In the darkness behind my lids, I puzzled that over. It didn't make any sense. By the time anyone saw those words, the Black Tower would by definition already be open.

Seasons preserve us. *Nothing must unseal the Door.* The earth seemed to shift under me, reality itself tilting into a dizzying new perspective.

The Gloaming Lore had never meant the door to the Black Tower.

"It's a gate," I gasped. I kept my eyes squeezed shut, afraid I'd lose my tenuous sense of the words if I opened them. "The obelisk. It was the Door all along."

"What? How do you know?" Ashe demanded, as Bastian excitedly exclaimed, "Oh, that could be it!"

"Someone left a message written in life magic inside the tower walls, so only a member of my family could see it." I didn't mention the part about the entire tower being effectively a chimera, not yet; this was hard enough to believe as it was. Footsteps and the rustle of clothes sounded as the others gathered around me.

"I knew it was a good idea to recruit you!" Foxglove crowed. "What does it say?"

"The gate must remain closed."

It didn't sound nearly important enough when I said it in my feeble human voice. They didn't understand the urgency, the dread, the centuries burdening this single commandment. I shook my head, took in a deep breath, and tried again.

This time, some of the power in the room slipped into my

lungs. My voice reverberated in the walls themselves, as if the Black Tower said it with me.

"The Gate Must Remain Closed."

A shiver traced its path across my skin.

"Grace of Mercy," Kessa swore.

"That was cursed spooky," Ashe said.

"Sorry. I don't know why that happened." It was all I could do to keep my eyes closed; I was more than a bit unnerved. "The gate to where?" I wondered aloud.

A slithering, grinding sound grew within the tower walls, grating on my nerves like nails against slate. I clapped my hands over my ears.

"What's wrong, Ryx?" came Kessa's muffled voice, and she touched my arm, lightly.

"Can't you hear? No, I suppose you can't." It was the latticework of bone that ran through the walls. The words shifted and blurred, running into each other as the chimera changed its form, letters twining and untwining to form new shapes.

An answer, writ in bone.

Slowly, slowly, new words formed, traced in ancient magic and nameless bone. Stark letters spelled out a truth so awful it stole my breath and dropped me to my knees.

"Ryx?" Kessa shook my shoulder. "Ryx, are you all right?"

This was what we had been guarding, all along. This was what I had unleashed.

"No," I whispered. "It can't be."

But I knew—*knew*, by the blood that ran in my veins—that the tower's answer was true.

THE GATE TO THE NINE HELLS.

FIFTEEN

"We need to get out of here," I said, my voice scraping roughly through my throat. "Out, now, and seal this chamber."

I lurched to my feet, shaking off Kessa's concerned hand. I'd opened my eyes to the scarlet-drenched room, but still the tower's answer burned itself into my senses. I couldn't unsee it, couldn't unlearn it. The pressure and heat in the air became too much, now that I knew what power lay behind them; I struggled against the need to breathe it in.

Foxglove took one look at my face and nodded, his bright eyes gone grim. "All right. Out!"

"But—" Bastian's pencil hovered over his notebook.

Ashe grabbed him by the back of the jacket, like a mother cat corralling a kitten. "I swear, you'd try to sketch a chimera while it was eating you. Come on."

They hurried out into the hallway without another question; thank the Graces I was dealing with people who didn't have to be convinced that magic could be dangerous. I slipped through the door on Foxglove's heels, then spun at once to slap my hand against the seal. My heart pounded to rattle my rib cage as the great obsidian slab slowly ground shut, the bloody light beyond it narrowing to a sliver and finally winking out.

My breathing rasped harsh and loud in the dusty alcove, echoing down the damp corridor of the old stone keep. The Rookery gathered around me, uncertainty and excitement and fear palpable in the air.

"What was it, Ryx?" Foxglove asked, his voice low and intense. "What did you see?"

Only this, and nothing more: nothing must unseal the Door.

It would have been nice if the Gloaming Lore had warned us *why*. Then maybe I could have been more careful. I would have listened to Whisper and killed Lamiel rather than let her come so close to the obelisk. Stayed far away from it myself. Convinced my grandmother to bury this madness beneath a hundred feet of stone, rather than trusting magical seals and words of warning.

Keep your secrets, guard your lore—but the Rookery were all staring at me expectantly, blissfully unaware of the horror that stood before them. My grandmother must have known; she must have accepted that the Rookery would eventually find out when she called on them for help. I lifted a trembling hand to my face, the awful truth rising up from my chest like a bubble of black poison, ready to burst through my lips.

This secret was too big to carry alone. Its weight was crushing me already.

"It's a portal to the Nine Hells." The words flew from my tongue, and now I could never recall them.

Ashe let out a bark of a laugh that cut off abruptly halfway through. "Pox, you're serious."

"Holy Graces preserve us," Foxglove whispered. His hand lifted instinctively to an artifice charm that pinned his cravat, as if whatever small power it possessed could protect him.

Kessa hesitated, glancing from me to Bastian, whose hands covered his mouth, brown eyes wide. "It can't be. The Hells are a story, an overly dramatic metaphor—they aren't real. Are they?"

"Real enough," I said hoarsely, slumping against the cold stone wall. "You felt the power in there. We were wondering what could be so terrible that they'd need to construct an entire tower out of obsidian and cover it with seals and wards to contain it. Well, now we know."

Foxglove, usually so poised, swayed on his feet as if he might faint. "The voices. Sweet Grace of Mercy. Those were demons."

Bastian shook his head, eyes wide and lost. "I can't believe it. No, I don't *want* to believe it. If this is true—if that's a gate to the Hells, and it's been *opened*, what does that mean?"

"It means," I said, my voice raw and strained, "if we make one wrong step here, we could unleash the Dark Days once more."

Bastian pulled books from his trunk in the crowded Rookery sitting room, where we'd retreated to huddle in our profound spiritual terror in privacy. He barely glanced at titles before setting them aside with far less than his usual care; his long, elegant fingers trembled on their covers.

"Every culture in Eruvia has a story of the Dark Days, when demons came forth from the Nine Hells to subjugate the earth. *Every culture.* Plenty of scholars have theorized that this must point to a true historic event."

"They're just stories," Kessa insisted. She drew closer to Ashe as if for comfort, and Ashe wrapped an arm protectively around her. "They're too exaggerated to be true. People made up the Demon of Corruption to explain sickness and rot, the Demon of Disaster to explain volcanoes and blizzards, and so on; and then they invented the Hells because those demons had to come from *somewhere*. Only the superstitious and the gullible think they're real."

"What if they are, though?" Bastian lifted his gaze from a

book, his eyes dark and troubled. "Even if the Hells aren't what we think they are, that doesn't mean they're not *something*."

I leaned against the wall by the hearth, shivering, arms wrapped around myself in a desperate attempt to regain some warmth. All I could think of was the terrible power that had poured through me both times I touched that seal—when I opened the gate. *Hellfire.*

"Graces know I don't want to believe it," Foxglove said, pacing. "But Bastian has a point. If you follow a story to its roots, you often find truth there. How many times have we used local legends to trace down forgotten artifacts or buried curses?"

"It's real," I said quietly. "I don't know if the stories are true, but the gate is real."

Bastian paused, a book in his hands, his chin quivering with some barely contained emotion. "I have to admit, even though it's part of my religion, I always assumed the story of the Dark Days was an allegory." A strained laugh burst out of him. "Times were hard, but we developed all these good things like art and charity to help us through them. Not *literal demons* coming into the world through an *actual gate to the Nine Hells* which is *still around*."

"I never doubted the Hells were real," Foxglove said darkly. "I grew up in the poorest part of Raverra during a plague year. I saw plenty of the Nine Hells on earth."

"Well, Ryx apparently had them in her cupboard all this time." Ashe shook her head. "We just had spiders in ours."

Kessa let out a great huff of breath at that. "That's right. If this is hard for me to accept, I can only imagine you must be ready to spit up your own brain in a jar, Ryx."

Ashe grunted. "Yeah, if it *is* a gate to the Nine Hells, I'd hate to be the one who opened it."

Kessa made a noise of protest and punched Ashe's arm.

"Thanks." I rubbed my forehead, which was more than half

an excuse to cover my eyes. "I assure you, I'd already thought of that."

I didn't know what to feel beyond pure shock. We'd slipped into the wrong world somehow, some strange place of dream or story. Surely we'd snap back to the real, rational world at any moment.

But I knew it was true. I'd found my answer, writ in bone. The deep instincts that tied me to the land knew it was no lie.

"Aha!" Bastian lifted up a book, triumphant. "Here it is. Diaghra's *Translations of Ancient Ostan Tablets*."

Foxglove's brows lifted. "I'd assumed you were digging for a book of legends of the Dark Days."

"Oh, certainly, but I always do prefer to find as close to a primary source as possible." Bastian paged eagerly through the book. "Most of the stories place the Dark Days at about four thousand years ago. Vaskandar and the continental Serene Empire didn't have much in the way of writing then, but Osta did. There's an account on a fragmentary tablet found in one of the oldest temples in Osta—likely not contemporaneous, but probably within a century or two, which is—"

"Skip the introduction," Ashe interrupted. "Get to the part where you tell us how to lock the damned gate and maybe stab some demons."

Bastian ignored her. "From the north came the Nine Demons," he read, "and they spread across the land in plague and misery, terror and death. Neither great armies nor works of potent magic could stand against them. All was ruin."

Sudden guilt twisted my stomach, sharp and fierce. This was what I'd risked unleashing again.

"The people lost themselves to despair," Bastian read on, while the rest of us exchanged somber glances. "The Nine Demons ruled for a hundred years, and life became a suffering to be endured." He lifted his eyes from the page. "I'm not certain what this next part means."

"Just read it," Foxglove said, fidgeting with his cuffs.

"Very well." He squinted dubiously at the page. "Some among the demons wore the masks of kings and queens. And there were those courageous ones who strove to slay them. But if one mask became broken, the demon without delay put on another. Therefore all attempts at their destruction proved in vain."

"I'll bet 'masks' means possession," Ashe suggested. "A lot of the old stories of the Dark Days in my part of Vaskandar are tragic tales about people getting possessed by demons and their friends needing to kill them."

Kessa grimaced. "That seems excessively awful."

"They're demons," Ashe said. "They're supposed to be awful."

I raked my fingers through my braid, unraveling it so I could do it up again and give my hands something to do besides twist against each other in my lap.

"Possession shows up again and again in the legends," Foxglove said, fingering the pouches at his belt. "In the Empire, too. We'd best assume it's a danger we may have to face."

"There's more." Bastian's voice had gone hoarse. He reached out, searching blindly, and Kessa put a cup of water into his hand; he drank a long swallow and continued. "The Great Sage of Parha discovered that the demons had come from a realm of light and fire through a pass in the distant mountains of the north." Bastian tapped the page. "If my recollection of Ancient Ostan is accurate, they use the same word for *pass* and *gate*."

Kessa sank back in her chair as if the spirit left her. "And here we are, in the foothills of the northern mountains, with a gate to light and fire locked up behind the most excessive wards I've ever seen. All right, you're beginning to convince me. And I need a drink."

"The Sage of Parha." Foxglove frowned, rubbing his chin. "My Ostan grandmother sometimes used that name for the Grace of Wisdom."

"There are some Ostans who believe the Graces were extraordinary people rather than divine beings, yes," Bastian said, with a careful glance at Foxglove as if measuring his reaction to this possible blasphemy.

"The Vaskandran legends of the Dark Days don't include the Graces at all," Kessa said, with an apologetic shrug for the Raverrans. "They speak of heroes who drove back the demons, but the stories say they were Vaskandran mages, not divine beings."

"Or not mages," Ashe put in. "I like the ones where they're regular people."

"One way or another, forgive me, but I don't think we can rely on your Graces to save us," Kessa said. "Whatever they were, or are, they're not here now."

It was an uncomfortable thought; my mother had raised me to make offerings to the Nine Graces and pray to them when I was in need, but had scoffed at demons and Hells, saying they were made up to scare people into obedience. The idea that the Hells were real and *here*, and the Graces beyond reach in the uncertain realm of divinity or myth, was terrifying.

I shook my head. "The message of the Graces was never that they would come and save us." Everyone looked at me; I took a deep, ragged breath. "If you're Raverran, you know how it is. You pray to the Graces for strength—for wisdom or courage, for luck or mercy. In the end, though, it's up to you to get it done. No one will do it for you. That's the Raverran way."

Foxglove nodded, his lips shaping the ghost of a smile. "So it is. And anyone who says it'll be easy is trying to sell you something."

"What's the Vaskandran way?" Bastian asked, with the nervous tone of someone not sure he liked the answer he had and hoping for a better one. "What do *you* do when everything is terrible?"

Kessa and Ashe exchanged a long glance. It was a more complicated question than Bastian probably realized. In Vaskandar, the Witch Lords regularly delivered miracles to avert the worst cruelty the turning seasons could deliver, from counteracting drought to quelling bandits. They were certainly more accessible and present than the Graces. But in some domains, the Witch Lord was the reason everything was terrible in the first place, and then no amount of Raverran-style cleverness and pluck could save you.

At last, Kessa said, "We endure."

Bastian swallowed visibly. "That's not reassuring, either."

Ashe poked his side. "Since we'd rather not endure another round of Dark Days, does your rock say anything about how they got rid of the demons and closed the gate?"

Bastian closed his book, shaking his head. "No. The tablet is broken, and the rest of it was never found."

"It's all right," Kessa said, lifting her chin. "We've got a gate to the Nine Hells in Ryx's tower, and that's extremely unfortunate, but it's closed. It was closed for thousands of years before our brief little indiscretions, and it's closed now. The Nine Demons don't appear to have come sweeping through to plunge the world into the Dark Days again."

"That we know of," Ashe added.

"Fair." Bastian took a deep breath. "All right. What do we do now?"

Foxglove's pacing stilled. "Technically," he said, with a grave glance around at all the members of the Rookery, "when we discover a threat to national security, it's my obligation to report it to my superiors in the Empire and Vaskandar."

My heart tried to jump up my throat. "You can't tell them

we've got a gate to the Nine Hells in Gloamingard. Everyone will declare war on Morgrain in a panic."

Kessa frowned. "She's got a point. Think how hard it was to talk down the Serene Empire from attacking their own client state when Calsida was slow to hand over that doomsday elixir, or how willing the Witch Lords are to saddle up the war chimeras anytime we find a Skinwitch. It's also our duty to avert these sorts of diplomatic problems, after all—and if we're speaking of technicalities, this gate hasn't been a threat to anyone's national security for four thousand years."

"Because it was a secret," Foxglove pointed out. "People may not know it's a gate, but they know it's powerful and dangerous. If nothing else, the Zenith Society will be sniffing around after it soon enough."

Kessa grimaced. "Can you imagine what they'd do with that gate? They'd be lining up like it was free-drinks day at the local tavern to see which of them could make bargains with all Nine Demons first."

"They're a Raverran political faction, aren't they?" I had to be missing something. "Raverran culture paints demons as abhorrent—pure evil. Would they really go so far?"

The Rookery exchanged meaningful glances; Bastian had gone an odd pale shade, almost greenish. Unspoken history hung thick in the air.

"Some of their members may honestly believe they're just a political faction," Kessa said, with a careful glance at Bastian. "But the core of the Zenith Society is something far worse. They've indulged in all sorts of repugnant magical experiments, collected highly illegal artifacts, and even tried to pull off a coup a few years ago."

"A coup!" I didn't think the Raverran government was particularly lenient about that sort of thing. "How are they still around?"

"We—or the Council of Nine, rather—obliterated the branch that was behind the coup." Foxglove's hand rested briefly on his pistol. "The rest of the Zenith Society swore they knew nothing about it, and were simply scholars of magic and concerned patriots with no interest in treason. They had enough influential members that the Council accepted this and left the rest of the society intact, but some of us are skeptical."

"Some of us have very good reason to be skeptical," Kessa muttered darkly.

Bastian still looked as if he might faint. "If the Zenith Society learns of the gate, they'll do anything to get control over it. I *know* them. They're desperate for some ultimate edge over Vaskandar, and they'll think this is the answer to their prayers."

"Anyone who thinks the Graces would give them the Hells in answer to their prayers has been seriously derelict in their attention to the shrinekeepers," Foxglove said dryly.

Kessa laid a calming hand on Bastian's arm and gave Foxglove a meaningful stare. "Maybe we *should* wait before reporting this. And not only because of the Zenith Society, much as thwarting those poxweasels is a good enough reason for me. Ryx is right; if we let this information loose at the wrong time, we'll start an international panic that'll make that time someone unleashed blood hornets at a harvest festival look like a courtly dance."

"Give us time," I urged them. "Let me sort out the current diplomatic crisis before we start a new one. I've got to meet with the envoys in an hour to talk about Windhome Island, for Graces' sake. We don't even really know what this discovery *means* yet; let's not make any irrevocable decisions about how to act on it when we haven't had time to think it through."

Bastian tapped his pencil against his notebook. "This *is* still technically just a theory. We don't have to report theories."

Silence fell on the room. The Rookery exchanged meaningful

gazes, the conversation continuing unspoken between them. I held my breath.

Finally, Foxglove leaned heavily on the mantel and sighed. "I can't put this off long."

"Just until we've got a solution," Kessa suggested. "They're *far* less likely to panic if we've already fixed it."

"How *do* we fix this?" Foxglove asked, the full impossibility of the situation weighing on his words.

"I'll get to work researching," Bastian said, digging into his chest for more books with the desperation of a man seeking escape. "The better I understand the enchantments, the more options we can come up with for reinforcing the seals, or possibly even destroying the gate."

"Feel free to search Gloamingard's library for anything relevant," I offered. "I'll check my grandmother's papers to see if she's got any notes on the Black Tower." I suspected that all my family's advice on the matter had already been carved into the castle walls in the Gloaming Lore, which mostly focused on never opening the Door in the first place, but I'd give that some further thought, too.

Kessa tapped her lips. "I'll make friends with the support staff in the diplomatic delegations—the clerks and guards and such—to see if I can get us some warning before they make any moves or figure this out."

Foxglove rubbed his hands. "I'll study our sketches of the Black Tower and the obelisk. And I'll also sit down with Lady Celia and a glass of wine and have a little chat about the Zenith Society. I want to find out how deeply they've infiltrated the imperial government."

I rose, full of grim determination. I knew what I had to do, and I had less than an hour to fit it in, though I wasn't looking forward to it.

"Where are you going?" Kessa asked, her head cocked questioningly.

"To talk to my aunt," I said.

Karrigan shook her head, dappled shadows sliding across her face. "A gate to the Hells themselves. Blood of the Eldest. *That's* what she wouldn't tell me."

We'd met in the deserted Aspen Hall, beneath the whispering leaves. It was as good a place as any to have a conversation without being overheard; the empty space around us ensured that no one could get close without being seen.

"I'm sorry." I wrapped my arms around myself against the nighttime draft weaving cold fingers through the hall. "It went undisturbed for four thousand years, until I stumbled into it."

Karrigan grunted. "Don't flatter yourself. Four thousand years? Maybe more like forty."

I stared at her uneasily. "What do you mean?"

"Don't you think it's odd that our family has held this castle for *four millennia*?" Karrigan swept a broad gesture to encompass all of Gloamingard with her bear-claw gloves. "From the Dark Days through the bandit kings to the rise of the Witch Lords, we've guarded the Black Tower and passed down the Gloaming Lore, and no one has taken this place from us. It's not as if this little hill provides some impenetrable defense. How do you think we did that?"

Her scarlet-ringed eyes pierced through any comforting *what ifs* or *maybes* I might have thought to utter. She was right. A growing dread built in my stomach. "The Gloaming Lore—"

"Says not to open the gate. But that doesn't mean there's no way to use the power." Karrigan started pacing, her boots striking hard notes from the wooden floor. "Do you know what my mother said when I asked her, years ago, if she'd ever been in the Black Tower?"

"No." The word came out strangled.

"'Once.'" The fur of my aunt's mantle lifted in response to her agitation, like a beast's hackles rising; it made her look fierce and wild and dangerous. "She's been in there, Ryx. I asked her why, and she got this cold and distant look, and I knew she didn't want to tell me. She said there was a terrible secret in there, to be used only in the time of greatest need. To be *used*, do you hear me?"

"We can't use it," I objected, horrified. "It's the power of the *Nine Hells*."

"Oh, it's eager enough to be used." She stopped her pacing and turned to face me, a strange light in her eyes. "I barely touched that obelisk, and I heard something calling to me, offering all *kinds* of things."

"That was a *demon*," I hissed. "For blood's sake, Aunt Karrigan, remember the Gloaming Lore. *Give no cunning voices heed, make no bargains born of greed—*"

"Never for greed." Her voice went deep and grave. "To protect Morgrain. To protect the Black Tower itself, and the secret it holds. Our ancestors must have done it dozens of times."

"Are you trying to tell me that our family has always been allied with demons?" The idea made me sick—the deep, sinking, terrible sickness of an ugly old truth.

History didn't leave one family in power for millennia without some telling advantage. Before the rise of the Witch Lords, Morgrain had survived eras of feuding bandit kings and the marauding Storm Queens, and our family had always held Gloamingard. *Always*. That stability had been a point of pride—but if the foundation we stood on was the pits of the Hells, surely that tainted everything we'd built.

"Maybe," Karrigan said. "Or maybe there's some way to use the power that bleeds out of that gate without getting demons involved at all."

"We don't know that," I objected. "We can't risk it."

Karrigan dropped her voice until I could barely hear it over the rustle of the aspen leaves. "We've got enemies circling us, waiting to be sure we're defenseless before they rip us apart. And there's still no sign of my mother." She took a deep, uneven breath. "We need every advantage we can get, Ryx. And if that means allying ourselves with demons, so be it."

SIXTEEN

No, I promised myself as I strode back toward my rooms through a dusty forgotten hallway in a section of the Great Lodge that had been sealed off by newer construction, anger at my aunt propelling me like the crest of a wave. *Absolutely not, under any circumstances.* By the Graces, there were some lines it should go without saying that you simply didn't cross.

Oh, I could see the logic. If it came down to it—if there were an army at the gates, and Gloamingard was about to fall—it would be hard to say no to whatever demon's bargain the gate could offer. I wasn't sure I could stand by and let Odan and Gaven and little Kip and everyone in the castle die if I had access to the power to protect them. We had to make sure it never came to that.

"I did warn you," came Whisper's voice, liquid and deadly soft behind me.

I turned to find a pair of yellow eyes glowing at me from a shadowed hollow between cobwebby antlers mounted over a doorway behind me. Luminescent flowers tucked in niches in the walls provided enough ghostly light to pick out the words carved down one side of the door frame in curling, elaborate letters: *Keep your trust through wits or war—nothing must unseal the Door.*

I shook my head, unable to unravel the tangle of feelings roiling in my chest. "You should have told me what that cursed stone was in the beginning."

"Of course I didn't tell you. I worked very hard to try to keep you from finding out." He leaped down casually to the floor, a falling shadow, landing with a puff of dust. "But you wouldn't leave it alone, and now you know. And what *I* need to know, Ryx, is what you plan to do about it."

The menace underlying his tone chilled me. I might consider Whisper my friend, but he'd made it clear enough that friendship had its limits.

"I only wish I had a plan," I said honestly. "I'm in shock."

He wove a slow circle around me in the dim corridor. "Because of what the bones told you?" he asked, too casually. "Or have other things occurred to you?"

"What, is there something even worse?" We were in one of my hidden routes through the castle, but even so, I glanced around and dropped my voice. "The Door is a *gate to the Nine Hells*. Do I need something more to be shocked at?"

"Not *a* gate," Whisper corrected. "*The* gate. To the best of my knowledge, there's only the one."

"Well, that's a great consolation." I slid down the log wall, dragging a clean swath through the dust, and came to rest on the age-smooth floorboards with my knees drawn up to my chest. "As for what I'm going to do about it, I don't know. I have to do *something*, because my aunt's plan is terrible. Soon every nation and domain in Eruvia will have designs on that gate, and Morgrain will drown in war. They'll raze Gloamingard to the ground if we don't stop them."

"I am disinclined to allow them to do that." Whisper stretched, a long sinuous shadow, his claws flexing into view through his dark fur. "This place is my home, and I like it the way it is. I suspect your grandmother feels the same."

"But she's not here." Fear tied knots upon knots in my belly. "Do you know where she is?"

He paused. "Not precisely."

"She's not..." I swallowed. "She hasn't gone through the gate, has she?"

"Of course not." He flicked a disdainful ear. "Passing through that gate would kill a human instantly, even one so powerful as your grandmother. She's not so foolish."

"What *is* on the other side of the gate, exactly?" I tried to sound casual, and avoided meeting his eyes. There was no sense reminding him that he hadn't wanted me to know about it.

He was silent so long, I had to look. He was an animal-shaped piece of darkness cut from the faint pearly glow of the flowers. His bushy tail swished across the boards behind him, restless, thinking.

"That," he said at last, "is an odd question for you to ask a mere chimera."

"You know many things, remember?" I pointed out ironically, arching a brow.

"Why do you want to know?"

I almost asked, *Why do you care?* But we'd run circles around each other enough already. "Does this have to do with your promise?"

He glanced away. "Maybe."

"I need to understand what I did when I touched that stone." I shrugged uncomfortably. "We have to figure out a way to make sure that gate never opens again." And to keep my aunt from giving in to the temptation to use it.

Whisper seemed to consider this. "Knowing more about the Hells will help you find a way to make all the meddling humans leave the gate alone?"

"Yes."

"Yourself included?"

I shuddered. "I'd rather not have anything to do with that gate again. The sooner I can be done with it forever, the better."

"Good." His eyes narrowed. "First you must understand that this world, the one we live in right now, consists mostly of matter, with magical energy running all through it like water. It pools in some places, flows in others, and is present in very nearly everything to at least some small degree."

What had blasted through that slim crack in the gate had been raw power, more pure and intense than anything I could ever remember experiencing. "So the far side is mostly magic," I guessed.

"All," Whisper corrected. "What you call the Hells is a layer of our own reality, like a buried aquifer, in which there is no matter whatsoever—only pure and limitless magical energy."

"And demons," I murmured.

Whisper's tail swished along the floor. "And nine demons, yes."

"What are they?" I asked, afraid of the answer. "If there's no matter in the Hells..."

Whisper strolled over to sniff a dead moth beneath the window, his back to me. "You humans are so full of questions."

"Whisper." I restrained myself from reaching for him. "I have to know if I..."

He batted the husk of the moth. "Yes?"

I swallowed. "If I might have let one through."

"It's not impossible," he said, going still. "Demons are creatures of pure energy, with no forms of their own. A human would see no more than a flicker of heat shimmer, or perhaps feel a faint gust of breeze, if that."

My fists clenched in my lap. "Until it possessed someone."

"Until it possessed someone, yes."

"Hells have mercy," I breathed.

Whisper's eyes gleamed at me in the shadows. "You'd best hope they do."

It was all I could do to try to focus on the conversation at my meetings with the Alevaran and Raverran delegations that evening. Thank the Graces Jannah was there to take notes, and my role at this point was mostly to nod and listen to their concerns. The terrible knowledge of what lay in the Black Tower burned in the back of my mind, and I had to avoid Aurelio's concerned eyes for fear that somehow he'd read the truth in mine.

It was hard to believe that any of this mattered now. That a petty conflict between nations over some barely inhabitable island was even relevant when I'd opened a portal to the Nine Hells in this very castle. But it had to matter. It would be difficult enough to maintain the peace on the strongest and most stable foundation once news of the gate got out. If Eruvia's balance was already rocking when this blow hit home, we'd never stop the tumble into war.

"A question, Exalted Ryxander."

It was Severin, leaning across the Round Room table with the hypnotic grace of a venomous snake.

"Yes?" I asked warily, tearing my thoughts away from the Black Tower to bring my full attention to bear on him. I could commit no less, with Severin of Alevar.

So much depended on whether he was playing some clever and convoluted game of his own—aimed at succeeding his brother, perhaps, or undermining him somehow—or if he was truly nothing more than the Shrike Lord's tool. He was too fascinating, too easy to stare at—and his sharp cheekbones, dark fall of silky hair, and the occasional gleam of wicked humor in his eyes were all frankly unfair ingredients in his poisoned cocktail.

But I didn't have time to unravel the knot of him, curse it. I needed to get this treaty signed quickly, before anyone found out the truth about the obelisk.

"You just came from the Black Tower, yes? How is the Rookery's investigation progressing? No further fatalities, I hope?" Severin's tone held its usual edge of irony, but there was nothing disinterested about the intensity in his half-hooded eyes.

I struggled to keep my face completely blank and neutral. "It's proceeding quickly, but I don't want to get distracted. We're here to discuss Windhome Island."

"I don't care about Windhome Island," he said. "My brother wanted it for Lamiel, since immortality is the best wedding gift. Now that you've removed that option, he has other priorities."

"So you have no objection to complying with the Serene Empire's stipulations for withdrawing all physical and magical presence from the island?" I countered.

Severin executed a languorous shrug that stirred the dark waterfall of his hair. "Only the objections anyone would have to paying up front for merchandise that hasn't been delivered. Unless you've handed over Exalted Lamiel's murderer and I missed it."

"We're not discussing what you want from Morgrain right now," I reminded him, an edge of frustration sharpening my voice. "These negotiations are with the Empire."

"We're not discussing what *I* want at all." His gaze held mine, then flicked sideways toward Voreth, who stood behind his shoulder, hands wrapped on his bone staff. "I assure you that our interest in these talks has everything to do with Morgrain."

That glance had been deliberate, heavy with meaning. Seasons, I was too rattled right now for more dancing.

"Your brother might be well served to have a bit more concern about the imperial warships aimed at his coast," I suggested.

"You don't know my brother." Some shadow flickered through his eyes. "You're assuming that Alevar wants to avoid a war. He's spent his life preparing for it."

That probably wasn't a bluff. Alevar was known for being a

militant domain; they maintained a standing human army and were said to have impressive reserves of war chimeras as well. It made them a coveted military ally, which was a problem—too many domains had mutual defense agreements with the Shrike Lord.

Still, there were limits.

"Surely the Shrike Lord isn't mad enough to take on the Serene Empire by himself," I said. "As for Morgrain, it's axiomatic that you can't defeat a Witch Lord in their own domain."

"Oh?" Severin flashed his teeth; the fleeting vulnerability was gone, if I hadn't imagined it in the first place. "One does wonder what might have happened to the Lady of Owls. It seems odd that she can't be bothered to show up for the negotiations. Or the Rookery's investigation of her magical secrets. Or the murder of one of her guests."

"Her business is her own." I attempted a mysterious expression, but my cheeks began inexorably warming, curse them. "I assure you, she's quite well."

"Oh, good." The smile that stretched his lips held no trace of friendliness. "I'm sure you wouldn't want your neighbors to get the impression that Morgrain is a failed domain, with no Witch Lord and no clear heir."

"Our neighbors wouldn't make such a basic mistake," I said. "Any more than *you* would make the mistake of sitting down at the negotiation table tomorrow with an experienced Raverran diplomat without having done any preparation." I gestured pointedly at the map of Windhome Island on the table between us.

Breath hissed through Voreth's teeth. Severin, however, broke into a laugh.

"Well then," he said, leaning back in his chair, "I suppose we'd better get back to the matter at hand."

My shoulders remained rigid with tension through the rest of the meeting. I might have fended him away from the most dangerous topics for now, but there was bound to be a reckoning soon.

If I couldn't figure out what Severin wanted before then—not his brother, not Voreth who followed him like a watchdog, but Severin himself—I suspected that wouldn't end well.

"Hey, Ryx."

I froze. As the last of my diplomatic guests had disappeared from the Round Room, I'd let my mask drop, slumping in my chair and putting my face in my hands. But that was Ardith's voice, coming from the doorway.

I straightened, greeting them with a smile that I allowed to be tired, since it was better if they thought I'd been slouching with exhaustion rather than with despair.

"Hello, Ardith. Having trouble finding your room?" I had no doubt that they knew exactly where their room was and were snooping around, but I might as well maintain the polite fiction.

Ardith's usual cheeky grin was conspicuously absent. They glanced around, then entered the room with only an echo of their customary swagger.

"I wanted to find you after the reception, but you were busy with the Rookery, so I thought I'd wait in ambush here and maybe eavesdrop on your diplomatic talks a little." They shrugged. "The diplomatic talks were boring, though."

I ran my conversations with Severin and Celia through my head, trying to recall if I'd said anything I wouldn't want the Fox Lord to know. "What did you want to talk about?"

"Karrigan. She was a complete ass to you at the reception." A surprising amount of heat warmed Ardith's words. "There's nothing wrong with getting help from the Empire."

I'd almost forgotten my confrontation with Aunt Karrigan.

The reception felt like a thousand years ago—a more innocent time, before I knew what lay in the Black Tower. "Thanks."

Ardith shrugged, a touch uncomfortably, as if sincerity were an ill-fitting garment. "I wouldn't be here if a Raverran alchemist hadn't helped my father and my da. There are some things the Empire does better than us, that's all, just like there are some things we do better than them."

"You've been waiting around outside the Round Room for hours just to tell me this?" Gratitude unfolded crumpled petals in my heart, a welcome relief from dread.

"Mostly, yes." They hesitated a moment, then grimaced. "I've got my job to do here, you know. I'd rather just lounge around drinking your beer and eating your food and telling jokes, but my father and the others sent me here for a purpose. If it looks like you're going to bungle the negotiations and get Vaskandar into a war with the Serene Empire, or if that artifact turns out to be a serious threat to the peace and the Rookery can't deal with it, I may have to do or say some things on behalf of my father and his allies that are...let's say less than completely friendly." Ardith spread their hands helplessly. "I wanted to make sure you knew it wasn't personal. That I like you, and I'm not going to get snooty at you about the jess, but I *am* here for a reason."

I closed my eyes for a moment, struggling with a mix of disappointment and frustration and the ever-building sense of incredible pressure on every single thing I did or said. Ardith liked me; I supposed that was something, even if they ultimately had to bring the wrath of the Conclave down upon my domain and everything I cared about.

"I understand," I said wearily. "I have my duties, too. And I like you as well, Ardith."

They flashed a bright grin at that. "Of course you do. It's because I'm so charming. See you at the negotiations tomorrow."

"You're not invited to the negotiations."

"I am now. Semi-official observer." Ardith shrugged an unapologetic apology. "I've cleared it with the envoys. It'll be fine."

I had dwindling hope that it would be fine. At this point, I'd accept anything less than a disaster.

The Bone Atrium had once been the main castle entrance, when the Mantis Lord ruled Morgrain; there was still no avoiding it, as it squarely straddled the center of many of the most heavily trafficked routes through the castle. The place was a soaring and impressive space worked with a complex filigree of magic-sculpted bone, punctuated by the jutting points of ribs, with the orderly regimented lines of vertebrae marking cornices and borders. As a child I'd loved its excessive ornamentation, and thought it was one of the most beautiful rooms in Gloamingard; then I'd learned it was built of thousands upon thousands of real bones, fused and shaped by the Mantis Lord's power—including those of his human enemies.

By now I was so used to it I didn't think much about how visitors might react. It took me a few moments to realize why Bastian and Foxglove kept flicking wide-eyed glances around them as we discussed our strategy for the imminent negotiation session.

"We won't mention the artifact unless someone else brings it up," I said, keeping my voice low, "and I'll let you two deflect any direct questions with technical details if they do."

Bastian nodded, swallowing visibly, his gaze riveted on something behind my head. I glanced over my shoulder to where a grinning human skull formed the keystone of a window arch and belatedly realized that maybe this wasn't an ideal place to gather before proceeding to the meeting room after all. Raverrans had a rather less cavalier attitude toward human remains than Vaskandrans did.

"Oh, that's...Well, the Mantis Lord had, ah, his own aesthetic." I laughed awkwardly, which was probably the wrong thing to do.

"So he did," Foxglove agreed, with great restraint. "Will your aunt be joining us for the negotiations?"

By the careful tone of his voice and the meaningful look he gave me, I suspected Foxglove shared my opinions about the sort of impact my aunt's presence would have on delicate talks with Raverrans.

"I didn't mention this session to her," I confessed. "She hasn't been involved in the process, so I'm afraid it simply didn't occur to me to see if she might like to be included."

Foxglove's lips quirked in a knowing smile. Hopefully my aunt would be more easily fooled.

"Have you made any progress on the obelisk?" I asked, dropping my voice to keep any odd echoes from carrying it beyond the three of us.

Bastian frowned. By the deep hollows under his and Foxglove's eyes, I suspected they'd been up most of the night—Graces knew I had been. "We've confirmed that it's a gate of some sort," he said. "And what came through it was raw magical energy. None of my research has turned up anything *else* it could open onto, though that begs the question of what exactly the Hells are."

"It's difficult to accept." Foxglove's voice went softer than I'd yet heard him speak. Stubble shadowed his cheeks this morning, with a few speckles of silver in it. "There are woodcuts of the Nine Hells in a book in the Temple of Wisdom library I went to as a child. One of the shrinekeepers used to show them to me to try to convince me to stay out of trouble." He shook his head, whether at the shrinekeeper's folly or at the horror of the Hells made real. "They were all fire and shadows and terrible phantoms, with the grinning faces of demons shaped from the smoke. I had nightmares about them, but I got into trouble anyway."

"Well, that's what life is, isn't it?" Bastian let out a nervous sort of laugh. "You learn that the world isn't what you thought it was. That your greatest truths are only stories, and the nightmares you thought were lies are truth."

That was darker than I'd expected from Bastian. He'd seemed so full of cheerful enthusiasm. My eyebrows climbed up my forehead.

Foxglove apparently felt the same way. "I'm surprised to hear such cynicism from you."

"I don't mean it cynically." He bit his lip, seeming to think about it; an odd, purplish flush crept up his neck, then receded. "Ryx, you may not know that I had a mentor who paid for my education at the University of Raverra. A sponsor who recognized my talent when he found me selling simple potions in the village fair."

"Aphrodisiacs," Foxglove murmured, his mouth quirking at the corner. "It's always aphrodisiacs." I struggled to smother a laugh.

"Well, that's where the money is," Bastian said, without so much as a blush. "The point is, there was a time when he ... he betrayed me." He stumbled on the word, and looked down at his boots, clasping his notebook to his chest. "I thought the world was a benevolent place that worked a particular way. I thought I could rely on certain things to always be true, and certain people to be trustworthy. I was wrong. I learned the world was a very different place, and I ... I was a very different person, too, than I'd thought."

Foxglove laid a gentle hand on his shoulder. Bastian shivered, but clasped his hand in apparent gratitude. A pale echo of his grief opened in sympathy in my chest, and I wondered what had happened to scar him this way.

"Anyway," Bastian said, his voice steady again as he lifted eyes full of a surprising quiet strength to meet mine, "this is like that.

Nothing is safe anymore. Things we took for granted aren't reliable or even real. I suppose I'd rather find out the Hells are real than that my friends are false."

I couldn't help an odd twist of envy. I'd never had enough friends to discover them false, true, or middling. I wondered if I should reach out to him—there was something open and aching in his expression—but I still had only begun to learn all the subtle rules of human touch.

A murmur of voices approached from one of the several corridors leading into the Bone Atrium. We straightened and moved slightly apart, as if we'd been doing something improper rather than simply having a meaningful conversation.

Lady Celia and Severin strolled into the room together, speaking in what appeared to be a cordial fashion, with Voreth and Aurelio staring daggers at each other behind them. Hope leaped in my chest; if they were talking, that was a good start. We might get this Windhome agreement signed by noon. Before the truth could escape our careful guard.

Suddenly Odan burst into the room from the direction of the Birch Gate. He paused inside the doorway, taking a second to gather his dignity and his breath. My heart plummeted. Blood and ashes, we didn't need another emergency now.

"Exalted Warden," he addressed me with a bow, barely keeping his fingers from flicking out in the warding sign while our guests watched. "Your cousin has just arrived at the castle gate."

All right, that *might* not be an emergency, but it was certainly an unwelcome complication. "Which cousin?"

"Exalted Vikal." Odan didn't quite smother a grimace. I struggled to keep my own face blank. Vikal was seventeen, flamboyant, and unlikely to bring a level head and mature perspective to this delicate situation. "I know you're busy, Exalted Warden, but he insists on bringing his weasel into the castle, and I don't have the authority to tell him no."

Usually our Furwitch guests were welcome to bring their animal companions into the castle, so long as they took responsibility for their behavior. Vikal was a gifted creator of chimeras with a flair for the dramatic, however, so Odan could be using the term *weasel* loosely.

"We're about to begin a meeting," I said. "Perhaps my aunt—"

I broke off as a tremendous racket sounded in the corridor behind Odan. And the chaos that was Vikal exploded into the room.

It was bad enough that he was riding a giant weasel, vividly striped in black and white, which bounded to the exact center of the room, scattering yelping Raverrans and annoyed Vaskandrans alike. Of *course* he also trailed a cloud of iridescent purple butterflies from his shoulders like a living cape. As a crowning touch, their wings emitted a high chiming sound, so that music followed him wherever he went.

"Ryxander!" Vikal cried, sliding down his weasel's shoulder when it had barely scrabbled to a halt. "I have a grievance to settle with you!"

I stood my ground as he strode up to me, trailing butterflies. He'd dyed his hair the same purple as their wings and outlined his eyes with the black paint currently fashionable with young mages; his mage mark stood out in a lighter shade of violet, almost lavender. Seventeen years old and the Warden of six villages, he was the perfect picture of an atheling poised to someday become a Witch Lord in his own right.

For once, with my Raverran guests gaping at him and his oversized weasel chimera in shock, embarrassment burned my cheeks instead of envy. Seasons spare us, he had power over life itself, and he used it to show off and make himself a nuisance.

"Hello, Vikal," I said, my tone pointedly polite in the hopes he'd take the hint. "It's my pleasure to welcome you to Gloamingard."

"You call this a welcome?" He flung an arm wide, scattering

butterflies. "Lancer and I rode for *hours* to get here, since I got the message. She's *exhausted*. And I'm told she's not welcome in my own family's castle?"

The weasel in question was sniffing the air, eyes bright and fierce, claws tearing up the Bone Atrium floor. Lady Celia had withdrawn to the far side of the room behind Aurelio, who had his hand on his pistol; Bastian had turned practically green. The Vaskandrans, more used to such displays, waited with resigned patience for the show to be over—except for Ardith, who must have come in during Vikal's rather distracting arrival. They grinned, hands thrust in their pockets, enjoying the spectacle.

"We don't have anywhere to put her in the castle," I said reasonably. "She won't fit, and she'll damage the place. Please tell her to let Odan and the stablehands put her in one of the special stalls, and—"

"In a *barn*? My Lancer?" Vikal threw a possessive arm over the weasel's shoulders; she bumped him with her whiskered nose.

I infused my voice with steel. "I have guests here from Alevar and the Serene Empire for a delicate diplomatic negotiation, Vikal. For now, at least, the barn will suffice."

Vikal tossed his purple hair. "*Fine*, then. Lancer, go with Odan."

Odan, his back rigid, offered a hand for Lancer to sniff, which she did with great enthusiasm. She followed him as he led the way with what dignity he could muster from the Bone Atrium.

The place felt bigger and infinitely quieter without a huge carnivore taking up the center of it. The butterflies mostly settled on Vikal's shoulders, forming a shifting mantle. Lady Celia hesitantly started back toward us, a wry *Well, that was exciting* smile tugging at her lips.

"Hello, Vikal," said Ardith. "Nice weasel."

Vikal lifted his chin proudly. "Honored Ardith. Of course she is."

I let out a long breath. "Now, Vikal, please be welcome. I have to attend to my guests, but your usual room—"

"This can't wait!" Vikal spun from Ardith, ignoring the others as if we were alone in the Bone Atrium. I could only assume he hadn't noticed Severin's mage mark, since even Vikal wouldn't completely neglect the courtesy due his peer; Severin, to his credit, raised no more fuss than a single eyebrow, though Voreth looked ready to explode with indignation. "What about the message I received? What do you have to say about *that*?"

"I have no idea what message you're talking about. Vikal—"

"*The* message!" Butterflies lifted from Vikal's shoulders in a singing cloud again as he spread his arms in agitation. "You can't just send something like that and pretend it doesn't exist!"

"I didn't send you any message." Foreboding began to unfold within me like a dark flower. "If it's family business, we can discuss it later."

"I have it right here." Vikal produced a slip of paper from his vestcoat pocket with a flourish and proceeded to read it in tones that shook echoes from the bones around us. "Come at once. We've discovered that the Black Tower—"

"Vikal, *later*," I snapped, grabbing at the message in alarm.

He never listened to me, though. None of my cousins did. He dodged my lunge, holding the paper higher, his voice only cresting louder, determined not to let me spoil his dramatic moment.

"—holds a *portal to the Nine Hells*."

Sweet Grace of Mercy.

A terrible silence fell over the Bone Atrium.

SEVENTEEN

Foxglove whispered a curse, so softly I doubted anyone else heard it.

All at once, everyone's face turned toward me. Lady Celia's normally bronze complexion went waxy pale; Ardith's expression hovered uncertainly at the edge of a smile, as if this might be a joke. Severin's eyes widened, as if Lamiel's ghost had just appeared to him.

The silence shattered into chaos, as everyone started yelling at once.

I couldn't pull any sense from the words and phrases scattered like shards of broken glass, but half of them seemed to be profanity. Vikal stood in the center of it all, hands on his hips, drinking in the scene he'd made.

Pox and ashes. I could laugh at him, denying the truth and dismissing his message as foolishness, and at least half the room would believe me—but I'd have lied to them, and when Foxglove made his report, they'd know it. Which he'd have to do soon now that the rumor was irretrievably out. Curse my cousin for a self-absorbed fool.

For a moment, all I could do was stare back at the distraught faces around me, just as horrified as they were. Half of me wanted to flee, and the other half wanted to strangle Vikal.

Instead, I raised my hands, and to my great surprise, the room fell silent. Whether I liked it or not, I had everyone's attention.

"First of all," I said, "Vikal, I didn't send you that note. I would very much like to know who did. It seems like a cruel trick." That much was all true, at least.

Vikal shrugged, his butterfly-covered shoulders chiming. "I assumed it was you. If not, then I don't know."

"Not me," Ardith said, lifting their hands. "I like a *good* joke. This one is terrible."

"Who cares who sent it?" It was Lady Celia, all her polite polish gone. "My lady, tell us! Is there any truth to this?"

I struggled to think of a way to buy us more time without openly lying to them. "We're still investigating the artifact. We don't know its nature yet."

"That's not a no." Lady Celia pressed a trembling hand to her chest. "Graces preserve us."

Voreth banged his staff against the floor. "How *dare* you keep knowledge of such a dangerous power from your neighbors? Do you mean to tell me Alevar has been standing on the brink of the Hells themselves for who knows how long, and you never saw fit to mention it to us?!"

"Of course they didn't mention it," Severin said, shaking his head. "It sounds utterly mad. It *is* utter madness."

"I assure you, it sounds mad to me, too." I tried a skeptical sort of smile, as if to imply that of course it couldn't be true, but I suspected I was showing too much strain. "This notion is as shocking to me as it is to you."

"If you'll permit me to interject," Foxglove said, his voice smooth and commanding, "this remains an untested theory. The Rookery has a duty to report the truth, but we still don't know what the truth *is*, so please contain any urges you may have to panic." Cautious relief showed on some faces. "We're investigating, but we haven't yet drawn any definite conclusions. We don't want to cause undue upset over one theory among many that may not prove to be true." He spoke slowly and with emphasis, catching the eyes of each person in the room in turn, radiating calm.

"I knew it," Vikal breathed. "I always knew we were guarding the greatest power and the greatest mystery the world has ever seen."

Oh, I definitely needed to strangle him.

Lady Celia whirled on Foxglove. "You take this seriously, though? It's a real possibility?"

Foxglove hesitated, exchanging glances with Bastian. Hells, they probably had rules forbidding them to outright lie to government agents about this sort of thing. "It's far too early to venture a guess about that," he said. "We have to investigate every theory, but we can't yet be certain it's false, my lady."

"How does one become certain?" Ardith asked, with morbid fascination. "Send someone in and see if they come out possessed?"

"We can't take the chance," Lady Celia declared, an edge of fear in her voice. "We're talking about a gate to the *Hells*. When I tell the doge and the Council, they're going to mobilize every Falcon in the Empire to destroy it, even if we have to scour this place down to the bedrock."

"Try it and see what happens," growled a voice like thunder.

Oh, Hells, no. My stomach seemed to drop down a well.

Aunt Karrigan strode into the room, fur mantle bristling on her shoulders, mage mark blazing bloodred. She ignored everyone else and stormed straight up to Lady Celia; Aurelio stepped up to put himself half between them.

I started toward them. "Aunt Karrigan—"

"Try it," she repeated, soft as the first warning flakes of a blizzard. "Then we can all find out what happens when you unleash the Nine Hells. Because I'll do that before I let Morgrain fall."

Well, pox. She could have spit in the envoys' faces and it'd be less likely to start a war.

Lady Celia drew in a sharp breath; Voreth looked as if smoke might start pouring from his mouth.

"*Enough!*" I barked.

It worked. They all turned to look at me. "I know everyone is upset, and with good reason. But now is not the time for rash action. We have to think about this rationally, rather than reacting from blind fear."

Lady Celia nodded slowly; she began to gather her usual calm poise back around her like a cloak. My aunt looked as if she might say something, but visibly swallowed it.

"But running about screaming and waving your arms in the air is so *satisfying* at a time like this," Ardith protested.

I ignored them. "We don't know that this *is* a gate to the Hells," I continued. Never mind that I was pretty cursed sure; I couldn't prove it, and that was good enough if it helped de-escalate the situation. "Regardless, it's currently inactive and sealed away behind some staggeringly impressive wards. It hasn't done any harm in four thousand years." I wished I were certain that was true.

"Fair enough," Severin said, "but you can't ask us to forget about this and pretend we never heard it. The chimera is out of the cage."

Bastian winced at that. Severin was right. There was no going back to the way things had been.

"All I ask is that we hold off on taking any action until the Rookery can analyze the information and present you with conclusions." I glanced hopefully at Foxglove.

"I don't know how this unconfirmed theory got leaked to

Exalted Vikal," Foxglove said, stepping forward, "but I believe I can have a report ready for you tomorrow. I'll contact my superiors with our initial information today, to prevent the further spread of rumors"—he threw a dagger of a glance at Vikal—"and I suggest you do the same. We can discuss the matter more tomorrow, armed with a calm outlook and better information."

"Very well," Lady Celia said, and offered us a clipped bow. "Tomorrow."

"So long as no one triggers an apocalypse before then," Severin added, a touch of strain underlying the irony in his voice.

The Bone Atrium emptied all too quickly, the envoys and the Rookery rushing to send messages to their governments. Nobody questioned that the negotiation session we'd been gathering for was canceled. My chance at nailing down a peace agreement before anyone found out about the gate slipped away forever. I didn't even try to keep them; I could gather them back together after the panic wore off and they could think again.

Ardith lingered last; their habitual grin remained in place like a shield, but no humor reached their eyes.

"This is one of those times when I may have to do something you don't like," they said. "Sorry, Ryx."

That could mean anything, but given our previous conversation, I had a decent guess. "Don't let them call a Conclave." Apprehension squeezed my lungs. "It'll be the end of Morgrain if they do."

Ardith tilted their head. "So it's real? Seasons spare us—I was holding out hope your cousin was a bit mad, and you and Foxglove didn't want to tell him so to his face."

Pox. I'd as much as admitted it was real with my reaction. I tried to work my tongue around a denial, but Ardith was no fool.

"Guess I'm glad you weren't willing to open it for a box of sweets." They shook their head. "I can't look the other way on this. I like you, I like Morgrain, I like Gloamingard—but this is serious. I can't go back to my father and the others and tell them 'Oh, it's all right, it's just the Nine Hells, Ryx has got it under control.'"

"What if the Rookery says it's under control?" I asked, desperate. "They're the official eyes and hands of both Vaskandar and the Empire in matters like this. If they're able to declare with absolute certainty that there's no danger the gate will open—"

"Karrigan threatened to unleash it on the Serene Empire," Ardith pointed out, with a sort of sympathetic grimace. "That doesn't help your position. My father and his allies work to sustain the peace, and demons fighting warlocks is basically the exact opposite of peace. They'll want to take immediate action to stop this."

I didn't know what form *immediate action* might take, but I had a suspicion they wouldn't be throwing Morgrain a delightful tea party.

"Karrigan can't open the gate," I said, throwing caution aside. I had to allay the Witch Lords' concerns somehow. "It doesn't react to her. It only reacts to me, because my magic is flawed. And I assure you that nothing the seasons can bring will make me open it."

Ardith chewed their lip a moment, hazel eyes thoughtful. "Maybe if the Rookery finds some way to guarantee no one can activate it," they said dubiously. "They might be willing to wait in that case. I still don't see how you're getting out of a Conclave on this one, though."

"Give me time," I urged them. "Give the Rookery time. I know you like to act the part of the irresponsible rascal, but your father listens to you."

"Don't give away my cover like that," Ardith laughed, glancing around in an exaggerated fashion. "Fine, fine. Let me think about this. But if you want me to wait for the Rookery, then they'd better act fast."

"I'm fairly certain they already know that," I said grimly.

As Ardith left, I spotted Odan waiting unobtrusively near one of the doorways. I had no idea how long he'd been there, but by the tension creasing his face, he'd overheard enough. I joined him on the discreet side of a femur-fluted pillar.

"Are you all right, Odan?" I asked him.

He offered me a stiff bow. "Never fear, Exalted Warden. I'll keep the family's secrets as I always have."

"That's not what I asked." I wasn't sure Odan was quite my friend—he worked for me, and that defined a certain set of barriers and pathways between us that had little to do with friendship—but he'd been here for me in a thousand small ways for most of my life, and I cared about him. "I'm sorry that you had to find out this way."

"Ah." His gray mustache worked for a moment. "Exalted Warden, I have lived and served in this castle for nearly sixty years. I may not be of your bloodline, but I can read the Gloaming Lore as well as you can." His posture was always stiff as a sword, but he seemed to draw himself up even further. "I consider myself a guardian, too."

"You certainly are." I flicked a glance in the direction Vikal had gone and let a touch of exasperation show in my face. "More so than those of the bloodline who don't live here."

The mustache skewed slightly. "Even so, Warden. Seeing to the integrity of the old stone keep is one of my duties; I've walked past the Black Tower and felt my skin crawl, and once or twice I've thought I heard whispers. I've known for a very long time that something terrible was in there." He shook his head. "Suffice to say that while I may not have known exactly what we've been guarding, nor am I entirely surprised."

"All right, then." I let out a long breath. "I don't know whether anyone among the castle staff heard that confrontation; it wasn't exactly quiet."

"I'll try to discreetly find out, Warden."

"Obviously we don't want this to spread if we can possibly stop it." We wouldn't be able to keep this secret for long, though. The staff would hear the envoys talking, feel the tension in the air, and draw their own conclusions. "If you think someone might have figured it out, or even have suspicions, talk with them. Make sure they know that this isn't something to gossip about."

"Of course, Warden. I've also already talked to the staff about avoiding gossip of any kind while the envoys are here, and I have a few people listening for me in case rumors start to spread. I was thinking more of the lady's absence and Exalted Lamiel's death, but the same precautions should serve us here as well."

"Perfect. Thank you, Odan. I don't know what I'd do without you."

He snorted. "With all respect, Exalted Warden, you'd make a mess of things."

"That I would."

I took my leave and headed off toward my rooms; much as I didn't want to, I had some letters to write.

As I passed a flower-framed window that looked out into one of Gloamingard's many small courtyards, I noticed a flash of gold embroidery and paused, my heart speeding up. Severin and Voreth stood among the rosebushes in the bold morning sunlight. A mockingbird waited patiently on a branch while Severin finished scrawling out a letter, presumably for his brother. By the set of Voreth's shoulders and the way he gripped his staff, I suspected they were arguing.

I could hardly let an opportunity like this pass by.

I ducked into a disused sitting room and through the back of a seemingly boarded-up fireplace, then slipped through the dusty space between walls until I came to a place where a low spear of white daylight interrupted the close darkness. It was the hole where the water pipe for a long-gone fountain had pierced the castle wall, and it happened to come out in the courtyard right next to where Severin and Voreth were standing. I knelt down, taking shallow breaths in the musty air, and applied my eye to the hole.

"—an actual gate to the Hells," Severin was saying, his hands trembling as he attempted to stuff his letter into a tiny message tube. "This changes everything."

"This changes nothing," Voreth snapped. "Our most exalted lord ordered you to get him either the murderer or that artifact, and those orders stand."

Severin laughed, but there was an edge to it. "Oh, come on, Voreth. Even my brother isn't mad enough to want an artifact whose sole function is access to the Nine Hells." He paused. "At least, I *hope* he's not."

Grace of Mercy, I hoped not, too. The last thing we needed was the Shrike Lord deliberately drawing on the power of the Nine Hells or allying himself with demons.

"The Shrike Lord has made it clear that vengeance is his priority now," Voreth said, his tone too commanding for an underling, bordering on insolent. Severin significantly outranked him; he must have some other hold or authority over the Shrike Lord's heir, to speak to him like that. "If Morgrain will not hand over the killer, then this artifact seems as if it would serve quite well to grant him the vengeance he desires."

The space between the walls seemed to get colder, as if a winter wind had found its way through the tiny round gap.

"What is *wrong* with you, Voreth?" Severin demanded incredulously. "Seasons spare us, I swear you'd drown a baby if you thought my brother wanted it."

"I serve the Shrike Lord," Voreth said, staring pointedly at Severin. "As do you, Exalted Atheling."

Severin finished preparing the message and let out a long, pained breath. "As do I," he agreed. "I suppose we'd better make sure that Morgrain hands over the killer, then."

Blood and ashes. Somehow, things kept getting worse.

Whispers hissed through the halls of the castle. Tension seethed palpably beneath the calm surface of its everyday activities, like water just shy of boiling. And it was my job to somehow keep this kettle from overflowing.

I wrote to my father and my uncle, and after some hesitation penned brief messages to the doge of Raverra and some of Morgrain's closest allies among the Witch Lords as well, attempting to project the reassuring impression that someone was in charge here in Gloamingard and that whatever ancient menaces we might be developing exciting new theories about, they had been well under control for millennia and continued to be so.

I wished I believed a word of it myself.

A knock sounded at my door when I was halfway through drafting a note to the Fox Lord. I wasn't sure who I expected— Odan, with a report on the guard shifts I'd asked him to post at the entrances to the old stone keep, or perhaps Jannah with a new batch of letters or some tidbits of useful gossip or minor espionage. But it was Aurelio who stood in the doorway, his face strained, barely able to manage a smile.

"Ryx," he greeted me. "Do you mind if we talk?"

"Come in." My room wasn't really set up for guests, since in the past I hadn't dared host anyone in such a confined space;

I gestured him to the simple wooden chair by the tiny square table where I sometimes had meals in my room, then perched on the edge of my bed. "What's troubling you?" I realized the moment it left my mouth how foolish the question was.

He gave a hollow laugh. "Oh, nothing. Everything is all roses and dandelions. Ryx, I don't know what to do."

There was a quiet desperation in the slump of his shoulders, the catch in his voice. *Oh, Hells. I should comfort him.* I had absolutely no experience comforting anyone whatsoever.

I reached out and patted him on the shoulder, twice, my palm flat and rigid. My heart floundered in my chest. I had never been so certain I was doing something wrong.

"It seems like the end of the world," I said, "but we have to remember that this gate has been there since the Dark Days, and nothing has happened." Best not to mention that I'd done something to trigger it and it was now leaking. "It's not really an emergency at all."

Aurelio shoved a clawed hand through his auburn forelock. "That doesn't matter. What matters is that Vaskandar has the power of the Nine Demons at its command. Don't you see?"

"That's not true," I objected.

"Your aunt literally threatened the Serene Empire with the power of the Hells." Aurelio spread his hands. "It doesn't matter what you believe the truth to be. The fact is, you have that power, and Karrigan at least won't hesitate to try to use it."

This again. I rubbed my forehead, wishing I could unravel time and stop Karrigan from saying that. "And the Empire can't afford not to assume she can do it."

"There are only two possibilities from a Raverran perspective, both of them terrible." Aurelio put his head miserably in his hands. "Either you *can* control the power, in which case there's a terrifying and unanswerable weapon in the hands of a nation with a habit of invading us, or you *can't* control it. And that's even worse, because then you could unleash the Dark Days on us at any moment through sheer accident."

When he put it that way, I'd be inclined to raze Gloamingard to the ground myself in the Empire's place. "I'll talk to Karrigan," I said, dreading the conversation already. "At the very least hopefully I can convince her to calm down her rhetoric."

"That's not enough." Aurelio shook his head with a heaviness as if a great weight lay upon it. "This is a power that could destroy the world. Raverra *can't* sit back and trust Vaskandar to handle this. We *have* to do something."

"That's what the Rookery is for." I leaned toward him, narrowing the space between us to a couple of feet. I succeeded in catching his eyes, and he lifted his face from his hands; there was no hope there, but by the Graces, I'd do what I could to kindle some. "They'll find some way to make sure the demons can't come through the gate again, and to keep us all safe from the power of the gate. They're experts. They deal with things like this all the time."

Aurelio snorted, a bit of life coming back to his eyes. "No they don't."

"Well, maybe not *quite* like this. But give them a chance." I gave him a tired smile. "If anyone can handle it, they can."

"We'd better hope so," Aurelio said, his face grave and pale. "Because if they fail, there may not be anyone around to give them a second chance."

EIGHTEEN

I'd never before set foot in the room Aunt Karrigan lived in when she visited Gloamingard. It was in one of the tree towers, an airy chamber shaped from three living trunks and a connecting lattice of intricately wrought branches. It was like being inside some combination of a treehouse and a shadow lantern, with the light filtering green and golden through the boughs. Layers of rich, bumpy mosses carpeted the floor, scattered with tiny star-shaped flowers, and a curtain of silvery vines draped the bed. A sleeping owl roosted on one of its posts, and a mink dozed on a chair cushion in a sunny spot; it opened one bright, sleepy eye to watch me as I entered.

Before the jess, I couldn't have set foot in here without leaving a wake of death.

By the way Karrigan's eyes flicked to the golden bracelet on my wrist, then back up to my face, she was all too aware of that. She grunted a dubious sort of welcome and let me in, but didn't invite me to sit.

Of course not. She preferred not to acknowledge my existence at all. Too bad for her; I was the Warden of Gloamingard, and if she didn't want to deal with me, she shouldn't have come here.

"We need to talk," I said stiffly. "Morgrain is in trouble."

Karrigan lifted a pale brow. "That's an understatement. I've just received a bird from one of our Wardens on the coast reporting that half the imperial fleet that was pointed at Alevar has set course for Morgrain."

I let out a surprised huff. That hadn't taken long; it had only been a few hours since the confrontation in the Bone Atrium. But the Serene Empire had courier-lamp networks that let them communicate instantly. Once Celia's initial message made it to the border, they had no need to wait for birds to fly back and forth.

"All the more reason that we need to work together to improve our relations with the Empire," I said. Then I hesitated, unsure how to frame this. "I know you're not fond of me—"

Karrigan barked a short, harsh laugh. "Do you think I blame you for existing?" She shook her head, mouth flattening. "No, I know full well that's your father's fault."

I stared at her, stunned, all my carefully marshaled words about avoiding warlike rhetoric spilling from my head like sand from a split bag.

"Well, that's . . . honest of you," I managed.

Aunt Karrigan shook her head and crossed the room to a cabinet shaped from the living wood of the tree tower, opening it to remove a crystal bottle and two cups. "Don't ask me to pretend you're not a problem. I was *relieved* when your mage mark started showing up, given your mother's worthless bloodline. Thought chance had saved our family from embarrassment." Amber liquid cascaded musically into the cups as she poured with careful precision. "Then you got sick, and I was as broken up as anyone about it. We all thought you were going to die. And I won't lie to you, Ryxander. It would have been better for the domain if you had."

My breath stopped as if she'd driven a knife into my lungs. I'd always suspected some of my family felt this way, but no one had ever said it to my face. How was I supposed to respond to that?

Especially because I knew it was true.

Karrigan put the bottle back into the cupboard, her hands lingering on the smooth wood as she closed the door. "I don't know what Mother did to save you, but here you are. I had to have two more children just as a *buffer* to make sure there was no way you could inherit the domain—and I love them more than life, but pox take it, I thought I was done with that—and every time I visit Gloamingard I hear about some outbuilding collapsed because you leaned on it, or a fire started, or another poor unlucky bastard dead or nearly so. All because my idiot brother didn't do his duty as an atheling and marry someone appropriate to his rank."

My jaw ached from clenching. I liked it better when she ignored me. "Do you have a point?" I asked, letting acid drip from my words.

"Yes." My aunt handed me one cup, keeping the other for herself. I took it in surprise, the heady scent of honey wine tickling my nose. "None of it's your fault. I don't hate you. Of course we can work together."

Dark humor gleamed in her eyes as she lifted her cup to me, then took a long swallow. I briefly considered finding out for the first time what it was like to punch someone before stuffing all the complex churn of feelings down into a bottle with everything else.

I set down my cup without drinking. "We've got Alevar poised to invade, the Empire preparing to wipe us off the map out of sheer panic, and the Nine Hells themselves in danger of breaking loose in the Black Tower. We need to walk a careful line if we want to keep this from destroying Morgrain."

"We need my mother to call off whatever cursed joke she's playing and get back here," Karrigan growled.

"You think she's disappeared as a *joke*?"

"To make things happen." Karrigan waved an impatient hand. "She's done this before. When your uncle and I were fighting over who would be her heir, or when some of her Wardens were misusing their power. Thought it would be funny to disappear and let us show our true colors, see what we did with her gone. Then she'd appear again and hold us all accountable, like winter falling hard and sudden. It's one of her favorite tricks."

This was news to me. I'd seen my grandmother do this in miniature, showing up late to a meeting with diplomatic guests while she eavesdropped from one of Gloamingard's hidden places to see what they'd say in her absence, but never on this scale.

"It's hard to believe Grandmother would let things get this bad without intervening," I said slowly.

"Oh, she'll show up soon enough. You wait." Karrigan shook her head. "And I'm saving up words for when she does."

"In the meantime, it's up to us to do what we can," I said. "And forgive me, but I'm not counting Vikal."

Aunt Karrigan grunted agreement. "Your uncle gave him far too much rein. I won't say more than that about kin."

I tried to ignore that she'd said far more than that about me. "Have you heard from the rest of the family?"

"I wrote my husbands and children and told them to stay away from Gloamingard, act like nothing was wrong, and tend to their own lands. They'll follow my orders. And your father's staying out of it and keeping his head down, as usual." She scowled. "Tarn, on the other hand, is making noise about whether I can handle this. I'm sure he sent Vikal here to keep an eye on me."

"*Vikal?*" I asked incredulously. "He's not fit to keep an eye on a sleeping dog." Never mind that most of the family would trust Vikal with more responsibility than me. He was a child in a way I'd never had the luxury to be.

Karrigan snorted. "He was what Tarn had available in the area."

I picked up my cup just to have something to turn in my nervous fingers. "The last thing we need is the whole family flocking here. That'll send a signal that something's wrong. We have to look as if Grandmother is still in control." It was the one thing that might make Alevar and the Empire hesitate before invading us.

"Then tell your father to back me," Karrigan urged. "If he does, Tarn will have to follow. Let me be the face of Morgrain while Mother is gone."

So that was why she'd poured me honey wine and gone to such trouble to assure me she didn't hate me. She wanted something from me.

I swished the golden liquid in my cup, staring at the patterns of light and shadow swirling in it. The damnable truth was that I was the one who should be the face of Morgrain at Gloamingard right now. I was the Warden, I was the one who could diplomatically handle our guests, and I was the one working with the Rookery to handle the gate.

But Karrigan was a real mage, respected by the rest of our family and our Witch Lord neighbors. Her presence here would reassure them in a way mine never could.

"You can be the face of Morgrain," I said slowly, "so long as that face is a mask I'm wearing."

Karrigan stiffened. "I'm not anyone's puppet."

"No," I agreed, "but you don't know what's happening politically in the Serene Empire and the domains beyond Morgrain right now. And forgive me, but you're making mistakes. You need me to guide you."

"Then guide me," she snapped.

I let out a slow breath. "Alevar is probably a lost cause, though we should do what we can to mollify them. Under no circumstances can we afford to set off the Empire."

My aunt took a long drink. "You're telling me not to threaten them."

"Yes."

"And to shut up about using the gate."

"That above all else." I would have loved to launch into a tirade about the damage she'd done, but Karrigan was far too comfortable in a shouting match. I needed her to listen to me. "Raverrans aren't Witch Lords. If they decide to bring their warlocks against us, they won't give us a second warning—they'll strike hard and fast and entirely by surprise, and we'll wake up to find half our coastline gone."

Karrigan sighed. "I'll be honest, Ryx. Vaskandran politics are easy. You say what you mean, you make a show of strength, and everyone is sensible enough to back off and not attack you in your own domain. Pay your grievances fairly, use your favors wisely, and you can't go wrong." She took one last sip and set her empty cup down on a nearby table with a bang. "With these Raverrans, it's different. They like to dance around the truth and hide their strength. I've got no patience for it."

"I'd noticed," I said dryly.

She stepped closer and laid a hand on my shoulder. It was a weighty but surprisingly gentle touch, with her bear-claw gloves off. "Fine. I'll be your mask. You handle them. I'll step back out of your way. They're your mother's people. I hate to admit it, but you know what you're doing."

An odd warmth grew beneath my breastbone. She was using me, and I knew it—if she bungled relations with the Empire too badly, she'd be out of the succession for sure, and she was essentially agreeing to let me clean up her mess while she took the credit—but the compliment was genuine. If she was using me, that meant she acknowledged I had a use.

And after all, I was using her, too. Maybe for the two of us, that was what family meant.

"I'll try not to let you down," I said.

I spoke to Lady Celia and Severin next, sounding them out on whether we might try to proceed with the Windhome negotiations that afternoon; I thought I managed to at least convince them that settling the dispute still mattered. After that I dug around in my grandmother's desk, looking for any kind of notes or clues about the Black Tower, but she'd never been the type to write things down. Odan found me and warned me that many of the staff already had an idea that something was wrong, and were on edge; I told him to distribute a cask of my grandmother's enchanted springwine reserve as thanks for their fortitude in this trying time. Gaven came to complain that Vikal's weasel had tried to bite a stable boy. Jannah let me know that messages were starting to come in from Wardens across the domain who'd heard rumors of my grandmother's disappearance, seeking information and reassurance.

Everything was coming apart in my hands like an old garment washed one time too many. Graces help me, but I had no idea how to salvage this.

I was on my way to check in with the Rookery, passing one of the massive tree towers that stood before the main entrance to the old stone keep, when a terrible groaning shudder ran through its bark. High above, its branches thrashed with distress. A pair of chamber servants ran from its arched doorway, shrieking, barely pausing to flick their fingers in the warding sign before running past me.

"What in the Nine Hells," I said aloud. A chill struck me as I realized that wasn't necessarily just a figure of speech around here anymore.

I sprinted through the tower, ducking beneath artfully draped curtains of moss and dodging more fleeing inhabitants, grateful that my jess let me move at full speed. I burst out of the far side to find a tangle of branches choking what had once been an airy hall between the tower and the gates of the old keep.

Violet butterflies filled the air, but the tortured creaks of protesting wood drowned out their soft chiming. Vikal stood at the center of the snarl, one hand laid against the trunk of the great ancient tree, growing spindly new branches out of its side. They twisted together with no semblance of order, jutting in every direction; Vikal scowled with concentration, the pink tip of his tongue held carefully between his teeth.

"Vikal! What are you *doing*?" I demanded.

"Sealing the Door," he said, lifting his chin, "as the Gloaming Lore commands us."

Graces grant me patience. This was what happened when you raised someone with power to believe they were accountable to no one. I imagined Ashe giving me a cynical, knowing look. *Mages*.

"Vikal," I said through my teeth, "you're not sealing the Door. You're making a mess of my castle, and you need to stop."

Vikal sniffed. "I wouldn't expect you to understand, since your magic is such a useless mockery that you gave it to the Empire." He cast a betrayed glance at the delicate golden braid of the jess encircling my wrist.

A muscle in my temple twitched. I had to restrain myself at all times, learning exquisite control at an age when most children were still running amok and throwing tantrums; and here Vikal stood in the midst of a mad, living manifestation of his emotions, making a mess of everything, without a second's thought for how it would impact everyone around him.

"You're a Furwitch," I said through my teeth. "And you're certainly not an architect. You don't have any idea what you're doing." The great tree trembled, and my alarm spiked sharply. "You could undermine the whole castle. Stop this at once!"

"Better that than undermine our purpose." Vikal's face twisted in contempt. "Don't presume to command me, you murderous freak."

That did it. I stepped forward, reveling in the newfound freedom of the jess on my wrist, and slapped him across the face.

It was a gentle slap, because my instincts rebelled against touching him. Vikal's hand still flew up to his cheek, black-rimmed eyes widening in shock.

"Vikal." I wrestled my voice down to something soft and calm, feeling bad about the slap already. "I'll command you all I want, because in this castle I have the authority to do so. I am the Warden of Gloamingard, appointed by the Lady of Owls herself. Put that tree back exactly the way it was, right now."

I'd meant my quiet voice to be soothing, but apparently it had the opposite effect; Vikal's eyes widened further, and he stepped back in apparent alarm. "Fine! Fine. I'll fix it. I was only trying to help."

I rubbed my forehead, suddenly weary. It wasn't his fault he'd been so spoiled. "You're young, Vikal. But you should know by now not to interfere with another Warden's territory without permission."

Vikal let out a gusty sigh. The butterflies settled back on his shoulders, and the branches began to slowly, carefully retract back into the massive trunk from which he'd grown them.

"It makes no sense," he complained. "Why did Grandmother trust *you* to be Warden of something as important as Gloamingard? All I have are six tiny villages."

I blinked at him. He couldn't be serious—but he was. Beneath his arrogance, vulnerability lurked in the too-tight corners of his mouth, in the bright sheen on his eyes.

Blood of the Eldest. He was jealous of *me*.

I'd always assumed my grandmother had done it to throw me a meaningless, empty title to maintain the pretense I was a real atheling. Gloamingard didn't technically need a Warden, since the Lady of Owls resided here herself. But I wasn't about to tell Vikal that—not now, when I needed him to accept that I was in charge.

"Maybe because she knows you're not ready," I said, which was probably true. Our grandmother was no fool. "Being a Warden isn't about having the power to rearrange the scenery or turn the wildlife into chimeras, Vikal. It's about being a good steward of the land and a protector of the people. It's only by service to the domain that we can earn our rulership of it."

Vikal sniffed his disdain of me, but too much uncertainty showed in his face for it to be convincing. "What would you know about the duties of a mage?"

"More than you, apparently." Six villages, by the Eldest. "Grandmother already has a thorn barrier sealing the old keep, and the Rookery has to be able to get in and out. If you truly want to guard the Black Tower and follow the Gloaming Lore, you can..." He seemed to be listening urgently. I supposed he was as desperate for a way to help as I was. "You can set small animals to watch the passages here, to warn us if someone tries to sneak into the old stone keep without permission," I decided. "The wards will keep intruders out of the tower, but if they get close enough, they might be able to communicate with the demons, and that would be bad. Can you post lookouts for me?"

Vikal nodded, his shoulders swelling. "Of course. No one will get past my guardians."

All he wanted was to feel useful and needed. I supposed I

could understand that. "Good. I knew I could rely on you, Vikal."

"And I know you can't do it yourself, because your magic is broken and useless," he added.

For one fleeting moment there, I'd almost liked him. "Thanks," I said.

He flashed me a grin as sharp-toothed as one his own weasel might give and turned to focus on cleaning up his mess.

"I'm not sure we can have a plan for the gate that will satisfy the Serene Empire by tomorrow," Bastian said in a low, worried voice, as we walked together to the Old Great Hall for dinner. The rest of the Rookery had gone on ahead; I maintained distance between Bastian and me, out of habit. "It's such an old, complicated, powerful enchantment, and there are pieces of it I don't understand. I need to study it more."

That was worrisome. After talking to Ardith and Aurelio, I wasn't sure how much time we had. "We have to give them *something*," I objected. "And Foxglove seemed confident enough."

"Yes, well." Bastian cleared his throat. "Something you must understand about Foxglove is that his philosophy is to do whatever it takes to accomplish the mission. I fear that a bit of exaggeration is well within the range of methods he condones."

"You don't sound like you entirely approve," I observed.

Bastian gave me a sideways glance from his warm, liquid brown eyes. "I confess I've never subscribed to the idea that the ends justify the means," he admitted, his voice roughening. "That philosophy is what led me to, ah, part ways with the mentor who sponsored me at the university."

"Ah," I said. "That sounds unpleasant."

"It was." Bastian shivered. "Fortunately, Foxglove is different.

You can usually rely on him to listen when you tell him he's going too far, and he won't make you do anything you're not comfortable with. Though sometimes you do have to stand up for yourself and tell him that."

He seemed anxious—whether to clarify the difference or to warn me, I wasn't entirely sure. "Sounds like your mentor put you in a difficult spot," I said.

Bastian's olive skin paled to a sickly greenish shade at the memory. "I was a fool to ever trust him," he said. "Suffice to say I've learned now that when someone makes your dreams come true, there's always a price."

"What..." I hesitated, reluctant to pry into something so painful, but desperately curious. "What did he..."

"*Ryx*," a familiar voice hissed from behind me, wild and urgent as I'd never heard it before.

I spun to find Whisper crouched in the hallway, hackles up, ears back. Bastian gave me a startled look; I'd never been certain exactly how Whisper talked, or whether everyone could hear him.

"Whisper! What's wrong?"

"Come quickly! Before she notices!" He spun without waiting for my reply and bounded off down the corridor.

I stared after him for a second, frozen.

"Ryx?" Bastian asked, sounding puzzled. "Is everything all right?"

The only other time I'd seen Whisper that worked up was over the gate opening.

"No," I said, and broke into a run after him. Bastian followed at my heels, almost audibly swallowing questions.

We chased Whisper down a short corridor; he dodged around the first corner we came to, barely a stone's throw from the Old Great Hall. We rounded it after him and almost crashed into each other as we stumbled to a sudden halt.

Bastian let out a cry of alarm and dismay. My mind went stark and empty as a field of winter snow, smothering and final. I clutched the wall in my desperate attempts to avoid stepping in the blood.

There was a lot of blood.

Aunt Karrigan lay sprawled on the floor before us, her fur mantle dark and stiff with it, her iron-gold braids half down and drinking it up. Several arrows stuck from her chest, and her throat was a wet crimson ruin. Her eyes gazed up at nothing, her mage mark gone dull and flat.

I should have sensed the life in her, from this close; she was a part of Morgrain, like me. I should have felt the furious aura of her power. But there was nothing. The floor might as well have been empty.

She was dead.

NINETEEN

I couldn't move. Not as Bastian called for help, his voice strained with panic. Not as Whisper fled bounding from the commotion, his tail bristling, task done. A sound built and built in the back of my throat, a silent high-pitched cry, but I couldn't release it. The terrible, bloody ruin of my aunt's body paralyzed me completely.

This couldn't be right. There had to be some mistake. Aunt Karrigan was too powerful and permanent a fixture in my life; she couldn't be dead. And she most certainly couldn't be murdered— not here, in Gloamingard Castle itself, the safest place for one of our family in all Eruvia.

Vikal burst into the corridor and dropped to his knees with an inarticulate cry, clawing at his hair. For once, there was no deliberate drama in the gesture—the uncomprehending fear and grief in his eyes were genuine, and made him look twelve years old. The tear inside my chest ripped wider.

A rumbling shook the floor. From down the stone corridor, past my aunt's body, a great groaning sounded.

Before she notices. Dread unfolded like a dark flower inside me.

Whisper had meant my grandmother.

Screams rose up in the distance, raw with terror. Gloamingard

Castle was alive, and all of Morgrain was waking in fury. Someone had killed my grandmother's child, and her domain howled for vengeance.

That howl echoed inside my own rib cage, full of crushing loss and a rage that could level mountains.

"Holy Hells," I gasped, swaying on my feet in the force of it. "Bastian, she's going to kill them all."

He stared at me in uncomprehending horror.

A rush of people came pelting up the hallway, some shrieking in fear—castle staff, our diplomatic guests, the rest of the Rookery—all fleeing the Old Great Hall behind us for their lives. Vines slithered after them like snakes, climbing the walls, leaves shaking with rage.

This corridor was stone, which was probably why the murderer had ambushed my aunt here—there was no life for her vivomancy to use to defend herself—but it was far from safe. Beyond my aunt's blood-soaked body, branches clawed down the hallway like reaching fingers, growing from the massive tree tower that housed my aunt's room.

"Grandmother, no!" I called, grief roughening my voice.

Severin and Ardith stood side by side at the rear of the crowd, attempting to push back the encroaching vines with their magic. A Witch Lord's control over her domain was absolute, however, and the ivy reached for them with strangling curls.

One tendril wrapped around Odan's throat, and I cried out in anguish as he choked after air. I grabbed at it in desperation, trying to help him, but it remained slick and whippy and quite alive in my hands. Hells take it, I didn't know how to kill something when it took more than a touch.

Severin seized the vine, his hands beside mine, and it relaxed its hold for just a second—enough for Odan to throw it off and fall to his knees, gasping. Gray-ringed eyes met mine for one brief instant, inscrutable, before he turned back to the fight.

The need to help burned like fire in my veins. If Aurelio released my power, I could try to kill all the attacking plants—but I'd be just as likely to kill some of the people packed into the corridor around me. There had to be *something* I could do, curse it.

A vine formed into a hard, sharp spear, stabbing at Kessa; before I could so much as move, Ashe sliced it in two, her sword leaving a sizzling trail of smoke in the air behind it.

The cauterized end of the vine twitched on the ground, and Ashe severed another and another, moving quick as lightning, her eyes almost glowing with intense focus. For a brief moment, hope kindled in my chest; she might be enough.

But the vines rose up again, green shoots pushing past the blackened ends. My grandmother was a Witch Lord, and not easily thwarted by the rules of nature.

"Graces preserve us!" Lady Celia cried, clutching a dagger in one hand and a wirework artifice pendant with the other. "Get the Lady of Owls to call them off!"

"Grandmother, please!" I directed my begging toward the branches that now reached across Aunt Karrigan's body, growing and spreading like cracks in the ice, tips sharp as sorrow and just as deadly. "It's me, Ryx! Vikal and I are here, too. And these are your guests, your staff, your friends. You don't want to hurt us."

The branches hesitated.

My cheeks were hot and stiff with tears; I hadn't realized I was crying. I reached out, feeling my grandmother's presence strong around me. A mad, destructive wrath reverberated through the castle like a deep bass note, with the high wild keen of grief layered above it. The vines reared back, leaves hissing, swaying furiously.

"Come back, Grandmother," I whispered, stretching toward the nearest branch. "Please. I need you."

The ivy reaching from the Great Hall dropped to the floor and recoiled, flowing away like water. The branches coming from up the corridor retreated, too, pulling back into themselves with a groaning of wood.

She had heard me. She had listened. And now she was leaving again.

My hand dropped back to my side, empty, something tearing away inside me as if caught on the receding branches.

It seemed impossible that my aunt hadn't moved through the whole thing. That she still lay there in her blood, arrows bristling from her, with nothing to say about this disastrous turn of events.

I slumped against the wall, breathing hard, throat aching, as the corridor erupted into noise around me.

There was a cup of tea in my hand. I wasn't certain how it had gotten there.

I had said something to the crowd, there in the bloody hallway; I didn't remember what, but it must have sounded authoritative enough, because most of them left. Severin had spoken some word to me in parting, his voice intense and shaken, but my horror-numb brain hadn't absorbed enough to even know whether his comment was nasty or sympathetic.

Vikal had stayed, crumpled into a ball and crying like a child, and I'd stood there struggling, unable to find words, unpracticed in gestures of comfort, trying desperately not to look at what was left of my aunt. Finally Odan appeared and sent us both away with the grim, closed expression of a man who had cleaned up dead bodies before. Which he probably had. There was Lamiel, at the very least, and I'd always suspected that not all of the people who'd dropped from my accidental touch as a child had survived.

I'd wandered back to the Old Great Hall and sat at the empty high table, staring into space. And now there was tea in front of me. Lavender, by the scent of it.

I blinked at the steam rising from its surface and looked up to find Kessa staring worriedly at me from across the table.

"I'm sorry," she said. "About your aunt."

I shook my head, swathed in a sort of dull horror. "We weren't close. I don't think she liked me much." I wrapped a hand around the teacup to feel its warmth. "She was my father's sister. We almost understood each other this afternoon. How am I supposed to fix everything that was broken between us if she's dead?"

Kessa reached for my hand, tentatively; I snatched it back out of instinct, heart pounding. She held my gaze, her brown eyes deep and soft, and I reached back out and let her fold her warm hands around my cold one.

"Family is complicated," she said quietly. "Seasons know I don't get along with all of mine. But no one should ever have to lose someone they love like *that*."

The intensity in her voice startled me. I looked closer at her face, shaking off the fog on my senses; strain showed around her eyes and mouth.

"Have you..." I trailed off, unsure how to ask.

Kessa stared at the steam rising from my cup for a moment. Then she sighed and pulled out a brown glass bottle from beneath her chair, pouring herself a cup of something dark amber and strong enough that I could smell it from across the table.

"You don't have to tell me," I said hurriedly.

She shook her head, a sad half smile brushing her lips brief as a dragonfly's wings, and took a long swallow. "My brother."

"I'm sorry." The words sat like lead on my tongue, completely inadequate.

Kessa rubbed her own shoulder, as if it ached. "He's why I hate the Zenith Society. The wretched stingroaches murdered him after we stumbled across some of their ugly secrets."

"Hells. I didn't know. I'd hate them, too."

"Poor Loren. He was such a sweet boy, so excited to be in Raverra with his big sister." She took another drink. "He didn't know I was a spy; I was working for our Witch Lord back then, all petty political missions. I'd brought Loren to help with my cover, because family traveling together is always less suspicious. I was..." She trailed off, making a face. "I'm not sure you'd have liked the person I was back then, Ryx."

"Oh, I don't know," I said. "If she turned into you, she couldn't have been too bad."

Kessa flashed me a brilliant, heart-stopping smile, but the sadness behind it broke something deep in my chest. Hells, I couldn't take this.

"That's kind, but she was a shallow little wretch, far too impressed with her own cleverness." Kessa sighed. "Anyway, I came back to our lodgings from a night of triumphant follow-up snooping, all full of what a wonderful spy I was, and found him murdered in his bed." Another long draft, her throat moving again and again. "So I know there are some things you can't forget."

"Yes," I said hoarsely. If I closed my eyes, I would see Karrigan's red-drenched throat, her flat dull eyes. I pulled my hand back from Kessa's; her touch was too much, too pure. "I'm sorry. I don't know what to say." I tried to sound gentle, to make up for taking my hand away.

"You don't have to say anything," she said. "We can just sit here and drink our respective beverages and feel awful together."

For a few minutes, we did that. Somehow, it helped, a little.

"Vikal doesn't deserve this," I said after a while. Karrigan and I each had our share of crimes, but Vikal was just a bit of an idiot in the way of the young. "I'm not sure he's lost anyone before. I want to help him—he's family—but he, ah, expresses his emotions very differently than I do, and I don't know how."

"Let him talk," Kessa suggested, putting down her cup with

the exaggerated care of the moderately drunk. "If he wants to, that is. Just listen, and let him talk. Or if he doesn't want to, then do something simple with him, so he's not alone."

I glanced down at my cup. "Like drinking tea."

Kessa's mouth slid toward a smile, and she flicked a nail against her bottle. "Or something, yes."

Footsteps echoed in the Old Great Hall. Odan approached, weary lines carved deep into his face. He stopped ten feet away from me, as he always had, and bowed.

"Exalted Warden," he reported, his tone crisp as usual. "The Lady of Owls has roused the domain, and the castle is cut off. Wolves and bears prowl outside, and the trees are restless with fury. The guests perceive themselves to be trapped and are distressed."

I pushed back my chair from the table and rose, as if I were pulling myself up from heavy wet sand. "I'll talk to them."

Kessa frowned. "Good Graces, woman, you need rest. Can't someone else?"

I shook my head. "I'm the Warden of Gloamingard. It's my duty. I don't have time to mourn."

"Ryx. Um. I'm sorry about your aunt."

This was exactly what I'd wanted to avoid. I'd ghosted through the walls by my old hidden paths up to my room, and had my dinner brought to me there, though I had no appetite— but Ardith, so good at lurking around in wait for me, had caught me in the halls on my way back from the privy.

I grunted. I had no words left for my guests. Tomorrow I could deal with them; tomorrow I could get back to all the politics and doom and crisis. Today I was done.

Ardith shuffled their feet. "Listen, I'm not good at feelings and sympathy and such, but let me know if there's anything I can do for you."

I stopped and turned to face them. Perhaps I had words after all. "Your father must be happy," I said.

Ardith blinked. "What?"

"Lady Celia, too, I'm sure. No more need to worry that she'll go through with her threats to use the gate." I couldn't keep the anger entirely repressed from my voice. I had no reason to think that Ardith was the murderer—but I had no reason to think that they weren't, either.

"Oh, Hells. I didn't kill her, Ryx." Ardith lifted their hands, hazel eyes widening.

"And your father? Did he send someone to do it, if he didn't want to get your hands dirty?" I slashed the air. "Or did one of his allies? You can't pretend none of them have ever resorted to murder."

Ardith grimaced. "You're not wrong that my father and his friends will breathe a bit easier without Karrigan shouting about unleashing demons on people. Nor will I deny that murder may be in their toolkit. If they were behind this one, though, I don't know anything about it. I swear to you, it's the truth."

"Tell it to my grandmother," I said. "I doubt she'll wait for the next Conclave to claim her grievance."

Ardith went pale enough that their freckles stood out like blood against their skin. They glanced warily at the walls, as if the wood might come alive and sprout weapons to attack them—which was a reasonable fear, if they might have anything to do with Karrigan's death.

"Look, I only wanted you to know that whoever did it—yes, even if it was my father—that wasn't right." Ardith straightened, their voice hardening. "Killing someone is one thing, but that's not how you do it. Karrigan didn't deserve that death. So if you need a bit more time, take it. I've told my father things are stable here, and that there's no need to rush to call a Conclave right now, or to take any other kind of action."

"And he'll listen to you?" I raised an eyebrow.

"Yes." Ardith didn't hesitate. "He makes his own choices and lays his own plans, and he doesn't always tell me about them. But he wouldn't put me in a position like this and then second-guess me. If I tell him he can wait, he'll wait—at least a little while." They grimaced. "But admittedly not for long, so maybe don't grieve for days and days."

I couldn't bring myself to thank them. Not when they might have been involved, even peripherally, in my aunt's death. But I gave a mute jerk of a nod before turning to head to my room.

We gave Aunt Karrigan to the forest at dawn.

An atheling's service to the land did not end in death. We covered the bloodstained ruin of her empty shell only with branches, so that the wild creatures of Morgrain could find her mortal flesh and return it to the cycle of life. I laid my own pine branch with a numb, sick feeling; when I lifted my eyes, I found the trees full of owls, awake and staring down with fierce yellow eyes. My grandmother's presence was heavy around us, watching, mourning, angry.

Kessa laid a hand on my shoulder as I stepped back to join the somber circle in the forest clearing that had gone still and safe for us to give Karrigan her final farewell. I managed not to flinch this time as she gave me a gentle squeeze and then let go.

Vikal didn't meet my eyes as he stepped forward to place his branch. His butterflies lay quiescent on his shoulders, their wings barely stirring. I'd tried to talk to him last night, but he hadn't answered his door, even though I'd sensed him in there.

When he took his place again, he lifted his head and stared

around at the gathering—mostly long-time castle staff and family. I'd had to explain to Lady Celia that there would be no funeral, no grand ceremony like they would have in Raverra, no influx of family and friends—not even Karrigan's children and husbands. For Vaskandrans it was the living person who mattered; they would have moved mountains to visit a dying loved one, but the idea of making a journey to take one last look at an empty shell was strange. Aunt Karrigan was already gone; it was too late.

"We will not forget this grievance," Vikal declared. His eyes sat in deep black pools of paint, and his mage mark burned all the brighter with his fury. "We will not forgive. We will have our vengeance, if we must take it with tooth and claw."

I stirred uneasily. It wasn't the most diplomatic statement to make during peace negotiations, even if I understood the sentiment. Once again, Vikal lived with all his feelings outside his body, in a way I never could dare to.

He had a point, though. The truth remained, no matter how hard I tried to avoid looking at it: Aunt Karrigan's life had been *taken*. And the person who killed her was probably one of our guests at the castle.

A hush fell across the clearing. The trees bowed as if a wind swept through them, and the owls spread their wings. I shuddered at the grief and fury boiling under the surface of the land.

"I should lay another branch for my father," I murmured, and stooped to pick one up from the waiting pile, wiping my eyes.

A broad, strong, familiar hand covered mine.

"No need," rumbled a voice deep as the roots of an ancient oak tree. "I'll do it myself."

"I can't believe she's gone." My father leaned heavily against a rough pine trunk, as if he might sink into it for comfort.

"I didn't think anything could kill her," I said.

"Me either. She was too stubborn, too grouchy, too much of a pest." He rubbed his forehead. "Seasons, I'll miss her."

Everyone else had left, retreating nervously to the castle as the forest started growing restless again once Karrigan's rite was done. My father and I had wandered into the trees until the sad pile of branches was out of sight.

His buttery hair fell thick and unkempt to his shoulders, and unaccustomed shadows and lines dragged at the familiar shape of his face. Other than that, he was the same as always: big and square-shouldered, with a deep quiet about him. No matter how anyone raged at him—Karrigan in her moods, or me when I'd gone through a phase of being furious that he'd sent me off to foster at Gloamingard—that silence simply absorbed it all, until you were left feeling foolish and spent.

"How did you get here so fast?" I asked. "Did Mamma come, too?"

"No. It's too dangerous right now." He shook his head. "The whole domain is seething. And I was on my way before I heard about Karrigan."

"Why?" I realized as I said it that one possible reason clasped my wrist in cold metal and tucked my hands instinctively behind my back.

My father noticed. He gave me a stern look. "That's not why. But Karrigan told me about your new jewelry."

Pox. He was bound to find out eventually, but I'd been hoping to put it off. "I don't want anyone else to die because of me, Da. And besides, it's my choice."

"Let me see it." He held out his broad hand.

Don't act like you're ashamed. I reached out a rigid hand to show him, red jewels winking in the complex golden wirework of the jess. It shouldn't be on an atheling's wrist, and I knew it.

My father studied it a moment, touching the slim twists of

metal with a gentle finger. "You're right. It's your choice. And if it means you're not living in fear of killing someone, it's a good one."

Some of the knots in my back eased a little. I leaned experimentally next to him; the pine bark poked rough and surprisingly hard through my vestcoat. I shifted to lean against the familiar, comforting warmth of my father's broad shoulder instead.

"Thanks for understanding, Da."

"Your mother has a lot of opinions." He chuckled. "I convinced her to wait a few days to calm down before sharing them with you, but you might get a letter."

I grimaced. "I'm sure. But if you didn't come for the jess or for Karrigan, why are you here?"

"Because this has gone far enough." Determination settled in his voice, like a great standing stone set deliberately in a precise spot. "Someone needs to find your grandmother and make her take the domain back in hand."

And of course he'd decided it would be him. He was the peacemaker, the truth speaker, the one who soothed tempers and told his siblings when they were out of line. There was so much I wanted to talk about with him—matters of family and politics and the fate of the domain, much of it things he'd spent his life trying to avoid—but he meant to disappear into the wilderness.

"What does Uncle Tarn think?" I asked.

"You know him." My father blew a soft breath between his lips. "He never criticizes our mother. He did ask me to make sure Vikal was all right; he was wondering whether he should come here himself."

"No!" I straightened away from the tree. "He needs to stay away. For one thing, we need to preserve the succession. We don't know why Aunt Karrigan was murdered—if it was because she was threatening the Empire, or if Alevar was taking some sort of twisted vengeance for Lamiel, or if someone is try-ing to weaken our domain by killing off athelings. For another, this situation is enough of a mess without throwing more family into it."

"I don't like leaving you here all alone." My father's jaw set stubbornly. "I've got no head for politics like you and your mother do, but I know enough to understand that our neighbor Witch Lords are always watching for signs of weakness. They'll notice that there's no mage-marked atheling in Gloamingard, and they'll assume—"

"They'll assume that Grandmother is still in command," I cut him off. *No mage-marked atheling.* My own father didn't consider me one of them. "They've seen her raise the land in response to Karrigan's death. So long as we act like nothing's wrong, they have no reason to believe she won't defend her domain. If the family comes rushing here like there's a void to fill, they'll pounce on us like cats on a fluttering bird."

"If you say so." He pushed a hand wearily through the tangles of his hair. It hurt my heart to see him looking so tired. "I'm glad you're the one handling this, Ryx. Your grandmother chose you as Warden of Gloamingard for a reason."

I couldn't help a self-deprecating huff. "To keep me out of trouble."

"If she'd wanted to do that, she would have made you War-den of some lonely tower out in the wilderness, with no people around." He squeezed my hand in his big, calloused one. "She gave you the most important castle in Morgrain, and our most important duty. Because she knew you could do it."

A bitter voice told me he was saying that for the same rea-son Karrigan had, out of gratitude that he didn't have to deal with this mess himself. I didn't speak it aloud, though. Just like I didn't tell him that I doubted I could save us from war, or that the Door struck a deep terror in me like nothing else I'd ever known, or about the sickening guilt of killing Lamiel.

Those were things a child might do, who could count on comfort from her father. Mine had only been around to offer comfort for several visits a year, and I'd learned long ago to get on with life without it.

Instead, I sighed. "All right. You find Grandmother, and I'll keep things from falling apart at Gloamingard until you bring her back."

He nodded. "I know you will."

My father didn't even set foot in Gloamingard. He must have known it would draw him in and refuse to let him go, keeping him from his mission. It was Odan who walked back to the castle with me.

I'd been surprised and touched to find him waiting by the road, solid and dependable, gaze solemn beneath his bushy gray brows. We started up the dusty road in silence, under a heartbreakingly blue late-summer sky, the first chill of autumn slipping up our sleeves and down our collars.

"What do we do now, Odan?" I asked him, letting my weariness show at last. Odan understood the dangers besetting Gloamingard as well as I did, and it seemed ridiculous to try to put on a front of strength for a man who'd caught me drawing on the walls as a child and seen me cry over a dragonfly that made an ill-advised perch on my shoulder.

"What we always have, Exalted Warden," he said, calm and sure as the rock that poked like weathered bones through the lush grass sheathing the hill.

I thought about that. "Guard the tower, ward the stone."

"Of course, Warden. Nothing has changed."

I took a long, deep breath of the fresh, autumn-tinged air. For all the restlessness upon the land, it still smelled like Morgrain: ancient stone and sun-warmed grass, pine and damp leaves and a distant whiff of sheep.

Home. I'd do whatever it took to keep it safe.

"I suppose you're right."

TWENTY

Much as it might have seemed like the world stopped when I found Aunt Karrigan murdered, it unfortunately did me no such courtesy. The air around Gloamingard's towers grew thick with birds delivering messages. Whispers ran through the halls, and at breakfast the Old Great Hall practically trembled with tension.

I had Odan call my noble guests into the Round Room, and asked Foxglove to join us as well. I arrived last; conversation fell silent as I approached the table. Everyone was trying to look at me and not look at me at the same time. Well, I was used to that; it was almost comforting that this time it was because I was the Warden of a castle beset by murder, threatened by war, and housing a gate to the Nine Hells rather than due to any personal or magical failings.

Almost.

Lady Celia sipped her cup of coffee with careful precision; I could practically see her holding back a thousand things she wanted to ask or say, judging a mere hour after my aunt's funeral to be too soon for business. Severin's sideways glances were harder to read, shuttered and thoughtful. Aurelio just looked miserable, smart enough to see everything tumbling toward war around him but powerless to stop it.

I refused to believe that we were powerless.

I leaned on the table with both palms. All eyes swiveled to lock onto me.

"I promised you answers yesterday," I said. "Thank you for your patience as my family reels from this terrible tragedy, but this is too serious a matter to postpone. I'm going to tell you what I can."

Ardith leaned their elbows on the table. "We're listening."

"First of all, yes, it's a gate to the Nine Hells." Wide-eyed glances flicked around the room, but no one breathed as I continued. "However, the Rookery assures me that the wards containing it are holding, as they have for four thousand years, so there is no immediate danger to us in the castle or to Eruvia. Is that correct, Foxglove?"

He rose, bowing with smooth grace to the dignitaries at the table. "Indeed. The wards are all structurally sound. For the moment, the situation is stable."

Vikal nodded sagely, as if he'd been personally responsible for the wards. "My family's work has endured far worse," he said. I was sure he had no idea what he was talking about; he was just making things up.

"As the imperial adviser on magic to this delegation, I'd love to see the gate myself," Aurelio said, with a quick glance at Lady Celia.

"I can't allow that," I replied flatly. Aurelio flushed. I felt bad for him, but I had to cut that line of thought off now. "Much as I would love to bring you all in on the Rookery's research, we have to be very careful. I can't guarantee the safety of anyone who enters the tower, and the wards themselves are dangerous. And it's not only that." I scanned their faces, letting some of the hard, cold weight I'd been carrying since yesterday come out in my voice. "Someone here is a spy. They learned the nature of the gate and sent that message to Vikal. And someone here is a murderer, who killed my aunt."

"And Exalted Lamiel," Voreth added.

I couldn't bring myself to agree, but I gave a tiny jerk of a nod before I thought through the implications of even that degree of assent. "I can't trust any of you," I said bluntly. "I'm sorry. I wish I could. But it would be utter foolishness for me to open up the Black Tower to such treachery."

Severin rose, with the graceful menace of a big cat stretching. "Ah, yes, we certainly couldn't let someone who would condone murder have access to the gate. So you understand why Alevar can't trust Morgrain with the Black Tower, either."

A murmur ran around the table. Curse him, this wasn't what I needed right now.

"Alevar doesn't have a choice." I met his stare, mage mark to mage mark. Challenge flowed between us like a racing current, tingling along my nerves. "Whether we like it or not—and I assure you, I'm not thrilled with the situation myself—this gate is in Gloamingard, under Morgrain's protection."

"Artifacts can be moved." Severin gave a languid shrug. "Castles can change hands."

"I'm already aware that the Shrike Lord is looking for an excuse to invade us," I snapped.

"Oh, he doesn't require an excuse."

I glared at Severin in frustration. I genuinely couldn't tell if he meant it as a threat or a warning.

Ardith leaned back in their chair, hands laced behind their head. "I have to say, defending yourself or settling a grievance is one thing. Invading to seize the gate by force is more likely to set off a general scramble that we'll all regret." They paused. "Not that I usually mind having regrets. It means I'm alive."

"The Serene Empire might feel compelled to get involved should such a *scramble* ensue," Lady Celia said ominously.

Lovely. Three thinly veiled threats of war in about one minute. That had to be some kind of record.

"We came here to avoid a global conflict. Let's not set one off instead." I gestured to Foxglove. "If you can't bring yourself to trust us, trust the Rookery. They serve not one country or one lord, but all of Eruvia. I believe they can come up with a solution to the gate problem that will satisfy everyone."

Foxglove's eyebrow twitched; I had to silently admit that might be an exaggeration, but they had a better chance at doing so than most.

"None of us want the Dark Days to come again," he said, his voice deep and grave. "Our priority is to ensure that they never will."

The mention of the Dark Days cast a sobering quiet across the room. I leaped into it. "We can't take risks with this. We have to put aside threats and bravado and solve this problem together, regardless of our differences, to ensure that what lies in the Black Tower will never threaten the future of Eruvia." Their faces remained stiff, closed; I had no idea whether I was getting through to them.

Vikal, seasons bless him, banged a fist on the table, scattering butterflies. "You know I'm with you, Ryxander," he declared. My heart warmed despite myself.

Lady Celia's expression, however, remained grim as a sea cliff. "The Empire will not wait much longer," she said. "If the Rookery cannot remove the threat the gate presents soon, Raverra will take its own steps to resolve the matter." Her tone left no doubt what those steps might be.

"My brother isn't known for his patience." Severin spoke with an odd care, holding my gaze. "He's already put his own preparations in motion."

There was some warning or extra meaning in his choice of words; I was sure of it. Did he mean the Shrike Lord was already moving troops or courting allies? Or—holy Hells. He could be talking about Karrigan's murder.

"I imagine the Conclave will act, too," Ardith put in, their mouth quirking up on one side. "There's just something about a gate to the Nine Hells that gets the blood moving."

All of them were poised to fall on Morgrain like starving dogs on a bone. Seasons spare us. We had imperial warships bearing down on us, and I'd bet my jess the Shrike Lord had troops and battle chimeras lined up on the border. Once regional violence broke out, the Eldest themselves might feel compelled to take a hand.

My grandmother might be powerful, but she couldn't stand against the rest of Eruvia united. Most likely all that was holding our neighbors back from invading us right now was the time it took to get forces in place.

"We can have a full report on the gate with options for possible solutions ready tomorrow afternoon," Foxglove promised. I struggled not to shoot him an incredulous glance at the time frame. He could read the room as well as I could, and he was saying what he needed to say.

Ardith cocked one eyebrow at Lady Celia, then the other at Severin. "Well? Can Alevar and the Empire wait a day or two before hauling off and lobbing chimeras and cannon fire around over some musty old artifact that's been sitting there harmlessly for four thousand years?"

Lady Celia nodded, all graciousness. "Of course."

Severin hesitated. Voreth leaned down and whispered in his ear; Severin brushed him away with an annoyed expression, as if he were a fly.

"I'm not rash enough to make such promises for my brother,"

he said. "However, I suspect he's unlikely to invade before tomorrow."

Like as not the Shrike Lord simply was smart enough to know that a fight over Morgrain was coming, and that if he waited for someone else to start it, he greatly increased his chances of coming out the winner. Anger simmered in my belly that they could sit here at my table, my aunt's murderer likely among them, and quarrel over Morgrain's bones.

I had to stay calm. If I didn't, I might tip the balance into violence myself.

Ardith dusted their hands briskly together. "Well, no global war this morning, then! Good job, everyone!"

"We'll meet again tomorrow," I said. "Today the Rookery and I will focus on the gate and on investigating the murder."

"Murders," Voreth muttered.

I ignored him. "When we meet, remember why you came here. Peace is too important to cast aside. We should first conclude an agreement over the Windhome Island incident, to get that accomplished and move on. Once that's safely signed, we can discuss the gate."

Everyone seemed to at least accept this plan, whether or not they liked it. The tension in the room eased; the table broke up into smaller conversations, with Ardith talking to Severin and Celia questioning Foxglove.

I sank back into my seat. Blood of the Eldest, we'd just given my aunt to the forest that morning; it would have been nice to make it through the afternoon without needing to convince half of Eruvia not to annihilate my home.

Aurelio slid into the chair beside me, head bowed. "I'm sorry about your aunt."

A wave of bittersweet gratitude coursed through me. Aurelio was the only one of my guests thus far outside of Ardith and the Rookery to offer me the simple kindness of condolences. "Thank you," I said.

He lifted a puzzled frown to meet me. "For what?"

"For acknowledging that I'm a human, with human feelings." Never mind that right now, I'd rather not deal with the mess of them churning in their bottle.

Aurelio hesitated. "I . . . I gather that you and your aunt didn't, uh, always get along."

That's right, I'd griped to him about my family before. And there had been the all-too-public jess incident at the reception, too. "Aunt Karrigan wasn't interested in getting along."

"This may not be much consolation, but . . ." Aurelio grimaced, clearly struggling to find a good way to put this. "Well, my father says sometimes only the Grace of Wisdom can see the reason bad things happen, but that doesn't mean there isn't one."

I rubbed my forehead. "I'm well aware that her rash statements about using the power of the Hells may be the reason she was murdered, if that's what you mean. That only makes it sadder and more pointless. She couldn't have used the power if she wanted to."

Aurelio went still. "Oh? But you activated it. I saw you."

This was a lucky chance to slip information to the Serene Empire that would help them see Morgrain as less of a threat—and they'd be more likely to believe it if I made it look like a thoughtless admission to a friend, too. I didn't like to use Aurelio this way, but Morgrain's security was more important.

"There are no instructions on that artifact," I said. "She had no idea how to use it. I'm the only one who's been able to get any kind of a reaction from that thing, and only because of a fluke of my broken magic." Of course, the demons whispering to her through the gate might have been happy to tell her how to use their power, but there was no need to mention that.

"Well." Aurelio's brows flew up, then descended back into

a frown. "That's not what we thought was going on at all. That's…a relief, I suppose."

He looked as if he might have more questions, but Lady Celia called him over to where she sat talking with Foxglove. I could only hope I'd helped soothe some of the Empire's fears.

Now I needed a way to soothe mine. I took a sip of black tea, but it had steeped too long in my cup and gone bitter.

Ardith dropped into the chair Aurelio vacated. Their usual cheeky grin was absent; somber lines drew their face into a new shape, as if the murder had transformed them into someone else—or stripped their mask away and revealed who they'd been all along.

"Listen," they said, their voice low and more serious than usual, "I'm going to be blunt with you, Ryx, because you seem like someone who would prefer honesty."

"I do, generally, yes," I said, bracing myself.

"This whole situation is a disaster. We're all peeing down our legs over the gate. After that meeting, it seems sure as death a fight is going to break out over it—which my father is going to be less than thrilled about, let me tell you—and I think we can all agree that there's one charming individual we particularly don't want to win."

"The Shrike Lord," I guessed. My fingers dug into the arms of my chair at the thought of him strolling into the Black Tower, victorious.

"Damned right. He's dangerous." For once, Ardith wasn't smiling. They kept their voice so close to a whisper that I could barely hear it, and their back turned to where Severin and Voreth sat on the far side of the room. "He's one of the few Witch Lords with a standing army, and he's got legions of war chimeras with custom venoms meant to take out mages, which is hardly neighborly. There are even rumors that he murdered his dear father in order to ascend to his position as Witch Lord."

"I'm glad you agree he's a problem." I flicked a glance toward Severin, but he remained deep in conversation with Lady Celia.

"My father was already watching him as a threat to the peace. We can't let him get his hands on the gate." Ardith shook their head.

"Then back Morgrain," I urged them. "Convince your father and his allies to declare that they'll defend us."

Ardith let out a long sigh. "Sorry, Ryx. That's too uncertain. If there's a fight, *anyone* could wind up with the gate in the end. We can't roll the dice on this one." They grimaced. "I'm afraid you're not going to like this, but we have to solve the problem at the source."

Before I could ask what in the Nine Hells that meant, Severin approached, breaking into the conversation with an unapologetic smirk.

"Conspiring against me, Ardith?"

"Naturally." Ardith flashed their teeth at him, their entire demeanor changing. "Who else here is fun enough to conspire against?"

"See, there's the problem with diplomatic gatherings like this. Insufficient fun." Severin spread his hands. "Perhaps you'd prefer it if we resolved our disputes with dice or cards? Everyone for themselves, and winner takes the gate?"

"That would hardly be appropriate, Exalted Atheling," Voreth objected from his place at Severin's shoulder.

Severin sighed, closing his eyes as if Voreth's words pained him. "I am allowed, upon occasion, to make a joke."

Voreth stiffened, his hands tightening on his bone staff. "You might perhaps consider the gravity of your position, and the trust your brother has placed in you by sending you here in his stead, Exalted Atheling."

Severin exchanged a meaningful look with Ardith. "Ah, I see. I'm *not* allowed to make a joke. Very well." He turned to me. "We remain unimpressed with the amount of effort you're putting into investigating Exalted Lamiel's death. It's almost as if you have something to hide."

"Well, now we have another murder to investigate." I gave him and Voreth my coldest look; Alevar was high on my list of suspects. "Given its importance to all of Eruvia, it's true that we've been focusing on the gate first."

"Then surely you can share more information with us," Voreth said, his eyes lighting avidly. "The Rookery has spent so much time analyzing it, but told us so little."

He'd certainly been willing to pivot to the gate quickly. I didn't like the eagerness in his face. "Your lord's interest in the Black Tower seems excessive for a man who claims to want nothing more than justice," I observed.

"Justice is most easily executed by those with power," Severin said.

"Power more easily twists justice to tyranny," I countered.

He grinned. "*Tyrant* is merely a name history's losers call its winners."

"Ah, but history's villains are those who misuse power." Hells, I was enjoying this too much.

"It seems we've come full circle, and are back at the beginning." Severin's dark eyes sparkled with suppressed humor. He looked cursed good when he smiled like that.

Voreth twisted his staff in his hands as if he imagined driving it into someone's heart. "My lord is interested in the gate because it remains inextricably tied to the murder of his betrothed," he declared. Severin threw him a glance like a poisoned dagger for the interruption, but he didn't seem to notice. "I, myself, am skeptical that this artifact is truly a gate to the Nine Hells. How are we to know this isn't just a rumor you've spread to attempt to obfuscate the true nature of Morgrain's secret source of power?"

"Oh, I don't know, Ryx seemed pretty upset that someone

sent that message to her weasel-riding cousin," Ardith observed, their hands jammed in their vestcoat pockets. "And claiming it was a gate to the Hells would be a phenomenally stupid way to try to draw *less* attention to it."

"Well, your secret is out now." Severin flashed a sharp smile. "And you've seen the reaction. All of Eruvia will turn on you like a pack of starving rats. Morgrain will need allies."

"Against *you*," I retorted, before I could think better of it.

Something flickered across Severin's face—something he quickly repressed as Voreth scowled over his shoulder. "If necessary," he agreed. "You have two easy ways to keep Alevar on your side, Exalted Ryxander: give us the murderer or give us control of the gate. I suggest your family wastes no time in settling on one of them."

"There *is* no murderer and you're not getting the gate," I said firmly. Best not to allow any doubt on either of those points.

Severin let out a long, dramatic sigh. "Well, that *is* unfortunate. You're part Raverran, aren't you? What is it they say in the Empire?" He clasped my hand between both of his in a mockery of benediction, his touch sending a jolt along my nerves. "Grace of Luck go with you."

I started to snatch my hand back in outrage, but something scratchy tickled my palm. A piece of paper, folded tightly into a tiny square. I curled my fist around it and glared at him. "You're the one who's stretching his luck, Exalted Atheling."

He laughed. "I try, my lady. I do try."

And with that, Severin bowed mockingly and moved off. Voreth trailed behind him, shooting me an unreadable glance over his shoulder.

I waited until everyone had trickled out of the Round Room at last and I was completely alone before unfolding the slip of paper. It looked like a corner torn off of something else; the handwriting was hurried and inelegant, but legible enough.

Meet me at midnight in the stable yard. Tell no one. We have much to discuss.

Well, *that* was almost laughably suspicious.

I refolded the paper and stuffed it into my vestcoat pocket, next to the gloves I still carried there just in case. It was probably a trap; I shouldn't go.

But by the Graces, whatever he was up to, I wanted to find out.

TWENTY-ONE

It was hard to force myself to listen to Bastian discuss the murder scene without letting my thoughts slide into an awful black hole of memory. I strove to cling to his words as if they were precious shards of something sharp but fragile.

"...She must have died mere moments before we arrived. She may still have been alive when Ryx's chimera came to get us."

Hells have mercy. I squeezed my eyes shut, but waiting behind my lids was the image of my aunt lying pale and empty on the floor, arrow fletchings hovering over her bloody wounds like flies.

Are you all right? Kessa mouthed from the far side of the fresh sprawl of notes and papers cluttering the Rookery sitting room.

I nodded. I wasn't, of course. But I had to be.

"Plus," Bastian was saying, "it seems there was a paralytic poison on the arrowheads. An alchemical one, strong enough to work on a powerful vivomancer despite their natural resistance."

She'd been awake up until the end, in terrible pain, knowing she was going to die. *Oh, Aunt Karrigan.*

"Interesting that they used a bow," Kessa mused. "I believe they consider them archaic in the Serene Empire, but mages use bows instead of guns sometimes in Vaskandar because a vivomancer can enhance wood but not metal."

Foxglove shook his head. "Bows are quieter. Imperial assassins still use them sometimes."

"If I wanted to pin a murder on a mage, I'd use a bow," Ashe said.

Bastian lifted a hand as if he were in a classroom. "An alchemical poison like that wouldn't be easy to get in Vaskandar," he said. "It certainly isn't something a Vaskandran would randomly carry around with them, while I could see the Raverran delegation bringing a kit of assorted alchemical supplies. If it *was* a Vaskandran, I'd think they brought the poison here with the express intent of killing a mage."

"All the more reason to think it was the same person who murdered Lamiel," Foxglove said.

I stirred, unease coiling in my belly. "No. It wasn't the same person."

"What do you mean?" Foxglove asked.

This had gone far enough. I met his eyes squarely. "I killed Lamiel."

Everyone gaped at me. Even Ashe's eyebrows went up.

"I didn't mean to," I added, my chest constricting at the looks on their faces. "She grabbed me when I was trying to block her from getting to the gate. I was actually trying very hard *not* to kill her. Regardless, I sure as Hells didn't kill my aunt."

My heart galloped erratically as a three-legged colt. Now they knew. They could take my jess and turn me in to Alevar—but that wasn't what I feared most. They were some of the only friends I had, and the thought of losing them was more terrifying than the gate waiting with all its sinister potential in the Black Tower.

Ashe let out a low whistle.

"That explains some things," Foxglove murmured. The look he gave me was strange, soft and sad around the edges—almost one of recognition.

"Are you going to turn me in?" I asked, my shoulders rigid with tension.

Ashe snorted. "Why would we do that?"

"Well..." I hated to remind them if they'd forgotten. I gestured reluctantly to Foxglove. "You did promise Severin to help find Lamiel's killer."

He nodded. "So I did. And I have."

Every muscle in my abdomen knotted tight as a fist.

Kessa half rose from her seat, wagging a finger at Foxglove. "You'd better not be thinking of some clever scheme involving turning Ryx over to the Shrike Lord. Sometimes your schemes go wrong, and I won't forgive you if you get her killed."

"Of course not!" Foxglove appeared genuinely scandalized. "I promised to investigate. I didn't say I'd tell him the results of my investigation. It was her aunt who promised to hand over the killer; I'm not bound by her word. I do think of these things, you know."

Kessa visibly relaxed. "Oh, good. I thought you'd lost your senses for a moment."

"Wouldn't be the first time," Ashe muttered.

My shoulders sagged with relief. Merciful Graces, they didn't hate me. "I can't deny I'm glad to hear it," I admitted. "More importantly, now you won't have bad information in your investigation. *Our* investigation." I straightened, my determination returning. "But I don't want any of this to distract us from dealing with the gate. Even my aunt's murder isn't as important as making sure that thing is sealed or destroyed."

"A noble sentiment," Foxglove said, "but I rather suspect the matters are interconnected. Exalted Karrigan threatened to use it, and now she's dead."

"Right after she threatened the Serene Empire," Bastian noted. "Raverra *is* fond of making dramatic examples of its enemies."

"Are we taking bets?" Kessa asked. "My money's on the Shrike

Lord. He wants the gate, and he wants vengeance; either way, he has no love for your family, Ryx."

Foxglove stroked his chin. "It's too early to throw around guesses. We need to gather more information."

I suddenly remembered Severin's invitation. "I may have a chance to find out more about the Shrike Lord's plans. His brother wants to meet with me in private."

Foxglove raised an eyebrow. "It could be a trap. Did he pick the place and time?"

"Yes." I thought of his note: *Tell no one.* To Hells with that. "Midnight tonight, in the stable yard."

Ashe grunted. "Sounds like a setup to me."

"I thought so, myself." I chewed my lip. The fact that Severin didn't seem to agree perfectly with the Shrike Lord didn't mean I could trust him. The enemy of my enemy wasn't automatically my friend—no matter how pretty his hair was. Not to mention that his hints that he didn't get along with his brother could themselves be an act.

If it *was* a trap, and I sprung it, we'd certainly learn something. And if it wasn't, well, then I'd learn something, too.

"I want to do it," I said. "Do you think you could keep me safe?"

"Hells, yes." Ashe stretched, grinning. "I'll get there first, check it out, and lurk in wait. If he tries anything, I'll cut him in half."

"I'll go, too," Foxglove offered. "Give us a half an hour head start, and don't look for us. He'll notice if you're glancing around too much. Just trust that we're there."

It helped immensely to know that they would be watching over me, ready to swoop down like the Grace of Victory if this turned out to be a trap. "Thank you."

Of course, if it was a trap, I'd still be walking right into it.

As I made my way through Gloamingard's night-dark halls, I couldn't help but remember the last time I'd prowled them alone at night, following Lamiel to the Black Tower. *Graces keep me from making another terrible mistake.* But this time I had my jess, and Foxglove and Ashe would be watching over me in the stable yard.

Besides, I'd take any opportunity I could get to find out what was going on in the mind of Severin of Alevar.

Most likely this was a trick, and he would try to coax information out of me or gain some inside access to the gate. Still, he'd dropped hints that he might not be entirely on his brother's side. I didn't want to get pulled into some Alevaran intrigue, but if Severin represented a wedge in the door to peace, well, I'd be a fool not to lean on that as hard as I could.

Some idiot fluttering part of me wondered if there might be another reason he wanted to meet alone—the same foolish piece that warmed my belly when I remembered how little space we'd held between us when we danced. Or that longed to run my fingers through all that silky hair.

The bitterest irony was that if the situation were different, that fancy might not have been entirely irrational. I had a jess now; courtship wasn't entirely out of the question. Severin and I held nearly equal rank, and an alliance with the heir to our most aggressive neighboring domain would be good for Morgrain. Both of us came from powerful magical bloodlines. My family would approve.

Except for the small fact that he'd publicly demanded my death. And his brother seemed bent on going to war with us. And I had little reason to believe he wasn't precisely the vicious sneering bastard he pretended to be.

Nothing about this was going to have the grace to be simple, curse it.

I was almost to the Birch Gate now, passing through the Bone Atrium, where the moonlight fell in scissored pieces through a latticework of bone. A cold draft brushed across my skin.

A backlit figure stood in the far door, waiting for me. Holding something. I froze, trying to pull more details out of the darkness. It could be Foxglove, come to warn me off, or Severin, taking the same route to our meeting place—but greeting them by either name could alert anyone else in the area to a presence best kept secret.

"Hello?" I called.

Beneath my own voice I heard a soft sound, a thrum and hiss.

And then a sickening *thwack* as a sharp impact struck my thigh.

I staggered and dropped to a knee, gasping with pain and shock. The world reeled, the moment shattered.

Something had pierced cloth and skin and muscle, and it was *still there*, lodged where it shouldn't be, a great broken shard of pain embedded deep in my leg. Obscenities tumbled in an incoherent mess from my mouth. I grabbed at the spot instinctively, and my fingers met wet warmth and smooth wood.

An arrow. Grace of Mercy, that was an arrow shaft sticking out of me. I stared at the white unforgiving line of it in the moonlight, the hard-edged flecks of feathers hovering at the end, and the black sheen of blood spreading around it.

The soft searing sound of parting air came again.

I threw myself to the side, my heart exploding with panic; the second arrow skidded off my collarbone, spinning across the floor. There was more blood and more pain, but I barely noticed it in the wild surge of fear and outrage that burst through me, fierce and unreasoning.

Someone was trying to kill me, to actually cursed *kill* me, and I was not going to cooperate.

I rolled and flung myself behind a bone-sculpted column, ignoring the agonizing jab from the arrow still in my leg, and managed a strangled squawk for help. Something was wrong—something worse even than the shaft sticking out of my thigh.

My limbs didn't want to move. I landed in an untidy tangle, my injured leg sticking out from behind the column. I tried to pull it back, but it barely twitched.

I couldn't lift my head. Could hardly force myself to breathe.

I stared at the arrow quivering in my leg, at the patterns of shadow across the bone-stitched ceiling, my heart pounding with a frenzy as if its only hope to keep on beating was to escape my chest.

Poison. Sweet Hell of Death—I was paralyzed.

This was how Aunt Karrigan had died.

Footsteps sounded on the floor, coming closer, slow and cautious. Giving the poison time to work.

Coming to cut my throat.

TWENTY-TWO

I silently cursed the cold weight of the jess on my wrist. The one time in my entire life that I could have used my broken magic, and it was denied to me.

Fear sent energy blazing down my limbs, enough to outrun a deer or toss a boulder—but I couldn't move. Rage pounded in my veins until I could have ripped this murderer's heart out with my fingernails, but I couldn't even claw my hands.

Get up, Ryx. Get up. *They're coming to kill you. Maybe a dozen more footsteps, and you're going to die.*

I strove with all my will, every furious and terrified ounce of my being, to move one finger. To make a sound. To overpower the jess and rip my magic free.

Nothing happened. All I could do was lie here bleeding.

Wait. *Blood.* Maybe there was something I could try after all.

I turned my fear, my pain, my panicky thwarted energy inward, at the profound and indelible connection binding my blood to the land.

And to my grandmother.

Come on, Grandmother, wherever you are. Notice that I'm hurt. I need you.

The footsteps sounded closer and closer on the bone-inlaid floor. I strained to move, but my body wouldn't respond. A knife scraped from its sheath.

I couldn't even scream to let out all the fear burning in my lungs. *Grandmother! Please!*

The lacy patterns of moonlight on the floor began to shift and swarm, like a cloud of butterflies made of light.

The footsteps stopped. On the far side of the pillar, my attacker sucked in a sharp gasp.

I couldn't see what happened next, but a vast crashing and splintering of bone echoed through the atrium, mixed with a muffled scream of terror and the panicked patter of fleeing steps.

My vision blurred, and a wave of bittersweet relief and love and grief washed over me. *Grandmother.* She hadn't abandoned me. Through the pain, and the pure horrible frustration of paralysis, and the alarming creeping lassitude that stole through me as blood kept leaking from my leg and shoulder, that was what mattered.

A shadow fell over me as a silent shape blocked out the moonlight.

Twin orange circles blazed from a face pale with anger and distant as the stars. *She was here.* My heart leaped high enough to touch the distant bone ceiling.

But something was wrong.

It was my grandmother's face, but a wildness lit her eyes that I'd never seen before. Something about the way she held herself was off, as if she were favoring an injury.

"Ryx," she said, with exasperation. "How do you always manage to get yourself into so much trouble?"

And she bent with swift and unhesitating fluidity and ripped the arrow from my leg.

I screamed, and the world collapsed into darkness in a sickening, giddy plunge.

For a time, I wasn't so much unconscious as far away.

My body was damaged, poisoned, failing, and nearly irrelevant. I needed to get up, open my eyes, and catch hold of my grandmother before she could disappear again. I needed to run after my attacker and try to glimpse their face. To see if it was Severin, and I'd blundered into a trap like a fool.

I was dimly aware of a voice cursing, and later of being carried—I tried to struggle in a wild panic for a moment, terrified that I would kill whoever held me, but I still couldn't move. I was a dead awkward weight, and the cursing changed tone with bitter effort, until light shone through my eyelids and more voices cried in alarm.

Time passed like a dream, and too many people were touching me, and I thought there must be corpses piling up like leaves after a storm. I needed to get up, *get up*—there was so much to do—but my body was useless, broken like my magic.

Once someone woke me enough to make me drink, shaking my good shoulder. It wasn't water. A whole sequence of different bitter swallows of not-water followed, each tingling with magic all the way down.

The world sharpened into enough focus at last that the pain in my leg and shoulder bothered me again. I was lying in my own bed, not on the Bone Atrium floor, and the world was warm with daylight. I opened my eyes.

Of all the people I might have expected to find sitting in my window seat, boots up on my favorite cushion, Ashe was not one of them. She was staring at the sun-drenched ceiling, her pale spiky head tipped back and nestled in her laced fingers, a dreamy expression softening her face. The moment I turned my head and made the pillow rustle, she snapped to attention, fluidly upright, eyes sharpening to their usual cusp-of-violence intensity.

"Huh, you're awake. That was quick." She shook her head. "Damned mages. You should take weeks to heal like the rest of us. It'd keep you more honest."

I tested my arm; it moved, but fresh pain stabbed through my shoulder beneath the bandages swathing my wound. I winced. I didn't feel quite confident enough to try anything with my leg, where the pain went deeper. A queasy fuzz about my senses suggested I was under the effects of more than one potion.

I glanced out the window at the bright blue sky. "Please tell me it hasn't been more than a day."

"Now I want to tell you it's been a month just to watch your face." Ashe snorted at my uncertain expression. "No, it's just past noon. You've had a long night's sleep, but no more."

I tried to sit up, but an overwhelming spike of pain in my leg dropped me gasping back to my pillows.

"My grandmother!" I managed after a moment. "I saw her." She had been so *real*, the least dreamlike part of that nightmare, the blaze of her eyes familiar as my own face. "Is she back?"

Ashe shook her head. "If the Lady of Owls was here, she didn't stick around—but she left a mark on the Bone Atrium, for sure. Spikes everywhere." She made stabbing motions with her fingers. "Everyone assumed she did it from afar."

"No, she was *here*. I saw her." Unease fluttered through me like a ragged moth as I remembered the odd look in her eyes. "She saved me." And ripped the arrow from my leg with brutal unconcern.

"Saved you and left you bleeding out on the floor. Nice family you've got."

All at once Ashe rose, swift and graceful, hand on her sword hilt, staring at the door with blank intensity. A soft knock sounded on the far side.

"It's us," came Foxglove's muffled voice. "Please don't kill me when I open the door, Ashe."

Ashe sighed and flopped back into her seat. "Oh, fine."

The rest of the Rookery plus Aurelio squeezed in, expressions ranging from grave to shaken. I tried to ease myself upright to receive them, but pain flashed white-hot through my leg.

Bastian waved his hands urgently at me. "No, no, you're not ready to sit up yet."

"Apparently." I sank back into the pillows, defeated, as the others took up perches around the room.

"Excellent. You're awake." Foxglove rubbed his hands. "Did you see who attacked you?" The others leaned forward, listening.

I shook my head, a shuddery feeling trying to rise up within me. I'd been trying not to think about the attack itself—the shocking first moment of impact, the sickening realization that someone had come there with the express intention of hurting me, of *killing* me.

"No. It was dark, and everything happened so quickly. But..." I hesitated. "I was on my way to meet Severin."

Foxglove winced. "I must apologize. I've been cursing myself this whole time. We were all set up and in position to protect you in the stable yard, and you got nearly murdered on the way there."

"Missed out on a perfectly good fight," Ashe sighed.

"You couldn't have known." I waved my hand. "For that matter, neither could anyone else. Right? Severin was the only one who knew about our meeting." A surge of anger swept through me—at Severin, for his betrayal, but more at myself for trusting him.

"That bastard," Aurelio said, through his teeth. "I wish I'd been there to guard your back, Ryx. I'd have loved the excuse to point my pistol at that smug face."

The Rookery were all looking at me oddly.

Foxglove cleared his throat. "You may both want to reserve your ire for other targets."

"What do you mean?" I asked.

"Ryx," Kessa said, gently as if she were breaking bad news, "much as I hate to destroy a truly beautiful animosity, it was Severin who found you and brought you to us for help."

My whole world seemed to tilt and rotate, like a puzzle piece I'd been looking at the wrong way. "Not…It wasn't my grandmother?"

"No." Bastian exchanged uneasy glances with Foxglove. "Exalted Severin saved your life, Ryx. When you pulled that arrow out of your leg, you really made a mess. You were bleeding all over him when he dragged you in. Luckily I keep us stocked with common medical potions, or I might not have been able to save you."

"I didn't…" I swallowed, my throat hot and painful. I couldn't bring myself to tell an entire room full of people that my own grandmother had left me to die. No, she wouldn't do that—she must have heard Severin coming and vanished, not wanting him to see her. "I suppose I must have misjudged him."

Aurelio shook his head, apparently in just as much shock. "But he wants Ryx dead, as Lady Lamiel's killer."

Foxglove flicked a startled glance at me, confirming that Aurelio knew; I returned a tiny nod. "So far as I'm aware, Alevar blames Morgrain in a general sense, but they don't suspect Ryx specifically."

Kessa tapped her lips. "He could have set the whole thing up to attack you and then look like he was saving you," she suggested. "To gain your trust. Very dramatic. I've done things like that on a lesser scale, without the attempted murder."

"I don't think whoever shot me would have risked coming back after my grandmother showed up," I said, remembering the pure terror in their departing scream.

Bastian pulled out his notebook. "The arrows had the same fletching as the ones that killed Exalted Karrigan," he reported, "and the heads were coated in the same paralytic poison. I think it's a safe bet that the murderer—or would-be murderer, in your case—was the same."

A queasy shudder ran through me at how close I'd come to dying exactly as Aunt Karrigan had. I hated to imagine her just as frightened as I'd been, in pain and helpless—but my grandmother hadn't been on alert for someone attacking her heirs yet, and Karrigan had died forsaken and alone.

"We should expect another attack," Foxglove said grimly.

"Oh, I'm looking forward to it." Ashe grinned. "I hope you like company, Ryx, because I'm going to stick to you like a burr. You're my best hope of a decent fight on this mission."

"I should warn Vikal." Pain and potions crumbled my voice at the edges. I hated how weak it sounded, but even this brief conversation had exhausted me. Kessa and Bastian exchanged *we should go* glances.

"Don't we have any real clues?" Aurelio pressed. "It could have been anyone."

"Anyone except Severin, it seems," I amended. It would make for cursed awkward diplomacy, knowing any of my noble guests might have tried to kill me—except perhaps for the one who had openly called for my death.

A gentle tapping drew our attention to the window. A gray jay stood on the sill, cocking its head, a slip of paper clutched in its beak.

I gathered myself to get up, but Ashe gave me a glare and opened the window for it instead. The bird fluttered to my hand and dropped a torn-off scrap of paper into my waiting palm before flying back out into the near-autumn chill.

I turned the scrap over, all too aware of everyone watching me.

When you're well enough, it said, *let's try again. We need to talk privately.*

"Seasons spare us," I muttered. "It's from Severin."

Severin wasn't the only one to send me a bird. A steady stream of them came and went through my window over the next couple of hours. I communicated from my bed with my family, the concerned Wardens of villages and towns all over Morgrain who couldn't calm the land they guarded, and even a few Witch Lords. All of the responsibilities of running the domain were falling on me now, with none of the power of a Witch Lord to back it up. I couldn't even send birds back on my own; I had to stack my letters in a tray for Jannah.

It didn't help that the pain dulled my wits and set my pen to trembling. Or that I had to keep closing my eyes and forcing myself to take slow, measured breaths to banish sudden memories of the sound of the arrow hitting my leg and the terrible helplessness of lying paralyzed on the Bone Atrium floor.

After one such spell, Ashe's voice cut across the silence, making me jump and almost spill the ink balanced on my lap desk.

"First time anyone's tried to kill you, huh?"

I'd almost forgotten she was there. She'd been dozing in her perch in my window, chin on her chest, unwilling to leave in the hope that an assassin would appear. Now she watched me with her ice-blue eyes narrowed to slits.

"Yes," I admitted. "Usually I'm worried about hurting people, not the other way around."

Ashe grunted. "Athelings. You'd probably never been in real danger before in your life, with a whole damned domain looking out for you."

I nodded ruefully. "I've been afraid plenty of times. But never truly for my own life. I don't…" I shivered. "I never thought before about how fragile we are. How much has to go right every single moment for our bodies to keep on living."

"Welcome to the world the rest of us have been living in." Ashe stretched her wiry frame, the brilliant sunlight catching in the tufts of her near-white hair. "I swear I don't know how you mages think you can rule over us when you don't even know what it means to be human."

"I'm human," I protested.

"Never said you weren't."

I chewed that over for a bit in silence. The ache in my leg deepened in a way that made me suspect my pain-killing potion was wearing off. It had been nice while it lasted—potions had never worked on me before, so when I managed to injure myself I had to tough it out.

"I've been thinking," I said at last, "about why someone would want to kill me."

She lifted pale brows. "Looks to me like they're killing off your family."

"Maybe. I'm sending messages to all my relatives to warn them, just in case." I thought of my father, out looking for my grandmother—but he was probably safest of all of us right now, because he'd be hardest to find. "They could be targeting us because we can get through the wards on the Black Tower, or it could be someone with a grudge against our family, like Alevar. There are other possibilities, though."

Ashe nodded sagely. "Always lots of reasons to murder some-one."

"Alevar is the obvious suspect, even with Severin saving me—I could easily see him and Voreth having a falling out over methods—but they're almost *too* obvious. Ardith kept talking about needing to take steps I wouldn't like to preserve the peace." I shifted on my pillows, but the growing ache in my leg and shoulder made every position uncomfortable. "I don't like to think it was them, but I can't rule out the possibility. The Serene Empire might be murdering its way toward a more malleable negotiating partner, or killing off anyone who they think could activate the gate before they move their warlocks in to destroy it."

"Lots of options," Ashe agreed. "Not my job to figure it out."

"I need to try to meet with Severin again." I picked up the torn scrap of his note from my letter tray and ran it through my fingers. "Though since it was a trap last time—"

"I doubt it was a trap."

"Maybe not *Severin's* trap, but *someone* certainly ambushed me," I amended.

Ashe snorted. "That wasn't an ambush. At least, not a competent one. If they knew where you were going to be, they could have set up in a much better spot. Up on a balcony or somewhere with cover, where you'd have no chance of seeing them. And they'd have picked someplace less trafficked. No, that was someone who took an opportunity when they saw you wandering around alone at night."

I shivered. "You think it's safe to meet with him, then?"

"Oh, I hope not." Ashe patted Answer's hilt, grinning.

"I suppose it doesn't matter whether it's safe." I drew in a deep breath, shaking off fears like cobwebs. "I *have* to meet with him. Just in case that's exactly what the assassin was trying to stop."

TWENTY-THREE

I'm glad you didn't die," Vikal said.

I had no idea how to respond to that. Not the words, or his presence here in my room for the first time ever, or the deep hollows of grief and anger carved into his face. I was forcibly reminded that he was four years younger than me, even though in some ways this expression was the most mature I'd ever seen on him.

"Thank you," I said at last. And I meant it. I hadn't known he cared enough to be glad.

Ashe pretended to doze in the windowsill, her sword across her lap. Vikal ignored her completely, dropping into a chair by my bedside with an attitude of utter exhaustion.

"I hope the worthless wretch tries to come after me next." Fury simmered in his voice. "I'll feed their heart to Lancer. You might be a bit useless, but you're *family*."

"Thanks." This time, I let the word drip sarcasm. "I hope you'll forgive me if I try to catch them before they make another attempt, though. Much as I'd love to see you strangle them, you're your father's heir. You need to stay safe."

Vikal sniffed. "I'm not afraid."

"And that's part of the problem." I leaned back into my

pillows; dealing with Vikal was exhausting at the best of times. "You're not only yourself, Vikal. You're a Warden whose villages depend on you for protection and prosperity, health and bounty. You're an heir who might, if the Grace of Luck turns truly against us and the seasons are full of spite, inherit the whole domain of Morgrain. And you're a royal whose murder could spark a war. You can't run around taking stupid risks. You should be tending to your domain and your people."

He stiffened. Butterflies opened and closed their wings on his shoulders, flickering shades of purple. For a moment, I thought he was going to tell me he could be as stupid as he wanted, because he was a proper atheling.

But his shoulders drooped, and he sighed. "I suppose you're right." He dropped his voice so low I almost couldn't hear him. "I don't want anyone else to die, Ryx."

"Me either." I didn't want to think about death—not now—and I could see Vikal working himself up for some morose philosophical discussion I wasn't in the mood for. I leaned toward him and murmured, "I saw Grandmother."

That did it. His eyes snapped up to mine. "You're sure?"

"Yes. In the Bone Atrium, before I passed out."

"Ash and ruin. I didn't realize she was *here*." He banged a fist down on his own leg. "And she didn't talk to me!"

"She barely talked to me, either." *She left me bleeding to death on the floor.* "She seemed . . . strange." I didn't know how to voice the terrible suspicion that had been growing in the back of my mind since I'd seen her, like the shadow of the hills at sunset stretching to claim Gloamingard for the night. I wasn't at all sure Vikal was the right person to tell, for that matter—but he was family. At this point, that made him one of very few people I could trust.

Vikal frowned. "Strange how?"

"Not herself." I took a shaky breath and tried again. "I don't

know; I only saw her for a few seconds. I can't help thinking...
She tried to deal with the gate on her own, right after I opened
it. She went into the Black Tower and disappeared. What if
she's..." I couldn't finish. The word locked in my throat, too
awful to speak.

"What if she's what?" Vikal leaned close, his eyes bright.

I managed a dry, strangled whisper. "What if she's possessed?"

Vikal stared at me. Seconds slipped past, unbreathing, unblinking, time continuing to run obliviously on even after I'd stopped
it by uttering my worst fear.

Laugh at me. Go on, please. I needed him to dismiss the idea as
foolish. To tell me that with his functioning magic enhancing
his connection to our grandmother, he could tell it wasn't so.
That if I were a proper atheling, I'd know she was fine.

Instead he stared at me in silence, his eyes growing wider and
wider. Ashe had lifted her head, too, no longer pretending to
sleep.

"That's the question, isn't it?" a silky voice said.

I stifled a yelp as Whisper jumped up onto my bed. "Hells
take you, knock or something."

Vikal leaped to his feet, his mage mark glowing a feverish
violet. "Do you know, creature? *Do you know what happened to
my grandmother?*"

Whisper glanced up at him through slitted yellow eyes, and
the whole room seemed to jolt and shudder, as if invisible lightning had struck it. Vikal reeled back, pale with the shock of that
single look.

An inch of bright steel flashed across the room. Ashe eased
Answer back into its sheath, her gaze riveted on Whisper.

"Politely, human." Whisper's voice was pure cold menace.
Vikal jerked his head in a nod, eyes wide.

"You know something." All the fear and grief I'd stuffed
down inside threatened to boil up and burst out of me; I knotted

my hands in my sheets as if I could grab and squeeze it all back in. "Whisper, she's my grandmother. *Tell me.* Please."

His ears swiveled toward me. "There are certain things I can't talk about with you."

"Because of your promise?"

He didn't answer, which I took as confirmation. I drew a shaky breath. "If there's any chance that my grandmother, the Witch Lord of Morgrain, is *possessed by a demon*, I think whoever you made that promise to would understand if you bent it a little." I tried to keep my voice even and failed utterly. "And if she *is* possessed, you realize I'm going to find out soon anyway, one way or another."

Whisper considered this, his tail lashing behind him.

"I don't know what promise you're talking about." Ashe looked back and forth between us, her hand still on her sword hilt. "But I think I can safely say *holy Hells on a stick*."

"Don't trust it, Ryx," Vikal blurted. "My father warned me never to trust it. No one even knows who made it, or why it slinks around Gloamingard. It's *dangerous*. I don't know why Grandmother didn't get rid of it ages ago."

I kept my eyes locked on Whisper's, which narrowed in annoyance. "I've always trusted Whisper," I said. It was true, though I knew it was foolish of me; nothing Vikal had said was wrong. "We're friends."

Whisper ignored Ashe and Vikal both, keeping his attention fixed on me as if we were the only two in the room. He didn't blink; I barely breathed.

"Consider," he said at last, his voice soft and lazy as always, "that there are three things that can happen when a demon attempts to possess a host."

I went very still, afraid any motion or sound I made might stop him from speaking. His voice seemed to draw the shadows deeper in my room, turning the sunlight coming through the windows pale and wan.

"If the host possesses unremarkable magical strength, the demon can take them by force," Whisper continued. "This is most common. In such cases, the demon destroys the host's consciousness, effectively killing them."

"My grandmother isn't weak," Vikal protested. Whisper flicked an ear in his direction, and he flinched. "Sir."

"Indeed," Whisper agreed. "I have little doubt she could repel such an invasion. The contest might take some time, however, especially if she were distracted by other pressing events."

"She could be fighting off a demon even now," I breathed, horrified at the idea. Events were certainly pressing. Blood of the Eldest, that would explain why she'd disappeared.

"But if she is, she'll win," Vikal insisted.

"It seems likely."

"What's the second possible outcome?" I asked, dreading the answer.

"If a human is foolish enough to invite the demon in willingly, there is no contest, of course. In these cases, the demon and the host share the body, taking turns. Either can seize control at will."

"Grandmother would never do that," I said, with confidence. No matter how badly she wanted whatever the demon could offer, she wouldn't risk the safety of her domain.

"What's the third option?" Vikal asked, his voice husky.

Whisper remained silent, staring at me through unreadable yellow eyes, and for a moment I thought he wouldn't answer. At last, his ear flicked as if brushing away an insect, and he spoke.

"Sometimes, rarely, a demon and its host possess complementary natures." His voice fell on my ears softly as snow at twilight. "When that happens, they meld together. Neither demon nor host can tell anymore which mind is which; they are inextricably intertwined." He shook himself, as if he'd gotten wet. "This is no more desirable for the demon than it is for the host."

Vikal and I exchanged a look of bottomless horror.

"But this is rare, you said," Vikal pressed.

"Rare enough that demons still consider it worth the risk to possess people, but not uncommon enough that they switch hosts frequently or lightly." He licked a paw. "I suppose it would be similar to the risk that a horse a human rides might throw them, or that a well-crewed ship might sink."

Vikal's fists clenched by his sides. "So if a demon is involved at all, which it may not be, she's probably just caught up in battling it and distracted by the complete disaster going on here in Gloamingard."

Guilt plucked at me with cold hands. My plea for help might have made it harder for her to fight off demonic possession. No wonder she'd pulled the arrow out and left in a hurry.

"That would make an awful amount of sense," I said. "It would explain why she's disappeared and doesn't seem to want to be found." And it would explain that strange look in her eyes, too.

Vikal's butterflies flocked in a great chiming cloud to his shoulders, as if he gathered them like a great breath. "We have to do everything we can to take care of this gate business by ourselves, so she can focus on her fight. We can't count on her to come back and fix everything."

"We can handle this on our own," I agreed. "The gate, the diplomatic mess, Alevar and the Empire."

Vikal nodded, his jaw set. "I'll help."

I didn't contradict him, but uneasiness settled over me like a cloak. Sincerity shone from his eyes; but for all his power, Vikal was useless as a diplomat, and he was in danger here. I needed to figure out how to protect him—but without him realizing he was being protected.

"You won't be doing it all alone," Ashe put in. "The Rookery has your back." She shook her head. "Which is a damned good thing, because I'll tell you frankly that I've been in some messes that'd turn your hair white—but never one quite like this."

"Nor have I," Whisper said. "And that should make you afraid."

TWENTY-FOUR

I eased my weight onto my injured leg, holding on to my bed-post; pain stabbed through my thigh, and I let out a soft curse.

"You're right," I grumbled to Kessa. "I'm going to need a cane."

"Are you sure this is a good idea?" She handed me the cane she'd brought me from their theatrical props. A vivomancer had shaped it, perhaps Kessa herself, topping it with a rook's head formed by magic from the wood. "You were nearly killed last night. No one will think you're lazy if you postpone the Wind-home negotiations another day."

"We can't," I said. "At this point, we're racing against the spread of rumors about the gate—not to mention the warships bearing down on our coast or the Alevaran troops gathering at our border. We have to gather any scraps of peace we can before all of Eruvia descends into panic and chaos."

"Still, don't be one of those would-be-hero idiots and push yourself until you collapse. We vivomancers heal fast, yes, but Ashe could tell you that we're not as tough as we think we are." She grimaced. "She'd probably back it up with some unnecessarily graphic anecdotes, too."

It was just as well Kessa had shooed Ashe off to get some food, promising to keep me safe for the necessary half an hour, or no doubt we'd be hearing those even now. I took a few practice steps with the cane; it was hard to get the rhythm of it right, and it hurt to put any weight on my leg at all, even through the potions.

"Ashe is about the toughest person alive," I said, "so her perspective may be skewed."

"Ashe?" Kessa snorted. "Hardly. She's a big baby. She may be prickly, but she's sweet as honey cake if you can get past her guard." Her expression went soft, even though her voice stayed businesslike and exasperated.

I raised a skeptical eyebrow. "I'd trust your assessment of anyone else, but not where Ashe is concerned. She hardly treats you like she treats other people."

To my astonishment, Kessa's cheeks went ruddy. "What do you mean?"

Well, this is awkward. "She, ah... I'm sorry, I just assumed— was I wrong about you two?"

Kessa gave me a confused stare. Just as I started to wonder if she were playing a joke on me, she dropped all at once into a chair as if I'd stunned her. "Oh! You thought—oh. Did you think we were a couple?" She laughed, but her cheeks stayed bright red.

"Well, I thought you at least fancied each other." I tried an apologetic grin.

"I, ah, wouldn't know about that." Kessa reached for the pitcher by my bed, poured herself a cup of water, and took a long drink as if it were strong wine. "You think she fancies me?"

I struggled to keep from laughing. "Do you mean you hadn't noticed? I thought you were a spy!"

"You've been reading too many stories of seductive masters of espionage." Kessa smiled, pulling her reactions mostly under control again. "I assure you, being able to make all the lords swoon with one smoldering wink isn't actually a requirement for the job. As it happens, I'm rarely attracted to anyone, and even then not physically, so I'm terrible at spotting when people are attracted to *me*."

"I can't tell, either, but for lack of practice," I said. That sounded nicer than *because most people are terrified of me*. "The one girl who was ever interested practically had to smack me in the face with it." I ached at the bittersweet memory of the revelation that Rillim—lovely, witty Rillim—felt the same spark kindling between us that I did.

"The funny part is that I can spot it when people are attracted to *others*, mind you!" Kessa wagged a finger in my direction. "Like you and that Severin. What are you *thinking*? He's trouble."

Hells. Now I was blushing. "He's pretty trouble."

"So's a viper."

"I can appreciate how pretty he is without being foolish enough to get involved with him." I didn't want to think about him right now—not the lush dark river of his hair, or the sardonic gleam in his eyes, or the fact that he'd apparently saved my life. "Is Ashe one of those rare exceptions you're attracted to? I can't help but notice that if there's a room full of people, your eyes keep going back to her."

"She's pretty," Kessa muttered into her cup. "And graceful, and competent, and funny. I do really like her."

I spread a hand. "Well, she certainly likes you."

"You think so?" Kessa's eyes went bright and speculative. "Well. *Well.* I'll keep that in mind."

"She's not subtle about it." I laughed. "But then, I suppose Ashe rarely is."

I was joking with a friend about another friend. I wasn't sure I'd ever done this before in my life. It felt *amazing*. Everything might be going to the Nine Hells, but in this room in this one moment, I'd never been happier.

"*That* I'll grant you." Kessa grinned. "Though I maintain that she's not as tough as you think."

"She's a creature of pure destruction," I protested.

Kessa flipped a dismissive hand. "She just knows that sometimes you have to destroy in order to protect."

The words struck me with unexpected impact; pieces fell together in my mind, like a broken vase reassembling itself. *Destroy in order to protect.*

That one phrase opened up a clear path through all the dangers besieging me: the forces converging against Morgrain, the killer hunting my family, the terrible threat of the gate. I only had to resolve to take it.

"Yes," I murmured. "Sometimes you do."

Kessa tilted her head. "What?"

"Come on," I said, resolution filling me as I gripped the head of my cane. "Let's go meet the envoys."

I ignored the throbbing of my leg and leaned closer to watch Lady Celia press her heavy golden seal to the bottom of the document Severin had just signed. She lifted it, and the Raverran winged horse shimmered in iridescent alchemical wax next to Alevar's shrike. I settled my elbows on the table and let out a long, soft sigh of relief.

It had been hard to drag myself here on a leg that wouldn't support me and stabbed with pain whenever I moved it. It had been harder still to force the envoys to talk about Windhome Island and *only* about Windhome Island, without straying into the more dramatic territory of gates to the Nine Hells or deadly grievances or murder. Hardest of all had been sitting here in a room with my noble guests knowing that one of them had probably tried to kill me last night and was hiding disappointment to see me up and alive today.

That knowledge put a bar of iron-hard tension across my

shoulders and a lump of apprehension beneath my breastbone. It kept me scanning faces during the meeting as the envoys hashed out details, looking for the slightest sign of malice cast in my direction. Even with my new resolution fueling me, it was utterly exhausting.

"The doge and Council will need to sign the final version, of course," Lady Celia said, handing her copy of the agreement to an aide for safekeeping, "but I don't anticipate any difficulties. Frankly, we have larger issues on our plates than Windhome Island now."

That was the bitter aftertaste to the victory I'd worked so hard to achieve. Mediating peace between Alevar and the Serene Empire didn't do Morgrain much good if the reason they were able to set aside their differences was because they both wanted to be free to turn their military might against Gloamingard.

I had to take other steps to protect my home.

"Very well," I said, bracing myself. "Let's talk about the gate."

"Oh, yes," Ardith agreed, perking up and putting away the book they'd been reading less than subtly in the corner. They hadn't been invited to this negotiation session but had showed up anyway. "We can't forget about the gate."

Foxglove, who had waited patiently through the negotiations, folded his hands across a leather portfolio of notes on the table before him. I'd barely had time to consult with him on the way here, but he'd cautiously approved my plan.

I took a deep breath. "Now, I know we all have a stake in this—"

"My personal stake is not wanting to have to bow down before my new demon overlords," Ardith said.

I ignored them. "But no one has a greater one than Morgrain." Vikal lifted his head at that, as if he heard horns. He'd asked to be there for the gate discussion, and since he was acting as his father's voice, I hadn't found a way to say no. "*We* have guarded the Black Tower for millennia. *We* are watching as you line up chimeras on our border and ships in our waters. And to be blunt, *we* will ultimately decide what to do about the gate."

Severin lifted an eyebrow. There was something different in the gaze he leveled at me today—some shadow that hadn't been there before last night. But when he spoke, his voice held nothing but soft, unmistakable menace.

"I think, Exalted Ryxander, that you'll find that's not the case."

"For once, I agree with Lord Severin." Lady Celia rose with a rustle of silk, her expression hard as steel. "You may have guarded this relic, but that doesn't give you the right to decide unilaterally what to do with a *portal to the Hells* that sits nearly on our border. The doge and the Council of Nine have instructed me to inform you that if the Serene Empire determines this gate to be a threat, Raverra will deploy all of its warlocks to raze this castle to the ground."

My spine tingled as if some ancient instinct tried to raise hackles there. She was a guest in my house, and she dared threaten to destroy it. I forced down my anger and waited; they were all setting up my next point beautifully.

Ardith's eyes narrowed, like a cat only pretending to be lazy. "You might find that some Witch Lords would object to that. Unprovoked attack on Vaskandran soil and all. Not to mention that if the smoke cleared and the gate was still standing, your greedy paws would be on it, and we can't allow that."

"You see?" I gestured around the table. "Now that you know this gate exists, you prepare to unleash rivers of blood fighting over it. If Morgrain falls, you'll attack whoever holds the Black Tower next. Chaos and death will engulf Eruvia, as sure as if we flung wide the gate and ushered in the Dark Days ourselves. There's only one way to prevent it." I paused; I knew what I had to say next, but it felt like blasphemy. Who was I to make a choice like this? I'd only known the Black Tower's secret for a few days.

I was the Warden of Gloamingard, that was who. No one else could make this decision.

The words fell heavy as lead from my lips. "We have to destroy the gate."

"Destroy it!" Aurelio cried, nearly leaping from his seat. "We barely know what it *is* yet. You can't destroy the most important magical discovery of the millennia without at least studying it first!"

Lady Celia sank back into her seat, her eyes glittering thoughtfully. "No, Aurelio," she said. "Lady Ryxander is right. This piece has to get taken off the board, or the game is over."

"It's our family legacy," Vikal objected, his expression deeply troubled. "To destroy it would be to throw away millennia of purpose and tradition." The butterflies on his shoulders fanned their wings only slowly, nearly quiescent—he was thinking about this and listening. That was significant, given that he'd be reporting back to his father.

"No," I said, only to him, meeting his violet-ringed eyes. "You know our purpose. *Only this, and nothing more: nothing must unseal the Door.* If we find a way to close it forever, our traditions and purpose are utterly fulfilled."

Vikal frowned, hunkering down in his chair to think that over. I'd take it.

Ardith folded their hands on the table. "Destroying the gate is the only way you're going to get out of a Conclave over this," they said. "The Eldest themselves are calling one. No one will agree on what to do, of course, and it'll all descend into war, like you described. Destroying it before the Conclave is a neat trick—like stuffing the last apple cake into your mouth and yelling 'What are you going to do *now*?!' I like it." They lifted a cautionary finger, cynicism flattening the humor from their hazel eyes. "But I don't know that the Eldest will like it."

"The Eldest aren't here," I said, my heart thundering against my breastbone at my temerity. Voreth's breath hissed through his teeth.

"*I'm* here." Severin rose, with the graceful reluctance of the sun cresting the hills on the winter solstice. "And I don't have to write to my brother to tell you that *he* won't like it."

"That's unfortunate." I willed myself not to flush as I met his piercing dark eyes. "However, as Gloamingard does not lie within Alevar, he doesn't get to decide."

"Any mapmaker can tell you that borders move," Severin warned.

"The same mapmaker would inform you that it takes time to redraw them," I shot back. "We have no reason to hesitate in this."

"Do you not? What does the Lady of Owls say about this plan of yours?" He glanced pointedly around the room, as if expecting to see her.

That was the biggest flaw in my plan; curse him for seizing on it. If my grandmother didn't want us to destroy the gate, she could prevent us with as little effort as it would take me to swat a fly. I had to divert him, lest others in the room started thinking about all the people who might have the power to stop us: my grandmother, the Rookery's superiors in Vaskandar and the Serene Empire, the Eldest, or even my Uncle Tarn if he got enough of my family behind him.

"If she were here," I said, "she'd ask why the Shrike Lord thinks he can meddle in her domain."

"Because he has a grievance to claim." Severin's voice went heavy as he said it. "You may have forgotten Exalted Lamiel, but he has not. If you cannot deliver her murderer as promised, he claims the Black Tower as compensation for her death."

"Out of the question," I said flatly.

Aurelio half rose from his seat, glaring at Severin. "You can't just demand the gate in recompense for a death no one but you even believes was a murder. That's absurd!"

"More to the point," Lady Celia said, leaning over the table and spearing it with a finger as if it were a conquered enemy, "you cannot treat this artifact as a bartering chip at all, because it's a *gate to the Hells*." She swept us all with a stony glare. "We can't delay in dealing with this. Do you have any idea the panic this will cause in the Empire if word gets out to the general population? Even if it stays securely locked up and sealed away?" She shook her head. "You don't, because I can't begin to imagine it myself. We are a rational, secular people, but this strikes at the heart of everything we fear most. The Serene Empire is built on order. Do you recall what the Nine Demons are?"

Ardith frowned, clearly searching their memory of the old stories. "Madness, Despair, and Nightmares... I remember those because we nicknamed three of my da's old aunts after them."

"Disaster, Discord, and Death," Vikal offered, his voice husky with portent. A chill settled in my bones at the stark, ominous grandeur of the names. *This* was what we trifled with unleashing.

"Carnage," Aurelio put in helpfully. "And I'm forgetting the last two."

"Corruption and Hunger," Lady Celia finished. "They are chaos, plain and simple. Forces of destruction and ruin. Enemies of civilization, and of all humankind. Just nine of them were enough to plunge the world into centuries of darkness." Her voice had dropped nearly to a whisper. Now she struck the table, loud enough to make me jump. "You can't *trade* that. You can't use that or control it. But people are damnable greedy fools, so that won't stop them from trying. We *must* destroy the gate as soon as possible."

Severin's mouth quirked as if Lady Celia's implication that his brother was a greedy fool amused him, even as Voreth scowled. The urgency with which Celia emphasized moving quickly, however, made me suspect she might be more concerned about forces within her own government.

"With all respect, Lady Celia, as your military-appointed adviser on magic, I feel we *can't* move hastily on this," Aurelio objected. "It's too important a decision to rush."

"I agree with this Raverran," Vikal said. "And I know my father would, as well. For four thousand years our family has guarded the Black Tower. You cannot cast aside so deep a tradition on a moment's whim."

"Someone's decided not to wait to act," Ardith pointed out. "Given the rash of murders and all."

"Lady Celia is right. We can't delay." I turned to Foxglove. This was the part I wished I'd had more time to talk to him about. "How long before you have a working plan to destroy the gate?"

I could see the desire to tell the envoys what they wanted to hear warring with realism in his face. "We're in the process of designing an enchantment," he said, choosing each word with care. "The difficult part is that any tampering with the gate has to circumvent its protections, which are formidable. We might have a working solution by as early as tomorrow evening."

Lady Celia looked relieved. "That's not so long."

Severin's brows drew together as if he was less than sanguine about Foxglove's reply. "No," he said. "It isn't."

"Fine." I tried to meet the gaze of everyone in the room in turn. I couldn't forget that one of them had conspired to kill me; it put extra steel in my voice. "I ask you to hold off on any dramatic action until then."

For a moment, it looked like I might have at least that much consensus. But Severin let out a long, pained sigh.

"I'm afraid that I have my instructions," he said, "and much as I respect your stance against drama, I cannot oblige."

Pox. I had a suspicion where this was going. Voreth looked entirely too pleased all of a sudden. "Exalted Severin—"

He raised his voice, letting it ring from the walls. "Be it known that the Shrike Lord can wait no longer. He has a true grievance, and he will see it paid."

Lady Celia frowned in confusion, exchanging glances with Aurelio. I knew what was coming, and I steeled myself, abdominal muscles tightening; there was no way to warn my gentler Raverran guests.

Severin pushed back his sleeve and pulled a bone knife from his belt. Grimacing, he drew a shallow line of blood across the back of his upraised forearm. A slim thread of scarlet dribbled down from it as Lady Celia exclaimed in alarm.

"On behalf of my brother the Shrike Lord," he said, his voice rough at the edges, "I call for the Rite of Blood and Water."

Hells. There was no backing down now, no delays, no clever tricks or evasion. Within a day, I'd have to address his grievance one way or another—or throw it back in his face.

I offered him the slightest bow I could manage from my seat, my ire rising further with each red bead that dripped from Severin's arm. He met my gaze, but there was no defiance in his expression; if anything, he looked tired.

"I hear your grievance." I tried to keep my voice grave and formal, but it came out sharp-edged nonetheless. "And will see it answered tomorrow at dusk."

"What in the Graces' names just happened?" Lady Celia asked through her teeth.

Severin had swept out of the room, Voreth trailing behind him. Everyone else had immediately fallen into startled conversation;

Lady Celia had set herself beside me at once, Aurelio following pale-faced and shaken.

"He invoked the Rite of Blood and Water." I rubbed my forehead as if I could scrub away this additional complication. "It's a custom to force settlement of a grievance or dispute. Everyone with a stake in the matter gets their say—all of us here will have a chance to speak—and at the end, we either bind ourselves to an agreement or the grievance is declared unresolved."

She frowned. "Why does resolving a dispute require dramatic public bleeding?"

Because this is Vaskandar. "To represent that if the grievance can't be resolved, there will be blood. Traditionally a duel, but when nations invoke the rite, it means war."

"Graces grant me patience." Lady Celia shook her head in frustration. "After all we went through to sign that peace."

"I know," I said, with feeling.

"This had better not delay the destruction of the gate," she warned, lowering her voice. "If certain political parties get the upper hand in the Council of Nine, they might take action to stop you."

Lovely. Yet another thing to worry about. "The Rookery is moving as fast as they can."

"I'll talk to them." She rose to corner Foxglove, leaving me with Aurelio.

For an awkward moment, we just stared at each other, both too overwhelmed to speak. My painkillers were wearing off, and I wanted desperately to go lie down; the deep pools of shadow under his eyes suggested he needed rest nearly as badly as I did.

"I'm glad you're all right," he said at last, emotion roughening his voice. I shouldn't be happy that he'd been worried, but a warm, comforting feeling bloomed in my belly anyway.

I managed a smile. "Me too."

And I *was* all right, no matter how much it might feel otherwise. I was hurt, and everything I cared about teetered on the brink of a bottomless cliff, but we hadn't tipped over the edge yet. We could still recover.

Aurelio stared at my jess, then at the hands folded in his lap. "It's been hard," he said. "For you more than anyone, I know. I must confess I'm in a bit of a difficult place, and I don't know what to do."

"I know what you mean." Greatly daring, I reached out and touched the back of his hand, brief as a bird pecking at an uncertain seed. I was probably doing this wrong again. "Disaster is hanging over us like a mountain, and it feels like any tiny misstep will send it tumbling down on our heads."

"Yes." The hand I'd touched curled into a fist. "I thought this would be easy—Grace of Mercy, I was just supposed to be here as a magical science adviser. Now there's all this pressure on me, coming from Raverra." He swallowed. "My mentor has such high expectations of me, as if he thinks I can somehow fix this whole situation with the gate all by myself."

"That's the terrible thing, though." I let out a shaky breath, not quite a laugh. "That's exactly what we have to do."

"Lord Urso says we shouldn't destroy the gate." Aurelio's voice went sad and wistful. "I hate being on opposite sides from you. We're supposed to be partners."

Hells. I'd been so caught up in my duties as a Warden, and to my family and even the Rookery, that I hadn't spent nearly enough time building my partnership with Aurelio. We might well be together for life; I owed him better.

"We *are* partners, Aurelio. Even if we're not always on the same side." I held out my hand, the jess gleaming on my wrist.

He hesitated, then clasped it briefly before letting go with a wan smile. "Thanks, Ryx."

"Now, forget what Lord Urso says," I urged him. "What do

you think about the gate?" I didn't know what kind of authority Aurelio had; if the military had sent him to advise Lady Celia, his role could have some teeth to it. And if swaying him might reach back to his mentor and his political circles, well, it would be lovely to be certain the Serene Empire was on our side.

Aurelio's shoulders bowed as if a heavy pack had settled on them. "I don't know. I mean, it's a gate to the *Nine Hells*. It doesn't seem like any good could come of it." He lifted his head. "But Lord Urso says that fear is always the biggest barrier to discovery. People used to be afraid that luminaries would start fires, or that food warmed in an alchemically powered oven would wind up poisoned. If we brought the scholarly power of the Empire to bear, maybe we could find a way to use that limitless magical energy without opening the gate. Or even if we could just learn more about the nature of magic from studying it, we could change the world."

"Changing the world is exactly what I'm afraid of." I shuddered. "The Rookery have been reading up on the Dark Days, and they tell me that half the population of Eruvia died in the first ten years. The survivors had to endure a century of plague and nightmare, suffering and horror and madness, living as playthings for the Nine Demons as their friends and family kept dying all around them. We're lucky humanity wasn't wiped out entirely."

"Still, if we were careful—"

"We won't have the chance. You heard everyone; if we don't destroy the gate, we get a global war. Even if that weren't the case, we couldn't study it—we can't let anyone *near* it." I dropped my voice to an urgent whisper. "If you get too close, you can hear voices coming from the gate, Aurelio. Even when it's closed."

His eyes widened. "Demons?"

"Yes. My aunt heard them whispering to her." The thought

set a profound uneasiness swirling in my gut. "There's no way to study it safely. My ancestors sealed it off for a reason."

"I need to think about that." He sounded profoundly disturbed.

"Please do."

Aurelio had no sooner left to join Lady Celia, frowning in a thoughtful manner I found encouraging, when Ardith plunked down in his place.

"The Rite of Blood and Water, huh." They shook their head. "That complicates things."

"I noticed," I said through my teeth. I knew Ardith could use a bow; I tried to match their voice and shape against my attacker, but I hadn't gotten a good look, and everyone sounded the same when they were screaming in mortal terror.

"I was hoping that I could stay out of your way and let you and the Rookery take care of the gate. Do my job by doing nothing, you know?" They sighed. "Now that Alevar has called the rite, I'm bound to get orders from above. Half the Conclave is getting in on this now. And I'd lay you a wager that not all the Eldest are going to back destroying the gate."

"Why not?" I spread my hands in frustration. "It goes to the Nine Hells! There's nothing good about it!"

"Foxglove's report apparently said something about the Hells being tied in to the natural flow of magic—the source, part of the cycle, I don't know. I honestly didn't read it. Too technical for me." Ardith shrugged. "You know Witch Lords, though. The older they get, the more they hate change, and they have very strong feelings about natural cycles and magic. I should warn you that they're probably going to at least want a delay until the Conclave can discuss this."

"It's not the Conclave's decision," I snapped. It came out more harshly than I meant, but the swelling ache in my leg was beginning to fray my temper.

Ardith arched their ginger brows. "If you think you can stand up to the Eldest, whatever potions they've been giving you are good stuff." They rose, giving my good shoulder a slap that I supposed was meant as friendly. "Anyway, now I've warned you. My apologies in advance for any small role I may play in destroying everything you hold dear, and all that. See you at the rite."

I lifted a hand to massage my temple. "Thanks, Ardith. See you at the rite."

Hell of Discord—I'd almost had this under control for a moment. Now everything was collapsing beneath my touch once again. The Rookery had best come up with that enchantment quickly, before it all fell apart completely.

"This is a terrible idea," I muttered, testing the draw on the slim sword at my hip. It was riding a little too far forward for my taste; I settled my belt more to the left and a bit lower.

It felt wrong to wear a sword around Gloamingard. This castle was supposed to be the safest place in Eruvia for me. My experience was limited entirely to practice; my mother had thought it would be good for me to learn the rapier as an ironically less lethal option for self-defense than my bare hands.

"You won't need it," Ashe said cheerfully. "If he so much as sneezes aggressively in your direction, Foxglove and I will have him dead on the floor before you can say 'seasons bless you.'"

"Rule Three, Ashe," Foxglove reminded her airily. "No killing when wounding will suffice."

Ashe sighed. "Fine."

Foxglove pointed sternly to her sword hilt. "Take that off and swap it for something less lethal."

"You're no fun. I haven't gotten to use that one yet." Ashe twisted the obsidian pommel, wrapped in golden wire and shining black beads, and it came off; she handed it to Foxglove. "Give me the blue one, then."

Foxglove swapped the obsidian orb for a matching one with blue crystal beads from one of his pouches. "I'm not giving the black one back until after the envoys go home. You don't need killing enchantments on your sword at a diplomatic event."

"Yes, I don't want any more of the Shrike Lord's kin murdered in my castle," I said fervently. "And please do stay out of sight unless I call for help. Just in case Severin actually has a good reason for wanting privacy." My curiosity itched to find out at last what that reason might be.

Ashe clapped my shoulder. "Foxglove and I are professionals, remember. You'll never know we're there."

The two of them withdrew from the Old Great Hall, the shadows swallowing them before they left the room. I remained alone, leaning on the smooth wooden head of my cane, feeling small in the big, drafty space. Shafts of moonlight pierced the darkness, falling from high windows in the hall; it was getting close to midnight.

I'd picked the Old Great Hall because it was part of the log-built lodge section of Gloamingard, from the era of the Lady of Badgers; most vivomancers couldn't work dead wood quickly, but a Witch Lord could mold anything that had once lived and grown in their domain with a thought from a hundred miles away. Severin had seen what my grandmother had done to the Bone Atrium, making it sprout deadly lances in every direction; this location was an implicit threat should he—or anyone else— try to kill me again.

And that threat was a bluff. The last thing I wanted was for my grandmother to have to intervene. Not if it could put her at a disadvantage in a battle with a demon.

Still, every muscle in my body had gone rigid, anticipating the impact of an arrow strike. My ears strained for the twang of a bowstring, and the breathy tearing of the air that followed. Even with alchemical potions and salves speeding my healing beyond the already quick recovery rate of a vivomancer—or whatever I was—my leg and shoulder still ached, reminding me how close I'd come to dying the last time I planned to meet Severin alone in the middle of the night.

At long last, footsteps sounded in the main doorway. I twisted nervously at my jess, wishing for a fleeting moment I'd asked Aurelio to release my power, just to be safe.

Severin stepped into one of the beams of moonlight.

TWENTY-FIVE

Severin moved with the hesitant grace of a deer entering a clearing, his head tilted to listen.

"Exalted Ryxander?" he called softly.

"Here," I replied, my voice hoarse with strain.

He passed between light and shadow, eyes shining in the silvery light. He didn't seem to be carrying any weapon beyond a dagger at his hip. My heartbeat began to slow from its frenetic ready-to-be-murdered pace to a mere rapidity more appropriate for a midnight meeting with an enemy.

His gaze marked my cane, and the bandages peeking from under my collar. A sort of grimace stole across his face. "I'm sorry this didn't work out last time."

"Beginning with an understatement, are we, Exalted Atheling?" The blunt words burst out before I could think better of them.

To my surprise, he laughed. It held a bitter edge, but his amusement seemed genuine. "Would you prefer something more grandiose? Shall I posture in a villainous fashion and make thinly veiled threats against your family?" He shook his head. "Much as I've enjoyed our sparring, there's no audience here to perform for. That's the entire point."

"Do you claim to come offering truth, then?"

"Truth is perhaps overly ambitious. Certainly something closer to it than the nonsense I have to spout in a more official capacity." He stepped in closer; I could have reached out and touched his chest. His voice dropped to barely above a whisper. "I'll get to the point. My brother must not have the gate, under any circumstances."

All the words and phrases I held prepared in my arsenal for a response failed at once. "What?"

A self-mocking smile twisted his lips. "Not what you expected? Good. One does have a reputation to maintain."

I cleared my throat. "You made it rather clear that the Shrike Lord wanted the gate for himself."

"Oh, he does, I assure you. But no matter what else happens here, we can't let him have it."

I'd expected some subterfuge, but this was too much of an about-face. There had to be a catch. "Is this some power play? Next you'll be telling me that *you* would be a far more responsible guardian for it."

Severin snorted. "A randomly selected Raverran street urchin would be a better guardian. Power seems to bring out my brother's cruel streak, alas." He rubbed his temple, a seemingly unconscious gesture; the moonlight picked out a faint scar that ran from under his hairline and down across his cheekbone to his jaw. This close, I could make out more scars across his throat, faint and blurred with time, as if someone had tried to garrote him with a rope of brambles. "Believe me, I'm not here as his envoy out of love for him."

Grace of Mercy. And I'd thought *my* family relations were complicated. "Yet you still demand the gate on his behalf in public," I said, wary of a trap.

"I have to. You may have noticed he's got Voreth attached to me like an extra shadow. If my brother catches me doing anything to thwart him, he'll..." Severin looked away, the scars jumping on his neck. "Suffice to say that if you think he'll have mercy on me because I'm family, you don't know my brother. He's kind enough to those who serve him, but those who oppose him he crushes utterly."

"But you're his heir," I objected.

Severin let out a humorless bark of a laugh. "Only because I swore to him I had no ambition to take the domain for myself, and because I helped him kill our father."

I clenched both hands tight on the head of my cane, willing myself not to take a step back, but I couldn't help leaning away a little. "You *what*?"

"Don't look at me like that. The man was a monster." When I still couldn't wrestle my expression away from horror, Severin sighed. "Look, my brother and I were unexpected twins. My father was a firm believer in the old wisdom that a Witch Lord should have only one heir, but our mother wouldn't let him kill one of us to avert the possibility of a contested domain. The day after our mother died, my father called us into his study and told us that one of us would have to kill the other, and he'd name the survivor his heir. He didn't care which."

I covered my mouth. "All right, you win, that's horrible," I said through my fingers.

"It's one small example of the encompassing charm and thoughtfulness that defined his life." Severin shrugged. "I didn't want to kill my brother, so I convinced him to kill our father instead. Which may seem only tangentially relevant to our discussion, but my *point*, my lady, is that I am only here speaking to you because I have never challenged my brother. That is the condition for my continued existence." A shiver traced his shoulders. "I'm taking an enormous risk just talking to you. Please understand the importance of discretion."

"I can be discreet." I still wasn't certain I believed him. He'd already proven himself well capable of acting a part. It cost me nothing to keep his secret, however, and if he wasn't lying, it might save his life. "Why are you trusting me with this?"

Severin hesitated, as if I'd caught him doing something embarrassing. An odd smile pulled at the corner of his mouth. "Voreth told me you threatened to set your chimeras on him," he said at last.

"What? Oh." That's right; I'd done that when he hit Kip. Remembered anger lit a coal in my belly. "He deserved it."

"I'm sure he did." Severin made an odd aborted gesture, his hand lifting briefly and dropping back to his side. "I saw how hard you worked to rein in your aunt before she could insult your guests, and all the care you put into things like making certain there were both Vaskandran and Raverran influences at the reception. But you were willing to throw all that diplomatic work away to protect some servant boy." He shook his head. "It was completely mad. I admired you for it."

Heat flushed my neck. "I protect my own."

"Suffice to say it gave me hope that you wouldn't betray me for political expediency."

"I won't," I promised. *Unless you betray me first.* "But if you still have to demand the gate on your brother's behalf at the Rite of Blood and Water, what are you suggesting we do? Simply ensure you fail to acquire it for him? We hope to destroy it within a couple of days, so that shouldn't be difficult."

"That's well and good if you can do it, but it won't avoid a war. If I return to Alevar empty-handed after the rite, I can guarantee you he'll invade your domain." He hesitated, then reluctantly added, "And things will go rather unpleasantly for me, as well."

"If he thinks he can successfully invade Morgrain without an alliance backing him, he's a fool," I said sharply.

"He's got the alliance already." Severin's words sank into me like lead shot. "But I have an idea. I don't know who actually killed Lamiel. If you know, don't tell me! Maybe it was someone you can't turn over, like the Lady of Owls herself."

I knew I was utterly failing at keeping my expression neutral, but couldn't begin to guess exactly what sort of face I was making. It was tight and twisted in all the wrong places, and Graces only knew what he must think. "Exalted—"

"Wait, hear me out!" He lifted a hand. "If you turn over someone as the culprit—*anyone*, a criminal, an enemy, it doesn't matter—I can take them and leave, my primary task accomplished. My brother will be pleased, and he'll have no excuse to start a war. His demands will be met, his grievance fulfilled. And he'll be so busy torturing the poor bastard to death that he'll forget all about the gate for long enough to give you plenty of time to destroy it."

I clenched my hands so hard on my cane that pain stabbed through my shoulder. "I am not going to condemn someone to a horrible death for the sake of political convenience," I said through my teeth.

"Not for politics! To save lives." For a moment I thought he would reach for my hand, pleading, but he checked himself. Instead he caught my eyes; his burned with desperate intensity. "I'm not asking you to sacrifice an innocent. Pick someone who you'd condemn to death anyway."

This entire situation was a mess, but I was sure of one thing: I wasn't going to let someone else die in my stead. "Gloamingard Castle doesn't have dungeons full of handy condemned criminals. And besides, I won't throw aside my principles so easily."

A wry, sad smile lit unexpectedly on Severin's face. "Oh, there's nothing easy about it. I assure you, I've lost my principles rather painfully, and over many years."

I frowned at him. "Then how can I trust you?"

"You can't." He spread his hands helplessly. "You shouldn't. And I'm not asking you to. I'm only telling you we have the same problem, and proposing a solution."

"We need a different solution," I said stubbornly.

"Fine, then. What marvelously principled solution would you propose?"

He crossed his arms and waited, challenge in his eyes.

I was half tempted to propose slapping that smirk off his lips. This was no joking matter. But I couldn't let him see how he upset me, or he might guess why—and while his confidences and proposals were all very well, there was no way I'd trust him with the knowledge that I was the one his brother wanted to kill.

Before I could come up with a suitably clever reply, something caught my attention in the shadows behind Severin.

A figure, lean and sharp, with a shock of pale hair. Two blazing orange circles staring out of the darkness at me.

Grandmother.

"So this is the one who lured you into a trap last night." Her words cut through the darkness, low and lethal as an assassin's knife thrust.

Severin's eyes went wide with fear. He turned, slowly, to face her. "Most Exalted," he said. "I swear to you there was no trap of mine. I was on my way to meet Exalted Ryxander and found her already hurt."

My grandmother advanced, slow and certain as death itself. The oppressive wave of her power pushed before her, sweeping over both of us, waking a resonating shiver from the walls, the floor, my own blood and bones.

"Are you the one who killed my daughter, Shrike boy?" she whispered. Her voice was all edges, a handful of broken glass.

Severin stepped back, waxy pale. "No, Most Exalted."

"Grandmother," I said, "Exalted Severin helped me last night.

He may have saved my life." I hated to admit it, because it meant a serious debt, a major favor—but I couldn't leave him to her wrath when he hadn't earned it.

Her orange-ringed gaze fell on me. A smile pulled her lips taut, all teeth and menace.

It wasn't her smile.

"I'm not certain I care," she said. "Someone killed my daughter and hurt my grandchild, and I want blood."

"Oh sweet Hells," Severin breathed, so softly I barely heard him.

My heart thudded against my breastbone. I stepped in front of him, planting my cane before me as if to mark a line I wouldn't let her cross.

Not that I had the power to slow her down, let alone stop her.

"Grandmother," I said, trying to keep my voice calm and reasonable, "I know you're fighting your own battle. Leave finding the killer to us for now. Once you've won, *then* you can have your vengeance."

"My own battle?" She cocked her head as if listening; it tilted a shade too far. The moonlight caught a wicked gleam in her eyes. "Is that what you think? You misunderstand."

All the breath seemed to leave my lungs. I had to speak, had to do something to keep the moment from spiraling into murder, but all I could do was stare in horror as realization seeped into me like cold, dark water.

"There was never a battle," she said softly. She came closer still, emerging from a patch of shadow into a brilliant band of silver light. "I braced for one, but it didn't come. There was no winner, no loser. We're all in this Hell called life together, Ryx."

My skin crawled. This close, I could feel it—the same raw, wild power that had blasted from the gate. It ran beneath my grandmother's more familiar presence—the whiff of grass and stones and ancient pines, of snow in the high hills and roots growing beneath the earth, of sleek fur and soft feathers and all the furious innocence of living things. This was different: a pure, hot crackling like the heart of lightning.

There was no dividing line between the two of them. The presences were one.

She was a demon.

TWENTY-SIX

Without quite taking my eyes off my grandmother, I whispered over my shoulder to Severin: "Get out of here."

He didn't answer, but there came a faint scuffing of moving feet, and his high frightened breathing began to withdraw. Thank the Graces he had the sense not to turn and run; she'd have been on him in an instant, like a pouncing cat. I had to keep my grandmother's attention until he was out of her sight and hope the demon's fancy would latch on to something else.

"What happened to you?" I asked her, not bothering to hide the grief roughening my voice.

"You let me through the gate." She bowed to me, stiff and mocking. "I owe you a favor for that." Her eyes narrowed. "But you also let a demon through into my castle, so it seems you owe me a grievance, and it balances out. You do have a remarkable talent for disaster, Ryx."

She'd come close enough that I could have reached out and touched her. Her stance was all wrong, too far on her toes, ready to launch into motion when she should have stood solid and grounded. A wild light gleamed in her eyes.

Suddenly her brows twitched down in a frown, and she reached toward my shoulder. "You're hurt."

"Of course I am. You saw." My voice shook. This was a nightmare, too terrible to be real; I'd wake up and find my grandmother whole and herself, sitting by me and offering a cup of lavender tea.

"Mortal bodies break so easily." She laid two fingers on my collarbone, gentle as the brush of a bird's wing. I flinched, but it was the same warm touch I'd always known.

Magic swarmed into me from her fingers, crawling like a thousand fire ants, and my shoulder and leg blazed with pain.

I barely choked back a cry. The last thing I needed was Ashe and Foxglove bursting in and attacking my grandmother; she'd kill them both. I swayed on my feet, dizzy from the jolt of energy. My grandmother caught my elbow, steadying me, her hand hard as a claw.

My wounds were gone. I could put my weight on my leg without so much as a twinge. She'd healed me completely.

I stared at her in horror. "How...? You're not a Skinwitch. Your power shouldn't work on humans."

She laughed—a rich, warm chuckle, as if I'd told a fine joke. "Oh, Ryx. Of course I'm not a Skinwitch. Think about it. Why can't a Greenwitch or a Furwitch use their power on humans?"

"Because their magic rebels. It recognizes their fellow humanity." It was my grandmother herself who'd explained this to me, gently, the first time someone accused me of being a Skinwitch, to reassure me it wasn't true. Her own words spilled out of my mouth, regurgitated in bitter misery from my memory. "You can't consciously use vivomancy on yourself or any fellow human, because your power instinctively twists away. You can use it unconsciously, however, like when vivomancers heal more quickly." *So you're not a Skinwitch, Ryx*, she'd told me. *You don't control your power; that's why it works on humans. If you ever gain control of it, you won't be able to kill people with it even if you want to.*

My grandmother wiped the last of the laughter from her eyes.

"That's right. But of course, I'm not really human anymore, am I?" As she lowered her hand, her face hardened, and the sense of palpable menace around her sharpened again. "And so I can cast aside all the petty little things that hold a human back."

A yawning black gulf of despair opened beneath me, the edges crumbling under my feet. It would be so easy to fall in, to be overwhelmed, to burst into tears or collapse in a numb pile of shock.

I couldn't do that—not now. Morgrain needed me. My grandmother needed me. I was the one person standing here in this terrible moment who had any chance of shaking something good out of it.

"You're still human," I said quietly. "You're still my grandmother. You wouldn't want vengeance if you didn't care about us."

"Of course I care." Her eyes narrowed, and orange fires glowed in them. "But you know better than anyone that sometimes your hand falls ungently on that which you love."

Oh Hells. For the first time in my life, a deep, visceral fear of her thrilled through my blood, resonating through the profound link we shared. "You wouldn't do anything to hurt your family or your domain," I said, trying to force confidence into my voice. "You will always protect Morgrain."

"Oh, I will." Her voice dripped the promise of blood. She reached out and laid a cold, iron-hard hand on the side of my face. "When I find the one who killed my child, I will turn them inside out and keep them alive while my owls eat their innards."

I tried again, desperate. "Morgrain needs you. The truth about the gate is out, and we're hovering on the brink of war."

"Let them bring war." Her mage mark formed wheels of twisting light in her eyes, burning an afterimage into my brain. "I'll destroy them so utterly it'll make the War of Ashes look like a children's party. If they hurt what I love, I'll scour them from the face of the earth."

I stared at her in horror. There was no bravado in her voice; it was bald statement of fact. She could do it.

She grinned. It was too sharp, too wide, but the mischief in it was familiar, and it broke my heart. "Still," she said, "it'd be more fun to trick them into fighting each other instead of us."

Something about her tone froze my breath in my lungs. "It was you," I whispered.

She cocked her head in question, bands of shadow sliding across her face.

"You sent the bird telling Vikal about the gate." I stepped back, pressing my fingers to my mouth. "You were the one who sent the message to Ardith that brought them here, too, about the Black Tower being open."

"I always did like Ardith. They're a creature of chaos." A mix of exasperation and affection colored my grandmother's voice. She sounded like herself. But then she laughed, and it was a demon's laugh. "I knew they'd stir things up."

A creature of chaos. She'd deliberately let loose the secret about the gate—the one thing certain to set all the nations of Eruvia at each other's throats.

"You're the Demon of Discord," I whispered.

I stood in the Old Great Hall after my grandmother left, gone as suddenly and silently as her namesake owls into the night shadows. I held myself utterly still, as if any movement might cause me to come apart in a thousand skittering pieces. The horrifying implications of what I'd unleashed fell on me one after another, hard and heavy as masonry blocks.

I rubbed my forehead, squeezing my eyes shut on the hot tears brimming in them. "Think," I muttered. "Think."

I had to take this one piece at a time. Even the Grace of

Victory couldn't destroy the gate *and* find a murderer *and* avert a war *and* restore my grandmother *and* keep the Shrike Lord off our backs all at once. I needed to pick one thing I could do, one step I could take, and do everything in my power to forget about the rest until that step was done.

My grandmother is the Demon of Discord, and it's all my fault.

"Sweet Grace of Mercy," I groaned, pushing my fingers up into my hairline.

"Hey. Were you going to leave us waiting forever?" Ashe's whisper echoed through the hall.

Ashe and Foxglove leaned on the balcony railing above me, peering down, near invisible in a patch of shadow.

"Severin *is* gone, yes?" Foxglove glanced around the room. "We hadn't heard voices for a while, so we came to make certain you were still alive."

They didn't know. They had no idea that one of the Nine Demons was already loose in this world, and things were so much worse than we'd thought.

"I—yes, he's gone." I took a deep, shuddering breath. *One thing at a time.* "I need to talk to Vikal. Now."

Vikal stared at me a moment in shocked silence, his face blank as new snow, the news I'd just told him not yet written on it. Then pain twisted his features into a knot. He banged his fist against the wall of his guest room, startling a few butterflies that had lit there for the night. He shook out his hand, then punched the wall again, harder; I winced at the impact.

"Curse everything. The whole world can go to the Hell of Nightmares. I'm done with it." He'd taken off his eye paint to get ready for bed, and without it his face seemed younger and more vulnerable. "First Aunt Karrigan, then you almost died, and now *this*."

"I'm sorry." My voice came out ragged at the edges. "This is my fault. I'm the one who let it through the gate."

Vikal whirled on me, the violet rings of his mage mark intense in twin pools of brimming tears. "Then you can go to the Nine Hells, too. And Lamiel, for meddling with the gate, and Grandmother, for never telling us anything, and for favoring you so much. All of you can go to the Hells together."

"Fine," I said through my teeth. "But first we've got a lot to do."

Vikal shook his head, stunned. "Do? What can we do? We're just third-generation athelings. Grandmother is the *Witch Lord*, with the domain in the palm of her hand, and *she* couldn't do anything about this gate."

"Yes. Grandmother is the Witch Lord, with the domain in the palm of her hand." I said each word with bruising force, because they hurt me too much to handle them gently. "And she's a *demon*."

"Blood of the Eldest." Vikal sank suddenly down into a chair, almost missing it.

Now he was beginning to see what had haunted me all the way through the halls of Gloamingard on the way to his room. What I hadn't even told Ashe and Foxglove yet, who waited outside, because Vikal was family and needed to hear it first.

"She can use her power on humans now." I drove the worst of it ruthlessly home. "We'd better *hope* she stays away. If she decides to take up the rule of Morgrain again, no one will be able to resist her commands."

"And how do you expect us to fix this?" Vikal flung his arms wide, as if to show me the impossibility of the situation.

I knew too well how bad it was. "We can't," I said softly. "Not now. All we can do is keep it from getting worse."

"It can't get any worse," Vikal said despairingly, staring at his feet.

"Oh, it can." I crouched down to meet his eyes. "Vikal, listen to me. You're an atheling, with a bond to the land and a duty to your people. You need to rise to the challenge and protect them now."

For a moment, I thought he would protest; I could see the complaint hovering on his lips, and in his helpless eyes. But his face twisted, he took a deep breath, and resolve settled on him like a cloak. "Fine. Tell me what to do."

I clapped his shoulder, an odd pride stirring in me. "First, you need to go warn the others."

He blanched. "My father. Hell of Nightmares, I have to tell my father that his mother is a demon."

"And mine, too," I said, swallowing a hard lump. "I can't entrust this message to anyone else. Only family. He's looking for Grandmother now, and he's too stubborn to stop, so we have to lie to him. Tell him she's a demon, so that he's warned, but tell him she's somewhere else—on the far end of the domain—whatever it takes to keep him from confronting her. Because you *know* that won't go well."

"Eldest, no," Vikal groaned, pushing his hands into his purple hair. "Your father is even more bullheaded than Grandmother. It'd be a disaster. I'll send the message, and I'll warn all our cousins, too."

"And be ready to act," I said grimly. "You and the rest—our fathers, our cousins, your siblings. If Grandmother misuses her power over the land, you'll be the only ones who can counteract her." *You*, not *we*: the words sat bitterly on my tongue. In this moment, all my family had to rise up together to deal with the threat of a lifetime, doing an atheling's duty as none had ever needed to before, and I couldn't be part of it.

Vikal nodded with grim resolve, purpose kindling in his eyes. "I'll do it. Morgrain can count on me, Ryxander."

"Good."

"What..." He hesitated, the awkwardness of the question bothering him for once. "What will you do?"

"I'll stay here and try to handle the political end and guard the gate," I said. "We can't risk anyone in the line of succession getting possessed, in case we figure out some way to get control of the domain away from Grandmother." I didn't mention the unspoken truth that the reason I didn't count was because if I was ever at a real risk of inheriting the domain, they'd have to kill me anyway, to protect Morgrain from my destroying magic. "That's crucial—please make sure everyone in the family knows to stay away and defend their own lands. It'll be the only way we have a chance of reacting to Grandmother if the demon makes a move."

"All right." Understanding shadowed his eyes; he knew that I was admitting I was expendable. "And you'll handle the Empire and the Shrike Lord?"

Part of me wanted to throw back my head and laugh until I cried. Instead I nodded, grave and solemn. "I will."

To my shock, Vikal reached out and let his hand fall awkwardly on my shoulder. "I'm glad you're the Warden of Gloamingard, Ryx," he said, a grudging edge in his voice. "It's good that you're handling the politics. I can create a glorious chimera, and I know how to keep the land and livestock healthy in my villages, but I don't know how to convince foreigners to do what I want when I can't just order them around. I'm glad you're here."

"Thanks." I managed a smile. "I'm glad you're here, too. The rest of the family will listen to you, and I know you'll do a fine job protecting Morgrain."

Vikal gave me a fierce nod. "I'll leave at once; I've enhanced Lancer's eyes so she can see at night. Stay safe, don't die, and seal the Door."

I couldn't begin to understand the feelings churning in my stomach. The wrenching loss and horror over my grandmother was only beginning to take root—but now, for the first time, I felt that Vikal and I were truly family.

"You too, Vikal," I said softly. "Stay safe."

The flickering orange light of the fire in the Rookery sitting room cast harsh and changing shadows over their faces as they listened. When I was done, a grim, breathless silence prevailed.

Even Foxglove couldn't stay standing in the face of my dire news. He sank into a chair, his face gray-tinged. "A demon loose in the world. Graces preserve us all."

"That's terrifying enough to banish sleep forever, but her dominion over the land makes it even worse." Kessa shook her head as if dazed by the sheer horrifying scope of the problem; Ashe shifted closer to her. "I'm trying to think whether there's anything we could do to sever that connection, so that we're just dealing with one of the Nine Demons rather than a demon *Witch Lord*."

"Just," Ashe grunted, with a humorless laugh.

I shook my head. "In theory my uncle could travel around blooding the stones and trying to usurp her claim over the land, but she'd sense him doing it and stop him immediately. The Eldest might be strong enough to contest her for the domain— but they might not. We don't really know how powerful demons are. And I don't want to tell the Eldest she's a demon, because there's a chance they'd decide the safest solution is to destroy Morgrain."

"There's something to that," Ashe said, fingering Answer's hilt. "Bit extreme, but it might work."

"I don't think we need to go *that* far quite yet," Kessa said, giving Ashe a stern glance. "If we can't break her hold over the domain, what *can* we do?"

"There's got to be some way we can save her." I looked pleadingly at Bastian. He was the scholar; he must know something that could help. "Some way to make her human again."

He winced as if my words burned him, turning his face away. A flush crept up his neck. "I don't know. Some things aren't easily undone."

"Ryx," Foxglove said, his voice soft as the first flakes of winter. "We may need to look at other solutions."

"We'll save her," I insisted.

The stare Foxglove leveled at me cut deeper than the assassin's arrow had. "We can't leave a demon as Witch Lord of Morgrain."

"Let's be clear on one thing," said a soft voice, smooth as silk and far stronger. "You don't have a choice."

TWENTY-SEVEN

W hisper prowled into the middle of the room from some patch of shadow, nonchalant as if he'd been there the whole time. Ashe had half drawn Answer when he spoke; she slid it back into its sheath with a click.

"Stupid chimeras," she muttered.

"Is he a chimera?" Kessa exclaimed, delighted. "He's so—" I shook my head frantically at her, and she caught herself, clamping her lips shut on whatever offensively endearing adjective she'd been about to apply.

Whisper's tail flicked with annoyance. "I came to stop you from making a lethal mistake. I can leave if you prefer."

Foxglove bowed, deep and gracious as if Whisper were a visiting king. I supposed he'd seen stranger things. "My apologies. We're listening."

Whisper leaped up onto the mantel, putting himself above everyone, and settled himself with regal poise. "First of all, demons can't die. Second, while you could in theory destroy her host and force her to choose another one, you lack the power to challenge a Witch Lord *or* one of the Nine Demons, let alone a being who is both."

"What can we do?" I asked, nails digging into my leg, finding itching scar tissue where a serious wound had been an hour ago. "Resign ourselves to face the Dark Days all over again?"

Whisper flicked a dismissive ear. "One demon hardly constitutes an apocalypse. Or rather, it depends on which demon."

Bastian started counting on shaking fingers. "Nightmares, Despair, Carnage, Madness, Disaster, Discord, Corruption, Hunger, and Death. All the options are terrible."

"I assure you, some of them are better than others." Whisper licked a paw.

"She's the Demon of Discord," I said, the admission weighing in my stomach like a stone. "She spread the word about the gate to the Hells to create chaos, and she's trying to incite conflict in the area. And she didn't deny it when I called her by that name."

"It seems likely," Whisper agreed, his voice soft as shadows falling.

"Forgive me, but why are you telling us this?" Foxglove asked, eyeing Whisper warily. "I've asked around about you—"

"Have you." Whisper's tone was icy.

"It's my job." Foxglove gave him a courteous bow—but he also hooked his thumbs in his belt, near his pistol and his pouches full of artifice devices. My pulse quickened. Whatever Foxglove had heard about Whisper, it was enough to make him nervous, though he hid it well. "Suffice to say, you're not known for going out of your way to be helpful."

Whisper's tail swished with annoyance. "I am not a pet or a servant, to spend my days *helping* humans. I have my own priorities. But those priorities are not served by you blundering around in complete ignorance, fouling everything up. Not when matters as volatile as the gate and the Nine Demons are concerned."

Or he simply wanted to control what information we had. He'd certainly tried to steer me away from certain subjects before. Either way, it only begged the question of how he knew so much about the Hells in the first place.

Still, I wasn't going to argue about his motives now, when for once he was in the mood to share.

Ashe ran her fingers along the twists of artifice wire on her sword hilt, as if she itched to draw it. "All right, if you're answering questions—how bad are the demons exactly? I've hunted chimeras that could wreck a town by themselves, but the stories of the Dark Days talk about fantastic stuff—rivers running with blood, day turning to night, earthquakes and hurricanes, the dead rising up from the earth, plagues that wiped out whole domains."

"The plagues were the Demon of Corruption." Whisper's lips lifted from his teeth, as if the name were distasteful. "The earthquakes and hurricanes were the Demon of Disaster. The rest were most likely Madness or Nightmare, though I suppose the rivers of blood could be the Demon of Carnage if it was literal rather than illusory."

My stomach sank into a dark, giddy abyss. "They can actually *do* things like that?"

"Naturally." He began cleaning a paw. "Some prefer to avoid such gauche displays, however. Discord, you'll be happy to know, is usually subtler."

"Lovely." I raked nervous fingers through the end of my braid, unraveling it. "So no rivers of blood from her, but we'd better watch out for, what... broken alliances and pointless wars? Economic collapse? General lawlessness?"

"Discord's schemes are often complex, and they keep changing in midcourse." Whisper's tail swished in disapproval. "She's unpredictable by nature. She does generally take delight in turning mortals against each other to achieve her goals."

Ashe grunted. "Better than Carnage, I suppose."

A grim silence fell over the room for a moment, broken only

by the popping of the fire. The urgent energy of fear began draining out of me, and standing suddenly took more strength than I had left. I sank down on the hard edge of the hearthstone.

"I'm sorry the Rookery got drawn into this," I murmured. "This is probably going to get very messy before it's over."

Kessa grimaced. "I can't deny this mission is turning out to be about as much harmless fun as a bucket of stingroaches, but don't be sorry. This is our duty. Your grandmother knew it would happen; that's why she sent you to get us. Dealing with danger-ous magic is our job—even if it's never been quite this appall-ingly dangerous before."

Your grandmother knew it would happen. My hands clenched on my knees.

"If she knew she would get possessed—if she knew that I let a demon through..." Of course she'd known. That was why she sent me to get the Rookery in person, rather than sending a bird; to get me away from the demon. That was why she went into the Black Tower alone. She knew she'd have a better chance than anyone to fight it off and avoid possession, so she went in there to face it herself.

Only she hadn't fought it off. They must have proven unex-pectedly compatible, Whisper's third option, and their spirits had fused. And now the grandmother who'd raised me was a demon, and the Witch Lord of Morgrain was a malevolent being straight from the Nine Hells.

"I don't know what to do," I whispered.

Ashe snorted. "That's all right. We never do. We just blunder along making things worse until we figure out a way to fix it all brilliantly at the last minute, then pretend it was our plan the whole time."

"Ashe," Foxglove scolded. "Don't give away our secrets."

"She's one of us now." Ashe shrugged.

The thought brought a spark of warmth to the cold that had

settled in my chest. "That's right. And you're experts at this sort of thing."

"Maybe not this *exact* sort of thing." Kessa offered a rueful smile. "No one has had to deal with a demon in four thousand years, and I have to admit I'm flat-out terrified. Still, your grandmother was right to call us; if there's one thing I've learned in my time with the Rookery, it's that we always find a way in the end."

"But there may not *be* a way to restore my grandmother," I said, hating to voice the quiet truth that had been gnawing a black hole in my chest. "If she's merged with the demon, I'm not sure that can be undone." I looked up at Whisper, questioning.

His tail tip flicked once, twice, then settled around his paws.

"Everyone changes," he said at last. "Change is the essence of life. And once you've changed, nothing can make you again what you were before."

That meant no. I swallowed a small noise before it could claw its way up out of my aching throat.

Bastian's face twisted with a pain that I neither expected nor understood. Then Ashe let out a long, rough sigh, as if she hated to do this.

"Once," she said softly, "long ago, there was a girl who cut out her heart."

Everyone turned to look at her. Ashe stared into the fire, seemingly oblivious to the attention, and kept talking in a quiet, mesmerizing voice. "She was a killer, and her heart got in the way of her work. So she left it on the floor behind her." The firelight flickered warm fingers across Ashe's face, lingering in her eyes. "Her work came easier after that, but she forgot why it mattered. She carried on, empty and hollow and slowly dying from the inside out, all without a heart."

Foxglove closed his eyes and rubbed his temple, as if remembering an old pain. Kessa stared at Ashe, rapt, her eyes soft and distant, black hair falling like night itself around her face.

"Go on," I whispered.

"She would have gotten herself killed, sooner or later," Ashe continued. "Probably sooner, because anyone who'll cut her own heart out takes pretty poor care of herself. But along came someone behind her, all unexpected—a wise and kind girl. And the kind girl was carrying a jar."

An odd little smile quirked Bastian's lips, and he glanced from Ashe to Kessa and back again.

"She handed the killer the jar," Ashe said, so softly. "And she said, 'You dropped this.' The killer opened the jar up. And you know what she found there, don't you?"

"Her heart," I breathed.

Ashe nodded, still studiously watching the fire. "She'd kept it safe. And the killer stared into that jar for a long time. At last, she picked her heart up and put it back in the empty hollow in her chest."

"What's your point?" Foxglove asked, his voice too harsh, breaking the spell.

Ashe shrugged. "If I have to *say* the point of the story, it'll sound stupid. That's why we make stories. So we can say things without sounding like idiots."

"I get it," I said roughly. If my grandmother had lost who she was, or where she drew lines, or what mattered, it was up to those who loved her to give it all back—if we could. I glanced up at Whisper. "How much of her is my grandmother, and how much is the demon?"

Whisper's gleaming yellow eyes narrowed. "I couldn't begin to guess. I haven't had any direct interaction with her since the gate opened; she's been avoiding me. And it's not as if this has happened so often that we have a deep understanding of how it works."

He sounded annoyed enough that I believed him. Which meant it was up to me to find out.

I took a deep breath to steady the squirming and fluttering that persisted in my stomach. "All right. I'll try to lure her out to speak to me again, so I can get a sense of who she is now. How much she's still *herself*, and what her goals and plans are."

"And try to remind her that she loves you and Morgrain," Kessa suggested. "Or anything else you think might help her decide that she wants humanity alive and more or less intact."

Whisper's ears flicked back in disgust. "If we've come to the point in the conversation where you're attempting to save humanity with the power of love, it's time for me to depart."

"Not really," I said, embarrassed. "We're talking about strengthening the parts of her that are my grandmother, so that she's more herself and less the demon."

His tail swished. "Utter foolishness. I came here to keep you from jumping to certain unfortunate conclusions. I see you found others far more ridiculous, and I will leave you to it."

He leaped down from the mantel and prowled into the patch of shadow from which he'd come. We all watched him go, but I doubted anyone in the room could pinpoint the moment when the dark space beneath the table no longer contained a chimera.

I tried to pull the scattered mess of my thoughts together. "All right. This makes it even more important that we destroy the gate as soon as possible. Do we have a plan for how to do so yet?"

"Bearing in mind that I haven't been able to translate all of the runes and symbols on the obelisk, so my understanding may not be completely correct..." Bastian flipped through his notebook, frowning at his diagrams. "Aside from the many layers of wards in the Black Tower, the enchantment seems to have two main pieces. The stone itself opens and closes an aperture of sorts to the Nine Hells—that line down the middle that glowed so brightly when Ryx touched it—in a reasonably controlled fashion. And the seal carved across it is like a lock on the door, holding it shut."

"Can we leave the seal intact, but disenchant the gate?" Foxglove asked, leaning over his shoulder.

Bastian tapped one of the diagrams of the obelisk's runes. "This part here is the problem. There's a whole section of the gate enchantment dedicated to protection against tampering of any kind. If we try to perform a disenchantment, or to alter the artifice designs so it doesn't work anymore, the protections will kill us. They're cleverly designed and quite powerful."

Foxglove's eyes lifted to mine, lighting with a sudden spark. "We could use Ryx."

"You don't *use* people, Foxglove, remember?" Kessa chided him. "We've been over this."

My heart lurched unpleasantly at the thought of unsealing my magic. But we had much graver concerns now. "I'd be happy to lend my power, if it would let us destroy the gate."

Bastian peered at his notes. "I think so. The protections are wound deeply into the gate enchantment itself; if you touched the gate, you'd be draining the power of the gate *and* the protections at once."

"I'd want to be careful not to deplete the seal again, though." I shuddered at the memory of the terrible white light, all the more sickening now that I knew it had come from the Hells themselves.

"There's some danger that you'd get the seal as well," Bastian said, looking between his notebook and the diagrams on the table. "The enchantments are all connected. That *should* be moot, however, since if you've taken the power from the gate, it can't open regardless. It's not impossible that there'd be a brief moment when the way was at least partly open if the seal drains faster than the gate itself does, though."

We all exchanged worried glances. My skin prickled thinking about the potential consequences if anything went wrong. If I couldn't be trusted in my own kitchens, how could we contemplate letting me tamper with the artifact that had triggered the Dark Days themselves?

Foxglove started pacing. "Is it worth the risk? What do you think, rooks?"

"Do we have another way to destroy it?" I asked.

Bastian hesitated, then shook his head. "Maybe with more time. But not by tomorrow night. It'll be hard enough preparing the disenchantment itself by then, without having to come up with a way around the protections."

"I don't think we *have* more time." I bit my lip. If the Shrike Lord already had his alliance in place, he'd have no reason not to invade immediately after the Rite of Blood and Water—unless I found some way to satisfy his grievance. Those Raverran warships would arrive off our coast soon, and once they did, the aggressive faction would only need to gain a momentary upper hand to start laying waste to Morgrain. And the Eldest could decide to intervene at any time; they wouldn't need to bring armies. They could walk up to Gloamingard themselves and take the gate, and no one could stop them.

Except possibly my grandmother.

"What will we do," I said slowly, "if my grandmother decides not to let us destroy the gate?"

Ashe let out a long breath. "Normally here's where I'd offer to stab her for you. And that offer stands, mind you, but I'm not sure it would do much."

Bastian rolled his pencil between his fingers, frowning thoughtfully, as if this were some problem his professors had set him and not a matter of the survival of humanity. "I think we want to use the wards. The ones that keep out everyone but your family. They're quite powerful—probably designed to stop demons, now that I think of it—and Foxglove could modify them to keep out your grandmother as well fairly easily. We'd only need a bit of her hair, or something of that sort."

"I can get you some from her brush," I offered.

"All right." Foxglove rubbed his hands together. "We've got until tomorrow evening to get this disenchantment together. Ryx, I'm counting on you to get the nations of Eruvia to hold off on unleashing destruction upon us in the meantime."

"That's all going to depend on the results of the Rite of Blood and Water," I said uneasily. "The Vaskandrans will abide by the rite, and the Empire—well, they'll probably at least wait until after the rite to see who their enemies and allies are before doing anything."

"I have faith in you," Foxglove said, with a glib confidence I wished I could believe in.

"Wait." Bastian lifted a hand, a worried frown drawing his brows together. "There's one more problem. If Ryx unleashes her power, it'll likely drain her jess, too. We don't know when or even *if* it'll work again—and if it doesn't, the Serene Empire may not be willing to give her another."

Everyone turned to look at me. Kessa came and put a hand on my shoulder, her eyes grave.

"That's a lot for us to ask, and frankly I feel like a stingroach for doing it," she said. Her warm, gentle touch was an active reminder of everything I had to lose. "You don't have to take the risk if you don't want to."

Hell of Nightmares. It had been one thing to live my life needing to avoid touch and stay away from people when that was all I knew. I'd developed strategies to deal with it and tried not to dwell on what I was missing. Going back to that life after my brief, sweet taste of human contact would be like being thrust back out into a snowstorm after only a few moments inside by a warm fire.

It would be a cold I was used to, at least, if a bitter one.

"I'll do it."

TWENTY-EIGHT

It was hard to meet the eyes of my guests at breakfast, over platters of sausage and eggs and brown bread hot from the ovens. Surely the truth would somehow show on my face—the horrible secret that it was too late to keep demons from coming through to Eruvia, and some sort of reckoning with the Nine Hells was already upon us.

All the work I'd done to try to preserve the peace wouldn't matter. As soon as word got out about my grandmother, all of Eruvia would unite against us. Morgrain's best chance at survival was the protective wrath of a demon, and no amount of tattered hope for my grandmother's humanity could cast that as anything but a catastrophe.

Voreth's sharp voice cut through the gloomy haze of my thoughts. "One wonders, Exalted Ryxander, about the state of the roads."

I blinked at him, a bit of smoked sausage still impaled on the end of my fork. "The roads."

"Yes." His tone grew acid. "The roads out of Gloamingard. I'm told that the land is *still* roused in anger, and anyone not from Morgrain stepping so much as an inch off the roads is in danger for their lives. Are we your guests, or your prisoners? It seems every corner of this castle hides a new abuse of hospitality!"

I set my knife down, slowly. I might not have my grand-mother's ability to darken the skies with leaning branches when she was angry, or the thunderous magical presence the rest of my family could muster, but I was done humoring him.

"Hospitality," I said quietly. "It's interesting you should bring that up, Honored Voreth."

Ardith grinned and leaned back in their chair as if getting ready to watch a show. Voreth, perhaps used to less subtle signs of danger from his lord, took in a sneering breath to reply.

I didn't let him. "Because you are my *guests*," I said, raising my voice. "Every one of you at this table. And yet one of you sought my death." Abrupt silence fell. Aurelio froze with his cup halfway to his lips; Lady Celia set down her fork.

I knew I should stop, but I couldn't. My voice grew sharper, colder, a sword blade sliding up under Voreth's chin. "One of you, sitting right here at my table, eating my bread and drinking my tea, is responsible for the *murder* of my aunt."

Suddenly, no one could meet my eyes. Every one of them looked guilty as a dog in the midden heap. I leaned on the table, palms flat against the wood.

"Morgrain hasn't forgotten," I said, anger expanding my voice to fill the Old Great Hall, "and neither have I. We will bring that murderer to my grandmother's justice, I assure you all." I spread my arms, taking in the bountiful breakfast laid out on the table. "But here I am, hosting you as graciously as ever, even though I know that one of you is my enemy. Because, Honored Voreth, I am the Warden of Morgrain, and I have a duty to my land and my people. I can set aside my personal grievances until we settle the greater issue of the gate, which threatens the peace of the entire region." I offered the entire table a short, stiff bow. "I'm sorry if you find it difficult to do the same."

With outward calm, I went back to eating my breakfast.

Seasons, that felt good. This must be how my family felt all the time: unafraid to take an entire room of important people to task, secure in the knowledge of their power. I had no such certainty, and my position was more than a little precarious, but curse me if it wasn't incredibly freeing to decide that just for this one moment, I didn't care.

Despite my outburst, everyone lingered after breakfast. Lady Celia and Aurelio talked seriously with Foxglove and Bastian about the gate, while Kessa struck up a conversation with Voreth about the Graces only knew what; I had to stay, as host, and be a diplomat again.

Severin approached me, his face guarded as a locked door. Hells, how much had he heard when I talked to my grandmother last night? I ran memory through my fingers, desperately trying to sift out what he might know.

"Exalted Ryxander," he greeted me. "It appears I have to manage without Honored Voreth's counsel for a few minutes. I find myself deeply bereft." His eyes flicked to where Voreth spoke to Kessa, gesturing agitatedly with his bone staff. Kessa listened with every appearance of rapt attention; I wondered if she were distracting him on purpose. "Perhaps I could console myself with a few moments of your conversation."

"I'll do my best to comfort you in this difficult hour." My mouth tugged toward a smile despite the seriousness of the situation. Still, my heart thumped faster as we moved away from the table, out of range of potential eavesdroppers; if he knew my grandmother was a demon, any hopes I might have of wringing peace out of the Rite of Blood and Water were dashed.

"I see you've given up playing it diplomatically safe," he murmured, his voice pitched low beneath the echoing voices in the hall. He stood close to keep his words from carrying—so close

I couldn't help but remember the feel of his hand on my back when we danced. I wasn't used to staring into faces from this close range, and damn him, he had truly fine cheekbones.

"There's no sense playing it safe when times are so dangerous," I replied, striving to keep my voice even.

"That's an understatement." Severin glanced over his shoulder at Voreth, halfway across the room. "I take it by the fact that I wasn't killed in my bed last night that you persuaded the Lady of Owls of my innocence."

"'Innocence' is a strong term," I said tartly.

"Perhaps. You're hardly guiltless yourself. And your grandmother seemed to be positively itching to do some murder," Severin replied.

Itching to do some murder was far better than *a demon*. He must not have heard anything. My shoulders began to relax.

"Given that she seems not to like me," he continued, "I'm eager to help you find your attacker—to save my own skin, if nothing else."

"So that you can direct the blame where you see fit?" I asked him pointedly.

He glanced away. "I may not know you all that well," he said, his voice oddly husky, "but dragging you around while you were trying to bleed to death all over me made a certain impression. Believe it or not, I feel irrationally invested in finding the killer and keeping you alive. Contrariness, I suppose."

He swallowed; the morning sun shone golden on the curve of his throat. *Seasons spare me.* It was so easy to argue with him, and so hard not to feel dizzily drawn to him at the same time.

I bowed my head. "I do owe you a debt for helping me."

"That's not why..." He broke off, sighing. "Suffice to say I want to give you what information I have, since I'd rather not become the target of the ire of a vengeance-crazed Witch Lord."

I lifted an eyebrow. "I hope you're aware of the irony of *you* saying that to *me*."

"Appreciating the irony around me is the only way I make it through most days." He flashed a grin, but then his tone sobered. "I can tell you that the assassin wasn't sent by Alevar."

"Would you know if they had been?" I let my skepticism bleed through. "It seems to me you aren't the one in control of the Alevaran delegation."

Severin winced. "All right, I'm sure Voreth has orders I don't know about. But he's been speculating that the same person killed Lamiel and Exalted Karrigan, and he wouldn't believe that if he were behind your aunt's killing himself. You can rule us out."

That was all plausible enough, but it also served Severin's interests. "Funny how you ask me to take that on faith, when you told me last night not to trust you," I pointed out.

"Ah, there's the trouble." His smile was all sharp edges. "I'm an atheling of an enemy domain and I'm only helping you to save my own skin. Which is exactly why you can *believe* me, but by no means should you trust me."

"Oh? To save your skin, you say?" I put my hands on my hips. "If Voreth believes Karrigan and Lamiel's killer to be the same, how will it satisfy your brother if we find the assassin and my grandmother takes her vengeance? What will you bring back to Alevar for him? The corpse?"

Severin bit his lip; the uncertainty of the gesture startled me, but I didn't let my wary stance soften. Finally, he sighed. "No. He's going to want to do it himself."

"Then it seems to me we're still left with a vengeful Witch Lord."

"I suppose I'll have to convince Voreth that Lamiel's killer was different." He glared at me. "Which isn't good for you, because he'll go back to suspecting your family. You make yourself hard to help."

"I never asked for your help."

"I can leave you bleeding on the floor next time, if you like," he snapped.

I grimaced. "I didn't say I wasn't grateful for it."

Severin shook his head, setting the long glossy tail of his hair to dancing. "If we can't come up with a likely suspect for Lamiel's death, I'm going to have to demand the gate at the Rite of Blood and Water. Which I'm certain will make me dreadfully popular with the Serene Empire."

"Forgive me if I feel popularity is the least of our concerns, given the circumstances," I said.

"Maybe I could just not go home," he said wistfully. "I could stay here, in your cursed castle, trying not to get killed by your terrifying grandmother, keeping warm through the winter by the heat from the gate to the Hells in your tower."

My brows flew up. "Your brother is *that* bad to live with?"

The question seemed to catch him off guard. "He's..." He frowned, and his voice softened, picking up an odd catch. "He isn't always. He can be affectionate, charming, downright heroic when the mood strikes him. He saved me from an assassin once." Severin grimaced. "Best not to mention what he did to the assassin afterward."

"But you want to escape him?"

"He can't forget how he came to be the Witch Lord, and he's grown more and more suspicious of me. Now if I say or do the slightest thing he interprets as a challenge, he changes quicker than a trap closing." Severin grinned, but it didn't reach his eyes. "You may have noticed that I have trouble keeping my clever comments to myself. It's rather wearying going through life never knowing when you'll suddenly get flung across the room for some chance remark, or because you looked at him the wrong way."

I frowned. "And you don't stand up to him?"

I expected him to laugh at me, but Severin dropped his eyes. "You can't stand up to a Witch Lord in his own domain, Ryxander. You know that."

"Ryx," I corrected him.

"What?" He looked up, surprised.

"Call me Ryx. At least when Voreth's not around." I lifted a finger between us. "And you absolutely *can* stand up to a Witch Lord in their own domain, if you're willing to face the consequences."

Severin snorted. "I don't want to die, thank you."

"Then why don't you run?" I challenged him. "If you hate it there so much, why don't you go live somewhere else? There are plenty of other domains that would be happy to take in a powerful mage like you."

He shook his head. "It's not that easy."

"I never said it was."

His face was too close to mine. Our eyes locked, mage mark to mage mark, and it was as if some energy passed between us. Anger sparked in his eyes.

"*You* have a loving, supportive family," he hissed. "You have no idea what it's like."

I couldn't help myself; I laughed. "Loving and supportive? My aunt said our domain would be better off if I'd died as a child. My uncle has met my eyes maybe six times in my life. Vikal called me a murderous freak."

"But they never..." He stopped, and rubbed the scar that ran down from his temple. "How did we get here? We're supposed to be talking about how to stop my brother from invading your domain."

"Maybe if you were willing to stop appeasing him, that would be a good starting point."

I immediately regretted saying it. He'd just shown me a soft spot; now wasn't the time to jab him in it. Hurt flashed in Severin's eyes.

Before I could find some way to soften my words, Voreth strode toward us, a satisfied almost-smile sitting at odds with his sour face, no doubt pleased with whatever lecture he'd given Kessa. I spotted her behind him at the table, pouring herself a rather early glass of beer; she gave me a wink and made a face.

Severin's entire posture shifted as Voreth approached, tension returning to his shoulders and spine. "Let's talk again soon," he said. His voice was quiet, but a cold stiffness had returned to it. "And . . . thank you. For stopping her from killing me last night."

"Just paying back my favor," I said, tension flaring down my nerves as it finally sank in that he had carried me bodily around Gloamingard in those lean-muscled arms while I was unconscious.

"Is that all?" An odd catch entered his voice.

Before I could frame a reply or even try to read the fleeting vulnerability in his eyes, Voreth arrived, and the moment was gone.

The wind stroked shivers from the wild grasses that buried half the stone circle. Blue sky stretched above, and the lumpy green earth below; Gloamingard held the two braced apart, all claw-like points and sharp angles, crowning the hill on whose side I stood. A few lichen-scarred gray stones lay on their sides, bones half showing through the grass; a handful more still stood, leaning at odd angles.

This place had always drawn me. Now I was using it to try to draw out my grandmother.

I could barely make out the runes, faint as the line a child's finger might draw in dry sand. But I knew what they said, from all the days I had explored here when I was small, leaving a trail of dead withered grass behind me.

Nothing must unseal the Door.

Pieces of the Gloaming Lore poked from beneath the smothering earth, on these stones older even than the keep at the heart of the castle, from the time of the ancient republic that rose after the Dark Days and fell to the Storm Queens. At the center of the ring, a newer stone stood taller than the rest, the lines carved into it sharper and more deeply. It bore another piece of lore that had been added at the same time the old stone keep was built, in the time of the bandit kings, when strong walls were necessary and sufficed:

I stand before the light
And hold the dark at bay
I am the guard at the gloaming

I'd known this was where the castle's name came from, even as a child, but I'd assumed it had something to do with the way the light of dawn and sunset caught on the castle walls. Now, as I traced the words carved in rough rock with a bare finger, it all seemed so much clearer.

It was my family's task to stand before the terrible white light of the Hells and stop it from spreading, to keep the Dark Days from falling upon us again. To hold our secret place in the twilight shadows and guard against both dark and light.

Maybe I hadn't failed that trust after all. Not yet. It all depended on exactly how much of herself my grandmother retained.

"I suppose you're going to insist on doing this."

I glanced up, not really surprised, to find Whisper looming above me, perched on top of the center stone.

"You don't want me to talk to her," I said. "Interesting."

"It would be easier for me if you would stop trying to learn things you're only going to regret knowing."

I met his yellow eyes, unblinking. "Easier for you to do what, exactly?"

His tail swished back and forth, painting his thoughts on the rock, but he didn't answer.

Time to try being blunt. "You seem to know a great deal about demons, for a chimera."

"You seem to have a great many questions, for a human," he retorted.

I plucked a strand of grass and rolled it between my fingers, eyeing him with wary frustration. "I like you, Whisper. I trust you, even. But I don't know what you're trying to do. You've said yourself that we may not be on the same side. And now my grandmother is a demon. If your loyalty is to her, where does that leave us?"

He stared at me a long time, blinking only once. Finally, he spoke. "My loyalty is to myself."

"Well, that's something, anyway." I shook my head. That was even less reason I should trust him, but I couldn't help it. He might not often tell me the whole truth, but he'd never lied to me. "Yes, since you asked, I do insist on talking to my grandmother. I have to try to find some way to keep this all from unraveling into total disaster."

"You can't," he said softly.

My breath skipped roughly in my chest. "What do you mean?"

What did he know that I didn't? Had more demons already come through the gate? I couldn't take more bad news, not now, when everything I was trying to save already balanced on the edge of a cliff of futility.

"You always did like this place," came a hauntingly familiar voice, rough as the stones around me, deep as the roots of the earth, fathomless as the sky.

I turned, my heart aching with each beat as if she'd impaled it on a pike, and faced my grandmother.

TWENTY-NINE

She crouched atop one of the fallen stones with animal comfort, wind stirring her white hair. Herself and not herself. Human and demon.

I swallowed, my dry throat rasping. "We both did. It's peaceful here."

The fierce orange rings of her mage mark flicked up to Whisper. "And you? Joining our little family talk?"

Whisper gazed down at her, aloof, inscrutable. "I'm here to protect my promise."

"Huh." My grandmother's eyes narrowed. "That's going to be difficult now, you know."

"Nevertheless."

I barely heard them. I couldn't take my eyes off her face, seeking out and finding every familiar freckle, the laugh lines beside her eyes, the faint crease between her brows.

"I missed you," I blurted, and immediately felt like a fool.

Her eyes softened, a little. As much as they ever did. "But that's not why you're here, is it."

"No." I swallowed. "I'm here to talk."

"To spy," my grandmother corrected, her teeth shining sharp in the golden autumn light. "To find out my plans, my intentions, my secrets. To gain a hold over me, if you can." She tilted her head. "At least, I *hope* that's why you're here. I'd be very disappointed in you if it were simply a social visit."

I'd come here to find out who and what she was, but I was perilously close to wanting nothing more than a hug and a soothing word. To be a child again, here in this circle, clearing dirt and grass away from the stones so I could read the runes. Safe, protected, and oblivious to the dangers these very ruins warned me against.

But Whisper was right. Everyone changed, and nothing could make you again who you were before. I couldn't become a child under my grandmother's wing any more than I could return her to exactly who she had been.

I forced a smile. "Since you mention it, I don't suppose you'd like to tell me what you intend to do now? I'd love to be able to reassure the Rookery that you've got no ambitions greater than a bit of gardening, and Eruvia will never know you're here."

She chuckled, a sound that made my stomach drop half a story. "Oh, Eruvia will know."

"This isn't a joke," I said, urgency burning in my lungs beneath the words. "The Empire and the other Witch Lords are bound to learn about you soon. And when they do, if we can't assure them that you're not a threat, they'll—"

"Try to kill me?" my grandmother interjected. She laughed, a full-body laugh as if the idea were ridiculous, but it faded abruptly, and her expression turned sober. "Do you think I deserve to die for being a demon?"

"No," I said, instinctively and fiercely. "Of course you don't."

"I doubt many people will agree with you," she said, irony edging her voice.

I grimaced. "The Dark Days did leave deep scars on Eruvia's memory."

"The Dark Days?" The demon that was my grandmother

snorted her contempt. "The Dark Days were a mistake. We came through that gate knowing nothing about this world, with no way to understand what we were perceiving and experiencing. We were beings of pure energy, suddenly taking on physical forms in a world of matter and life. We flailed about with no idea what we were doing, each following our own nature and impulses. Without goals, without plans. And *still* we essentially destroyed civilization."

"And now?" I asked, hugging myself against the chill that originated not from the wind teasing my braid and vestcoat, but from deep within, called up by her words.

My grandmother looked about her, taking in the hillside in a proprietary, satisfied sort of way. "Now I am human," she said. "I have human desires and human loves. And I will protect what is mine."

"You could protect it better if there were peace in the region," I suggested.

The gaze she turned on me was strange, almost pitying. "There will be no peace, Ryx, and you know it."

"I won't accept that," I said stubbornly. "No matter how unlikely it seems, I have to try."

She tilted her head as if I were a curious animal, some stranger to her domain she'd never seen before. "I made a mistake with you, Ryx," she murmured.

"What do you mean?" The mad intensity was back in her eyes; I took an instinctive step away from it.

"I should never have taught you to suppress your power, to reject the damage you cause." She rose with a predator's slow grace, balanced on her stone, slim as a knife but far more deadly. "I should have raised you to embrace what you can do. To revel in the glorious wake of chaos you leave behind. I can see that now."

I fell back another step, into the shadow of the central stone, my heart stumbling. Her power unfolded invisibly around her, charging the cool dry air with the hum of an impending storm. I clamped a hand over the golden jess circling my wrist, instinctively protecting it. "I like it better this way, I assure you."

Whisper leaped down from his stone, landing on the wind-flattened grass beside me. He stretched, yawning to show his teeth.

"I think this has gone far enough," he said.

My grandmother chuckled, and the pressure of her power eased. "So protective."

"You asked me to be," Whisper said.

Ah. Perhaps that was it; his mysterious promise had been to keep me out of trouble. A strange disappointment tugged at me; it was so simple, so benign.

But no. I did risky things all the time, and he didn't seem to feel obliged to stop me—and he hadn't seemed concerned that the attempt on my life had endangered his promise. He was far more protective of the Black Tower and its secrets than he was of me. He must be referring to a more simple, mundane request, of the sort he could feel free to ignore when it was inconvenient.

My grandmother looked at me—truly *looked* at me, in the way she always had, where her eyes seemed to pierce through to my soul and absorb everything there was to know about me in one glance.

"So I did," she said softly. "Very well, Ryx. I suppose you've learned enough for one day. You can go back and give your friends your assessment on the dangers I pose."

She turned to go. I didn't want her to leave, even knowing she was a demon; even feeling the wrongness, the bright sharp edge in every movement and look.

"And what should I tell them?" I called after her, barely stopping myself from reaching out.

My grandmother glanced back over her shoulder. A sickle-sharp grin split her face, and her eyes burned with an unholy light.

"Tell them that it doesn't matter whether I'm a threat or not," she said. "Because if I am, there's nothing they can do to stop me."

Bastian stared at me, eyes wide. His teacup had frozen halfway to his mouth when I told him about my grandmother's sudden appearance in the stone circle, and had stayed there through my increasingly distraught description of our conversation.

"...And she was *right there*, Bastian. Right there in front of me, like she was never gone. It was her, and it wasn't." I swallowed a great scalding gulp of tea.

I wasn't sure Bastian had blinked more than about twice since I showed up at the Rookery guest quarters with the last vestiges of my precious control slipping through my fingers; I'd found him the only one there, with the others out on various business. *Stop*, I told myself. *This is too much. Look at his face.* But my mouth kept going, disgorging the whole messy tangle of my feelings on the paper-strewn table between us.

"I don't know what to do. She's not dead, so I can't mourn her. She's still my grandmother, so I can't hate her. She's also a *demon* who remembers causing the Dark Days, and I can't..." I gestured wildly around the room. The words that had tumbled out of me in an incoherent rush abandoned me all at once.

Bastian set his teacup down, slowly and carefully as if it might explode. "She still seems to care about you."

"*Yes.* That's part of what makes it so awful. She's still my grandmother, but she's not..." I shuddered. "Not human."

Bastian winced. He settled back in his chair, tugging at his jacket collar. "I suppose that depends on how you define humanity. The philosophers have different opinions on the subject."

"What do you mean?" I didn't honestly give two figs about

something as abstract as philosophy right now, but I was willing to clutch at any hope he had to offer.

"If I understand correctly, she's both herself and a demon." A strange, wistful smile crept onto his face. "One could argue that whether she still possesses *humanity* depends on how she makes her choices."

I twisted my teacup on its saucer for something to do with my hands. "I don't know, Bastian. I looked in her eyes for my grandmother, and I *found* her. But there was something else there, too. She wants to protect Morgrain, but there was this wildness, almost cruelty—I think she would do things now she never would have done before." I squeezed my eyes shut, then opened them again. "I don't know what choices she'll make. I'm not sure she knows, herself."

"Maybe," Bastian said, his voice husky with more emotion than I expected, "she's still figuring that out. Maybe she doesn't know how human she is, either. Maybe what happens now—how we all respond to her, how we talk to her, what choices she's faced with—will determine the answer to that question."

There was a quaver in his voice, and an odd flush had crept up his neck to his cheeks. I'd never seen him so passionate. For some reason, this mattered to him a great deal.

Curiosity shook me half out of the dark sinking pool I'd been caught in. I knew so little about Bastian—but he seemed to be struggling not to show how agitated this conversation was making him, so I wasn't sure now was the time to ask.

"I suppose," I said slowly, "the question isn't truly whether she's technically human. It's whether she's a good person." I thought that over and amended, "Or good enough."

Bastian nodded enthusiastically. "Yes. Like that fox chimera—you consider him a friend, don't you? Even though he's not human by any definition?"

He threw out the example as if he'd picked it randomly, but

something about the way he waited still and quivering for my reply suggested he cared far more about my answer than he was willing to admit.

Ah. Suddenly, a dozen small details made sense: Bastian's odd-colored flushes, his flinches at certain inexplicable moments—the way he waited for my reply so intently now, as if he had a great personal investment in the answer.

"Of course," I said. It was a bit more complicated than that with Whisper, but for Bastian's sake, I let no doubt enter my voice. "The fact that he's a chimera doesn't matter. He's my friend."

And I held Bastian's gaze, willing him to understand.

His eyes widened, showing whites all the way around. He opened his mouth, then closed it. "Oh! Oh. Ah, well."

A blush crept up his neck, and now that I was looking for it, I could tell that it was the wrong color. A shade too purple. And his skin bumped up in its wake, like gooseflesh—or scales.

"Who did this to you?" I started to reach toward his face but dropped my hand, still not sure when touch was helpful or allowed.

The fear in his eyes tore at my heart. He'd never been frightened of me, not when I admitted to killing Lamiel or when I unleashed the power of the gate, but he was frightened now. His chest heaved with quick breaths, and the flush didn't retreat as it always had in the past, but deepened almost to violet.

"I'm sorry," I said, inwardly cursing myself. "I shouldn't have said anything. I don't want to intrude."

He stared at me for a long moment, his pulse pounding visibly in his throat. Slowly some of the terror went out of his eyes.

"It was my sponsor," he said quietly. "The one who paid for my education."

I grimaced. "You'd mentioned he turned out not to be as benevolent as you'd thought, but I had no idea. That's terrible. He was a Skinwitch?"

Bastian shook his head. "No. He was a member of the Zenith Society. As was the Skinwitch. When I realized some of the things my mentor was asking me to research weren't ethical, I refused to help him anymore, and he turned me over to his colleague for his experiments." He managed to smile, somehow, almost apologetically; that smile felt like a bleeding wound in my chest. "He modified me for stealth. See?"

He scrunched up his face, and colors swept across his skin in waves, like a shaken sand painting. When they settled, he matched the woody hues of the log-walled room perfectly.

"That's impressive." I wasn't sure it was the right thing to say, but an awkward compliment seemed better than acting like it was something he should be ashamed of. Graces knew I'd been on the receiving end of that often enough myself. "I'm sorry you went through all that. For what it's worth, though, I like who you are now. And...you seem happy with the Rookery?"

"Oh, yes." He relaxed, and the colors of polished wood drained from his face, returning it to his normal olive shade. "They're the ones who rescued me and got that branch of the Zenith Society thrown in prison, years ago. They're my dear friends."

"And they know?"

He waved his hands as if to stop me from doing something dangerous. "Foxglove and Kessa, yes, but Ashe doesn't! Please don't tell her. She's a chimera hunter. She'd *probably* be fine, but..."

"I understand." I grimaced. "Believe me, as someone used to getting mistaken for a Skinwitch and treated accordingly, I do."

"So you understand why the question of humanity is so important to me." A wistfulness softened his eyes. "I *have* to believe that whether you're technically completely human doesn't matter."

"You're human enough," I said firmly. "More human than the ones who did this to you."

He ducked his head. "Maybe the Lady of Owls is human enough, too."

"A demon, though..." A shiver ran bone-deep through my whole body, as if I had a high fever. "That's different than a chimera. Do you truly think one of the *Nine Demons* can be redeemed?"

Bastian hesitated, his dark eyes clouded. "I suppose that depends on what they've done. Whether they're the same person now. And what choices they make from this point on."

I let out a long breath. Pox. That made sense, but it didn't make anything simpler. "I need to somehow get my grandmother to make human choices."

"Yes," Bastian agreed, smoothing the cover of his notebook as to soothe it. "Not only for her own sake, but for the future of Eruvia."

I struggled to sort out the chaos of my thoughts as I headed to find Odan and talk about setting up for the Rite of Blood and Water. It was all too much; I couldn't face the emotions that snarled within me whenever I thought about everything that had happened. One by one, I peeled threads from the tangle and stuffed them down somewhere deep inside, to deal with later: Lamiel's death, the gate, my aunt's murder, the nations converging on Gloamingard to destroy it, the attempt on my life.

My grandmother. My stride faltered, and the lurch of grief climbed up my throat and set my eyes to stinging.

I'd handed control of the domain I protected to the Demon of Discord and more or less destroyed the life of one of the people I loved most in the world. How in the Nine Hells was I supposed to bottle that up and move on?

I rubbed my eyes with ruthless vigor. I didn't have time for this. I had to focus on what I could *do*.

"Ryxander—Ryx! Wait!"

It was Severin's voice, low and urgent. I turned with a strange tingling surge along my nerves to find him hurrying after me, glancing over his shoulder.

"Voreth's in an argument with Honored Ardith," he said. "He'll realize they're just riling him up on purpose soon, and then he'll notice I'm gone. Is there somewhere we can talk where he won't find us?"

We were in a place where the Lady of Badgers' rough log walls overtook the Mantis Lord's Bone Palace. I stood on the bone side of the division, beneath arching ceiling beams of polished ivory and corner moldings of patterned vertebrae. Severin looked out of place on the warm, homey, simple side, slim and elegant in his long black vestcoat embroidered with a diagonal sweep of abstract feather designs in gold thread.

Someone had tried to kill me. I shouldn't talk to *anyone* in private, let alone the brother of my mortal enemy—but Severin had saved my life, and the urgency on his face was honest enough.

My mother always said the Grace of Luck favored those who took risks.

I slipped my fingers through a gap where a sawn-off log end didn't quite meet up with the first curving rib of bone. It only took a light tug to swing the entire section of logs open just enough to admit one person at a time.

"In here," I told him, and slipped through into a forgotten space of dust and shadows.

Severin followed without hesitation, and I pulled the hidden door shut behind us.

THIRTY

The place I took Severin wasn't some impressive secret chamber, but only a leftover bit of architecture that didn't fit the Lady of Badgers' plans, like so many odd places in Gloamingard. Once this had perhaps been the corner of a garden courtyard, but now only a narrow triangular shaft of outdoors remained, floored with moss and weeds. Twilight streamed down from several stories above us, and the air held the biting chill of a place that never saw direct sunlight. The log walls that had been built over the courtyard loomed on two sides; on the third, a fanciful arch bordered with bone-chip mosaics housed the rubble of a broken fountain that had been ruined for centuries. A startled bird crossed the light above, wings fluttering shadows down upon us.

Severin glanced up, around, and then at me in a kind of wonder. "Can you just open up a door anywhere?"

I laughed. "In Gloamingard? Not quite, but close enough. What do you want?"

It sounded too harsh, too businesslike, but I didn't have the gentleness in me for pleasant chatter right now. And Severin didn't look as if he wanted to waste any time, either.

"I have bad news," he said, his voice low, glancing instinctively around as if he expected Voreth would find us even here. "I found out who my brother's allies are against you. He's got one of the Eldest on his side."

Hell of Despair. I swayed as if he'd pushed me. "Which one?"

"The Elk Lord." Severin's fingers flicked out from his chest. "Apparently my brother convinced him that his grievance is valid, and he's concerned about your plans to close the gate."

I pulled my braid over my shoulder and began worrying fiercely at its tip. No matter how alarming it might be to imagine the phenomenal power of the Eldest turned against my home, I couldn't let fear overwhelm me; I had to think. The Elk Lord's vast domain lay north of Alevar, and old blood ties connected them. But the Eldest usually stayed out of local disputes, and the Elk Lord was a traditionalist and a stickler for protocol.

"He's using your brother's grievance as an excuse," I guessed. "This is about the gate for him, isn't it? He's one of the ones worried that closing it will disrupt the cycle of magic."

"It seems likely," Severin agreed. "You know how he hates change. He's made it clear he'll abide by the results of the Rite of Blood and Water, though. If my brother accepts payment for his grievance, the Elk Lord will have no proper cause to attack Morgrain, and he'll stay out of it."

Pox rot everything. I'd just about decided to tell the Shrike Lord to stuff his grievance at the rite this evening; he couldn't stop us from destroying the gate, and I'd hoped he was bluffing about having an alliance sufficient to back an invasion. If he had one of the Eldest on his side, that was no bluff, and we'd find out all too quickly whether my grandmother's arrogance about her ability to destroy anyone who trifled with Morgrain was warranted.

Revealing that she was a demon in the process when she unleashed powers that no Witch Lord should have. Which would turn all of Eruvia immediately against us and undo half the purpose of destroying the gate.

I pressed a hand to my temple. "This is not what I need right now."

"Unfortunately, you and my brother have different priorities." Severin took a breath. "Now, I have an idea. If you declare that Exalted Karrigan was the one who killed Lamiel, that will at the very least buy us some time."

I stared at him, not bothering to hide my disgust. "Truly? You're suggesting I blame my own departed kin for the death Exalted Lamiel brought on herself?"

Severin stiffened. "Only in the context of saving your domain from an invasion."

The situation might be dire, but there were some lines I couldn't cross. "I'm not accusing my dead aunt of a murder she didn't commit."

"Then pick someone else!" Severin threw his hands up, apparently as exasperated by me as I was by him. "Pick some local villager who died this week and claim they were a hired assassin! I don't care. We just need to give him a name. Someone he can't hurt, because they're already dead."

"It wouldn't be the truth," I insisted.

He stared at me as if I were some strange creature making cries unintelligible to humans. "The truth doesn't matter. Surely you can see that."

"It matters. Consequences might fall on the scapegoat's family. Their community would know it wasn't true, and I'd be showing my people that I don't value their honor. If word got out, no one would trust me to pay grievances fairly." I shook my head. "Shall I go on?"

Severin slashed the air with an impatient hand. "That's all ifs and maybes. We need to give my brother what he wants, or he'll—"

"Do we?" I cut in sharply. "Do we really need to appease him?"

"Yes!" Severin stepped closer to me, his hands lifting as if he wanted to grab my shoulders, but then they dropped to his sides. "You don't know what he's like, Ryx."

"You're right," I agreed, softening my voice. "I don't. I hope I never find out. And you should never have had to learn." I held his gaze. In this light, his storm-gray mage mark almost vanished into his dark irises; but it was still there, gleaming faintly like tarnished silver. "*That's* why I have to oppose him."

Severin winced and looked away, his gaze latching on to the ruined fountain as if it were of intense interest. "You are an incredibly difficult person. I'm trying to help you avert a war."

"Are you?" I tilted my head, watching the light stream over his sculpted face. "Everything you've suggested seems aimed at soothing your brother's wrath, which is more likely to save your own skin than prevent a war in the long run."

"You've caught me," he said, with forced lightness. "In this case, however, those interests happen to align."

I didn't believe him for a moment. "And if I told you that I'd thought of a way to avoid a war *without* giving your brother what he wants?" I challenged.

Severin blinked. "How?"

By getting the Shrike Lord's grievance declared invalid. The Elk Lord, cautious and honorable, would never commit himself to a publicly dubious cause. But if Severin would always act as his brother's dutiful agent, no matter how little he liked to do so, I couldn't tell him that—it would give him time to prepare to counter me at the rite.

"Your answer," I insisted. "Which would you choose, if you could only do one? Satisfy your brother's wrath, or keep him from invading Morgrain?"

"I..." Severin looked down at his own hands, curled into fists at his sides. He shook his head. "It's not that simple. It depends on the situation and the specifics; backing a foolish or shortsighted play accomplishes nothing. Do you have a plan, or are you just throwing out hypothetical questions?"

"I have a plan," I admitted. "I can't promise it's a good one. And if I told it to you, I'd put you in a position where you'd have to betray either me or the Shrike Lord."

Severin's mouth twisted. "And you don't trust me."

"No. I don't want to do that to you." I tried a smile, but it came out too soft, too painful around the edges. Curse him, he kept muddling feelings into my diplomacy. "Let me handle this. I'll take on the risk of your brother's wrath myself."

Severin let out a bitter sound, halfway between a laugh and a huff of disbelief. "It must be nice. To be so certain you can be brave, and that it will lead to anything but pain and death."

"I'm *not* sure." I pushed back loose tendrils of hair from my face, wishing I could as easily clear the cloud of dread that hovered over me. "To be honest, everything I do seems to lead to pain and death more often than not. Sometimes I think Aunt Karrigan was right, and that the world would be better off without me." Hells, I shouldn't have said that. He was looking at me so strangely, his face still, his eyes shadowed. I lifted my chin, determined not to flinch away. "But, Severin, I have to keep trying."

His brow furrowed. "I don't understand you at all."

He was one of the first people who'd bothered to try. A scalding tightness seized my throat.

"Oh, I'm easy to understand," I said. His dark eyes drank me in; I couldn't look away if I wanted to. "You, on the other hand, wear a lot of masks, Severin of Alevar. I'd love to find out what's under them. Do you even know yourself?"

I reached toward his face. I couldn't quite bring myself to cross the last few inches to the smooth, sharp line of his cheekbone.

He sucked in a breath as if I'd struck him. The twilight drew a line of shadow down to his jaw from his temple, along his faint old scar.

"Hells take you," he muttered.

I dropped my hand, disappointed.

He caught it in his cold, lean one and raised my palm to lay it, trembling, against his cheek. *So warm.*

"Help me," he said hoarsely. "Help me find out."

His life pulsed miraculously against my fingertips. The thrill that traveled up my arm from where I touched him wasn't magic, nor was the warmth that flooded me. The jess gleamed on my wrist like a promise.

"I have the scandalous suspicion," I breathed, "that beneath them all, you may be a good man."

His lips quirked toward a self-mocking smile. "Impossible."

Hells, his face was close. His eyes had gone soft and aching. I wanted to show him he was safe, here. That he didn't have to be vicious to survive, or let his brother shape who he was.

I couldn't do any of that while a huge lie stood between us.

"I'm sure of it," I said, my voice gone husky with emotion. "I'll show you how sure I am. Do you want to know the truth? Who really killed Lamiel?"

Something flickered in his eyes. He lifted a finger and laid it across my lips, a cool warning.

"No," he said. "Don't tell me."

I pulled back from his touch, the moment broken. "You saved my life," I said. "I owe you the truth."

"I don't want the truth," Severin whispered. "I'm too afraid of it. Because I know what the truth can do."

THIRTY-ONE

Three hours before dusk I was in my room, answering messages and writing letters and trying not to think about the upcoming Rite of Blood and Water, when a soft but decisive knock sounded at my door. I rose and opened it cautiously; Ashe had insisted on standing guard, so I didn't have any fear of assassins, but at this point I expected a new emergency every time I so much as opened a cupboard or heard someone call my name.

It was Foxglove. He lifted a bottle of wine and both eyebrows. "Need a drink?"

"I don't drink," I said. Though with the jess, I theoretically could, but I saw no reason to get sloppy in habits that might still save the lives around me.

Foxglove shrugged. "Want to watch me drink, then?"

"All right." I stepped aside for him, desperately curious as to what this might be about.

Foxglove strolled over to my breakfast table, hooked its single chair out with his foot, and had the wine bottle open almost before he finished settling in it.

"You and I, Ryx," he said, pouring himself a glass, "have a difficult decision to make tonight."

"Oh?" I pulled over my desk chair, the only other seat in the room, and sank down warily opposite him.

"About your grandmother," he said.

Well, pox. I didn't want to think about my grandmother. I froze, trapped.

"Specifically, what to tell the governments of Vaskandar and the Empire about her." Foxglove lifted his glass to me. "Sure you don't want some?"

"We can't tell them," I objected instinctively. "They'll all turn on Morgrain in a panic, just as they did over the gate."

"Believe me, I'm aware of the irony of Eruvia throwing itself into chaos in order to try to fight the Demon of Discord." Foxglove drained half his glass, then topped it off again. "I hope you can also see that we can't keep information this important to ourselves. We can't let the demon catch Eruvia unaware."

The demon. I couldn't call her that, or think of her like that; she was still my grandmother. I laced my fingers together on the table to keep my hands out of trouble.

"I don't trust them to make decisions for me about something this important," I said, forcing my voice flat. "Not the other Witch Lords, and not the doge and the Council of Nine."

"That's the crux of the problem," Foxglove agreed. He eyed his glass as if it were an old enemy, then downed another long swallow. "I made the mistake of putting blind trust in my superiors, once."

"Your superiors in the Rookery?"

"No." He paused a long moment, considering the glass in his hand. "My superiors in the imperial assassins."

"Oh!" I made absolutely certain not to push my chair back away from him, because I hated when people did that to me. "You must be, ah, very good."

The imperial assassins were an open secret, an implicit dagger hidden behind the Serene Empire's smile. No one seemed to know how many there were, or much about them, and none could point to an instance where the Empire had definitively used them, but everyone knew they existed. My mother had cynically surmised that the Empire might not even make use of their talents at all—the mere fact of their existence was enough to give that extra bit of leverage to certain negotiations.

Foxglove shrugged off the compliment. "I've lost my edge, these days. Let's just say there's a reason I hate the Zenith Society, and I understand your reluctance to trust the government better than you'd think. But they still need to know that there's a demon loose."

I pulled my braid over my shoulder and began reworking it, as if by unraveling my hair I could unravel the problem. "We still don't know what my grandmother's going to do, and we have no idea what the best way to respond is going to be. Right now she's not doing any harm."

Foxglove cocked one eyebrow. "She deliberately leaked information that could still cause a global war."

"All right, fine. But that's what she did when she was *playing*." I shivered. "We have a relatively stable situation now. If we attack her and make her angry—if we set something off before we have any idea how we're going to deal with her—it could get so very much worse."

Wine made its rising music as it flowed into Foxglove's cup. "I do sometimes wish it weren't my job to deal with these things."

"I know the feeling."

We both thought for a moment about the dark and terrible consequences if we bungled this—or at least, I assumed Foxglove thought about that. I was mostly staring into a random corner of my room in blank horror. Every time I tried to wrap my understanding around the idea that a demon was loose in Morgrain—never mind that she was also my grandmother—my mind shied away.

"Have you considered that you may find it easier to get backing for destroying the gate at the Rite of Blood and Water if people know there's a demon already in the world?" Foxglove asked. "Fear is a powerful motivator, and no one will want her to let more demons through." He took a more cautious sip of wine, his half-hooded eyes pensive. "Right now we've got Witch Lords wanting to avoid meddling with the gate and a major Raverran faction hot to study it. There's no guarantee I won't get orders any minute to leave it alone, and I have to follow them if I do. But this rite has enough representatives of imperial and Vaskandran governments involved that if they back us, we can go ahead and destroy it as soon as we have the enchantment ready, and it would take an unequivocal command at the highest levels to stop us."

"You have a point." I closed my eyes. It was too easy to imagine the fiery orange rings of my grandmother's mage mark watching us from the shadows in my room. "I'd vastly prefer not to play that card yet unless I have to, however."

Silence fell between us. Then Foxglove sighed. "I'll tell you what. I won't report anything to my superiors until after we destroy the gate. After all, we don't have any proof your grandmother is a demon, and I wouldn't want to alarm them with an unconfirmed theory."

"Thank you," I said, with feeling.

"As for the Rite of Blood and Water... Well." Foxglove emptied his glass and set it decisively on the table. "I'm trusting you to come up with a brilliant and clever plan sometime before sunset."

The sun was getting low, and I didn't have a brilliant and clever plan yet.

The Aspen Hall trembled with whispers. The golden leaves

above us shimmered in a wind that I certainly couldn't feel down on the floor, if it existed at all. Diplomats and aides stood in tight clusters of two and three, rumor and truth twined together around them like strands of smoke, hissing and spreading like wildfire.

The Rookery moved through the hall, lighting those flames and putting them out. Kessa soothed tempers with a touch or a laugh, bringing people drinks, calming and charming with her gracious smile. Foxglove and Bastian laid out the plan for destroying the gate with convincing logic and detail. Ashe lurked in the corners like the Demon of Death, her grin daring the murderer to try anything under her watch.

It was our last chance to privately try to get everyone on our side before the Rite of Blood and Water. Everyone could see the sun bleeding out on the crest of the hills through the windows. We were almost out of time.

There was at least one more person I needed to talk to before the rite began—one vital ally whose support I had to confirm.

Thirty years ago, when my grandmother made Odan her steward, some of the more ambitious mages in Morgrain were offended. She'd told me, with a chuckle, that some had even dared to ask her how she could have chosen *him* as her steward, when he had not a drop of magic in him and there were plenty of mages, marked and otherwise, eager for such a prestigious post.

My grandmother had told them that the choice was simple: she already had plenty of magic, and didn't need more. Odan had something she *did* need.

As a child, I'd never thought to ask what that was. Odan had so many clear virtues that he seemed an obvious choice; his excellence was a given. Now, however, I wondered. If the virtue she'd prized him for turned out to be, say, undying personal loyalty, I could be about to make a terrible mistake.

I pulled him aside in an empty corner of the Aspen Hall, dropping my voice barely above a whisper. "Odan, I need to warn you about something. No one else in the castle knows besides the Rookery—no one else *can* know, not yet, not even Jannah."

"Of course, Warden." Odan's gray brows descended like storm clouds. "This is about the Lady of Owls, isn't it?"

I stared at him. "How did you know?"

He shrugged, an uncomfortable movement. "I had a dream that I saw her, Exalted Warden. If it *was* a dream. The touch of the Hells is on her, isn't it?"

The knot in my throat tightened. I forced myself to nod. "If she comes back—returns to Gloamingard and starts giving orders—what will you do? She's still the Witch Lord."

He met my gaze squarely. "I told you before. I'm a guardian, the same as you. This castle is my charge." He shrugged off the horrifying implications of a demon Witch Lord as if they were irrelevant, mere dust that had fallen on his shoulders. "If her orders would harm the castle or the people in it, I won't obey, and I'll tell her so. That was the promise I made her when I took my post, Warden."

A rush of gratitude coursed through me, so strong my eyes stung. "It's good to know I can count on you, Odan. Listen— if all goes well at the Rite of Blood and Water, we're going to attempt to destroy the gate directly afterward. It's too dangerous to risk letting it fall into the hands of anyone who wouldn't guard it as vigilantly as you have."

He gave a slow nod. "I understand, Warden. If the lady appears while you're working on that, I'll see what I can do to distract her."

"Thank you." I took a deep breath. "I'd like you to increase the guard around the old stone keep. Cover every possible entrance with battle chimeras and human guards—use everyone we've got if you have to. I want guards on every window and door, every hole in the wall big enough for a cat to crawl through, every secret passage that leads there, every roof and tower and wall an enterprising person with a grappling hook could leap to or climb."

Odan nodded, shifting his weight to his toes with readiness. "I'll see it done, Warden. Good luck with the rite."

There was more I wanted to say—so much more—but we both had jobs to do. I returned his nod and let him go do his.

Severin prowled the hall like a restless panther on a leash, Voreth lurking behind him as always. Now that I'd begun to know him better, I could read the tension in the set of his shoulders, the uncertainty shadowing his eyes. Sympathy pinched my heart; I had to protect Morgrain first, but by the Graces, I'd do what I could to make sure he wouldn't face unpleasant consequences when he went back home.

If he went home. Small flames of anger licked up inside my ribs at the memory of his scars. Maybe I could convince him to stay here and escape his brother altogether.

Ardith sauntered over to me, rapier swinging at a jaunty angle on their hip. "Hullo, Ryx. Ready for the rite?"

"No," I admitted. "You?" I tried to keep my tone as casual as possible, forcing my breath not to quicken. It would be nice to someday once more be able to hold conversations with people I considered more or less my friends without wondering whether they had tried to kill me.

"Not even close," Ardith confessed. "I originally came here to take advantage of your hospitality and do a bit of low-pressure spying. It was supposed to be so relaxed that I didn't even have to hide that I was snooping, and could just lounge around making a nuisance of myself and drinking your beer. But my father and his allies keep giving me more responsibilities, and suddenly I'm representing half the Conclave in this idiotic rite."

This was doing nothing to slow my speeding pulse. "Ah. What have they asked you to do?"

Ardith grimaced. "The worst possible thing. Represent their interests to the best of my judgment. I *hate* using my judgment."

"I'd be happy to lend you mine," I suggested, with a smile I hoped was charming. "I'll gladly make all your decisions for you."

"I wish you could. That'd be easier than trying to sort out and balance all the things half a dozen different Witch Lords want me to do." Ardith sighed. "I shouldn't even be talking to you about it, but I wanted you to know I've got them all breathing down my neck, so don't take anything I say or do personally."

"Whenever you say things like that, I get this awful sinking feeling in my stomach," I confessed.

"Me too, Ryx. Me too." They flipped me a cheery wave. "Good luck! How bad can it get, right?...Don't answer that."

They wandered off to go talk to Severin and Voreth, which didn't set my mind at ease at all.

I scanned the hall for Kessa, hoping to ground my burgeoning worries against her common sense, and spotted her glossy black hair and crimson-trimmed vestcoat sticking out from behind one of the great aspens. She was talking earnestly with someone, and it took me a moment to recognize Ashe. Those athletic shoulders followed a vulnerable curve, and her spiky head ducked with what might even be shyness. As I watched, she reached out toward Kessa with a tenderness I was certain no enemy had ever seen from her, and their hands slid together.

I turned away at once, covering the smile that spread across my face. All right, *that* had saved my mood. Maybe tonight wasn't completely doomed after all.

"Ryx." Aurelio appeared at my elbow. "May I speak to you privately for a moment?"

"Of course. What is it?"

He glanced around, then beckoned me aside; we walked to the far end of the hall together, alone beneath the shifting golden leaves.

"I wanted to talk to you about the Rite of Blood and Water and the Rookery's plan for the gate," he said, his voice low. Worry clouded his eyes. "I'm concerned that everyone is going to make a terrible mistake."

"Aurelio, I can almost guarantee you that we're going to make a terrible mistake. There are no good ways out of this mess we're in."

"True enough, but we have to find the best way we can." He ruffled the back of his hair. "And you're the only one who can make sure that happens. You're the most powerful person in Gloamingard right now."

I laughed, startled into it. "I can think of several people who would disagree."

"Not when it comes to the gate." His gaze bored into mine, sincere and urgent. "As the last member of your family in Gloamingard, you're the only one here who can let people through the wards to destroy it. No one can do anything to it without you. Really, when you come down to it, you're the only one whose opinion matters."

"I don't think that's true, but all right." I had to make enough arguments tonight; I wasn't going to start one with Aurelio over whether I was as insignificant as I felt.

"Of course I have to put in my plea for you to make the right choice." He smiled an apology and spread his hands, as if to say *What can I do?*

More pressure. Exactly what I needed. "Aurelio..."

"Hear me out." He hesitated, as if he had to choose his next words very carefully. "I've been thinking about this and talking to Lord Urso. We have almost no understanding of the Hells, but it sounds as if they may be the source of all magic in the world. Don't you think it's a terrible idea to destroy the gate without fully understanding the implications?" He spread his hands. "The gate is contained now. Your ancestors kept it intact all these centuries for a reason. Let's not undo their work with a poorly considered decision."

It was the same argument Ardith had said some of the Witch Lords had been making. If they were coordinating with Aurelio and factions in Raverra, I might face unified opposition tonight, which was bad news.

I let out a long, tired breath. "Aurelio, you've got a valid point, and if we could somehow keep everyone from fighting over the gate, it might make sense to wait and study it. But even then, we'd be trusting that no one would gain access to it who would misuse it. Call me a cynic, but I don't think humanity has that kind of wisdom or restraint."

"Well, we do have to make sure it's in the right hands." His voice shifted, and I had the impression he was repeating points someone else had made to him. "That's one of the things that makes the gate irreplaceable, actually—that it appears to be a power source you don't need a particular inborn magical talent to access. So we can make sure the gate is controlled by people with wisdom and vision, rather than people who happen to be born with a random natural advantage. Power is power, after all; it's a tool to accomplish a goal. There are no evil means, only evil ends."

I snorted. "Now you're sounding like that Raverran cabal—the Zenith Society."

A strange, guarded expression crossed Aurelio's face. Cold realization hit my stomach like a swallow of seawater.

"Hells," I breathed. "You *are* a member of the Zenith Society."

THIRTY-TWO

It's not what you think," Aurelio said, reaching out as I backed up a step. "Ryx, listen to me. The Rookery has a skewed perspective on the Zenith Society—they had a bad run-in with one splinter faction, years ago. The rotten ones were purged then; those who remained were the ones who *didn't* get involved in shady business."

"Does Lady Celia know of your affiliation, then?" I demanded.

He grimaced. "She's from an opposing faction, so I've kept it quiet. But the Zenith Society isn't some sinister cabal—we're dedicated solely to the advancement of magical knowledge and the protection of the Serene Empire."

"Pure altruists, I'm sure," I said, letting the irony drip from my voice.

"Everything in Raverra is political. There's not one altruist in the whole city. But we've read the signs: border raids in Callamorne, Vaskandran forests that creep a few feet farther onto imperial soil every day, domains like Alevar building up standing armies, chimeras found deep in imperial territory, Lamiel's magical land-grabbing stunt on Windhome Island—the list goes on. We see war on the wind. We just want to ensure that the Serene Empire will never fall to Vaskandar, no matter how many Witch Lords unite their terrible power against us." He took a deep breath. "And for that, we need the gate."

"Look, I don't want to see anyone invade the Serene Empire, either," I hissed, struggling to keep my voice low as anger bubbled up in me. "But this isn't how we do it."

"Then how?" He sounded genuinely desperate, like he'd love to know. His eyes pleaded with me. "You're no fool, Ryx. You *know* Vaskandar will always keep trying to expand. We have hundreds of years of wars to prove it. This peace has been exceptional, but it can't last forever. We're seeing the beginning of the end right now, with these aggressions from the Shrike Lord; there are a handful of other Witch Lords beginning to push boundaries, too, seeking domains for their children and spouses and friends. And the Serene Empire has to be ready. *Morgrain* has to be ready."

"There's an ocean of difference between being ready to deal with invaders and using a *gate to the Hells* as a weapon," I said, frustrated. "You think the Witch Lords are bad because they use their connection to the land to oppress those without magic? Well, how will it be any better if your Zenith Society takes power using the strength of the Nine Demons? That's even worse!"

Aurelio stared at me, shadows passing through his eyes. "That's what I'm worried about," he said, his voice dropping almost to a whisper. "That's what I tried to tell Lord Urso. But he says that we're wise enough to use it only for good, and I—I have to believe him, Ryx."

Uneasy memories of Bastian's story stirred in my mind, and suddenly I was very afraid for Aurelio. "No you don't," I urged him. "Listen, I've heard stories about the Zenith Society finding bright and promising protégés from poor families and just… using them up. Lord Urso is *using* you, Aurelio."

His eyes dropped to the floor. "I know that," he said. "Do you think I don't know that?"

"Then leave him! You don't need him. You can—"

"Yes I do." He raised his eyes to meet mine, and there was anger in them. "You don't know, Ryx, because you were born to a powerful family. Sure, they treat you like garbage, but they feed you. You're the lady of a castle, for Graces' sake." He shook his head. "I owe Lord Urso everything. My father owes him everything. We were sleeping on a tenement floor when he started running errands for the Zenith Society and Lord Urso decided he had promise. I still remember what it was like, being hungry and having no food or any idea when I'd get any. I can't go back to that, Ryx. I can't send my father back to that."

"You'll just let him use you?" I asked, incredulous. "You know he's out for power, and treating you and your father as tools that can be cast aside, and you'll still do whatever he tells you?"

"What choice do I have?" Aurelio's voice cracked, and he turned his face away. "And besides, he's not wrong. Vaskandar *is* an existential threat to the Empire, and war *is* coming. I need to believe in him, Ryx. I have to work for him anyway, so I want—no, I *do* believe he's right."

"You have other choices." I reached out toward him. "You don't have to stay with him. You're not going to starve, Aurelio. You've got your own career, and you've got friends and connections who can help you."

He caught my extended hand in both of his. "You owe him, too, Ryx." Aurelio turned my wrist so the jess gleamed on it. "He's the one who used his connections to get me the authorization to give you this. If you act against the Zenith Society, he might pull the same strings to revoke that authorization and take it back."

He said it as a warning, not a threat, his voice anxious. Still, I snatched my hand back, struggling to hide my anger.

"I am the Warden of Gloamingard. I choose my actions for the good of the people of Morgrain."

"Then think carefully about where that good lies." He stuffed his hands in his pockets, as if they needed warming after how quickly I'd dropped them. "Don't overreact out of fear of old stories. Turn my words over in your mind for a while. And I beg you, when you step up to make your speech at the Rite of Blood and Water, make the right choice."

"I will do my best to do so," I said, my stomach sinking. I could lose him tonight—as an ally, as a friend. "I can only hope you do the same."

We gathered for the Rite of Blood and Water in the orchard at dusk, as long gray shadows enfolded the hill. It was a time of beginnings and endings, when the muted fires of sunset kindled and died in the west, but the cold light of the stars had yet to waken in the velvet sky. The door of day closed, the door of night opened, and only human hands could lift a steady light against the changing of the tide to darkness.

The rite demanded witness of earth and sky, and so we stood in the orchard, the living breath of the trees around us, the insects singing their tense song to the evening. Electric whispers raced around among the gathered people, punctuated by silences that hummed with possibility.

If Aurelio was to be believed, I held the evening's potential in my hands. It was a terrifying idea, given my record for catastrophes.

He stood with Lady Celia and her aides, all of them looking somewhat nervous at participating in a Vaskandran rite, the last light of sunset painting harsh shadows on their faces. He caught me watching him and returned my stare with one that burned with a silent plea; I glanced away first.

I was half inclined to report him to Lady Celia. I doubted she'd be happy to find out the Falconer advising her was a member of the Zenith Society, no matter what Aurelio said—though if opposing factions had appointed him her adviser, she might not be able to do much about it. I should tell the Rookery, at least. But he'd trusted me to keep his secret, and I couldn't bring myself to immediately turn around and break that trust. If he really was part of some harmless scholarly branch of the Zenith Society—or more likely, had been tricked into thinking so—I'd be a poor friend if I got him demoted or worse. Not to mention that denouncing him now would throw the rite into chaos, destroying my chances of achieving a consensus here. This called for delicacy I could best bring to bear *after* the rite. One crisis at a time.

Odan set up a small table and placed a goblet on it, one sculpted by magic from bone with delicate scenes of misty mountain lakes and trees trailing falling blossoms. I should have created the table myself on the spot as the host, drawing it up from the tree roots with magic—but Odan, being Odan, had thought ahead and brought one.

I stepped forward into the dying light and raised my arms. A hush fell on the orchard, with dozens of eyes turned on me as night shadows crept up the hill from the valleys below us. *I am the guard at the gloaming.*

"Exalted Severin has invoked the Rite of Blood and Water, on behalf of his brother, the Shrike Lord," I said. "We stand now at the falling of night to find a path that will bring us through to face the dawn as allies, not enemies. It has never been more important to do so, for the dawn that's coming may be terrible indeed—if we allow it to be." I paused, sweeping my gaze across the serious faces gathered around me, relying on my mage mark to grant my stare intensity. I envied my family's ability to rouse their magic like a lifting of hackles, so that all could feel it in the air.

"I, for one, have no intention of allowing it," I said firmly.

They strained to believe me; I could see it in their eyes, feel it in the air. They *wanted* peace, nearly every one of them. They wanted someone to tell them they could be safe.

My heart contracted in my chest. One of the Nine Demons walked the world once more, and none of us were safe. Any peace we forged here would be fragile as a bubble floating on a river. This hope was an illusion, and I knew it.

If it could avert war, it was an illusion that could save thousands of lives—at least for a little while.

"The issues before us are the disposition of the gate to the Nine Hells discovered under my family's ward in the Black Tower, and the resolution of the Shrike Lord's claim of grievance over Exalted Lamiel's death. Let all who have an interest in these matters drink from the goblet and propose their solution. In the end we will bind ourselves to a course of action, by blood or by water."

I stepped back from the table to make room for whoever would speak first. There came a brief pause; Severin conferred quietly with Voreth, and Ardith simply grinned, their hands stuffed in their pockets.

Lady Celia seized the waiting moment. She swept up to the table and took a neat, decisive sip from the clear water in the goblet before lifting her chin to address the gathering.

"We stand at the cusp of a crisis," she declared, her strong voice resonating through the orchard. "The Graces have given us a chance to avert the same fate that scarred our people's memory for millennia. We must seal this gate forever, and lock away the horror that has become synonymous in all our cultures with suffering and evil. To do anything else is rank madness. I propose on behalf of the Serene Empire that we follow the plan the Rookery has presented to us, and destroy the gate permanently."

She dipped a curt bow to the assembly and returned to her place in the rough half circle gathered around the table. I noticed that she didn't mention the fleet of warships that Jannah's birds reported was now in position off the coast of Morgrain, poised to rain destruction upon us if the Serene Empire didn't get its way.

A silence fell. For one brief moment, the wild hope kindled in my chest that no one would disagree, and we could resolve this simply and easily.

Then Severin took an audible breath, cutting like a sword across the quiet of the evening. When he strode forward, however, there was no hesitation in his pace, and no weakness or doubt in the gaze with which he raked the assembly after taking his ceremonial draft from the cup.

"I stand before you as a representative of my brother, the Shrike Lord," he said, with careful emphasis, as if to disavow any personal stake in the matter. "Know that there are only two settlements he will accept: either delivery of Exalted Lamiel's murderer into his hands, or ceding control of the gate to Alevar." A murmur of protest ran through the Raverran delegation, but he raised his voice over it. "If Morgrain can provide neither, then he and his allies will make war upon them to obtain his satisfaction. I offer you this path to peace: I propose that dominion over the gate be given to the Shrike Lord, who claims it in recompense for his beloved's death." Severin caught my eyes. "Unless, of course, Exalted Lamiel's murderer can be found and turned over to the Shrike Lord for justice, in which case I gladly withdraw this proposal."

He stepped back from the table with no more than a curt nod, and kept his eyes trained straight ahead as he walked back to his place at Voreth's side. A bitter taste lingered at the back of my mouth. He was going to play the part his brother had given him to the end, it would seem—and to be fair, with Voreth ready to step up in his place, to do otherwise would bring down the Shrike Lord's wrath upon him without accomplishing much.

"Does anyone else have a proposal for a solution?" I called out.

My eyes slid to Ardith, anticipating what they might say with something approaching dread. I almost missed it when Aurelio stepped forward, slow and deliberate, from his place at Lady Celia's side.

Celia's brows climbed her forehead as he approached the table; whatever he was about to do, he hadn't warned her. My middle tightened. *Don't do it,* I willed him silently. *This is enough of a mess already without you sticking your hand in it.*

He picked up the cup, regarded it a moment, and took a long sip. At last he turned to face his audience.

"No doubt I do my career no favors by saying this," he began, flashing an apologetic smile at the incredulous Lady Celia, "but there is a third option we must in good conscience consider. And as a Falconer—a steward of the Serene Empire's magical knowledge and might—it's my duty to lay it before you."

You mean Lord Urso told you to lay it before us. Lady Celia shook her head, jaw set. Next to me, Foxglove and Bastian exchanged glances.

Aurelio forged ahead. "When I joined the Falconers, I often found myself in the vicinity of artificers and alchemists and their projects. And my mentors taught me a very important lesson: if you don't understand something magical, *don't touch it.*" That drew scattered chuckles, and he grinned briefly before pulling his expression into something more stern and sober. "Never has Eruvia seen a more dangerous artifact than this gate. And while the Rookery's skills and knowledge are legendary, they've only had a few days to examine it. We need to be extremely careful, my friends, because the consequences of making a mistake could be dire indeed."

Hells. He was making too much sense. Some of the Raverran delegation were nodding, and Ardith listened attentively, their eyes bright.

Aurelio, to my horror, flung an arm in my direction. "Lady Ryxander is too modest to mention it, but her family has protected this gate without incident for *four thousand years*. Leaving it in their care is literally the only course of action *proven* not to lead to a recurrence of the Dark Days." He gripped the edges of the table like a podium, drawing himself up. "Instead of leaping to drastic and immediate action, I propose that we let Morgrain continue peacefully in their capacity as its guardians—but that we also put together an international team to study the gate. With all due caution, of course, and with the intent to share our discoveries for the benefit of all."

Fair words, but the last thing we needed was a parade of people coming close enough to the gate to hear the whispering voices of the demons. Especially since I had no doubt half of them would bring their own agendas and secret orders. My teeth ground together at the thought.

Aurelio spread his hands wide. "For the safety of Eruvia, we must not destroy this gate. Not until we understand it better, and know the consequences of our actions. Thank you."

He offered us all a deep bow and returned to his place. Lady Celia stood stiff and furious.

The sky had gone purple with dusk, and the lights I'd had Odan hang in the trees around us twinkled to life, bathing faces with the pale glow of luminaries and phosphorescent flowers. It was a thinner light, like old brittle ice, and it made everyone's faces tired and afraid.

I stepped forward, clearing my throat. "If there are no more proposals, then now is the time when any who would speak on this issue may do so, whether to back a proposal, argue against one, or bring up new considerations."

Ardith sauntered to the front without hesitation, smirking. *Oh Hells. Here it comes.*

"Well, looks like I'm the only one here officially undecided," they said. "Let the bribes roll in!"

Ashe chuckled. Voreth glared. I held my breath and waited

to see where this was going; Ardith was no more undecided than I was.

"Alas, I fear it's time to lay down my cards," they sighed. "I may be officially undecided, but *unofficially* I'm here to represent a mixed assortment of Witch Lords who've asked me to be their eyes here. And they have a whole list of concerns." Ardith produced a square of paper from their pocket, unfolded it with a flourish, and began to read. "Where is the Lady of Owls during all this? How can we be certain the enchantment to destroy the gate won't have horrific and spectacular magical backlash that kills us all?" They paused and looked up. "I have to admit I'm concerned about that one myself."

"Please. We *are* professionals," Foxglove murmured beside me, sounding mildly offended.

"There was that time in Callamorne," Ashe whispered. "*That* was pretty spectacular."

Foxglove brushed imaginary dust off his cuffs. "We agreed never to speak of that."

Ardith kept going. "What will happen to the flow of magic in this world if we seal the gate? Why—oh, anyway, it goes on." They crumpled up the paper. "The point is, they have questions. Some of them even have *good* questions! While they don't all agree on a course of action, there's a general consensus of alarm that one domain could make this sky-shaking revelation and then propose to wipe it out forever virtually in the same breath. They think it smells suspicious, like something is being covered up, and I have to agree." They grimaced in my direction. "Sorry, Ryx."

Feeling the crowd's eyes on me, I offered Ardith a stiff nod. Curse them for being too perceptive.

Ardith took a deep breath. "Suffice to say they want to call a Conclave to talk about this before we do anything too permanent. Whether they're willing to throw some power around to enforce it or not, I'll leave to your imagination."

They swept a cocky bow and all but strutted back to their place. Despair settled over me like falling snow; only Lady Celia seemed to back destroying the gate immediately, and Aurelio's speech made it clear that the Serene Empire was divided.

Foxglove smoothed his cravat and stepped forward, Bastian at his side. They took turns carefully and seriously presenting everything they'd been attempting to pound into the heads of the diplomats all night: the threat the gate presented, the Rookery's recommendation to destroy it, and the plan for doing so.

The crowd remained restless. In the thin, pale light, they looked concerned, but not convinced. Foxglove could see it, too; worry flickered in his amber-brown eyes. They weren't lining up on our side. They wouldn't let us destroy the gate.

That meant it was my turn to play my secret ace. Seasons witness, I didn't want to do this.

I stepped forward, dread building up an almost unbearable pressure in my chest. *Grandmother, forgive me.*

"There is one more matter you may want to consider," I told them.

THIRTY-THREE

The attention of all the assembled people focused on me like the heat of the sun coming out from behind a cloud. I approached the table; every step across the garden felt like a mile.

Grace of Wisdom, help me avert a disaster instead of causing one, just this once.

My grandmother's presence watched from the trees around us, ready, almost eager. She knew as well as I did the chaos I would sow if I told them the truth about her. The violence that would engulf the entire region as everyone turned on our domain—or, if she could arrange it, on each other.

As I took my place, I found my eyes drifting to meet Severin's. I, too, knew what the truth could do.

"Honored Ardith is right," I began. My voice came out uneven; my hands trembled. I clasped them behind my back. "There's something we've been holding back, for fear of starting a panic."

A hush fell across the orchard. I could see the question in their eyes: *How could it be worse?* Blood of the Eldest, if only they knew.

"There is a chance..." I swallowed. "No. I'm certain that a demon has already come through the gate."

Severin made an inarticulate noise. The crowd erupted in gasps and exclamations; Ardith clutched their own sleeves, paling, and Lady Celia reached out to steady herself on an aide's shoulder.

"So far as I know," I continued, my throat dry to cracking, "there's just the one. We need to make absolutely certain that this demon does not bring others through from the Nine Hells. And so I implore you, for the sake of Eruvia, to let us destroy the gate immediately."

The orchard erupted into shouts and questions. I lifted a hand, not done yet; they fell silent at once, straining desperately to hear whatever horrors I might utter next.

So far, I'd spoken only truth, and I'd like to keep it that way. But I had to be so very careful threading this next needle.

"I'm sure you've noticed my grandmother's absence," I said. "She is currently keeping this demon contained, and she is the reason why you've seen so little sign of its presence in this world." All technically true, but holy Hells, I felt like a liar. "It is *imperative* that she doesn't face a threat to her domain that would require her personal intervention, causing her to shift her focus to war at this critical time."

Murmurs swept through the crowd. Severin shook his head in a sort of stunned admiration, mouthing *This was your plan?*

"That's all I have to say on the matter right now," I called out. "Clearly this is another problem we must face and deal with, and there's a great deal of information to be shared and plans to be made and steps to be taken. At this rite, however, we deal only with the question of what to do with the gate. I don't want to distract from that all-important decision with a discussion that will take days. Let's focus on the question at hand and make our choice. Will you leave a gate to the Nine Hells in existence while a demon is on the loose with the means to open it and unleash the Dark Days upon us all? Or shall we destroy the gate and limit the damage, and *then* turn our full attention to dealing with this singular threat?"

I shrugged, as if the answer didn't matter to me. With a frightened uproar clamoring in my ears, I paced back to my spot next to the rest of the Rookery, my face turned up to the smooth purple sky to avoid meeting anyone's gaze.

The debate continued with new urgency. Every time it strayed to focusing on the demon, I stubbornly directed it back to the gate. My announcement seemed to have served its purpose; the idea of keeping the gate around to study it seemed much less appealing when more demons might come through at any minute.

Voreth demanded proof that a demon had truly come through; Ardith countered by demanding proof that one *hadn't*, but Foxglove officially vouched for the demon's existence on behalf of the Rookery before that could spiral too far. Aurelio kept shooting me betrayed looks, his mouth set in a straight line. Hells, he of all people should know it was nothing personal. My mother had told me more than once that in Raverra, it was best to keep friendship separate from politics.

When everyone seemed to have run out of new things to say, I stepped up to the table again. "The time has come for us all to decide where we stand," I declared. "Each party must bind ourselves to a resolution, with water or blood." I turned to the Raverrans, softening my voice to explain. "Water is a promise. It can be conditional; it can be renegotiated later. Blood is a vow. When you bind yourself with blood, the earth listens. You cannot change your mind."

Lady Celia nodded, her face schooled to polite understanding, her eyes a bit wide.

Ardith strolled up first, putting on a cocksure strut like armor. They took the bone cup and lifted it as if in a toast. "I've heard enough. I think it's safe to say that the Fox Lord now favors destroying the gate. You convinced me, Ryx. I can't claim to be quite as sure what the other Witch Lords would think, but let's not give the Conclave the chance to muck this up, shall we?" They took a long swallow of the clear water.

Lady Celia strode to the table next, with all the determination of a soldier going to war. She paused to consider the cup. "My resolution is powerful enough for blood, but since I speak on behalf of the Serene Empire, it is not my place to bind the doge and the Council of Nine with my vows. Let me state as clearly and firmly as I can that the Serene Empire strongly backs the Rookery's proposal to destroy the gate at once."

As she took her sip of water, she glared over the rim of the cup at Aurelio. He pressed his lips together in silence; she must have had words with him.

Severin stepped forward, and every muscle in my abdomen tensed. *Stand up to him*, I willed him silently. *Ignore that gargoyle glaring over your shoulder and break away from your brother's shadow.*

He stared at the cup a long time, his shoulders taut. One hand stole up and rubbed his neck, along the scars there.

"Come on," I whispered, hands clenched. "You can do this."

Severin reached out toward the cup. He glanced at me, his eyes clouded. Then he closed his hand, straightened his spine, and faced the crowd.

"My brother's will is clear," he said, his voice soft but carrying. "I understand the threat this gate poses, but as his envoy, I cannot agree to destroy it. Not unless I can return to Alevar with Exalted Lamiel's killer for the Shrike Lord's justice." He turned to me, his eyes pleading. "Exalted Ryxander. I have no choice but to ask you: Can you deliver that justice?"

All eyes turned to me. I let out a long sigh.

"I'd hoped to avoid this," I said. "But you give me no choice." I straightened, letting my voice ring out loud and clear. "The Shrike Lord's claim is false. I deny his grievance."

The Raverrans exchanged puzzled glances; the Vaskandrans drew in shocked breaths. Severin went pale as bone.

"On what basis?" Voreth snarled, his knuckles bulging on his staff.

"Exalted Lamiel broke the laws of hospitality." I pulled back my sleeve to show the long pink scar her dagger had left. "She trespassed in places she was told were forbidden and *stabbed me with a knife*. The only reason I have forborne from claiming a major grievance was out of respect for the Shrike Lord's grief." Voreth opened his mouth to protest, but I raised my voice. "She set a chimera on our people to distract from her crimes. It was *her* meddling that caused the gate to be opened. Morgrain could claim grievance after grievance from that night—and the Shrike Lord can claim *none*. No one murdered Lamiel; she tampered with dangerous powers and brought her death upon herself." I glared at Voreth, since I couldn't quite bring myself to meet Severin's eyes. I hoped to the Hells his brother wouldn't blame him for this. "You hold no valid grievance. I deny the Shrike Lord's claim."

Into the silence that fell, Ardith let out a loud whistle. "Well! That was comprehensive."

Voreth started forward. "You have no right to deny this claim! You're not even a proper atheling! You—"

Severin whirled on him, lips drawn back from his teeth. "You are not the Shrike Lord's envoy, Honored Voreth."

Rage darkened Voreth's face, but he bowed. "Forgive me, Exalted Atheling."

Severin turned to face me. Calculation narrowed his eyes. I tried to put an urgent message in mine: *I don't want this to hurt you. Help me figure out how to keep your brother's wrath from falling on you for this.*

No matter how the rite resolved, the Elk Lord wouldn't back the Shrike Lord after all the doubts I'd cast on his grievance; and after what I'd said about my grandmother and the demon, the Shrike Lord should have trouble finding other allies against us. I'd accomplished what I needed for Morgrain. Now I had to make sure Severin didn't bear the cost.

"I know nothing of the grievances you claim against the Shrike Lord," Severin said. His features still formed a perfect picture of arrogant disdain; he was good at this act, damn him.

"Your lack of knowledge makes them no less true, and no less relevant," I returned.

Severin hesitated. "Yet my brother *felt* Exalted Lamiel's death. Someone else was involved. My brother will know the full truth, and have his vengeance."

Ah. That was an angle I could work with, if a dangerous one. "If you have the truth, will you back the destruction of the gate?"

"If you direct me to the proper target of my brother's vengeance, then he may pursue his grievance against that individual in place of his grievance against Morgrain," Severin said carefully. "If he has no grievance against Morgrain, then I am forced to admit he has no claim on the gate."

"Very well." I took a deep breath. "Morgrain does not acknowledge your grievance, but nor will we withhold the truth. I will pledge to give you what information I have about Exalted Lamiel's death." I'd been willing to tell Severin the truth anyway, and I wasn't promising to tell anyone but him. "What you do with that information is up to you."

"Including the identity of this presence my brother felt?" Severin asked, reluctance dragging at his words.

Once I gave him my reply, I couldn't take it back. But it

would be unfair to force Severin to accept the consequences of his brother's wrath while evading them myself.

"Yes," I said.

Severin winced, so slightly I wouldn't have noticed if I hadn't spent more time than I was prepared to admit staring at his face. His voice dropped so low I could barely hear him. "Will you bind yourself with a blood vow? I'm afraid my brother will accept no less."

A blood vow was serious for anyone, but more so for an atheling with a blood tie to the land. There were all manner of stories describing gruesome fates for athelings who broke a blood oath, and I had no idea to what degree they were true.

Everyone was watching. Curse it, I was tired of ducking responsibility for Lamiel's death. It might have been her fault, but still, it wouldn't have happened if I'd made different choices.

"I will." I drew my dagger from its sheath. Kessa bit her lip, trying to catch my eyes, shaking her head. But I understood the potential consequences, and by the Graces and the Eldest, I was done running from this.

I drew the knife across the back of my arm, along the scar Lamiel had left, steeling myself for the hot lick of pain. Blood beaded along the shallow cut, and I let a few drops fall to the fertile earth.

Think, Ryx. Think about how you phrase this.

I locked eyes with Severin, my blue mage mark burning into his gray one. "I swear to you that before you leave Gloamingard, I will tell you the further details of Lamiel's death, including this other person involved."

That was as much maneuvering room as I could give myself. My vow was only to Severin, and he might not choose to pass the information on to his brother. And if he did, well, the Shrike Lord might kill me, but it put the matter off until we could deal with the gate, and that was the most important thing.

Still, I couldn't help a chill of foreboding at what I'd just bound myself to do. I might not consider Lamiel's death murder, but I doubted the Shrike Lord would agree. Aiming his vengeance against me rather than Morgrain would leave me no less dead at the end of it, and now he would finally know his target.

Severin inclined his head. "I receive your vow. The Shrike Lord's grievance against Morgrain is satisfied, for now. Let it be known that his deadly grievance against this individual, however, remains."

That would have to do. I nodded grim acknowledgment.

He lifted the bone cup to me. "I pledge Alevar's backing for destroying the gate, contingent on your fulfillment of that vow."

And he drank, slow and long.

"Then all agree," I declared, barely keeping my voice steady, "and this rite is concluded. The Rookery will proceed with destroying the gate, and afterward the Shrike Lord's grievance will be settled."

The tension in the orchard shifted. With the rite resolved, everyone began breaking up into clusters of buzzing conversation, talking agitatedly about the demon.

I withdrew from the light and the crowd, into the sheltering shadows of the orchard. Lady Celia would doubtless descend on me with questions in a moment, and Ardith would come sniffing after information; I had no desire to get pinned down by either of them. I laid my hand on the rough bark of an apple tree and took in a deep breath of its sweet scent.

"You've doomed me," a voice husked, startlingly close.

I spun in my dark corner of the orchard to find Aurelio standing there, his face barred and patched in black shadows from a gnarled old apple tree that blocked half the light. Even with his expression partly obscured, I could see the emotion twisting it.

Given that I had potentially just consigned myself to the very real doom of the Shrike Lord's vengeance, my patience for dramatics was thin. "No I haven't," I snapped. "For Graces' sake, Aurelio, I'm trying to save us from a demon invasion."

He shook his head, and there was something barely controlled in the motion, full of grief or pain that bordered on madness. "You don't understand. I can't let you destroy the gate, and go back to him a failure. I *can't*. Not just for myself, but for my father."

I went still. There was more going on here than I understood. "Aurelio, if you're not safe with Lord Urso, I can give you shelter here."

He laughed bitterly. "He's going to take your jess, you know. There's no way he'll let you keep it now."

My jess. Realization hit me like a bucket of swamp water, foul and cold.

I needed Aurelio to release my magic, or I couldn't drain the gate.

He had the power to stop us from destroying it. He didn't know it yet, because he hadn't heard the plan—but if I asked him to release me, he'd figure out why I must need my magic, and he'd never say the release word. Not so long as Lord Urso wanted otherwise.

I had to trick him. I hated to do it, when he was staring at me with eyes brimming with unshed tears, clearly worried about his father and in desperate need of help. If I deceived him into releasing me, that would be the end of our friendship. My power would drain the jess, and Aurelio and Lord Urso would certainly have no motivation to get me a new one. I'd be back to my old life forever, minus one of the few friends I'd ever had.

No crowds, no parties, no travel, no Rookery, no hope of romance. And my grandmother, the one person I'd relied on for human touch, was gone.

Hells, at this rate I'd be dead anyway. I swallowed a knot in my throat.

"He can't take my jess back!" It wasn't hard to sound upset at the idea. I put my hand protectively over my wrist for good measure. "Not now. I need my power suppressed to touch Fox-glove so I can let him through the Black Tower wards. Everyone is depending on me. I can't let them down."

The lie tasted bitter on my tongue. It had come so easily, and I despised myself for it. Especially as the struggle played out on Aurelio's face, balancing his mission against his friend's welfare.

His mouth resolved into a grim line, and he stepped back: one pace, two, three. Well out of reach.

"I'm sorry, Ryx," he said, regret in his voice. "I never wanted to hurt you. But we need that gate."

Hells, he was really going to do it. Panic leaped up in my chest, even though this was what I'd wanted. "Wait—"

Aurelio took a deep breath. "*Exsolvo.*"

The release word.

It was as if color rushed back into a world from which I had forgotten it had been drained. The air came alive with power around me: warmer, richer, more vibrant.

A great heady rush washed up my arm from the jess, tingling with exaltation, and it went cold on my wrist. I snatched my hand back halfway through reaching toward Aurelio, a muffled cry strangling in my throat. A leaf brushing my ankle withered, the life dwindling from it; I moved instinctively away before the whole plant could die.

"I'm sorry," Aurelio said, his voice catching as if he truly meant it. "I can't let you do this, Ryx. Now, if you'll help me, I can get you a new one."

For a moment, I pitied him. He was afraid, and desperate, and seemed to feel genuinely terrible about this. For a brief moment, I almost felt bad about what I was going to do.

But no. He'd been willing to damn me to a life without touch just to get me to do what he wanted. This was the price he paid for that choice.

I met his eyes, anger simmering beneath my skin, and yanked the jess off my wrist. Maybe it would be more prudent to let him think I was cowed, but I couldn't summon a convincing pretense of meekness or remorse right now.

"Help you do what? Betray my country? Everything I do, I do for Morgrain." I stuffed the useless jess defiantly in my vestcoat pocket.

His face went blank with shock for a brief moment before twisting to anger. "You tricked me! You *wanted* me to release you. Hells take you—you need your power to destroy the gate, don't you?"

He took half a step toward me, fury in his eyes, but I lifted my empty hands. "Aurelio, stop! I don't want to kill you."

He stopped. "I *trusted* you," he spat. "I thought you were my friend. How could you do this to me? If I fail Lord Urso, my father and I are finished!"

"For Graces' sake, losing your patron can't balance the scales with enabling the return of the Dark Days!" I didn't bother to strip the frustration from my voice. "Lord Urso isn't the ultimate arbiter of all fortune. You'll manage without him."

"No. You don't understand." Aurelio's face crumpled into despair. "The things my father's done for him—the things *I've* done for him—it's not just a matter of being poor again. He could put us in prison, or worse." A hard resolve entered the shadow-dappled lines of his face. "It's not too late. You can still help us."

I didn't like the new tone in his voice. Calmer, more controlled, almost cruel. "The only thing I'm helping with tonight is securing the future of Eruvia."

"Precisely. They still need you to destroy the gate. And you won't help them do it." He visibly mastered himself, smoothing the anger from his features, though hurt lingered in his eyes. "Because if you do try to help them destroy it—or if you tell anyone I'm with the Zenith Society, or do anything but cooperate with us fully—I'll tell Voreth who really killed Lamiel."

Defiant words withered in my lungs. Telling Severin in private was one thing; we could plan how to proceed together. Telling Voreth now would ensure a swift reaction from the Shrike Lord, unmitigated by Severin's interference. He might demand my head, send assassins, or accuse me of being a Skinwitch and get the Conclave involved—any of which could delay our destruction of the gate, not to mention get me killed. I glared at Aurelio in silent fury.

"Now, be smart," he said, his tone calm and reasonable once more. "This isn't a hard choice. All you have to do is come up with some reason why you can't drain the gate. Then you can tell Severin whatever lies you were planning, keep your secret, and keep your jess as well. Otherwise..." He shook his head. "I doubt the Shrike Lord will be merciful."

"You can go to the Nine Hells," I growled. "Aurelio, curse it, you're talking about *killing* me."

For a long moment, he was silent. Then he sighed, letting loose a breath as if he never expected to see it again. "I suppose I am. And I'm not proud of it. But I do what I have to, Ryx." His voice sharpened. "And you did lie to me. We were supposed to be *partners*. Well, the Falcon may have the power, but the Falconer holds the jess." He offered me a stiff, mocking bow. "Report back to me in an hour, and we'll talk about next steps."

For a moment, I considered slapping him. Just one smack

across his face, and he'd die regretting he'd threatened me; my secret would be safe. It was no less than he was threatening to do to me.

If I did, I'd be a murderer in truth.

I dug my nails into my palms and let him walk away.

THIRTY-FOUR

The faint whisper of a footstep in the grass and a brushing rustle of leaves warned me of someone's approach. I whirled barely in time, yanking myself back from Kessa's reaching hand.

"Don't!" I cried.

She froze, surprise turning to alarm on her face. I scrambled back out of her reach, heart beating wild against my sternum, grass withering beneath my footsteps.

"I'm not safe to touch." I lowered my voice, hoping to hide the tremor in it. "I had to trick Aurelio into releasing me."

Kessa's brows dipped together. "What? Why?"

I glanced around the orchard, my breath still coming fast. The diplomats had gathered into a knot of grave discussion; the Rookery had drawn together around Bastian and his notebook, clearly making plans. Kessa must have come to get me. Aurelio was talking to the Raverran delegation, all smiles, no doubt confident in my silence given the terrible threat he held over my head.

That stingroach. I pulled my gloves from my pocket, brushing against the inert wire of the jess, and yanked them on over rage-stiff fingers. The leather molded to my hands, familiar as an old curse.

"I need to talk to the Rookery," I said grimly. "In private. Right now."

"We don't have much time." I paced a short arc before the fireplace in the Rookery guest quarters, careful to keep several feet between me and the others. "Aurelio will realize I'm not submitting to his blackmail when I don't show up in an hour—less, now—and he'll reveal that I'm the one who killed Lamiel. And *that* will set off an immediate political disaster between Morgrain and Alevar, which will almost certainly interfere with our ability to destroy the gate."

Kessa shook her head, stunned. "I can't believe Aurelio is a member of the Zenith Society. I *liked* that wretched pustule."

"I can kill him right now," Ashe offered, grasping her sword hilt. "Won't take me five minutes."

"That would be murder," Bastian pointed out.

Ashe nodded. "Correct."

"Let's not get distracted," Foxglove said dryly. "We can deal with Aurelio after the gate. We're on a time limit; we have to do this now."

"Now?" Bastian flipped furiously through his notebook. "You mean, right this moment?"

"Yes. As soon as we can be ready. Even if we find some way to delay Aurelio, our political consensus could fall apart at any moment, and there are too many people who might be able to stop us if we don't get this done before they can react."

Kessa raised her brows at Foxglove. "Are you certain you're up for a disenchantment of this scale? Forgive me, but you don't even have the mage mark."

"If Ryx can drain the gate completely, it shouldn't matter how powerful he is," Bastian said. "There'll be no resistance. He can sever all the key points in the patterns so the power can't flow through them anymore. Then we can work on obliterating enough of the carvings that it can't be reestablished."

"Do we know where all those key points are?" Foxglove asked Bastian, peering over his shoulder at his notes. "I've been focusing on the politics rather than the magical analysis."

"Nearly." Bastian flipped through pages of his notebook with a worried frown. "I need a bit more time."

"How long?" Foxglove asked.

Bastian bit his lip. "Half an hour, maybe?"

Foxglove gave a curt nod. "All right. We can't wait, because Aurelio will try to stop us the moment he realizes what we're doing."

"I can make sure he doesn't," Ashe offered.

"He's an officer of the imperial Falconers, with powerful friends in the Serene Empire," Bastian objected. "We don't have the authority to do anything to him."

"We could apologize later," Ashe suggested.

"Let's not start any diplomatic incidents until *after* we get this gate closed," Foxglove said.

"What about Ryx?" Kessa asked, her brows drawn together in concern. "If we're destroying the gate, Aurelio will be desperate—he'll have no reason to hold back. He's bound to play his cards and tell her secret, and Voreth will demand her head in a pretty box to bring back to his master."

"I'll tell Severin first and hope he can hold Voreth off," I said. I didn't want to think about it right now; my stomach clenched up into a queasy ball when I did. "I made a vow, after all, and I've put off that reckoning long enough. Let's get my part with the gate done quickly, so that whatever happens, you can still destroy it."

Kessa looked for a moment as if she might argue. But Foxglove put a hand on her shoulder and shook his head. "Ryx is right, Kessa. That's a whole different round of the game. Gate first, political fight later."

Kessa nodded reluctantly, giving me a worried look.

A wave of overwhelming, bittersweet joy rolled through me.

Foxglove was trusting me with an important task. Kessa cared what happened to me. Ashe and Bastian didn't question whether I could do my part; they were content to rely on me. I was one of them.

They were my *friends*. This was what I'd always yearned for, without ever quite knowing what I wanted.

And I'd found it now, when I stood on the brink of losing everything.

Foxglove gave a sharp nod. "Right, then. Bastian, you and I will get our disenchantment ready as quickly as we can. Ryx, you go drain the gate before anything can stop you, so it'll be ready the moment we are."

I nodded, trying to look competent and confident, and not at all as if I were completely terrified of touching that obelisk again. I couldn't make myself speak.

"Kessa, you go with Ryx, and be ready to stall anyone who tries to interfere. Charm them into submission. Ashe, guard Kessa and Ryx. If anything goes awry—the gate isn't draining, Ardith sticks their nose in, Aurelio figures out what you're doing—come get the rest of us."

"If Aurelio tries to stop us, can I—"

"Rule Three," Kessa interrupted.

Ashe sighed. "Fine. I'll just hamstring him or something. Killjoy."

"All right." Foxglove rubbed his hands together, eyes gleaming, as if this were some exciting challenge and not a horrific nightmare with the potential to plunge all of Eruvia into the Dark Days once more if we made a mistake. "Let's do this."

We were about to enter the Hall of Chimes on the way to the old stone keep when Severin called after me down the corridor.

"Ryx! Ah, that is, Exalted Ryxander."

I turned, ignoring a knowing leer from Ashe, apprehension lurching in my gut. Severin hurried toward me quite alone, with no sign of his usual sneering shadow.

He caught up, out of breath. "I got away from Voreth for a moment and came to find you. Can we talk?"

I glanced at Kessa and Ashe; Kessa nodded and retreated down the hall, tugging Ashe with her. Bones clattered and tinkled gently above them, following their movements.

I wasn't ready for this. But then, I'd probably never be ready for this.

"Here for your promised payment?" I asked.

"No!" He reached out toward me as if he might grab my shoulder; his hand hung uncertainly in the air a moment, then dropped to his side. "Please tell me you have a clever and devious plan to fulfill that vow. Please tell me you're not going to do something stupid."

"That depends on how you define *clever* and *stupid*." I grimaced. "Anyway, it's not so bad. I only have to tell you how she died. I didn't agree to turn anyone over."

"That won't matter to my brother. He won't wait." Severin brushed the loose locks of hair back from his face in frustration. "He might even come kill whoever it is in person, and with your grandmother busy with that demon, there's no one here who could stop him."

The last thing we needed was my demon grandmother fighting a Witch Lord in Gloamingard while we tried to destroy the gate. "We'll find a way to weasel out of telling him," I said.

Severin shook his head. "That's easier said than done. Do you actually have a name of someone involved in her death? Or did you just make that up?"

I took a deep breath. "It's me, Severin. Lamiel grabbed me to get past the wards around the gate. I couldn't dodge her quickly enough, and she died."

His eyes went wide and white-edged. He shook his head mutely, staring at me.

"I didn't murder her," I said quietly. "But my magic killed her."

Severin pressed a hand to his temple. "No, no, this is terrible. It can't be you."

I spread my hands. "I've got no one else, Severin."

"We have to think of some way around this."

Kessa was waving me onward, making urgent faces. And she wasn't wrong. Once Aurelio told Voreth the truth, I'd get sucked into a political disaster, like it or not. My part in destroying the gate had to be done by then.

"We will," I assured Severin.

I turned to go, but he reached after me. "Wait!"

I dodged, swearing. "Aurelio deactivated my jess! You can't touch me unless you brace yourself against the pull of my magic, or you'll die like Lamiel did."

He kept his hand extended. "I'm braced," he said softly.

On a wild impulse I reached out, ignoring his hand, and laid my fingertips on his chest. For one, two, three beats of his heart, his pulse warmed my fingers through his vestcoat.

"I have to go," I said. "They can't destroy the gate without me, and we need to get this done before someone tries to stop us. Keep thinking of a way out of this mess, and I will, too."

Pulling my hand away felt as miserable as if I'd plunged it into ice water. I turned, cradling the lingering warmth on my fingertips, and hurried after Ashe and Kessa. Severin's eyes on my back burned as if the stormy rings of his mage mark seared my skin.

I'd wanted never to cross the threshold of the Black Tower again. And yet here I was once more.

The red glare seared its way into the back of my eyeballs,

runes and patterns burning into me. The throb of power in the air resonated horribly with the blood pulsing in my own veins. The tower watched me, alert, waiting, its vast presence looming over me. The air was so thick with menace and magic it was hard to breathe.

I stood before the stark black obelisk, just outside the final protective ring, my nerves jangling like a pocketful of dropped coins on a marble floor. *Run away*, every instinct screamed. *Run, before it's too late.*

"You can do this, Ryx," Kessa said softly from behind me. "Or at least, I hope you can, because I certainly can't."

I let out a strangled laugh. "I don't know if I can. I've never tried to do anything like it before." Not to mention that now that I was here in the flesh, standing before the gate with the oppressive weight of its power crushing down on me, the last thing I wanted in the whole world was to touch it again.

"I have faith in you." Kessa gave me a smile no less warm for the strain around the edges. "And more to the point, Bastian thinks you can do it. He's usually right about this sort of thing."

"We don't have time for you to doubt yourself," Ashe said bluntly, her eye on the door. "We need your part in this done before Aurelio drags you up in front of Voreth and tries to get you packed off to Alevar for a convenient gruesome execution."

"Ashe," Kessa said reprovingly. "Have some compassion."

"I never said we'd *let* him." She patted Answer's hilt.

"No, you're right. We don't have time." I drew in a deep breath of hot air; it had a metallic tang, sour in the back of my throat. "Stand back. I'm doing this."

Before I could think better of it, I stepped forward and— being careful to avoid the circular seal—laid my palm directly on the groove that ran down the center of the great black stone.

Heat blasted my face. The gate blazed to life, the groove lit to incandescence under my palm. Power rolled through me in a vast, shuddering wave, searing my nerves like lightning. A deep sound shook the tower, an unheard note vibrating every bone in my body and the stones beneath my feet, as if the ancient rocky hills themselves all uttered one low, long note together.

It was somehow worse, infinitely worse, knowing this light and heat and power came straight from the Nine Hells. I was touching the Hells themselves, drowning in their agonizing light. It glowed through my hand, showing the bones, as if my fragile mortal flesh was brittle paper on the verge of catching fire.

"Blood of the Eldest," Ashe swore.

"It's open," I gasped. "Kessa! Should I stop?"

"Bastian warned us this might happen." Her voice sounded strangely distant behind me. "Keep draining it! We have to depower the gate before the seal fails completely!"

Any second now the horrifying white radiance would dim, the heat would fade, the violent tide of power coursing through and past and around me would thin out. I bit back a scream at the great swelling roar of magic that seemed on the verge of shattering me to pieces, the sickening rush of overwhelming force that filled the Black Tower in a flood of raw, blistering light. *Only a little longer. Just endure it a moment longer.*

But the pain didn't stop. The noise didn't quiet, drowning out the prayer to the Graces that died on my tongue. The light blasted through my closed lids, and nothing could block the great resonating hum that threatened to shake apart my very bones.

Yes, whispered a voice like claws dragged through gravel. *A little wider...*

My eyes flew open. All I could see was an agony of white brilliance.

"This isn't right!" I cried. "It's not closing!"

Ashe swore. "I'll go get Bastian and Foxglove."

I tried to pull my hand away, but my palm stuck to the gate as if the black stone were some great magnet, the power coursing through it binding us together. "Hurry!" I screamed, in a panic now. "I can't stop!"

"She's on her way." Kessa's voice came from directly behind me, strong and calm, though surely that must be a mask she wore to reassure me. "Do you want me to try to help?"

"No! If you touch me, you'll die!" I grabbed my own wrist, tears drying at the corners of my eyes in the heat rolling off the stone. I couldn't even see my hand with all the light pouring through it. "Stay away! I need room."

"Got it," Kessa said, her voice coming from farther away. This time, she couldn't quite hide the edge of fear in it.

I hurled myself backward at the floor, as hard as I could, throwing the full weight of my body against whatever seal bound me to the stone.

Pain tore through my hand and up my arm. I slammed into the stone floor, falling across the blazing red circle of protective runes. A tingling rush ran through me, and the warding circle sputtered out.

I couldn't feel my hand, save for a buzzing ache, but it had come free. Relief washed through me like cool water.

But the line down the center of the obelisk still blazed, bright and terrible. My skin dried and cracked with the heat pouring from the stone. And an endless wave of power crashed unabated through the chamber, threatening to obliterate me with its sheer force.

I staggered to my feet, turning my half-blind eyes from the light. "Graces help us, it's *still* not closing! Kessa, what do we do?"

She stood riveted halfway to the door, her eyes fixed on the gate, tears on her cheeks reflecting the white glare. Both hands pressed to her mouth, and her whole body trembled.

"Ryx," she moaned. "Help me."

"What?" I started toward her, blinking away the insistent afterimage of the vertical line burned into my eyeballs. "Kessa, are you all right?"

She gave a sudden, sharp gasp and flung her arms wide, head tipped back, as if she might embrace the Black Tower itself. For a moment, I thought the sheer force of magic flowing from the gate had caught her, like a twig in the current, and might bear her away. I almost reached for her, but stopped myself.

"Kessa!"

Suddenly she relaxed, furling her fingers and unfurling them again, looking around her in apparent wonder. A terrible smile spread over her face, wild and cruel, stretching the sweet shape of her mouth in all the wrong directions.

It was not a human smile, by any definition.

THIRTY-FIVE

You're not Kessa," I whispered.

"Mmm," she agreed, rolling her shoulders as if settling a new coat. "Not for much longer, anyway. It'll take me a few minutes to finish killing her."

"Let her go!" I wanted to lunge at her, grab her, shake Kessa's own expression back onto that horridly grinning face—but I didn't dare touch her. Panic beat dark, frantic wings in my chest. "Get out of her right now, demon!"

The thing wearing Kessa blinked. "But you gave me this body as a gift. Did you not?" She stretched luxuriously, as if reveling in the feeling of having flesh. "You opened the gate for me, and there it was, waiting. I must thank you."

"She's not a *gift*!" I screamed it so loudly the power around us eddied invisibly with the force of my words, setting the floor to vibrating beneath me. "She's my friend!"

The demon laughed. It sounded nothing like Kessa's own musical laugh; it was all sharp broken pieces, like shaking a bag full of shattered glass.

"Then you should be more careful with your belongings," she said. "This body is mine now. Or will be in a moment, when

I finish destroying your friend's spirit." Her eyes danced, drinking up my anguish as if it were delicious.

I was out of time. I couldn't hesitate, couldn't balk, or Kessa would be gone forever. I could take a terrible chance and risk killing her, or I could let her die for certain.

My fear vanished, replaced by a rage cold as obsidian and vast as the Black Tower itself.

"No," I said, my voice coming from deep in my chest. The suffocating heat around us seemed to emanate not from the gate, but from the wrath burning within me; the glaring light of the Nine Hells at my back cast my long stark shadow before me. "I won't let you."

I reached out, grabbed her hand, and *pulled*.

"What—" She staggered into me, unsure of her balance in the unfamiliar body. I wrapped my arms around her in a tight hug, clasping her against my thundering heart, her hair tickling my nose.

What hummed beneath my touch was not the usual tingling rush of warmth, the soft unweaving sigh of a life dissolving into me. It was a rough crackle of energy, an electric surge of raw power, more like what I'd felt when I touched the gate. It writhed within my arms, struggling not to be drawn out of Kessa's body; it was like holding a bolt of lightning.

Please let this work. Kessa, please don't die.

"What are you *doing*?" she cried, stiffening and writhing in my arms. "Let me go!"

"Let Kessa go first," I hissed through my teeth.

Demons are creatures of pure energy, Whisper had said. And Bastian had told me, *You simply disrupt the energy of everything you touch, sometimes to the point of dissolution.*

I could only pray to the Graces that I wouldn't kill Kessa, or wind up possessed myself.

"You *dare*! Do you know who I am? Do you—" The demon

sucked in a sharp gasp, going rigid against me. "You! *I know what you are.*"

The hot, fierce power I'd clasped to me slipped up and out between my arms, tearing out of my grasp, leaving a trail of searing pain along my nerves. Kessa's body went suddenly limp, deadweight collapsing in my embrace like a puppet with the strings cut.

I flung myself away from her on a white-hot surge of fear, letting her tumble heavily to the hard floor. Her head struck the black stone, and she lay sprawled in a senseless tangle of limbs and skirts and streaming black hair.

He eyes were closed. I couldn't tell if she was breathing.

I dropped to my knees at her side, a whimper wrenched from my throat. Graces help me, had I killed her? I couldn't touch her to check, couldn't help her, could only kneel here making sounds of wordless animal grief, the harsh glare of the Nine Hells pouring over me.

She wasn't moving. Her chest didn't rise and fall.

I had no time to be broken. Bastian was a scholar, an alchemist, and halfway a physician; if anyone could help her, he could.

I staggered to my feet and ran for the door, half blind with tears, leaving Kessa's body on the Black Tower floor.

I ran as if the floor crumbled behind my heels into a bottomless abyss. As if ravens stabbed and pecked at my back, piercing through my rib cage to find my heart. I had to outpace my own thoughts, so that the full consequences of Kessa lying still and pale in the harsh white light of the Nine Hells wouldn't catch up to me.

I needed to find the Rookery. They'd probably never speak to me again after this, but that didn't matter. All that mattered was getting help for Kessa if there was any chance it wasn't too late.

I burst into the Bone Atrium and skidded to a stop as Ashe ran in through another door, the rest of the Rookery at her heels, leading them toward the Black Tower. Surprise flashed across her face.

"Ryx! Where's Kessa? Did you—"

"Hurry!" I gasped, doubling over. "Help Kessa! She's in the Black Tower!"

Ashe looked shocked. "You *left* her there?!"

"I . . ." There was no time. "I think I might have killed her." My voice stretched high and nearly hysterical, as something awful clawed its way up the back of my throat.

Foxglove swore and burst immediately into a run. Bastian barely spared me one wide-eyed glance full of shock and hurt and incomprehension before following him; it twisted like a knife between my ribs.

The look Ashe gave me burned with a wild, terrified, animal fury that teetered past the edge of madness.

"If she's dead," she hissed, "I'll kill you."

And she sprinted after the others.

I turned to follow them, dread at what I would find squeezing my chest, legs shaking. But before I could take a step, a voice rang out behind me.

"Exalted Ryxander! Stop where you are."

Voreth. Of course he caught up to me now, when I least wanted to do this. I swiveled to face him, my heart pounding.

He came striding toward me, his staff clacking on the floor. Black stripes of shadow slid across him as he passed beneath the slanting lances of bone that still crossed the atrium, stabbing down from the walls and ceiling. Behind him came half a dozen guards wearing Alevar colors.

And Aurelio, a bitter smile on his face, hands stuffed in his coat pockets.

"This isn't a good time, Voreth," I snapped. "I need to attend to an emergency."

"I overheard your little announcement." His lip pulled up

into a sneer. "You murdered one of the Rookery. Much like you did Exalted Lamiel."

The soldiers started to fan out in a wary arc, moving toward me. All my own guards and chimeras were stationed around the old stone keep, halfway across the castle, by my own orders; my staff and other guests would all be at dinner at this hour. There was no one in shouting distance who could defend me.

I knew I should be worried, but I couldn't bring myself to care. I only wanted to resolve this quickly so I could follow the Rookery and find out what had happened to Kessa. And the demon, holy Graces, I'd let another demon through.

"We can have this argument later," I snapped, moving toward the doorway the Rookery had taken. "Something went wrong with the gate, and there's another demon on the loose. I have to—"

"I *told* you," Aurelio interrupted, with heated vindication. "I warned you not to try to destroy it without studying it completely first. Now you see you should have listened to me."

"Forgive me if I don't take your word for it, Exalted Atheling," Voreth said, pacing closer to me. "You see, I've just learned you were lying to us all along, and that *you* killed Exalted Lamiel yourself. And now I've come to finally collect the murderer your aunt promised to deliver."

"Later," I snarled, and spun toward the door. I didn't have time for this.

Something hard swept my legs out from under me, and I crashed to the floor. I rolled onto my back, cursing—only to find Voreth's bone staff leveled at my throat, the tip sharpened by his magic to a spear's point.

"Now," he said softly.

Sheer frustrated fury boiled up in me. "You selfish idiot! Lives are at stake!"

"That's unfortunate," Voreth said, "but my lord's orders have priority."

Aurelio laid a hand on Voreth's arm. "You promised I could talk to her a moment first."

Voreth eyed Aurelio narrowly, but withdrew his staff. "I did."

I scrambled to my feet, half of a mind to make a run for it, but Voreth's soldiers had formed a loose ring around me. This was sheer folly, attacking me in my own castle—except that my grandmother was gone, my aunt was dead, and I had no way to call for help except with my own mortal voice. "Talk quickly," I snapped.

Voreth moved back to give us a semblance of privacy, but it was only a pretense, since Aurelio stayed prudently out of easy lunging range.

"I can still get you out of this, Ryx, if you're willing to cooperate." His voice was so low I could barely hear him.

"Out of what?" I asked furiously. "Being attacked in my own home?"

"Listen, I don't want you to get hurt." A muscle in his jaw twitched. "I never did. It was all I could manage to get the order for your death rescinded; Lord Urso said I was letting my feelings get in the way of the mission. But I could spare you again, no matter what he says, if you help me in return."

"What order for my death?" Nothing he was saying made sense, especially when all I could think about was Kessa and the demon who might still be out there. But something about his tone snagged my attention, and his words penetrated at last, like cold rain soaking through my clothes.

"Grace of Mercy," I whispered. "You're the one who tried to kill me."

He winced. "I didn't want to. I had my orders from Lord Urso, for the good of the Empire, and what could I do? I had to betray someone—either you, or my father and my mentor. And I like you, Ryx, but they're my *father* and my *mentor*."

I stared at him. There were no words for the contempt and fury churning in my stomach.

"I'm glad I failed," he said. "I'm not sure I could do it again, to be honest."

Red rage unfurled ragged wings in my chest. "You're the one who murdered Aunt Karrigan."

"To save Eruvia!" he hissed. "I'm sorry, Ryx, I truly am, but it's a *gate to the Hells*. We can't trust anyone else with control of it. Certainly not a Witch Lord, or a Witch Lord's heir."

"And you think I'd help *you* seize control of it?" My mouth was too dry to spit at him, but my lips peeled back from my teeth in a snarl. "Never. Not even to save my life."

Aurelio sighed. "I'm sorry to hear you say that."

Something sharp jabbed into my shoulder from behind. Curse it, I was so angry at Aurelio that I'd lost track of Voreth. I started to whirl on him, a strangely fresh scent flooding my senses—peppermint?

Darkness swooped across my mind like a dropped curtain, and I felt myself falling.

THIRTY-SIX

Voices sounded around me: low, rough, frustrated. Smooth wood slid beneath my back and legs, and my wrists ached— they were dragging me by someone's belt across the floor. I struggled to rise, but everything was still slow and groggy, as if my mind and body were drowning in molasses.

"How is she waking up already?!" That was Voreth, incredulous.

"Her freakish magic." Aurelio's voice. *He* was still here. "Looks like it unravels alchemy in about a minute or two."

I forced my eyes open. They wouldn't focus, but the vague blur of colors around me suggested the New Manor, near the Birch Gate. They were hauling me off to the Shrike Lord before anyone noticed, without waiting for Severin's approval or to see what was happening with the gate.

No. Panic flooded my veins like a jolt of lightning. I couldn't leave now. I had to go to Kessa. I had to make sure the gate could be destroyed. I had to warn the Rookery about the demon, and keep it from taking anyone else in the castle.

"You're making a mistake," I groaned. It came out slurred and muddled.

I tried to stagger to my feet. The strap on my wrists jerked, throwing me to the floor instead. I got my hands under me, ignoring the bruises, ready to push off and rise again. "Listen—"

Voreth's bone staff cracked hard across the back of my head, and I cried out, my face hitting the floor.

"You're as likely to kill her as knock her out that way," Aurelio said sharply.

"How am I supposed to keep her down, then?" Voreth demanded.

Pain stabbing through my head, I rolled onto my shoulder, levering myself up. "Listen to me," I tried again, desperate. "I need to know—"

Aurelio bent over me, his face attentive, as if he would hear me.

Something sharp pricked the lump of muscle between my shoulder and neck.

"We'll just have to keep trying, I guess." The words tumbled down a dark hole after me as I slipped back into unconsciousness.

There came a patchwork time of brief urgent glimpses: rough jabs of Voreth's staff, hard floors, arguing voices. It couldn't have been long, but with fear and desperation surging through me against the smothering sleep potion, every second stretched into an endless, agonizing struggle.

"Take the rest of the vial. I've got to see what's happening at the gate." Aurelio. Curse him. I reached for him with a numb, shaking hand, furious enough to kill, but with a sharp jab in my arm, I was gone again.

The scents of hay and horses, the jingle of harness, the cold clasp of metal on my wrists. *No. The demon. I have to warn everyone about the demon.*

"Hurry, before Exalted Severin returns with some foolish delay."

The creak of wheels, the scent of dust and pine, the clatter of hooves. Cold. Everything was cold, and bruises ached all over my body. *Kessa.*

"Straight down the middle of the road. Put one wheel in the forest, and if the Lady of Owls notices we've got her granddaughter in chains, we're all dead."

Hells, they were getting away from the castle. I struggled toward consciousness, like a swimmer rising toward the shimmering mirror light at the top of the water.

"...some kind of monster," an unfamiliar voice whispered. "Watch."

Something light and soft fell onto my face. A leaf. With a faint rustling crackle, it shriveled to a crisp against my skin.

"That's horrible," another voice murmured, with sickened awe.

"Right. And you heard what happened to Joss when he put the chains on. For blood's sake, don't touch her."

I heaved myself up in a panicked lurch, blinking sense out of light and shadow, the leaf fluttering down from my face. There came a great scramble of motion away from me.

They'd chained me in an open wagon bed, my hands behind my back. Two soldiers cringed at the far end of the wagon, faces pale with terror, leveling flintlock pistols at me. Moonlight filtered through the canopy of branches reaching over the road, and the warmer illumination of a pair of lanterns set shadows flaring across the guards' faces with the bouncing of the wagon. My head pounded, and dozens of minor cuts and bruises nagged at my attention as well, but all I could think of was what might be happening at the castle.

Hell of Nightmares. This couldn't be real. Not now. Fear tasted coppery in the back of my throat.

"I need to get back to Gloamingard at once," I blurted, my voice coming out high and strained. I tried to scramble up to my knees, but the chains yanked at my wrists, secured to the wagon.

"I'm afraid you're in no position to dictate orders, Exalted Ryxander." Voreth's voice floated out of the darkness, and he rode up beside the wagon, lip curled in a smile. "Besides, it seems to me that your help with the gate has consistently made matters worse. Gloamingard is far better off without you."

The truth of it struck me like a falling tree. I sank against the hard wagon boards, aching all through.

"Truly, the Shrike Lord will be doing Morgrain a service by killing you," Voreth went on, his tone amused. "I'd heard you were an embarrassment to your family, but you're more of a curse."

I couldn't muster a retort; he had a point.

And given that no one seemed to have come after me, my family and the Rookery might well agree with him.

I just had to make it to the forest, not ten feet away over the side of the wagon. On the road itself, ancient and powerful commands bound into the land by generations of Witch Lords ensured the safety of travelers. But so long as we were still in Morgrain, if I could make it so much as one step off the road, the trees and all the beasts of the wood should protect me from recapture.

I worked my wrists in their chains, without lifting my forehead from where I'd laid it in apparent despair on my knees. I could probably slither out if I wasn't afraid to lose a bit of skin in the process. The pistols were the issue. Even if I killed the guards in the wagon before leaping out—which I wasn't certain I was willing to do; they were just following orders—there were four more guards, all watching for trouble and ready to shoot me. The trees might keep them from following me into the woods, but they couldn't stop me from dying with a musket ball in my back. And I couldn't help anyone at Gloamingard if I were dead.

I needed a distraction. Something to pull their attention away from me long enough to make it to cover. I lifted my head, scanning the moonlight-scattered space between the columnar shadows of the trees.

A speck of ghostly green light drifted between the branches, then vanished.

I blinked, wondering if I'd imagined it. But it reappeared for a moment, along with another. And another. Green-gold sparks floating in the air, like stars come down to dance in the halls of the forest.

Autumn was the wrong time of year for fireflies.

"Oh Hells," I breathed, as my heart kicked into a gallop.

More and more appeared, filling the dappled air with tiny lights. The soldiers peered into the forest, some with wary gazes, others full of wonder. Part of me wanted to warn them, but I kept my lips clamped shut, frantically working my wrists against their chains.

"They're so beautiful," one man sighed.

"They could be dangerous," a woman snapped. "Be ready for…"

She swayed in her saddle and fell with a heavy thud to the road.

In the same moment, the soldiers riding in the wagon with me suddenly slumped over, pistols clattering from their hands. The rest of the guards fell one by one, reaching for their weapons; one sprawled over the neck of his horse, and another landed with a loose-limbed crunch that left me wincing.

Voreth cursed and reached for the bone staff slung across his back, but he slumped in the saddle before his fingers touched it. His horse swerved to stay under him. The other horses clattered to a confused halt, tails swishing nervously, ears flicking right and left; the wagon rumbled to a stop.

I braced for a sting, but none came.

A shadow dropped from a tree limb above, landing in the

wagon bed in a graceful crouch. The wagon creaked and rocked under the impact. My heart seemed to miss two beats, then leaped into a sprint trying to catch up.

Beneath a familiar pale crest of hair, two burning orange circles lifted to gaze at me.

"Hello, Ryx."

THIRTY-SEVEN

I swallowed. "Hello, Grandmother."

"Shall I kill all these people, do you think, for daring to put my grandchild in chains?" She tipped her head, considering. "Or shall I kill half of them, and make it look as if their comrades did it to them? That could be fun."

Hells have mercy. We'd already gone from hello to murder. I tried to delicately shift the subject. "Are you rescuing me?"

"Perhaps." Her eyes narrowed. "What will you do if I let you go?"

Run back to Gloamingard, warn them about the demon, and help destroy the gate. I couldn't tell her that. Our bond was too deep for me to lie to her, though; she'd know immediately if I did.

"I'd finish what I started," I said carefully.

My grandmother laughed. "Destroying the seal? Do you truly wish to unleash all nine of us? I personally find Carnage and Despair to be tedious, and would rather leave them in the Hells."

I stared at her warily, not sure what she meant.

Or had I somehow accidentally drained the seal alone, and left the gate intact? That might explain what had happened in the Black Tower. But the seal on the stone was clearly marked, and I hadn't touched it. If its precisely inscribed circle didn't delineate the binding enchantment's boundary, what did?

Ash and ruin. Hope drained out of me like wet sand from a ripped bag.

"The whole obelisk is the seal, isn't it?" I whispered. "It's not a gate at all. We were wrong."

My grandmother's teeth flashed in a too-wide grin. "What mortal would be mad enough to construct a gate to the Nine Hells? There was never a gate. There was a tear, a hole. The obelisk held it shut."

I surged halfway to my feet, forgetting my chains; they yanked me to my knees. "I've got to tell the Rookery. If they destroy it—"

"Then the passage to the Nine Hells will be thrown wide, as it was in the Dark Days." Her mouth curved in a secret smile, her lids drooping until her eyes became burning orange slits. "That could be amusing. We didn't know what we were doing the first time, blundering across the physical world like children learning to walk. We could accomplish so much more now."

It was as if the ground fell away beneath me, leaving me balanced on a knife's edge above a dizzying abyss. It was easy enough to think *My grandmother is a demon* or *We could unleash the Dark Days upon Eruvia once more.* They were statements too big and terrible to understand, like a storm raging outside a closed window while you sat comfortably by the fire, shivering at what you saw through the glass.

But the ancient mad gleam in her eyes was no distant storm, no fable of long ago. I was talking to one of the Nine Demons *right now.* And what I said to her might determine how many of the others we had to face. Every word I uttered could tip the balance between my grandmother and the demon, and save or doom thousands of lives.

"You still want to protect Morgrain," I said, holding her gaze. "I know you do, Grandmother."

"Of course. And protect it I shall, such that all the world trembles to see." She lifted a sly finger. "But peace is *boring*, Ryx. Chaos is better. I've been keeping mostly quiet because you haven't needed my help making things wonderfully messy. Until now." She sighed. "Now that you've gotten the humans to agree and work together, I suppose I'll have to stir things up again."

That didn't sound good. Hells, every turn this conversation took stumbled into some new danger I could unleash on Eruvia by inspiring the Demon of Discord's destructive whims.

I licked my lips, considering my next question. This would be easier if I weren't chained up in the back of a wagon, surrounded by unconscious enemies, with a splitting headache. "Do you know which demon came through the gate today?"

She cocked her head. "Do you know how *many* demons came through the gate today?"

A chill struck me like spilled ice water. "No."

"Neither do I. Though I expect we'll both find out." She extended a hand toward me, her expression turning sober. "Come with me, Ryx. We'll find out together. We're both creatures of chaos, you and I; we were never meant for peace."

"Come with you where?" I asked neutrally.

"To Gloamingard. To take what is ours." She looked up at the moon, seeming to revel in the touch of its silver light. "Or perhaps we'll go to Alevar, and see if we can pit Exalted Severin against his brother. With a bit of help, we could make it an even match, and then the Shrike Lord will have his hands too full with an attempted coup to bother us." She spread her arms wide, as if to embrace all the possibilities. "Or to the Serene City! We could crash all the best parties. No one would dare stop us. You could dance your partners to death in a fine silver gown, while lovely music played. Or we could call the Witch

Lords to Conclave, and kill them all, and let their heirs descend into war."

My throat went dry as old bone. "Those options, ah, may not be as appealing as you think."

"Why not?" My grandmother laid a gentle hand on my shoulder. "You owe them nothing, Ryx. Not Vikal, not the Rookery, not the diplomats back at the castle, not the people of Morgrain. They've scorned you, used you, made the warding sign against you. They gave you up without protest to go to a terrible death. Forget them, and come be what you were meant to be."

"A monster." My mouth twisted bitterly. "A murderer. A curse."

"Exactly. We'll be monsters together. Like always." She gave my shoulder an encouraging squeeze. "Why do you think I understood you so much better than your own parents did? A Witch Lord is a monster, too."

"And if I say no?" I gathered my courage as best I could, with both hands bound behind my back and my heart rattling in pieces in my chest. "If I say I'd rather seal the gate, keep the peace, and protect my people—what then?"

Shutters seemed to close in her face. "Then you're a sentimental fool."

"I've always been a fool," I said softly.

She sighed. "Ah, Ryx. Don't choose this. It'll hurt so much more if you do."

"I can't abandon my duty," I insisted. "Or my friends."

Her hand dropped from my shoulder. She rose in a single, fluid motion. "You'll change your mind soon enough," she said. "You'll have to, when he's killing you."

A hollowness opened behind my breastbone. "You're not going to just leave me here, are you?"

"Of course not!" She laughed, but I didn't dare feel relief. Not with that gleam in her eyes. "No, no. If you won't come with me, I want you pushed to the edge, Ryx. I want you shattered and broken, so all your lovely jagged shards can help me cut the world into new shapes."

She leaned down and patted my head with tender care. "And if I just leave you here, you'll escape," she whispered. "You always were resourceful. I have to do more than that."

Panic leaped in my chest. "Wait—"

"Good night, Ryx. And good luck."

A green spark flickered in the corner of my vision; something stung my temple. Consciousness jerked out from beneath me like a conjurer's tablecloth.

THIRTY-EIGHT

I woke to burning thirst and a world gone dead around me.

All I could feel was the boards of the wagon beneath my cheek, the chill dawn air harsh across the parched dryness of my lips. I had no sense of trees around me or grass beneath me, no sense of birds in the pearl-hued sky or the thousand small creatures sleeping in the earth. I might as well be floating in an empty void, or buried in a stone tomb.

I was no longer in Morgrain.

Despair crushed down on me, driving the breath from my chest, a sharp pain jabbing my ribs.

Except the pain was real, physical, and the wagon had stopped. *What the—*

"Hit her again," someone said.

A sharp blow struck my side. I rolled away from it as far as the chains let me, and up to a crouch to face the soldiers peering at me from the far end of the wagon bed. One of them pulled back a musket he'd clearly just used to jab me awake; fear strained his face. More guards glared at me, their fingers flicking out from their chests in the warding sign. Voreth leaned against his bone staff outside the wagon, regarding me with calculating eyes.

My pulse lurched into a sprint. This was bad. If I was in Alevar, my chance to escape had vanished. Instead of the land aiding me, it would hinder me. My captors no longer had to treat me with any kind of gentleness to keep from drawing my grandmother's attention and ire. Even my killing touch wouldn't get me far when every living thing was turned against me; if a wolf perished as it tore out my throat, or a tree branch withered as it pierced my heart, I'd be just as dead.

Being in Alevar meant that more than a day had passed since we'd left Gloamingard. Anything could have happened there. Kessa could be dead; the demon could have taken a new host and murdered everyone in the castle; the gate could be thrown open wide. It was Gloamingard's great moment of crisis, and its Warden had spent it unconscious in a wagon bed, of no use to anyone.

And no one had come after me. The knowledge stabbed between my ribs far more sharply than the throbbing pain of my new bruises. It wouldn't have been hard to overtake the wagon. Everyone had left me to die.

The *best* possibility was that no one cared about me. Any other alternative meant that the situation at Gloamingard was bad enough to keep anyone from following.

I liked to think Ashe would have already found me and killed me if Kessa were dead.

I squeezed my eyes shut, fighting back hot tears. I didn't want to look at angry, frightened soldiers right now, or Voreth's hateful face. I didn't have time to care about what they were going to do to me. I needed to get back home and tell the Rookery what I'd learned from my grandmother about the obelisk, curse it. Whether they still counted me a friend or not.

The hard muzzle of the musket shoved my chest, rocking me back on my heels.

"I require your full attention, Exalted Ryxander," said Voreth. "You will be coming into the presence of the Shrike Lord soon, and you need to understand how to behave."

"I don't give a dead rat how you think I should behave," I croaked. "I've got—"

Before I could finish, the musket drove into my stomach, forcing the air from my lungs. I curled over, gasping. One of the soldiers laughed nervously.

"You will show him respect and bow before him," Voreth said, his voice calm and even.

"Listen to me," I rasped, as soon as I had enough breath. "That doesn't matter right now. The gate—"

This time, the musket cracked across my jaw. I tumbled back against the wagon boards, all words knocked from my mind in a blinding flash of pain.

"Voreth! What are you doing? Stop this at once!"

My head snapped up, hope rising in me like a leaping flame. *Severin.*

He rode up to the wagon along the forest road, his horse snorting a greeting to its comrades. His usually sleek fall of dark hair hung loose and tangled, as if he'd ridden hard to get here. His black-and-gold coat was buttoned wrong.

He gave me one quick, anguished glance as he approached, and then averted his eyes. Graces, I couldn't play this game right now. Was that guilt over not coming sooner? Revulsion at the monster who'd murdered Kessa? Fear of telling me what horrible things had been happening at Gloamingard? I wanted to shake answers out of him.

Voreth bowed to him. "Exalted Atheling. After some difficulty on the road, I thought it important to make sure our captive understood that she is in Alevar now, and can expect no more gentleness."

Severin did not so much as glance in my direction. He dismounted, tossing his reins to a startled soldier, and strode over to Voreth, glaring. "You have no right. Her pain belongs to my brother. Every blow you strike, you are stealing from your lord."

A muscle in Voreth's cheek jumped, and his eyes widened. He bowed again, more deeply this time. "I thought, Exalted Atheling, that surely—"

"No," Severin interrupted him. "You clearly didn't think at all. If the captive is weakened from your care, she won't last as long. My brother wants a slow death. Have you even fed her?"

Voreth winced. "No, Exalted Atheling."

"See to it. If my brother is robbed of his due vengeance for Exalted Lamiel's death, I will make certain he knows who is at fault."

Voreth began snapping orders at his soldiers, and they scrambled out of the wagon and hurried to get me food and water. Under cover of the activity, Severin came and leaned against the wagon, meeting my eyes at last.

"Are you well?" he asked neutrally, with a glance over his shoulder at Voreth, who wasn't far.

"Did you come from Gloamingard?" I demanded, straining against my chains. "Is everyone all right? Is Kessa—"

"She's alive," he said quickly. "Not well, but alive."

Something rigid and brittle gave way inside me. I slumped, fighting back a great swelling cry that wanted to burst up out of my chest. *Alive.* I hadn't killed her. Thank the Graces.

"She was still unconscious when I left," he said, fast and low so Voreth wouldn't hear. "I'm sorry I didn't come after you sooner. Everyone was distracted by the situation with Kessa, and by the time I realized what had happened, Voreth had a long lead on me."

"We have to hurry," I said, my voice coming out breathy and trembling. I cleared my raw throat. "Another demon came through the gate—that's what attacked Kessa. And the gate is—"

Severin hissed. "Another demon! Seasons spare us." He glanced back over his shoulder toward Voreth, who approached now with soldiers carrying bread and water. Severin straightened, his expression hardening. "And you will find that begging for mercy does no good with my brother, Exalted Ryxander, but if you behave honorably you may earn enough of his respect to merit a swifter death."

A chunk of bread and a water flask thunked into the wagon in front of me. I stared at them, then looked up at Voreth. I was tempted to ignore him and keep blurting out my urgent secrets to Severin, but that would make it too clear that I saw him as an ally.

"You do realize I can't pick those up, right?" I rattled my chains at Voreth.

He turned away.

"Too weak a mage to survive contact with her, Voreth?" Severin taunted.

Voreth's lip curled. "If you're so concerned with her health— on your brother's behalf, of course—*you* can feed her."

"Or you could unchain me," I suggested.

Voreth walked away. Severin sighed, then leaped up into the wagon with nimble grace and pulled the stopper from the water flask.

"I'm sorry," he murmured, offering it to me.

"That doesn't matter now. We have to get back to Gloamingard and tell the Rookery not to—"

"We can't go back to Gloamingard." He wouldn't meet my eyes again. "I can't free you."

I stared at him in disbelief. Those four brutally simple words crushed the hope from me like a massive stone dropped on my chest. First my grandmother, now Severin. At least she had the excuse of being a demon.

"Let me go, Severin." Maybe, somehow, I'd misunderstood. "I need to get back to the castle and stop the Rookery from making a terrible mistake."

"I can't." The words were a bare ragged whisper, as if his throat were as dry as mine.

"You mean won't," I said, beyond the point of gentleness. "You're an atheling, for blood's sake. You outrank him."

"I'm not a good person, Ryx." He still held out the water flask, with a touch of desperation. "My brother never gave me that luxury. I've known every day of my life that he'll kill me the moment he thinks I'll defy him. If I let you go, if I do anything to protect you, he'll execute me in your place."

"So you're here to what?" I demanded furiously. "Help me feel a bit better before I die?"

"I don't know." His hand shook on the flask, and he looked up at last, frustration burning in his eyes. "I don't know what to do. My brother could stop us with a thought if I tried to help you escape. Just drink the water, all right?"

"I was counting on you." Hells, I should be kinder, but I was too exhausted and afraid and hurt to be kind. "Now you show up and you're cursed useless."

A spasm of pain or anger crossed his face. He threw the flask down; water seeped between the boards, wasted. "I'm trying to help you," he hissed.

"You're not very good at it."

He stood, disgust at one or both of us carving lines in his face. I pulled against my chains, afraid of missing my chance. "Severin, listen. You have to get a message back to Gloamingard. They *must not* destroy the obelisk. It's not a gate after all, it's a—"

"Are you done here?" Voreth asked, returning.

Severin looked at me, then at Voreth, his expression remote and cold. "Yes," he said. "I believe I am."

I didn't get another chance to talk to Severin; Voreth stayed between us, clearly suspicious. When my throat grew so dry that

I started coughing uncontrollably, they tossed me another water flask, and I had to bring it to my lips using my feet and knees.

Whenever I got the chance, I glared at Severin, past however many soldiers rode between us. *Send the message, you idiot. Tell them about the gate.*

His eyes always slid away from mine. Just like everyone else's had, all my years in Gloamingard. I supposed I must be uncomfortable to look at, bruised and battered and hungry as I was. Everything hurt.

It didn't help to remember that I was likely going to hurt a lot worse soon enough.

Through my exhausted haze, I tried to stay alert for opportunities to make a run for it. But Alevar was a low, wet country, and the roads our horses traveled were often raised causeways held in place by tree roots and surrounded by swamp. I wouldn't make it three paces before slimy things pulled me under the water and held me in their dead tangle to drown.

At least I could take bitter satisfaction in watching mosquitoes descend on the guards who'd beaten me in swarms; they died when they landed on my skin, of course. *Ha. One less life to give power to the Shrike Lord.* I'd take my petty victories where I could.

I still hadn't found a chance to escape when the Shrike Lord's castle reared up before us, a collection of sharp spires like pointed teeth bristling on a low hill. Clouds of birds circled above it, stark black silhouettes against a storm-gray sky.

What paltry options I had left vanished one by one as the wagon rolled through the maw of the gate into a stone courtyard. Thorny vines climbed the walls and sleek, brindle-furred chimeras, like a cross between weasels and panthers, prowled a restless guard. Deep, visceral fear tightened my gut at the mad predatory hunger in their eyes.

Now even my grandmother couldn't rescue me. Not from inside another Witch Lord's own castle. The last spark of hope

I'd been cradling in my heart sputtered and died, leaving gray ashes in my chest.

The wagon stopped. Two soldiers folded down the back, while others kept pistols trained on me. Severin climbed into the back of the wagon, then crouched down to face me with troubled eyes.

It was all I could do not to burst out in hysterical, panicky laughter. *Oh, I'm sure this is all very upsetting for you.*

"I have to unlock your chains," he said.

"So kind of you to do that *now*," I retorted.

"You're in my brother's castle." His voice was subdued, and he hunched his shoulders as if constantly expecting a blow. He rubbed at the scars on his neck. "He's watching us. I can feel his attention on you. Please come quietly."

"You want me to go meekly to my death?" I gave him a flat stare. "Why, so he'll pat you on the head and tell you you're a good brother?"

Severin winced. "I don't want you to get hurt."

"You are literally asking me to walk peacefully into the presence of a man whose stated intention is to torture me to death." I shook my head in wonder, because it was easier to be disgusted with Severin than to let in the fear that scrabbled at my mind with curving claws. "I honestly don't know if you're mocking me, or if you're such a hopeless pile of contradictions you can't help yourself."

Severin's face went rigid. "Fine. You're right. I'm a coward. That doesn't mean I *like* any of this."

"I'm sure your disapproval of the situation will be a great comfort to me." I dropped my voice to a bare whisper. "Did you send the message? Did you tell them about the gate?"

Severin's brows lifted in apparent surprise. "I haven't—"

"Do you require assistance, Exalted Atheling?" Voreth asked pointedly, appearing behind Severin. "Your brother is not known for his patience."

Severin grimaced, and his face went remote and haughty again. "I'm going to remove your chains now," he said. "I suggest you cooperate, or I'll find someone far less gentle to do it for me."

I let him unlock my chains. His hands trembled, and those disheveled strands of hair fell into his face as it bent next to mine.

"I'll do what I can for you," he whispered.

"Maybe you'll at least manage to return my corpse to Morgrain," I replied bitterly.

Then he stepped back, and I was loose. My shoulder muscles creaked as I brought my arms forward at last, rubbing my wrists. The chains had left red marks on my skin, but they bothered me less than the bruises on my ribs. Still, I was very aware of being whole and alive, with all my pieces intact and attached. For now.

Soldiers formed a ring around me, with long pikes and pistols. They tried to look grim, but it was fear I saw in their eyes, in their white knuckles, in the too-tense way they held themselves. I was free, with death in my hands. If I chose, I could kill at least a few of them before they finished me, and they knew it.

But they had been born into the Shrike Lord's service, and were only doing their jobs. And besides, I couldn't die until I got my message out. I walked with them peacefully enough, in the center of a ring of spears, chimeras circling beyond the soldiers with gleaming eyes and sharp white fangs.

Kessa is alive, I reminded myself. *There's hope we can salvage this. You have a job to do.*

A certain shivering unsteadiness stole up my legs, however, as they herded me with their spears into the Shrike Lord's throne hall.

THIRTY-NINE

Briars covered the soaring walls of the Shrike Lord's hall, black on gray stone, forming intricate abstract patterns that teased the mind with their negative space. The vaulted ceiling arched in ribs of curving wood, black to match the briars, over more gray stone. Every line in the place seemed to subtly converge toward the far end of the hall, where a few plain stone steps led to an austere black throne.

I couldn't help but notice that some of the briars decorating the hall wove through bits of bone: threading through a piece of rib cage here, a skull's eye socket there. All of the bones looked human. I shuddered.

The hall was far from empty. Courtiers and officials parted as we entered, opening a path to the throne for us. Their clothing was sober and practical, for a royal court, and their faces solemn. If they expected to enjoy this, it certainly didn't show in their faces.

The Shrike Lord sat on his throne, radiating the presence of a man who knows without question that he is in command of everything around him. His power filled the air with a pressure like an impending storm. He was in the briars on the walls, the hills at his border, the depthless swamps with all their ancient layers of decomposing history that stretched for miles around us. His was the strength of tangled whispering boughs, of open expanses of hissing marsh grasses beneath a clouded sky, of water deep and black enough to drown the greatest army. You could sink into his power forever, in layer after layer of darkness and ancient death, and never find a bottom.

And all those layers of his power reverberated with barely suppressed rage. I had never been so hated in my life. The very air I breathed wanted to choke me. I faltered, but made myself keep walking. Sweat slickened my palms.

It was unsettling to see his fine-chiseled face, so like Severin's, set in lines of brooding cruelty. His mage mark stood out stark white against his dark eyes, burning his hate into me from across the hall. He had dyed a broad storm-cloud gray streak into his hair, leaving it black on the sides like a shrike's mask; it swept back from his forehead and fell loose to his broad shoulders. Tattoos of intricately twisting briars wound up his bare arms, more heavily muscled than his brother's, and vanished into a close-cut black vestcoat that looked more like a military uniform than royal raiment. Only the gray cape flowing from his shoulders held an edge of silver, one bright gleam in his stark hall.

Voreth and Severin waited by their lord's side—Voreth kneeling at the bottom of the steps, and Severin standing one step up. I met Severin's haunted eyes, staring a challenge at him; he mouthed something at me, but I couldn't make it out. It had better not be *Sorry* again.

"So," the Shrike Lord said, his voice rich and resonant, filling the hall and vibrating in my bones. "This is Lamiel's killer."

The soldiers melted away from around me, as if they didn't want to be associated with me by proximity. I stood alone in a clear space halfway to the throne, the Shrike Lord's animosity bearing down on me with all the force of ancient stone, iron roots, and deadly talons. My vision dimmed under the weight of his power, and I found it suddenly hard to breathe. He wanted my legs to buckle beneath me; I could feel it. He wanted me to kneel.

I had touched the Hells themselves with my bare hand. I stood straight before him, setting myself grimly against the burden of massive magical power hanging so heavily in the air.

"Exalted Lamiel trespassed in forbidden places, abused our hospitality, and attacked me without cause," I said, my voice ringing from the thorn-clad walls. "I await your apology, Most Exalted."

Severin winced. The entire hall sucked in a sharp collective breath, a gasp edged with ragged fear. It suddenly seemed half-empty, the space growing even wider around me.

The smoldering presence in the air ignited to rage. It hit me in a great black wave, and I rocked on my feet with the force of it. *Maybe that wasn't the most diplomatic opening move.*

"Bravado does not become you." The Shrike Lord's voice remained controlled, despite the fury blistering the air. "My grievance far surpasses yours. You killed my betrothed while she was your guest, an envoy of peace to your house. Do you deny it?"

"No," I said, my voice thickening.

"You will die for this." He said it quietly, but every stone in the hall heard his words. His hands curled tighter on the arms of his throne, knuckles whitening. "You understand that. I will take your life as you took hers, and only then will my grievance be satisfied."

"I understand." I didn't accept it, even here at the heart of his power; it didn't seem real. His bleak logic, however, I recognized all too well. "There's something *you* need to understand, first."

"You will not profane the solemnity of your last moments with tedious insults, I hope," he said.

"No." I clenched my fists at my sides. I had to make him listen to me, no matter what. Or if he wouldn't listen, I had to get through to Severin. The atheling stood by his brother's throne, face ashen, eyes locked desperately on mine as if trying to send me some silent message.

I was done with his pleading looks. They were worth less than nothing if he didn't support them with action, and I was well past the point where I could bear to hope that he had some subtle plan. But by the Graces, he could convey a simple warning.

I drew in a breath. "You know of the artifact at Gloamingard. I've discovered that it's not a gate at all; it's a seal on an existing rip in the world. I need to get that message to the Rookery." The Shrike Lord's expression hadn't changed. Surely he must care about this—his domain would be affected, too, if the Nine Demons strode the world again. "We must strengthen the seal, not destroy it. Guard it, not fight each other to possess it. I could have killed half these soldiers, but I walked in here willingly for one reason: to urge you to help Morgrain guard the seal against any who would threaten or misuse it."

Severin's eyes widened while I spoke, then narrowed. I was sure he heard every word and understood their implications. The great sickening knot inside me relaxed a little; at least I'd passed on my information.

But the Shrike Lord's face remained stony, and the cloud of his anger grew no less oppressive in the air. If anything, it intensified.

"Do not think for a minute," he said, "that I care what you want."

"This is for the safety of all Eruvia, Alevar included," I insisted. "Not just Morgrain."

A sudden raw intensity flashed onto his face. "You dare much to suggest that I would lift a single finger to help the domain that slew the one person in the world I loved." Severin bowed his head at that, his hair swinging forward to hide his expression. "I will deal with the gate as I see fit, but your pleas I cast into oblivion. I do not hear them."

The Shrike Lord rose from his throne, his gray cloak falling around him. The briar vines on the walls began to shift, serpentine. Severin flinched away and closed his eyes.

"Enough words," the Shrike Lord said. "Now I claim my blood price, Exalted Ryxander of Morgrain."

I couldn't help myself. I stepped back, fear stabbing into my racing heart at the killing intent in those dark eyes. I searched frantically for some weapon, some trick, some last-minute ally, some word that could protect me, but there was nothing.

The briars slithered down off the walls, reaching for me, their black shadows falling across my face.

"Wait!" Severin cried, reaching out toward his brother.

The Shrike Lord flicked a contemptuous glance at him. "Do not demean yourself by pleading for her life, Severin."

"Of course not." The disdain in Severin's voice trembled on the edge of credibility. I held my breath, heart skittering in my chest like a dropped marble. "But she clearly knows a great deal about the gate. Don't you think you should get as much information out of her as possible before killing her?"

The Shrike Lord didn't take his cruel eyes off me. "No," he said softly. "I don't."

And all the reaching thorns struck at me at once.

I lashed out in instinctive panic, smacking one vine with the flat of my hand; it turned dead and brown, starting at the point where I'd touched it and spreading a good arm's length from there. Another vine touched my ankle and withered instantly. A wild thread of fierce hope slipped through me: I could fight him.

I turned to grab a third briar, its barbs pressing into my hand as it went dry and brittle at my touch. Another whipped suddenly at me, lightning fast; thorns tore my clothes and cut my skin as it lashed around my waist. As it died, it went hard as oak, its grip on me unyielding. *Pox, pox, pox.*

I struck out at another whipping branch in a rising terror, but now the dead ones were reaching for me, too. Dozens of them lifted up, swaying like rearing snakes, and descended on me all at once.

The vines seized me in their barbed grasp, coiling around my arms, my legs, my throat. Thorns hooked through my clothes and skin, winding around me. I choked back a scream; I didn't want to give the Shrike Lord the satisfaction.

"Ryx!" Severin cried, starting toward me.

His brother didn't even look; he'd expected this. The back of his hand crashed into Severin's face, knocking him down to the hard stone floor.

"You're lucky I'm willing to save you from treachery, brother," he said softly. Severin wiped blood from his mouth with a trembling hand.

The briars flexed like a great spiky fist around me and snapped back to the wall, flinging me flat against the stone.

A light flashed across my vision, and my breath whooshed out. For a moment I became nothing but a struggle to get air back into my lungs—nothing else mattered, not the briars pricking me or the throbbing of my skull or the Shrike Lord staring death at me or the crowd watching in terrified silence. Then I drew in a great hoarse gasp, and another, and with it a sustaining fury.

Only half the crowd remained, pressed back against the now-bare walls, no doubt more afraid to leave and risk the Shrike Lord's wrath than they were to stay. Severin wouldn't look at me as he climbed slowly up off the floor. But his brother watched, jaw set, satisfaction gleaming in his eyes.

"Pathetic," I croaked, as the thorn vines slithered around me, pinning me tight to the wall ten feet off the floor. "You're just a bully after all."

"Justice requires strength to punish the wicked," the Shrike Lord said. "It is a ruler's duty. Still, in this case, I confess that I'll take great pleasure in watching you bleed to death."

"You pretend to be an honorable man," I spat, "but there's no honor in gloating. It's petty and cruel."

That got a reaction. Something flared in his eyes—anger or guilty recognition. His lips peeled back from his teeth.

Sudden pain pierced me in half a dozen places as dagger-length thorns sprouted from the briar vines. This time, I couldn't keep from crying out. Wet warmth spread from each wound, the fabric of my clothes drinking up the blood. *Grace of Mercy, help me.*

Severin flinched and squeezed his eyes shut, his hands balled in tight fists at his sides.

"You're worth more than this," I gasped, hoping he'd know that I spoke to him and not his brother.

His shoulders bunched as if he wanted to strangle someone, his face twisted in self-loathing.

The Shrike Lord ignored him, watching me bleed with narrowed eyes. "The wonderful thing about vivomancers," he said, "is that they take so long to die."

I'm not a vivomancer, I tried to say, but a numbness spread through my veins, making my tongue too thick and clumsy. I could barely twitch my fingers, and my head drooped. *Poison.* Robbing my strength to move or speak.

It made sense, I supposed, through the haze of agony. He would hardly enjoy listening to his enemies shout insults down at him as they slowly perished on his walls.

Like I was doing.

The anger drained out of me, replaced at last by bone-deep, crushing despair. My grandmother had abandoned me, Severin was no help, and the Rookery was far away.

And now my life was trickling slowly away while the court of Alevar pretended not to see me, and the Shrike Lord watched with glittering malice in his white-ringed eyes.

FORTY

A long, red-tinged time later, someone spoke my name.
"Ryx. Wake up."

I dragged the ragged shreds of my awareness up from whatever murky pool of suffering they'd dissolved into for the past several hours and raised my head. The hall had emptied at last, the courtiers and even the Shrike Lord himself going off to bed. Severin had left with his brother, pale and downcast, blood still smearing his mouth.

The only people left in the hall were a pair of guards on the main door, presumably set there in case I tried to escape. They studiously avoided looking at me; neither of them had spoken. Oil lamps alternating with luminaries shone in niches around the throne hall, bathing the room in a mix of shadows and golden light.

"You don't have time for this, Ryx."

Whisper sat in the center of the floor, tail lashing with annoyance as if this were all somehow my fault.

The guards didn't seem to hear him or react to his presence in any way. I stared down at him, blood stiffening my clothes and the taste of copper in the back of my mouth, and wondered if he was a hallucination.

"By all means, carry on dying if you wish," he said, "but it seems rather self-indulgent given how much work you have to do."

The urge to wring his furry neck kindled sufficient spark in me to rasp out a few words. "This is...not my idea."

His ears twitched to catch my voice, though the soldiers on guard didn't react. "So you don't want to die here?"

It was a good question. Everyone I cared about had abandoned me. Everything I'd tried to do to help had only made things worse. Eruvia might well be better off without me. I had no reason to believe that survival would mean anything but more suffering.

But even with every breath making the thorns cut deeper, even with my blood running down the walls and pooling on the floor below me, even with every moment costing monumental effort just to make it through, I wasn't ready to let go of this life. Whisper was right; I had too much work to do. I was the Warden of Gloamingard, and my castle needed me.

And that wasn't the only reason. I didn't deserve to die here, curse it. I was worth more than this, too.

"No," I managed. "Not yet."

"Then you'd better stop lazing around." Whisper cocked his head, as if listening. "It'll be too late soon. Human bodies are so fragile."

So this was how it would end: bleeding to death while a chimera mocked me. My eyes drifted back shut. *I should have known.*

"Ryx." Whisper's indifference dropped like a shed cloak. "Don't fall asleep. You won't wake up. I can't rescue you—I need to stay neutral. You have to do this yourself."

And how do you expect me to do that? I wanted to ask, but it was too much.

"Fine." An edge of frustration came into Whisper's voice. "I wanted to avoid doing this at all costs. But if you're going to insist on being difficult, let's see if this wakes you up: Severin didn't send your message."

My eyes flew open. "What?!"

"The fool is too distracted trying to find a way to save you." Whisper watched me carefully, tail working behind him, measuring my reaction. "If you die here, the Rookery will destroy the seal, and the rest of the Nine Demons will come through and most likely possess them, since they'll be closest to the gate. Gloamingard will fall." He fixed me with his yellow gaze. "Your friends and your family will die."

The words seemed to break open something inside me, as if he'd spoken an incantation to shatter a seal. A vast, seething lake of fury and love welled up, driving out my pain and exhaustion and despair.

"I can't allow that."

"I'm afraid you'll have to do something about it, then." He rose and stretched. "Good luck. I've got my own business to attend to."

And in the blink of an eye, he was gone.

This surge of wild, desperate energy couldn't last long; all the damage done to me was still there, sure as the blood-slick thorns protruding from my left shoulder and wrist as I weakly turned my head to gaze past them toward the guards on the door. I had to get free somehow, and quickly, before this final burst of strength faded.

I could think of only one tool I had left.

All my life, I'd strained to hold back my broken magic. To keep it sealed away, like a hand balled tight into a fist, or an eye squeezed shut. My parents and my grandmother had done everything they could to train me to contain it; ultimately, they'd been unsuccessful, but that didn't mean all my striving had been without effect.

I took in a deep breath, ignoring the sickening stab of pain from a thorn in my side. And then I let it go, doing everything I could to uncurl that tightly clenched power within me.

Fractures ran along the briars, quick as forking lightning. A great rustling and crackling filled the room. The soldiers let out startled exclamations, reaching for their pistols.

For the first time in my life, I pushed my power outward.

The luminaries winked out, one after another, rapid as popping bubbles. The rush and tingle of magic raced through my limbs.

"Whatever you're doing, stop it now!" cried one of the guards, drawing her pistol and pointing it at me. The other whipped around, searching the room for an intruder.

The torches flared, then guttered out. Warmth flooded me, banishing some of the pain. Shards of wood rained to the floor as the briars began to crumble. The branches holding me sagged, and I cried out as the thorns twisted in my wounds.

The guards suddenly dropped, one after the other, limp and vacant. Dead as stones. Their lives flowed into me in a heady rush of strength.

Holy Hells. I'd gone too far.

In the distance, thunder rumbled.

Something vast and awful was unfolding in me, stretching tattered wings that had been cramped and caged for my whole life. I'd made a terrible mistake. Fear sang along my nerves, and I struggled against the crumbling briars that held me.

They shattered like sugar glass, cascading down in a great clattering wave of wood and dust. I fell, landing more or less on my feet—but they skidded out from beneath me, slipping on my own blood. I hit the ground, breathing hard, and couldn't get up. *No, no, no. Stop. This is too much.*

A deep, awful trembling started in the floor. No, not the floor—in the earth beneath it, far below. It ran up through me, through the walls, shaking every stone in the castle. Magic shivered through me in response.

"No!" I cried aloud, terrified.

"Ryx?" called a muffled voice from beyond the door, alarmed. *Severin*. If this kept escalating, in a moment I'd kill him, too.

I struggled to pull my magic back inside me, where it belonged. But it was raging free, awake and angry, stirring the earth and the sky to violence. It resisted, furious at being tamed for so long.

I won't let you kill anyone else.

With every ounce of will I possessed, gasping at the effort, I slowly clamped the fist of my power back shut.

The earth stilled. A dim spark flickered back to life in the luminaries. I lay on the floor, my breath coming quick and shallow, surrounded by scattered bits of dead wood.

Severin burst into the room, a slim dagger in his hand. He recoiled at the sight of the dead guards, then saw me and hurried over.

"Ryx! Hells, you're a mess."

"What else did you expect," I muttered hoarsely.

I tried to get up, but my left arm wasn't working, and my right was too weak to so much as lever myself up on one elbow. The edges of my vision crumbled like the brambles had, and everything seemed fuzzy and distant.

"Ash and ruin, you're covered in blood." He knelt by my side. "You've got to get out of here. Can you walk?"

I laughed. It took too much breath, and my head swam. "I can't even stand. I think the only life I've got left is what I stole from those poor dead bastards over there."

Severin glanced at them, then back at me. He bit his lip.

Before my foggy brain realized what he was doing, he laid his hands along both sides of my face, his touch warm and gentle. And he bent and placed a light, dry kiss at the top of my forehead.

A giddy rush of strength poured into me. Severin gasped in shock, his hands going rigid on my cheeks.

I rolled away from him, blurting panicky curses, but he caught my hand. Warmth and tingling energy surged up my arm.

"No, wait! It's all right," he said. "I won't let you take too much, I promise." He was doubled over on his knees, voice ragged with pain.

"Don't be a fool!" I yanked my hand from his. He was too drained to stop me. He barely caught himself from falling to the floor, with trembling arms.

"See, you're better already." He forced blue-tinged lips into an alarmingly vague and unsuccessful smirk. His eyes shone glassy and unfocused, and he swayed as if he might pass out.

"You *idiot*. You could have died!"

But he was right. My bleeding had stopped, there was strength in my limbs again, and the world didn't seem so far away. He'd taken a reckless risk, but it had worked.

"Come on," I said grimly, staggering to my feet. "Your brother is bound to have noticed what I did here."

Severin's smile widened. "In his sleep, perhaps. I drugged him."

I stared. "You *what*?!"

"Of course I did. Why do you think I played along with him? It was the only way I could think of to buy time to get you out of Alevar and beyond his reach. I don't know how long it will last, though." He dragged himself upright, leaning on the wall; he looked almost as bad as I felt. "We'll have to ride quickly."

"I can't ride horses," I pointed out grimly. "They'd die."

He let out a gust of breath. "And I don't know how to harness a carriage. All right. We'll have to run."

"This isn't going to work," Severin gasped, falling to his knees in the muddy road.

Branches tangled above us, knotting their fingers against a dark, mottled sky. It still felt wrong that I couldn't sense the life in the trees, or in the mud beneath my own stumbling feet.

Everything hurt, and I was breathing like I'd run a hard race, but we couldn't have made it more than a few miles from the Shrike Lord's castle.

"You shouldn't have touched me," I muttered, leaning against a dead tree to keep from joining Severin on my knees. My more-wounded leg trembled; I wasn't sure how much longer it would support my weight at all. "It's not like you're a cup of tea I can delicately sip from the top. I was unraveling your *life*."

"I'm feeling that," Severin groaned. Even in the darkness, he was too pale, his face gone the sickly ivory of the moon above us. "I'll admit I don't think I'd do it again."

There had been too many times when I'd briefly brushed against someone through clothes or gloves—a touch too fleeting and muffled to kill, but still enough to make my poor victim drop, their heart stuttering, gasping for breath or losing consciousness altogether. It inevitably took days of rest for them to fully recover. Severin had been trying to hide it, but I could tell he was in bad shape. If he kept pushing himself like this, I might kill him yet.

"You should go back," I said, worry knotting the words harder than I'd intended. "Pretend you were asleep the whole time. No one saw you help me escape. You're too badly hurt; you're never going to make it to the border."

"Neither will you," he said stubbornly, and dragged himself to his feet. "My brother is bound to wake up soon. He'll set every living thing in Alevar to find you and kill you. These swamps are full of deadly venomous snakes; you won't stand a chance."

"Then there's no point drawing you into it." I tried to cross my arms, but my left one still wouldn't move well enough; I winced at the stab of pain from my shoulder. "Besides, you need to warn the Rookery not to destroy the obelisk. We can't risk that information dying with us."

Severin's mouth twisted bitterly. "I finally do something to defy my brother, after all these years, and you're telling me to go back and pretend it never happened."

"Yes."

"To leave you to die, after I spent the past couple of days agonizing over how I could save you."

"I do plan to try my best to survive," I said wearily. "We don't have time to argue about this. Severin—"

His finger flew to his lips, eyes widening. I broke off and listened, every muscle tensing; if his brother had awakened, the next thing I felt might be the tree I was leaning against ripping my head off.

Hoofbeats. And voices, and rumbling wheels, perhaps a quarter mile distant.

Someone was traveling the Alevar trade road in the middle of the night.

"And here I thought spotting figures on the road ahead meant bandits, and I was finally going to get to stab someone," said a voice from the darkness, quite close by.

My heart jumped in startlement at first, but it kept going up and up, surging with joyous exaltation to reach the stars. "Ashe!"

The Rookery had arrived.

"I see our rescue plans will be unnecessary," Foxglove said from the high seat of a cabriolet I thought I recognized as belonging to Lady Celia. "A pity. They were remarkably clever and daring, if I do say so myself."

I barely heard him. I was staring past him to the person riding beside the cabriolet, wrapped in a warm cloak and looking more wan and tired than I'd ever seen her.

"*Kessa!*" I cried, wishing more than anything that I could fling my arms around her.

She waved and smiled, a little tentatively. "I'm back. Thank you for saving me."

I blinked. "Saving you? I almost killed you!"

"From the demon." She shuddered, and Ashe moved instinctively toward her, hovering like a fierce-eyed hawk.

"I'm sorry we didn't come sooner," Foxglove continued, his voice grave. "We were rather focused on making sure Kessa didn't die, and it was a near thing. I'm glad you're all right—I was afraid we'd be too late."

Bastian slid off his horse, approaching me with a frown. "I wouldn't say all right. Graces, Ryx, you're covered with blood."

A sharp, hissing rustle passed through the branches above, like a sudden wind—but the air hung heavy and still. I stepped away from the trees, nervous. Pattering raindrops began to drip down from the leaves overhead.

"Just rain," I sighed with relief.

The trees thrashed more violently, and something cried in the night.

Severin swore. "No. He's awake. And he's angry."

Ashe whirled, her sword in her hand, and pointed it down the road behind us. A figure stood there, a mere black silhouette in the darkness, a cloak flowing from his shoulders. I didn't have to see his face to feel the weight of power upon him, so great it seemed the whole world tilted dizzyingly toward him.

"Quite," said the Shrike Lord.

FORTY-ONE

The twin lines of trees flanking the road shifted with groans and creaks, shuffling to cut off our retreat should we have been foolish enough to think there would be any point in running. The Rookery horses shied and whinnied with alarm; only Kessa's stayed calm, from the soothing touch of her magic.

Every inch of me strained to bolt and run, but there was nowhere to go. All of Alevar was an extension of the Shrike Lord's will. I was like a mouse who had slipped through a cat's claws and made it halfway across the room only to be caught again. And now I'd drawn the Rookery into this mess with me.

The Shrike Lord advanced toward us, slow and menacing as the inexorable slide of time toward death.

"I am disappointed in you, Severin, that you would help my enemy. I thought you were a more loyal brother than that."

Severin stood frozen, his eyes wide with terror. He shook his head, his ready supply of sharp words apparently depleted at last.

"He's a more loyal brother than you deserve," I said fiercely.

"The words of the dead are meaningless," the Shrike Lord replied.

Ashe rolled her neck and stepped forward. "I've got an answer for that."

"Rule Four, Ashe!" Kessa hissed, clinging to her horse.

"He's not here to talk," Ashe protested.

"He's a *Witch Lord*," I whispered, wishing I could pull her back. "He's immortal. We'd better *hope* he's here to talk."

"I'm here for one purpose," the Shrike Lord said, still advancing. Damn it, I'd forgotten how sharp a Witch Lord's hearing could be. "To complete my vengeance. The rest of you can go."

He could have killed me without stirring from his bed. He must want to do it with his own hands.

Anger raised its weary head in me. I'd tried reasoning with him, and I'd tried diplomacy, and I'd bled out the last ounce of restraint I had on his wall.

"You want vengeance against Lamiel's killer?" I snarled. "Take it against yourself. You're the one who encouraged her to go looking for immortality anywhere she could find it, with no regard for the consequences."

A swinging tree branch struck me hard in the back, knocking me gasping to my knees. Mud oozed through my fingers as I struggled to get my wind back. The Shrike Lord didn't so much as blink.

Foxglove half rose in the rain-slick seat of his cabriolet and managed to pull off a credible bow even as he strove to control his carriage horse. "My lord, we came here to retrieve Exalted Ryxander for a reason. She is part of the Rookery and essential to our work. The Conclave gives us the right to—"

"Silence," the Shrike Lord said.

Something dropped from a tree branch above the cabriolet, landing in looping coils around Foxglove's neck. He flinched under its sudden weight, then went very still. I remembered what Severin had said about the swamps being full of deadly venomous snakes, and gooseflesh rose on my arms.

Another snake reared up between me and Bastian, massive and muscular, its triangular head weaving at him. He leaped backward with a startled oath, his skin going mottled as the shadows around us. Kessa reached for some weapon in her boot—and stifled a shriek as another snake, slim and delicate as a jess, glided up and around her wrist.

"Don't hurt them," I cried, rising from the muddy road. My wounded leg trembled under me, and rain slid cold fingers through my hair and down my face. "You have no grievance against any of them. Only me."

"Unlike you, I am no murderer, Exalted Ryxander." The Shrike Lord glanced at Ashe, who stood protectively between us, her sword out and ready. The ground beneath her feet suddenly gave way, the roots that held the road together above the swamp pulling back to let the earth crumble into a muddy hole. Ashe let out a curse and leaped to safety before she could tumble into it; a pair of trees bent down to cut her off from me, quick as a portcullis falling.

He'd neutralized the Rookery so quickly. At least they'd be safe this way—provided those snakes weren't too excitable. Worry for my friends sat like lead in my stomach as I raised my empty fists to face the Shrike Lord.

"Sorry. You're going to have to do *much* better than that."

It was Ashe, stepping into the Shrike Lord's way again. She'd somehow slipped through the trees that caged her. My heart leaped to see her bright and slim as her own drawn sword before me.

The Shrike Lord flicked a contemptuous hand; more trees reached for her, but Ashe dodged them with casual ease. Roots grabbed at her from below, but she leaped over them. A snake lunged at her, and she kicked it off the causeway.

"So slow," she taunted him. "Sure you're not the Turtle Lord?"

I scrambled away, opening up space, my heart pounding. Ashe was an insect to him; she couldn't hurt him, only annoy him. But he couldn't seem to swat her, either, and she was buying me time. I had to use it wisely.

"Listen, everyone," I called, desperate to at least pass on my message. "I met my grandmother on the way here. The entire obelisk is the seal on a tear in the world. If you destroy it, you'll open the way to the Nine Hells permanently."

"Curse it," Bastian exclaimed, loosening his collar. "I *knew* something in those artifice patterns didn't add up." He glanced over at where Ashe danced around the Shrike Lord; then he grimaced, made a casting-off motion, and seemed to vanish.

What the— Oh, right. He'd been modified for stealth. His guardian snake reared back its head in confusion, flicking the air with a forked tongue.

"Quickly," he whispered, suddenly beside me, all but invisible with a pattern of leafy shadows across his skin. I barely stifled a startled shriek. His burgundy jacket lay in the muddy road, the false front of his shirt crumpled with it. I couldn't feel any heat coming off him, even though he was far too close for safety; he must be able to regulate that, too. "Get out of here. We'll hold him off."

Foxglove beckoned me surreptitiously from his cabriolet, pocketing an artifice device shaped like a wire-wrapped tuning fork; the snake that had held him hostage lay draped around his shoulders as if it were a fashionable scarf, seemingly unconscious. Kessa had calmed his horses despite not being quite able to reach them; she sat stock-still on hers, sweating with concentration, still looking weak and pale from her brush with death.

The Rookery was not so easily defeated, after all. Hope spread its giddy wings in my chest. I had a chance.

I ran for the cabriolet, nerves singing. A wave of dizziness threatened to overwhelm me, my body protesting such quick movement after I'd lost so much blood and replaced it only with stolen life. *Just a few more steps—*

With a horrible groaning crash, a massive tree slammed down between me and the carriage, barely missing Foxglove and Kessa, completely barring my way. *Pox.* The horses reared and screamed, terrified. There came a splash from the water below the causeway, accompanied by a frightened yelp; Bastian became fully visible once more, knocked into the water and half pinned under the fallen tree's spreading branches.

I spun, panic buzzing in my brain, to face the Shrike Lord. He'd opened a gap several yards wide in the causeway, letting the water pour through it; Ashe stood on the far side, sword in hand, bouncing on her toes as if yearning to make the impossible jump. She couldn't reach me, either. Hell of Despair—I was on my own again.

The Shrike Lord had never slowed his advance. He strode inexorably closer, oblivious to the rain that poured over us both. He wasn't even breathing hard.

Of course he wasn't. He could have done much worse than this. He was barely trying. A shudder of exhausted fear shook me all the way up my spine.

Dozens of snakes crawled from the swamp, winding their way through the mud of the causeway, elegant and deadly in the dim gray light. I had no doubt all of them were lethally venomous; there was no way I was getting past them alive. I could only pray silently to the Graces that the Rookery would have the sense not to try anything too daring that would get them killed as well.

The Shrike Lord was almost upon me now, looming against the branch-twisted sky. Time to try talking, if I could force words past the fear and anger burning my nerves like acid. I took a shaky breath.

"I can't stop you from killing me," I began. "But if you have any sense, work *with* Morgrain after that. Eruvia needs—"

Suddenly I was kneeling in the mud again, pain exploding in my jaw. Kessa cried out my name.

I hadn't seen his fist coming; nothing had flickered in his eyes to warn me. *Hells have mercy.* He didn't need magic to kill me. He was fast as a cat and built of limber steel.

A long bone knife hissed out of its sheath at his side. "Lamiel was the one person in the world I loved." His voice caught on the last word with genuine grief. "Now that she's gone, I don't care if Eruvia goes to the Nine Hells."

I lifted groggy eyes to meet the blazing white rings of his mage mark. *At least let me die standing.* But my body was too broken, too exhausted, my hold on it slipping in the mud and the rain as a dull roaring filled my ears.

"I do," Severin said, and stepped between us.

"Get out of the way, Severin," the Shrike Lord said.

"No." Severin's voice was quiet but unshakable. I would never have known he was afraid if I couldn't see his hands, clenched white-knuckled behind his back. "Enough. You've hurt Ryx enough. Let her go help them close the damned gate."

The Shrike Lord surveyed his brother for a long moment as the rain poured down on both of them, his lips pressed together as if to hold back some word of anger or pain. I held my breath, not daring to interrupt with the slightest sound, even though I wanted to cheer for Severin.

The Shrike Lord whispered, "You were the only one I could trust. All those years, with our father trying to make us kill each other, you were my ally against him instead. And *now* you turn on me? Over *this*?" He waved his bone knife at me, incredulous. "I thought I'd taught you loyalty. I see that I was wrong."

Severin winced, his hand going involuntarily to the scar at his temple, but he didn't give ground. "I'm loyal enough to tell you that you can be better than this."

His brother's hand cracked across Severin's face. He staggered under the blow; I scrambled back to make sure he wouldn't stumble into me, rising from the mud at last.

A white-hot spike of anger flared through me. Power stirred beneath my skin, straining to blaze to life—to hurt the Shrike Lord as he'd hurt Severin.

Oh, Hells, no. I throttled it back, breathing hard, rain running down my cheeks.

Severin wiped blood from his split lip with a shaking hand. "You can be better than this," he repeated firmly.

The Shrike Lord raised his knife. "Get out of the way, Severin. Don't think for a moment that the blood we share protects you from me." The unnatural evenness of his voice had cracked at last, and it quavered with emotion.

"Oh, I've never held any illusions about that." Severin laughed bitterly. "But you did fool me into thinking you had a sense of honor, ruthless though it might be. Everyone else I've watched you execute was a criminal or a traitor, someone who genuinely tried to do you or Alevar harm. You know damned well Lamiel died because of her own stupid plot. If you kill Ryx now, it won't be justice. It'll be murder."

Severin must have known his brother would hit him again for that. He seemed to turn and flow with the punch, and I could only hope it didn't hurt him too badly. He straightened slowly, the rain plastering his shirt to his wiry shoulders.

"For the last time," the Shrike Lord growled, the trees around us quivering with his fury. "Move. Or I'll clear you from my path."

I stepped forward, anger shaking me like the last leaf in a hurricane, my power barely held in check. "Don't touch him again," I snarled. "Seasons witness, he's your *brother*. If you hit him again, I swear to you I will die making sure you remember it."

The Shrike Lord started to pull back his lip in a sneer of contempt. But as the frost-white rings of his mage mark fell on mine, something stopped him. He went very, very still.

He must have noticed when I let my power loose in his castle, even through his drugged sleep. He must have felt the rumbling deep in his earth, the stealing of his lives. He wasn't as afraid of it as I was—not by a long stretch—but it was enough to put a faint glimmer of caution in his eyes.

Severin's gaze never wavered from his brother's face. "Go ahead and move me," he said, his voice soft. "Kill me, if you want. But if you kill Ryx now, when the Rookery needs her to deal with the most serious threat Alevar has ever faced, I'll know you for a liar who only pretends to care about protecting his domain. And I'll know your measure is forever less than I thought it was."

The trees encircling us tossed as if in a high wind. Harsh cries and hisses came from the swamps around us. Kessa was down off her mount now on the far side of the fallen tree, shivering in the rain, desperately trying to soothe all of the Rookery horses at once; their attention stayed on her, but their ears flicked and their eyes rolled at all the furious noise. Ashe...I'd lost track of Ashe, and I hoped to the Nine Graces that didn't mean she was about to stab the Shrike Lord in the back or some such foolishness and ruin everything Severin was trying to do.

The two brothers stared at each other, eye to eye, mage mark to mage mark, for a long time. I didn't dare move. If I drew attention to myself, I had little doubt it would tip the balance in the wrong direction, and I'd be dead in a heartbeat.

Finally, the Shrike Lord turned away, his cloak shedding rain in a swirling arc, his back rigid.

"Get out of my domain," he said.

Severin's shoulders slumped, and his knees looked ready to buckle. "Fine."

"And don't come back, Severin. I'm through with you."

He winced at that, as if his brother had struck him again. "Just as well," he said, with forced lightness. "I'm tired of you, too."

The Shrike Lord began walking away. Without looking back, he called, "If I ever see that murderer again, I'll kill her."

It took me a moment to realize he was referring to me, and that this meant he wasn't going to kill me *now*. Relief crashed down on me in a giddy wave, and I swayed on my feet.

Severin waited until the darkness and the rain swallowed his brother from sight. Then he dropped suddenly to sit in the mud, ignoring what it did to his fine clothes, staring after his brother with a stunned expression.

"I finally did it," he whispered.

I reached out, hesitantly, and offered him my hand. He took it and looked up at me, his eyes gleaming in the moonlight.

"I stood up to him, Ryx. He exiled me from my home, but I stood up to him, and he didn't kill either of us."

"You were wonderful," I assured him. "Now let's get out of here, before he changes his mind."

It was a long, wet, bone-jarring ride through the night in Foxglove's cabriolet. He perched on the driver's seat, while Severin sat beside me, the only one who could safely do so; I kept a few inches between us anyway, since I didn't trust him to stay awake in his current state. I sat rigid with tension and armed with a stick, ready to poke him if he looked like he might nod off.

Everything hurt. My whole body felt sick and exhausted and broken. But my heart kept beating, wild and fierce, despite all the Shrike Lord's attempts to stop it. And I was surrounded by friends who'd cared enough to come to my rescue, after all.

"We sealed the door to the Black Tower as soon as we got Kessa out of there," Foxglove informed me as we raced through the night, the horses magically enhanced by Kessa and Severin to make the journey through the darkness without resting. "Fortunately, it seems anyone can *close* the door; you only have to have the right bloodline to open it. The gate was still glowing then, but the seal should have restored itself by now."

A shudder passed through me, blending with the rumble of the carriage. "And the demon?"

"No sign of it when we left," Foxglove said, but worry flattened his voice. "It may have gone back through the gate when you pulled it out of Kessa. I don't like the idea that it's still out there somewhere, but we have to face that it could be."

"And everyone in the castle is all right?" I asked, anxious. "Has Odan taken charge?"

"Yes. Somehow, we neglected to inform your family of your situation. We thought it would be better to quietly extract you from Alevar rather than getting atheling dramatics involved."

"Thank you," I said, with feeling. I was already light-headed from blood loss, and from the flight of potions Bastian had made me drink, but relief left me positively dizzy. Gloamingard was in good hands. "What about Ardith and the Raverrans? And that traitor Aurelio?"

"Hells take it, I knew there was something important I forgot in the chaos." Frustration stretched Foxglove's voice. "I'm sorry. We were so caught up with saving Kessa—and then you—that I didn't warn Lady Celia he was a member of the Zenith Society." He shook his head. "We didn't want the diplomats mucking around while we were gone, especially with another demon in play, so we asked them to leave the castle for safety reasons while we destroyed the gate. They were setting out when we left Gloamingard; Aurelio's back in the Serene Empire by now."

"He killed my aunt," I said through my teeth.

"Well." An ominous stillness came over Foxglove, like the black waters of a deep pool after the last ripples have faded. "Then he'll face a reckoning when we return."

"Exalted Warden. Thank the seasons you're home." Odan greeted us by the Birch Gate as the sun dipped down behind the western hills and the hard light of day softened into purple twilight shadows. His usual unruffled calm had a few cracks in it; his mustache was positively unkempt. "I've done my best in your absence, but these are challenging times and somewhat beyond the usual scope of my duties."

"Gloamingard could not have been in better hands, Odan. Thank you."

He took in our ragged appearance with a frown. Kessa leaned on Ashe for support, and I had to favor half a dozen healing wounds as I climbed down from the cabriolet; I winced at every motion until Severin came, worry tightening his face, and gave me his hand to help me down. The warmth of his touch was a welcome distraction from the pain.

"Exalted Atheling." Odan bowed deeply to him. "My apologies that I have no better reception prepared for our noble guest. I didn't expect we would be hosting you again so soon."

"I've had a change in plans," Severin said dryly.

"Our other guests have mostly departed," Odan told me. "The Raverran delegation left a couple of observers to verify that the gate was actually destroyed. I believe they're planning to call their warships home as soon as they have that confirmation."

"*That's* going to be an interesting discussion," I muttered. "Thanks, Odan."

I limped toward the Birch Gate; everyone fell in around me as if I were my grandmother—except giving me more room, of course—which was an odd feeling. "Any new emergencies while I was gone?"

Odan's mustache twitched. "It would seem that when you leave, everything is suddenly calm, Warden."

I lowered my voice. "Did the Rookery tell you about the second demon?"

"Yes, Warden. There's been no sign of it."

Kessa shivered. "Good. I hope that horrid monster went back to the Nine Hells."

Ashe put an arm around her shoulders, apparently without thinking. Kessa tucked herself in tighter against her side; Ashe's eyes grew bright and soft, and her expression ever so slightly panicked. I suppressed a smile.

"We should do something about the gate right away," I said, ignoring the trembling exhaustion in my legs and the dozen pains that stabbed me with each movement. "I don't want the Empire to decide we're taking too long and they should rain ruin down on us just to be sure, and every moment we delay is another that my grandmother might decide she has her own plans for the gate and intervene. What's the next closest thing to destroying it?"

"Changing the locks." Bastian exchanged glances with Foxglove. "We already had those plans to modify the Black Tower wards to keep out the Lady of Owls in addition to anyone not of your family. That way at least she can't open the gate and let the rest of the demons through."

"That's better than nothing," I said, with some relief. "How close are you to ready?"

"I'm ready to do the inner circle around the obelisk now." Foxglove pulled a small artifice device from one of his pouches: a ring of carefully twisted golden wire circling a rune-graved disk the size of a large coin. A thread of silver-white hair gleamed in the weave of gold. "I've got six of these done, which should be enough. Ryx, I'll need you to suppress the warding circle so I can alter it without its protections frying me. Bastian, I'll need some alchemical etching fluid and a stylus so I can carve some extra runes into the floor and mount these in the right places."

"What's the current status of the gate?" I asked Odan.

"The door to the Black Tower remains sealed," he said. "I couldn't venture a guess what it's like inside, Warden. I've kept the extra guards posted on the tower and the keep."

A chill struck me. "The demon I banished from Kessa could still be in there, waiting."

Odan's bristly gray brows contracted. "In that case, I'm especially glad that I denied Ensign Aurelio's request for a closer look at the Black Tower."

I stopped, stricken. "Aurelio? He's still here?"

"Yes, Exalted Warden. As the Raverran delegation's magical and military adviser, he stayed to observe for the Empire to make sure the gate was destroyed. I'll confess that I thought it was suspicious when he asked to see the Black Tower. I told him to wait for your return and pose that question to you, naturally."

Foxglove let out a hiss. "More than suspicious. I wish I'd called in some favors to have him locked up."

"Should have let me stab him," Ashe said.

Foreboding crested in me like a great wave. "If he was trying to get access to the gate, he must be planning some kind of move."

Foxglove cursed. "You're right."

And whatever that plan was, he'd probably realize he was running out of chances to put it into action when he heard the Rookery had returned.

"I think we need to get to the Black Tower right now," I said.

Foxglove met my eyes. His expression went grim, and he nodded. "Let's go."

As soon as we entered the old keep corridor that led to the Black Tower, I knew something was wrong. Reflected scarlet light washed the walls and floor of the dim hallway, and the gate's power pushed at my senses in a shuddering wave.

The door to the Black Tower was open.

"I thought you said the tower was sealed," I whispered to Odan as we all paused at the top of the stairs. Even the pulses of raw power rising from below couldn't drown out the rapid pounding of my heart.

"I did, Warden." His face fell into grim lines. "There should be guards here, too, but they're gone."

That couldn't be good. Graces preserve us, there was no possible reason for any of this that boded well at all.

"Odan," I said quietly, "I want you to evacuate the castle at once. Get everyone out—every last soul—as quickly as possible. Leave everything behind and just get the people out of here."

His jaw flexed, but he nodded. "Yes, Warden."

"Take them down to the town for now. You evacuate, too. We need at least one person free and clear from here who knows what's happening."

"If you command it, Warden."

"I do. Hurry, Odan. I'm counting on you."

"Of course, Warden. Good luck."

"We're going to need it," Kessa muttered as Odan's swift, purposeful footfalls receded down the dusty halls.

Ashe slid Answer from its sheath, her eyes fixed on the glow coming from the alcove. "Luck is overrated. I'd rather have good timing any day."

"I think our timing is terrible, actually," Kessa said, eyeing the corridor ahead with trepidation.

"Yup. So I guess we have to hope for luck. Let's do this." Ashe started forward on silent feet.

The rest of us followed. But I knew what we would see, even before we came to the alcove. Red light and dry heat poured through the open door, and two guards lay dead before it.

And within, there he stood at the gate—framed with scarlet light, his arms raised in invocation: Aurelio. *That rotten stingroach.*

"Oh no you don't," Ashe growled, and bounded into the Black Tower. The rest of us swarmed after her. The anger rising in me at his treachery was almost strong enough to match the oppressive weight of power that hit me as I entered the obsidian chamber.

Aurelio whirled to face us, dropping his arms, a strange smile on his face that didn't extend to his eyes. "Ah, there you are. I was worried you might be late."

"Wait," I called to Ashe, who was heading for him with murder in her stride. I'd noticed something that made ice crystallize inside my lungs, in painful opposition to the heat scorching my skin.

Aurelio stood *inside* the glowing circle of runes that surrounded the obelisk. The one that no one could pass but my family.

"Who let you through?" I asked him hoarsely.

Aurelio's grin spread wider, a cruel light coming into his eyes. "An old friend."

"'Friend' might be an exaggeration," said a far-too-familiar voice.

With the casual grace of a stretching cat, my grandmother slipped around from the back of the obelisk.

FORTY-TWO

My grandmother rested one lean shoulder against the obsidian slab, an amused smile quirking her mouth. Drinking up our shock like it was honey wine.

But it was Aurelio's face I couldn't stop staring at. I knew that cruel smile.

The second demon.

"You." I clenched my fists and stepped toward him. "When I threw you out of Kessa, you went and got Aurelio. Didn't you?"

"Not quite." Aurelio's expression flickered and changed, softening to something human, something desperate. "The demon didn't take me by force, Ryx. I invited it in."

Kessa backed away from him, her arms wrapped around herself.

Ashe stepped between them. "Only the Zenith Society would be that stupid."

"You willingly gave yourself to a *demon*?" I couldn't hide my disgust. "How could you possibly want—" An awful thought struck me. "Your mentor ordered you to do this, didn't he?"

Aurelio winced. "I had to, Ryx. I've gone too far to back down now." His eyes were strained, haunted. I couldn't help a certain horrified pity, even after all he'd done.

"You're right about one thing." I shook my head, furious at him for making such terrible choices. "You've gone too far."

"I may come to regret it." Aurelio gave a lopsided, strained shrug. "For now, we have an understanding. I give Hunger a body, and in return it gives me the power to protect the Serene Empire." His expression shifted again, stretching with inhuman glee. "And we want the same thing, after all: to throw the gate wide and drink in all the limitless strength it can give us."

Foxglove averted his face in seeming despair, but his amber eyes shone with a fierce light. He slipped a slim wire-wrapped device halfway out of one of his pouches, and a soft hum resonated in my skull—a noise muffling device, to thwart my grandmother's unnaturally good hearing. "Exalted Severin, run and tell Odan about the second demon," he whispered. "Make sure the knowledge gets out." Severin, who stood at the rear of our group and was barely inside the tower, nodded with tense agreement. "Everyone else, draw the demons away from the stone and keep them busy so Ryx and I can alter the ward. Remember that we're also buying time for Odan to evacuate the castle."

Severin faded back out through the door as if he'd never been here. Foxglove slipped the device back into his pouch and started drifting casually out to the side, poised to get into position as soon as the demons were distracted. The others fanned out and moved forward to take up more space and cover for him.

I couldn't try anything so sneaky; my grandmother had turned her full attention to me.

"I see you managed to escape after all, Ryx," she said. "Did you learn anything from the process?"

There was a certain edge to the question; her eyes narrowed analytically. *I want you shattered and broken*, she'd said in the forest. I thought of the luminaries flickering out in the Shrike Lord's throne hall and the guards dropping dead, and a rumble deep in the earth, and shivered.

"I learned that I can count on my friends more than I can rely on my power."

My grandmother made a face. "Ugh. We'll have to work on that. Come here, Ryx."

A retort died on my lips. My legs started moving on their own, with the sort of irresistible instinct that might yank my hand back from a fire. *Pox.*

"She's controlling me," I warned the others, tension singing through my nerves as my legs carried me inexorably forward. It was an awful sensation.

But I could work with this. I just had to get my grandmother out of the circle somehow, then contrive to casually step on it and keep her focus away from Foxglove. I might not have experience with this brand of subtlety, but a lifetime as a curiosity on the fringes of Vaskandran royal society had taught me a lot about redirecting attention.

None of which helped me stay calm as my feet kept drawing me nearer to the burning intensity of my grandmother's orange-ringed eyes.

Bastian fell back a step or two, tucking his notebook protectively to his chest. "I don't understand how you think you can open the gate," he said to Aurelio, "given the way the layered protections work. Even if the Lady of Owls can operate the enchantment as one of the guardian bloodline, won't the limiters intervene?"

Aurelio frowned. "Limiters?"

"Don't tell him," Kessa said sharply. "Let him try it." Both of them kept their focus entirely on Aurelio and my grandmother, nothing in their posture so much as acknowledging that Fox-glove was in the room—or Ashe either, as she fanned out to the other side, ready to make a move. If I didn't know them well, I'd think the edge in their voices was fear. Each acted their part with full confidence the others would do theirs, like fingers on the same hand.

And now they were counting on me to do mine. Resolve ran through my nerves like steel.

"You're bluffing," Aurelio said suspiciously. But he stepped forward, away from the gate and toward Bastian, as if he couldn't help himself.

"Right," Bastian agreed hastily, tucking his book behind his back. "You caught me. There are no limiters, of course."

Kessa put a hand on Bastian's shoulder. "You'd better get out of here with that notebook," she murmured, her voice carrying across the room despite its soft tones. She was an actress, after all. "If he figures out how to open another gate . . ."

I was fairly sure there was nothing in that notebook about opening new gates, and didn't remember anything about limiters, either, but Aurelio couldn't know that. As Bastian backed another step, the picture of growing alarm, a yearning ignited in Aurelio's eyes, and he strode quickly across the room. Reeled in neatly as a fish.

"Give me that book," he demanded.

Hunger, he'd said the demon was. Clever Bastian and Kessa, luring him out by making him *want* something.

I'd arrived in front of my grandmother. It was easy enough to stand with one foot on the protective circle; the runes flickered and dimmed.

"What do you want from me?" I asked, holding her eyes. Anything to keep her looking at my face and not toward where Foxglove slipped quietly around the room to the other side of the obelisk.

"It's not what I want *from* you." My grandmother stepped closer to touch my cheek with a gentle hand. "It's what I want *for* you."

"A bright future and a happy life?" I asked sarcastically. "Some cake and tea, and maybe a puppy?"

"You've been wasting yourself, Ryx. Skulking and hiding in the shadows, staying out of everyone's way." There was genuine affection in her voice, in her fingers as they brushed hair back from my face, and that made it all the more disturbing. "I only want you to stop holding back, stop burying your light for the sake of others."

Foxglove had crouched down behind the obelisk. I made certain to keep my eyes fixed on my grandmother's face, but I knew he must be working on the warding circle. I wished I had any idea how much time he needed for each of the six anchors. Every word of this conversation hurt like a splinter under my skin, but I had to draw it out for as long as I could.

"You're the one who taught me that everything I do should be for the sake of Morgrain," I said quietly.

Her eyes narrowed. "So I did."

Shouting and commotion broke out behind me, toward the door. I couldn't help myself; I turned to look.

Ashe had crept up behind Aurelio and driven her sword all the way through his chest. It protruded straight through his sternum, the blue crystals on the wire-wrapped pommel glowing with the power to punch through bone. Aurelio's back arched in apparent agony, and blood bubbled on his lips. Ashe's eyes held a cat's intense, lethal focus.

My heart lurched despite myself—he had been my friend once, even if he betrayed me. *Whatever happened to Rule Three?!*

Aurelio let out a contemptuous laugh, wet and terrible. Livid white sparks sprayed from the wound, crackling up Ashe's blade like lightning; she pulled it from his back with an oath of pain and surprise. He whirled to face her, the hole in his chest swarming with opalescent light.

"Do you really think demons are so easy to kill?" he demanded.

My grandmother's hand fell on my shoulder. She'd stepped up beside me—*so close* to being outside the circle. "Oh, this is fun," she said. "I think the Rookery will give him more trouble than he expects, but of course they can't win. Shall we watch?"

Bastian's hand moved so quickly it almost seemed to flicker, dipping in and out of his jacket with inhuman speed. Suddenly there was a flintlock pistol in his hand. A sharp crack hit my eardrums, and the scent of gunsmoke filled the air. I flinched at the sound.

Aurelio staggered. For one breath-catching moment, I hoped he might go down.

But he straightened, a smile straight from the Hells twisting his face, and reached toward Bastian. The air before his fingertips rippled with a pulse of power. *Sweet Grace of Mercy.*

Bastian's pistol clattered to the floor. He dropped to his knees, clutching the arm that had held it, and let out a strangled cry of pain.

"What did he do to him?" I demanded, my insides twisting at the look of agonized horror on Bastian's face.

"Ah, yes, making his own body consume itself." My grandmother nodded. "One of Hunger's oldest tricks."

I tried to run toward him, unthinking, but my legs locked in place. I would have fallen if not for my grandmother's gentle hand on my shoulder, holding me up. "I've got to help him," I protested, trying to hide my inward stab of alarm as I realized how close I'd come to stepping off the barrier circle.

"You can," my grandmother assured me. "If you let your power loose."

"I said *help*, not *kill*," I retorted angrily.

Ashe had lunged at Aurelio again, flicking lightning-fast cuts at his arms and legs; but the air in front of Aurelio shimmered, and her sword rebounded each time as if it had struck a steel shield. Kessa took advantage of his distraction to draw her dagger and stab down at the back of his neck, something close to hatred darkening her eyes. Her blade bounced off of his invisible shield, too.

It tore a deep wound in my chest to see the fear and bitter

memory in Kessa's face, and the desperate determination in Ashe's, and the agony in Bastian's—and to have to stand here and do nothing but watch.

But I had my own job, as the tingle of magic running up my leg from my carefully positioned foot reminded me. The others were accomplishing exactly what they wanted: buying Foxglove time.

Then Aurelio lifted his hand again, the air around it shimmering like black stone on a hot day.

"Ashe!" I cried. "*Look out!*"

She dropped back to a guard position, graceful and wary. Suddenly she stumbled. Blood began flowing all at once in alarming rivers down her arms and legs.

"*Ashe!*" Kessa shrieked, reaching toward her.

There was nothing she could do. The blood streamed not from any clear wounds, but straight through Ashe's skin, as if the demon called it out of her.

Ashe wavered on her feet, drenched in blood, and fell to her knees.

"Leave them alone," I shouted, every instinct straining to leave the circle and run to help them.

Or to do something more. The fury boiling like volcanic fire within me yearned to unfurl my power as I had in the Shrike Lord's castle. To unleash it on Aurelio and the demon he hosted, and Hells take the consequences.

My grandmother watched my face intently, her eyes gleaming.

Aurelio lifted his hand again. I tensed as if it were my own pain coming—but Severin burst through the door, a knife in his hand, and threw himself protectively in front of Bastian and Kessa.

There were no plants or animals here for him to work with. His magic was completely useless, and he knew it. His face was drawn with desperation, and his temples beaded with sweat. He'd run back here after warning the others, fully aware he couldn't do much more than slow the demons down with his death. *Oh, Severin.*

Aurelio barely seemed to notice him. He looked at his own shaking hands as Bastian groaned in agony on the floor and Ashe fell to one knee.

"This wasn't what I wanted," Aurelio moaned.

Suddenly a laugh came from his own throat, deep and wicked. "But it's exactly what you asked for."

"I thought they'd put up more of a fight than this," my grandmother sighed, surveying the battered remnants of the Rookery. The faint crease of a frown appeared between her brows. Before she could start counting people and perhaps begin wondering where Foxglove might be, I grabbed her arm, seizing her attention.

"You've got to stop Aurelio," I urged her. "Surely you don't want *him* to win here."

She cocked her head. "Why not?"

I was on the verge of blurting out that he'd killed her daughter, but realized just in time what a terrible mistake that would be. I needed to draw this out as long as possible, for Foxglove and Odan to do their work; unleashing my grandmother's full fury on Aurelio would likely bring things to a quick and violent end.

"Because he's an arrogant ass," I said instead.

My grandmother let out a short bark of a laugh. "He *is* an ass. Both of them, actually. Having a conversation with Hunger is impossible—everything is always about him."

"Why give him control of the gate?" Above all else, I had to keep her distracted; so much the better if I could sow division between the demons while I was at it.

"To see what he'll do with it." My grandmother shrugged. "Better to have him make an idiot of himself waving all that power around than have it sit locked up doing nothing."

"The Black Tower is *yours*," I insisted. "It's in *your* domain. If you let him have the gate, you're letting him have Morgrain."

My grandmother's lips twitched downward into a frown. "Of course he can't have Morgrain," she snapped. "Morgrain is mine, by blood and bone. I am its protector."

"If you give him the gate, you're setting him up in a seat of unassailable power right in the heart of your own domain. Can't you see that?"

A choking cry came from Severin, and I whipped my head around, my heart leaping fearfully.

Aurelio had him by the throat, a fierce grin on his face. Severin hung limp from his upraised hand, gray and wasted.

Like a corpse who'd died of starvation.

I let out a sharp cry of anguish, but Severin's hand twitched, and relief flooded me. He wasn't dead—not yet.

Ashe lunged from where she knelt on the floor, blood flying in a trail behind her, and sliced Answer across the backs of Aurelio's legs. With a howl, he fell to his knees, dropping Severin to lie motionless on the floor.

Bastian surged up from the ground, quick as lightning, using his good arm to fling a vial of some alchemical potion into Aurelio's face. Smoke rose up with a horrible sizzling sound and an acrid stench; Aurelio covered his face with clawed fingers, letting out a muffled scream.

Hell of Nightmares. It was too terrible watching them destroy each other, piece by piece. But the Rookery would not stay down. Ashe knelt panting in a pool of her own blood, waiting for another opening. Bastian downed a potion as he wove on his feet, face greenish and shining with sweat, body curled protectively around his withered arm. And Kessa was reaching out urgently to Ashe with a fistful of leaves, presumably some magically enhanced herb to help keep her from dying of blood loss. They were far from out of tricks. My heart surged with fierce pride to be part of their company.

"He's too arrogant." My grandmother shook her head, her eyes still on Aurelio. "He can heal himself, certainly, but he should never have let them do that. Too much damage and the body will die, and he'll have to waste time and energy seizing another."

"Will you really let him be just as careless with Morgrain?" I urged. I could see Foxglove out of the corner of my eye, working his way around the circle, lying almost flat to the ground in his gray coat to avoid catching my grandmother's attention. I had to get her to move away from the obelisk.

Suddenly, a blinding light flared from Aurelio, and heat blasted my face. Bastian, Ashe, and Kessa flew backward as if struck by a massive invisible hand, hitting the walls with boneless thuds. I flinched at the sound.

They collapsed to the glassy black floor like rag dolls. Not one of them stirred.

This time, they stayed down.

FORTY-THREE

My insides lurched with a sickening fear for my friends. Between their terrible magical injuries and the force with which they'd hit that wall, it was hard to imagine that they could survive. Every inch of me screamed to run to their aid—but if I lifted my foot from the circle on which I stood, the wards could kill Foxglove. A stifled whimper escaped my throat.

"How dare you greet me with such insolence," Aurelio hissed, in a voice not his own. "Humanity has forgotten much in four thousand years. I'll hang your carcasses over the castle gate as part of their first lesson."

My grandmother shook her head. "Ugh. Tasteless." She sauntered toward Aurelio, her teeth bared in a warning grin. "I think you forget who makes decorating decisions for Gloamingard."

Aurelio staggered to his feet, wincing; shimmering light crawled across the bloody backs of his knees. "You said we could be partners."

"I'm reconsidering," my grandmother said, her tone insultingly casual.

Foxglove moved from his position halfway behind the obelisk, carefully creeping out in the open. He lay down with his back to the door, looking as if he'd fallen there in the battle, shielding the quick motions of his hands from sight with his body. If either of the demons thought about it for a second, they'd realize the fight hadn't come this close to the gate; but hopefully he could at least avoid pulling attention out of the corners of their eyes this way.

"I need ten minutes," he whispered to me.

It might as well be a thousand years. But I nodded, dipping a neck rigid with tension. "I'll give it to you."

"If I might interject, I'm not excited at the idea of corpse-based decorating, either," Aurelio said, his voice human again and shaky with pain and shock. Perhaps he was having second thoughts about letting a demon share his body now that it was too late. *Idiot.* His fate might be terrible, but he'd jumped into it with his eyes open. "I don't want to rule anything or hurt anyone. I only want access to the gate so I can protect my home. If we can come to some kind of agreement—"

My grandmother laughed. "I'm the Demon of Discord, little boy. Agreement is against my nature."

"I should have seen this coming." His voice went hard and sharp.

"You should have, Hunger. We've done this dance before." My grandmother put her fists on her hips. "There is one difference. This time, I'm not *just* Discord. I'm also the Lady of Owls, and I do not share my domain."

"You let that *human* pollute your soul." Disgust twisted Aurelio's face, followed by surprise at the words that had left his own mouth.

"I did not allow or intend anything of the sort," my grandmother retorted. "As it happens, however, we were a fine match, and I like who I am now."

"And who are you?" Aurelio sneered—or Hunger did. "Neither human nor demon, but a mockery of both."

"I am the Witch Lord of Morgrain." Her voice took on a great and terrible resonance, as the Black Tower itself echoed her words with a deep rumbling of stone. "And this place is mine. Get out and find your own."

Foxglove slithered along the floor to the next spot on the circle, giving my feet a wide berth. "Two more," he whispered.

"Minutes or tokens?" I asked, barely moving my lips.

"Tokens," he replied. "Don't step off that circle until I'm done, no matter what."

My grandmother advanced on Aurelio, waving a dismissive hand at him. "Get out of here, boy, and take Hunger with you. I've had my fun playing with you; we're done."

"For now," the demon said with Aurelio's lips, sounding resigned. "Your whims could shift again tomorrow, and you know it."

"Perhaps. I'll find you if they do. But this gate is mine. Go, before I destroy your host and leave you cold and formless in the empty night."

Aurelio's eyes widened with a very human fear at that, and he turned and fled.

Pox. Apprehension spiked through me like a crackle of lightning. Foxglove still had two tokens to go, and now our last distraction was gone.

My grandmother turned slowly around. "What are you doing, Ryx?"

Menace lay under her voice like sheathed claws. She paced toward me, no mercy softening the hard shine in her eyes.

"Watching your ally hurt my friends and wondering how you can ask me to side with you." I broadened my stance in the weak hope that I could at least partially block Foxglove from her view.

"Did we not just discuss how I don't want anyone else tampering with my gate?" she asked pleasantly.

"Grace of Mercy," Foxglove breathed, so softly I almost couldn't hear him.

"We did," I admitted, desperately trying to think of a way to stall for just a few more minutes.

"I'm disappointed, Ryx." She shook her head. "After everything I've done for you."

"You turned me over to the Shrike Lord." I let anger color my voice, hoping to draw her into an argument. "You *knew* he planned to kill me. Why should I believe you have any good intentions toward me at this point?"

"You wound me. All I want is for you to come into your own." She paused, her eyes narrowing, and power and menace gathered in the air until I could hardly breathe from the pressure of it. "Perhaps the Shrike Lord simply didn't bring you close enough to death."

Graces help me. Here it comes. Every muscle in my body went rigid, bracing for pain.

"That's enough of that," said a new voice, languid as a snake uncoiling.

Whisper prowled through the door into the Black Tower, the red glare of the wards reflecting off his fierce angled eyes.

My grandmother turned to face him.

"I thought you always stayed neutral," she said, a strange note in her voice.

Wariness. Hells have mercy, she saw him as a threat.

"I do," Whisper agreed. "You'll note I didn't interfere with you and Hunger until now, even though I disapprove of tampering with the gate. But there is still the matter of my promise."

"You can't be serious," my grandmother snorted. "It's far too late for you to keep it."

Foxglove eased his way silently across the floor toward another spot in the circle. *One more*, he mouthed to me over his shoulder.

"I'm deadly serious. Do what else you will here. Unleash the rest of the demons if you wish. But in this one thing, never interfere with me."

"I'll do what I cursed well please with my own domain and my own granddaughter," my grandmother growled. "We're going to have words about this, *old friend*. Right after I kill these others and put an end to their meddling."

Whisper's tail tip flicked across the floor, brushing the Rookery's lives away as irrelevant. "Fair enough."

Hells. And for one moment, I'd thought he was keeping her occupied so that Foxglove could finish his work. I should have known better; he'd told me again and again that he couldn't take my side.

My grandmother turned toward Foxglove, lifting a hand.

"Wait," I cried, my heart pounding. "I'm not an idiot. I know you're talking about me. Grandmother, I'll do whatever you want—just don't hurt them. You win!" I threw up my hands. "I don't understand, though. What is it you want me to do?"

"I would think that would be obvious." She cast a sidelong glance at Whisper, who watched her narrowly, tail lashing a warning. "She asked me. You stay out of this."

"So long as you don't say anything that forces me to intervene," he agreed, his voice smooth as a silk garrote.

My grandmother turned her fiery orange eyes back to me. "You know what I want."

"For me to stop bottling up my power." I spread my arms, trying to keep her attention on me. "But I don't understand *why*."

She cast a sidelong look at Whisper. A sly smile tugged at one side of her mouth. "To set you free."

"Touching as that sentiment may be," I said, unable to keep the irony from my voice, "I don't *want* to kill and destroy everything around me."

My grandmother sighed. "And that's always been the problem with you."

I clenched my fists at my sides. A healing thorn wound in my wrist twinged—one that wouldn't be there if the grandmother I loved hadn't left me to die for, essentially, her own amusement.

It would be easier if she were gone. But this woman in front of me was still, at least in part, my grandmother, and that cut deepest of all.

Ashe's voice floated into my memory, soft and compelling: *And the kind girl was carrying a jar.*

Hells. I squeezed my eyes shut, then open again. If I didn't hold on to her heart for her, no one would.

"My power is not my nature," I said through my teeth. "I want to *protect* Eruvia, not wreak destruction on it for fun. And you might be a demon now, but that's not *your* nature, either. You'd do anything for the good of Morgrain and your family. You're my grandmother, and I know you, and that will always be true."

Pain tautened her face, and she stepped back as if I'd struck her.

"Ryx..." Her voice had gone rough and quiet, and a softness crept into her eyes.

"Done," Foxglove cried, flinging himself back from the circle and to his feet. "*Now*, Ryx!"

Inwardly cursing his timing, I stepped off the warding circle.

The runes and arcing lines carved into the floor began to glow again, faintly at first, with a sullen radiance like old embers. My grandmother's eyes narrowed, and she reached out toward the barrier.

Sparks flew from her fingertips; she snatched her hand back. Slowly, she turned, leveling her burning glare at me.

I'd never felt her anger before. Not like this. The full, terrifying measure of her predator's stare bored into me, merciless, with the weight of an entire domain crashing down on me behind it. I shrank back in instinctive fear, a mouse before the talons of a descending owl.

"You *tricked* me!" she snarled. "You said all that to distract me!"

"No! I meant every word of it." I reached out a pleading hand, my heart twisting.

My grandmother swept an arm back at Foxglove without looking. He went flying across the room and smashed into the obsidian wall, sliding down with a groan to lie still on the floor. Red light from the wards soaked all of the Rookery like spilled blood.

"I respect a good trick," my grandmother said through her teeth, "but there are consequences, Ryx."

She drew herself up, and it was as if all of Gloamingard sucked in a long breath, gathering power. I backed away from her, knowing too well there was nowhere I could run, my breath frozen in my throat.

"I know you, Ryx." Her voice held all the deep, eerie wildness of an owl's cry. "Better than you can imagine. And I know that nothing will hurt you more than watching your friends die." The mage mark in her eyes glowed like a molten wire as she caught my gaze, and my insides plunged. She meant it.

I should have been terrified, but it was as if my capacity for horror had already been exceeded. Now my inner vessel overflowed with something else—something clearer, stronger.

"No," I said, and my voice came out far more sure and steady than it had any right to.

My grandmother raised one white eyebrow. "No?"

"You won't." I walked toward her, past Whisper's languorous witness, until we stood face-to-face. "You won't hurt me, and you won't kill them. Because we care about each other too much."

"Please." Her lip lifted in distaste. "Spare me the sentiment. It doesn't suit you."

"Maybe not, but it's true." Finally, all doubt was gone from my heart. "You put up with me wrecking things in your castle for seventeen years. You treated me like your granddaughter, not like the family embarrassment. You taught me, and you brought me tea when I had nightmares. It makes no sense, but I can't stop loving you just because you're a demon, or even because you sent me off to the Shrike Lord's mercy." I shook my head, disgusted at myself. "I don't know that it's a strength, but that's the way it is. You're my family. And I'm yours. We're stuck with each other."

She grunted, a harsh sound, but one I knew well from when she was covering up a surge of emotion. "And why would this stop me from killing the Rookery? I don't give a rat's tail about any of them."

"Because if you did, I couldn't forgive you. And you *need* me." I reached out, feeling as daring as if I were about to pet a venomous snake, and lightly touched her shoulder. Just as she had for me, all those years, when no one else in this castle could. "You're afraid of your own children," I said softly. "You never showed yourself to Aunt Karrigan or Vikal after you became a demon, because you couldn't bear it if they hated you. You're terrified of losing them—but you know I understand about being a monster. You won't lose me just because you're half a demon now. But you *will* lose me if you kill my friends."

Her eyes narrowed to hard slits, her whole face tensing. She drew in a sharp breath through her teeth and turned away.

For a long moment, there was silence. My heartbeat drummed in my ears. The heat leaking from the gate baked my skin, and the red light and power in the air oppressed my senses until I was sure I would scream.

"Take them and get out," she said at last, her voice low and rough.

"What?" The word burst out before I could stop it.

"Take your friends and get out of this castle. Out of all of

Morgrain. If you stay here, you'll be a splinter in my mind, and I'll worry at you until you break." She strode toward the door, without looking back.

"You too, chimera," she added sharply. Whisper pretended not to hear her.

And then she was gone.

My knees gave way without warning, dumping me on the hard obsidian floor. Something between a gasp and a sob hit me in the chest. I had to get up, had to go help the others, but for one moment, my limbs were numb with shock and wouldn't answer me.

Kessa sprang up from where she had lain, so quickly she must have been faking unconsciousness. Herbs and what looked like a potion bottle already in hand, she raced without hesitation to Ashe, who sprawled still and pale in scarves and ribbons of blood. Bastian lifted his head weakly, cradling his arm, and called out, "Foxglove?"

"I'm fine." Foxglove winced as he heaved himself into a sitting position. "Broken wrist from a bad landing, maybe some ribs, probably a concussion. You?"

"I've felt better." Bastian's voice was rough with pain. "Downed a few potions, and I think I can brew something to fix my arm, but that was unpleasant. How's Ashe?"

"Alive," Kessa said grimly. "She's lost a lot of blood."

Bastian rose unsteadily and staggered in her direction. "I've got excellent potions for that. Though between Ashe and Ryx, we're going through them quickly! If we can get her to actually rest for a few days, she should recover."

I dragged myself to my feet and approached Severin. He lay curled on the floor, his lips nearly white, his cheeks sunken. His eyes flickered open, dull and glassy.

"Unnngh," he said.

"Are you all right?" I knelt next to him, not daring to touch him when he looked this bad.

"I'd like to stop having the energy sucked out of me for a while." He sat up with an effort, rubbing his temple. "I think I'm all right? It was less horrible than when *you* did it. Less my life, and more…" He waved a vague hand at his own body. "My strength. I think after some sleep and a few good meals I'll be fine."

"It's nice to know I have a more unpleasant effect on you than a demon does." I offered him a hand up, meeting his eyes to make sure he was braced for my touch before he took it.

"I understand the need to groom each other after a tussle like this," Whisper said, stretching, "but we should leave now. Neither the Lady of Owls nor the Demon of Discord were ever creatures of surpassing mercy, and if she changes her mind about letting you go, I can't be bothered to save you."

"I need to make sure Odan was able to get everyone out of the castle," I protested.

"You can do that from outside," Foxglove suggested. "Your grandmother will know if you don't leave, and I'm sure she's watching you."

"Good point," Kessa said. "I'd really rather not face down another demon today." She scooped up Ashe's limp form with surprising strength, cradling her gently against her chest. "Let's get out of here. We can regroup in the town—with alcohol. So much alcohol."

Severin lifted incredulous eyebrows. "We're going to leave a demon ruling as the Witch Lord of Morgrain?"

"We don't have a choice," Foxglove said grimly. "We've warded her off from the gate, and that's all we can do for now. We can't fight her, and much as I hate to admit it, there are limits to what one can accomplish with sneaking and diplomacy."

"Severin and Kessa," I said reluctantly, "once we get outside, can you send birds to the other Witch Lords, warning them about my grandmother? There's no keeping this secret anymore."

"We should warn the Serene Empire about that wretch Aurelio as well," Foxglove added. He shook his head. "We've got some hard, dark work ahead of us, but we need to be alive to do it. Let's go."

FORTY-FOUR

I'm sorry, Exalted Warden." Odan drew himself up with serene dignity, as if we stood in the Old Great Hall and not in the dusty yard of an inn at the edge of town. The light of the inn lanterns cast deep shadows across his face. "But I'm going back to the castle."

The babble of dozens of voices floating from the warm windows of the inn almost swallowed his words. Odan had assured me that the entire population of Gloamingard Castle crowded inside, here and at another inn down the street; he and Gaven were working on figuring out places for everyone to sleep. I wanted more than anything to step into the sweet golden light of that jam-packed taproom, to feel the heat of all those living bodies and see their familiar faces safe with my own eyes. But I couldn't. Standing in this inn yard was dangerous enough; I needed to be gone soon, before an accident could happen.

"I am, too," I told him, dropping my voice so that Kessa wouldn't hear as she set up a comfortable bed for Ashe in the back of the Rookery's wagon nearby. "I'm the Warden of Gloamingard. It's where I belong."

Odan shook his head. "No, Warden. You should go with the Rookery."

"I can't leave Morgrain now," I protested. "My people need me."

He leveled a frank stare at me from beneath the gray bulwarks of his brows. "Exalted Warden. Respectfully, right now, your people need the Rookery."

I winced. There was no denying that their talents were more likely to be of help in dealing with a demon Witch Lord than mine were. "Still, for me to run away now, when my duty is to stay and protect—"

"You misunderstand, Warden. Of course you'll protect us. Do you think I don't know you? I've helped raise you for seventeen years, since you came to Gloamingard. I *know* that you'll do your duty." His mustache bristled with the force of his words. My eyes stung. "You can only free something from a trap from outside the cage. *You* are the one best suited to help Morgrain, with the Rookery helping you. I can try to occupy the Lady of Owls and stall, and do what I can to guard the Door."

"But if you're alone in the castle with Grandmother..." I swallowed.

"The Lady of Owls and I have known each other a long time. I'll manage." Unbelievably, Odan smiled, his dark eyes crinkling. "You were always more useful than most of the rest of your family. I have faith in you, Warden. You won't forget us."

"Never," I agreed. A great yearning to hug him tore through me. Instead I pressed my gloved fist to my chest. "Then I entrust my beloved castle to its most faithful guardian. Take care of Gloamingard."

"I will," he promised.

I turned away so he wouldn't see the tears that burned hot tracks down my cheeks.

Castle Ilseine, just across the border in the imperial client state of Loreice, housed the Rookery's eastern headquarters—and it was

Gloamingard's opposite in every way. The low, sloping stone walls of its jutting triangular bastions formed a smooth, regular star shape crowning its hilltop, with long cannons lining the walls and precisely carved runes three rows deep beneath them. A courier-lamp spire jutted from the roof of the keep, like a needle aimed at the sky. It was crisp and sensible and orderly, rather than sprawling with chaotic, mismatched layers of history. It was undeniably *imperial*.

Its strangeness should have been exciting. I'd always wanted to see the Serene Empire—but not like this.

Blue-uniformed soldiers had welcomed the Rookery home with an efficient flurry of activity, whisking most of them off to see to their wounds. Foxglove was making reports, his arm in a sling. I'd joined him at first, but when they devolved toward the bureaucratic he'd sent me to my new room in the stone tower at the center of the fortress—a legacy of an older castle, and claimed entirely by the Rookery—to get some rest.

And here I'd found a certain furry riddle waiting for me, curled in the exact center of my bed, his pointed nose neatly pillowed on his bushy tail. One yellow eye opened in a thin gleaming slit, watching me.

Of course Whisper was here. Never mind that he hadn't traveled with us on the road from Gloamingard, or that we were in the middle of a warded and guarded fortress, or that the door had been locked. I was too exhausted to muster even a token crumb of surprise.

I slumped on the edge of the bed, aching all over, and scratched behind his ears.

Whisper made a pleased sound. "Ah, yes. Just there."

"I miss Gloamingard," I said softly. It was a longing that cut me deep inside, stabbing at the slightest movement of my thoughts. The castle's twisting halls and bristling towers, its mad hodgepodge of architectural styles and living trees, its thousand secret places—and most of all, my grandmother's presence filling it, calm and sure, her unspoken love sustaining me every day.

"This bed isn't as comfortable as the ones at home," Whisper agreed, flexing his claws into it to test the truth of his words. I sat with him for a while in silence, trying to think how to ask the question I'd put off for too long already.

Except it wasn't really a question anymore.

"You're not just a chimera, are you," I said at last.

"I never claimed to be."

We'd all assumed, generation after generation, that he was a leftover creation of some previous Witch Lord, haunting the castle to carry out some long-ago mission given him by perhaps the Sycamore Lord himself. Gloamingard had so many protections woven around the Door; it had only made sense that Whisper was one of them, guarding his own lore and his own secrets.

It had only recently occurred to me that his connection to the gate might be more direct.

"My grandmother said you were neutral," I ventured carefully.

"I don't take sides in other people's squabbles." Whisper flicked an ear in distaste.

"Yet you came with me, when we left Morgrain."

"The Lady of Owls evicted me," he said, his tone offended. "It *is* her territory, and I dislike direct conflict, so I left."

"That's not the only reason, though," I pressed. "Is it?"

Whisper's tail swished across the bedspread. For a moment I thought he wouldn't answer.

"I know you want me to help you," he said at last, his voice gone serious as if he wrapped silk carefully around each precious word. "But terrible as the Dark Days were for humans, I assure you that if the Nine Demons go to war with one another, it will be far, far worse. Your world might not survive it."

"And so you stay neutral."

"Yes."

I fell silent. It sunk in that I was scratching the soft fur of a being of myth and legend. People cursed by him, Vaskandrans told their most bone-chilling campfire stories about him, and the Serene Empire deemed him the embodiment of evil itself.

A demon.

My friend.

"I'm glad you came with me," I murmured, because I was.

Maybe my family had been right all these years, when they told me I shouldn't trust him. Maybe I was damned for liking him. But if he was a scourge of humankind, well, he was remarkably restrained in his intrinsic evil. And he was good company, in his own way.

"Someone has to keep an eye on you," he said.

He closed both of his, signaling an end to his willingness to answer questions.

That night I lay awake in my strange bed in this strange place, unable to sleep despite the deep exhaustion pulling at every piece of me. The light was wrong, a thin wash of pale haze from luminaries in the fortress courtyard bleeding into the moonlight. The sounds were wrong, with the occasional murmur of distant conversation, the calling of the watch, and the sweet hourly chiming of a mantel clock instead of the whisper of wind through leaves and the hooting of owls. And the world felt dead around me, my atheling's senses blind outside Morgrain, giving me the impression I lay in a lifeless tomb.

It was the undigested lump of worry in my stomach, however, that kept me awake. All I could think of were the people I'd left behind: poor Odan, alone in Gloamingard with a demon. Jannah and Gaven and little Kip and all the castle staff, suddenly bereft of their home in a domain at the crux of a crisis the likes of which the world hadn't seen in four thousand years. My father, too stubborn to stay out of trouble, and my mother, embroiled deep in the problems of a country not her own. All my family, who I'd left to clean up my mess after promising myself over and over that I'd handle it myself—even Vikal, seasons spare him, who deserved a chance to grow into his responsibility. And most of all, the people I was sworn to protect. No matter what Odan had said, I felt like I'd abandoned all of them.

Something pricked at my senses. A tiny spark of life.

Tap tap tap, it went at my window.

I leaped out of bed and rushed to throw open the casement, where a small screech owl waited, its yellow eyes blazing fiercely as my grandmother's. It dropped a message cylinder with one scaly talon, fluffed its feathers, and sailed off into the night.

I opened the tiny case with shaking hands, tearing the paper as I worked it out of the tube. This could be from anyone, I reminded myself. All vivomancers sent owls for nighttime messages, for obvious reasons. And my grandmother didn't need an owl to communicate with me—she could seize control of me from a hundred miles away and make me write her message to myself.

It wasn't a comforting thought.

At last I laid the torn paper on the moonlit windowsill, and a bittersweet rush of relief and longing hit me at the sight of my father's plain, blocky handwriting.

Your mother and I are fine.

Talked to Vikal and got your latest message about Gloamingard. Will stay away.

Working on getting everyone from the land around the castle moved elsewhere.

No news yet, but you know your grandmother. She'll make a move soon.

Your uncle and I will take care of the domain. You take care of yourself.

I'll keep in touch.

Love, Da

I pressed the mangled paper flat against my chest, eyes squeezed shut, as if I could push this tiny piece of Morgrain through skin and bone into my heart.

"Dealing with magical problems in Eruvia is an irregular business," Foxglove said. He paced the Rookery sitting room—an elegant place very much in the style of the Serene Empire, all velvet curtains and oil paintings and delicate furniture with brocade cushions. Morning light streamed in through the windows. "Some years, there's not much to do. This is not going to be one of those years."

Ashe snorted from where she lounged by the fire. She still looked pale—even more so than usual—but her eyes held an alert spark, and I had no doubt she was ready to stab any demons who needed stabbing. "You could say that."

"The Witch Lords will have their Conclave," Foxglove continued. "The doge and the Council of Nine are closeted in Raverra, attempting to come up with a plan to deal with this situation. Both the Empire and Vaskandar are likely to have missions for us."

"And questions," Bastian added, clutching his little notebook.

"So many questions. They woke me up before dawn to get on the courier lamps with the doge."

"So much for that trip to the shore I've been talking about." Kessa sighed. She sat by Ashe, running her fingers through the pale tufts of her hair. Ashe didn't seem to mind at all.

"My point is that we need all the help we can get." Foxglove turned to Severin, who perched on the edge of his seat, clearly uncomfortable with all the lavish imperial fabrics and paintings and artifice devices around him. "Do you still want to travel with us on our missions, at least for now?"

"Yes, if you'll have me." Severin flashed a self-mocking smile. "I may not be the best companion, but I have nowhere else to go, and I want to see this through."

He tensed, and I could tell he was waiting for a harsh dismissal. Whatever treatment he was used to from living with his brother all these years, a warm welcome was no part of it.

Kessa whooped and Bastian grinned. Severin's eyes widened in surprise. I flashed him a broad smile.

Ashe showed her teeth. "Don't let it go to your head, mage boy."

"You won't be able to join us officially," Foxglove warned. "The Rookery has to maintain a careful balance in its membership, to ensure we remain neutral. We got permission to add Ryx because she's half-Raverran, but the uncontested heir to a Vaskandran domain might be a bit much for our superiors to swallow."

"That's quite all right," Severin said, still looking bemused. "I like the idea of being unofficial for a change. It sounds relaxing."

Foxglove turned to me. "And Ryx. Is it too much to assume you still want to stay with us?"

"My first and overwhelming priority is helping Morgrain." My hands tightened in my lap, stretching the leather of my gloves. "I need to deal with my grandmother somehow, and hunt down Aurelio and deal with him, too, and find a way to close off the gate."

Kessa chuckled. "You do realize you just listed off our top priorities as well, right?"

"Well, then it shouldn't be a problem to stay with the Rookery awhile." I let my shoulders relax a little. "I can think of no better position from which to try to help my family and the people of Morgrain, and no better company to do it with."

Foxglove lifted his glass to me, then nodded to Bastian. "Tell her," he said.

Bastian reached into a pocket and pulled out something slender and gleaming: the jess Aurelio had given me, which I'd turned in upon our arrival at Castle Ilseine. Its red glass beads winked in the light.

"The power returned to it once it was out of your possession for a while," he said. "A jess isn't normally reusable, but in this case I think it will work."

Hope leaped in my chest. "I can have a jess again?"

"I've studied it and consulted with Mews artificers over the courier lamps," Bastian said. "When you were unleashed, you drained the jess completely. Now that its power has returned, we believe it will be as if it were newly created. You can have it back if you like, but anytime your Falconer unleashes you, you'll have to take it off and give it at least a day to return to full strength before someone puts it on you again. And each time will be like the first time—you don't need to have the same Falconer."

"Which is good, because we're certainly not inviting Aurelio back," Kessa said with a shudder.

"In fact," Foxglove said dryly, "I used that unfortunate incident as leverage to get the Mews to agree to a special exception. The Rookery can function as honorary Falconers in your case— so we don't need to bring another outsider into our councils, or fear another betrayal. If you want this jess, you can have it today."

"Yes. I want it." I couldn't keep my voice from trembling. Hells, they were going to make me cry, right here in front of everyone. I could touch people again. I wouldn't have to wall myself away in some isolated tower after all.

"Then the only question that remains is who you want for your Falconer," Foxglove said, spreading his arms as if to encompass the entire Rookery. "At least for now. We can switch things around if, say, we need to split up—it's downright convenient."

This was real. They were going to let me stay with them, one of their company, and I wouldn't have to hide on the fringes anymore. I'd lost my home, at least for now, and that wound wouldn't stop bleeding until I could return to Morgrain; and whenever I thought of my grandmother, a black wave overwhelmed me. But I still had a place to belong, and people to belong to, in a way I'd never really had at Gloamingard with my own family.

"I trust any and all of you," I said, my voice thickening. "I don't know how to choose."

"You don't want me," Ashe said. "I'd forget to release you. I've usually got other things on my mind."

"Take Kessa," Bastian suggested. "She's the most sociable of all of us, and you want to be stuck with someone who's a good conversationalist."

I laughed. "All right."

This time, it was Kessa who slid the golden bracelet over my hand, a smile dancing in her eyes. I held my breath as the cool metal settled on my wrist.

The pressure of the air seemed to shift, the colors in the room to grow not duller, but more subtle. It was as if a noise I had been hearing for so long I'd learned to tune it out went silent.

Kessa hesitated. "Is it safe now?"

"I think so," I said, nervous. I held out my open palm, expecting her to try a quick, brushing touch.

She threw her arms around me, squeezing me tight. Bastian chuckled; Ashe let out an explosive breath.

"I'm going to die young, Kessa," she muttered. "Have mercy."

Kessa released me, and I grinned at the Rookery, my heart full. Ashe clapped my shoulder, and Severin reached out to squeeze my hand, sending an entirely different sort of warm tingle across my palm.

I clung to this moment, desperate to keep it forever. Everyone's smiling faces welcoming me, rejoicing in each other. They didn't care that my magic was broken—no; they celebrated it. They were all broken too, in their own ways, and ultimately stronger for it.

"We've got work ahead of us," Foxglove said, his brows descending in a solemn valley over his piercing eyes. "I won't lie to you—we've never had the odds stacked this deep against us. I'll have to ask you to go into some dark and terrible places with me if we're going to have any hope of carrying light through to the other side."

"Oh, stuff the doom and despair, Foxglove." Ashe flashed sharp teeth at him. "You should know by now that I don't care how big and nasty our enemy is. I just jump in and start stabbing."

"We had noticed that, yes," Kessa said, with an air of affectionate weariness.

"I was getting to a point," Foxglove protested, with an injured look.

"I'm sure you were." Kessa patted him on the shoulder. "Alas, it's too late now. Ashe, let Foxglove make his point next time."

Severin and I exchanged a glance; amusement danced in his

eyes. He hadn't taken his hand back, and I wasn't going to let go until he did. A glowing warmth spread through me like tea with rich honey.

Foxglove didn't have to make his point; I knew what he'd been about to say.

None of us had to do this alone.

The story continues in . . .

THE QUICKSILVER COURT

Book Two of Rooks and Ruin

Coming in 2021!

ACKNOWLEDGMENTS

This book began as a series of excited messages back and forth with my agent, Naomi Davis, who is fantastic to brainstorm with as well as being the best champion any author could ask for. It grew and got better with feedback from my fabulous long-time beta reader, Natsuko Toyofuku, and critique partner, Deva Fagan. It flourished (after some hard work) under the insightful editorial guidance of my amazing editor, Sarah Guan, and my fantastic UK editor, Emily Byron; and it reached its final evolution with the help of my incredible new editor, Nivia Evans. This book would not have existed without all of them—or at the very least would have been a lot worse—and I am profoundly grateful.

I couldn't have done it without the unflagging support of my family. My husband, Jesse King, and my daughters, Maya and Kyra, encouraged me with patience and enthusiasm, taking on my chores when things got rough; Maya was my sounding board when I needed to talk through plot or character problems. My friends had my back as well, cheering me on through daily word-count updates and understanding when I had to disappear into the writing cave for a while. And I am reminded quite insistently (through vigorous headbutting) that I also received a great deal of "help" from my loyal dog, Freya, and our cats: Ninja, Star, and Tiggy.

An astounding amount of work goes into making a finished book. Entire universes cannot contain my delight at the gorgeous cover by Lisa Marie Pompilio and Peter Bollinger, or the wonderful map by Tim Paul. My gratitude goes out to my copyeditor, Kelley Frodel, for exacting attention to detail; my production editor, Bryn A. McDonald, for taking this book to its final form; and my publicist, Ellen Wright, for preparing its way into the world. Thank you to the entire Orbit team for taking such incredibly good care of my book baby.

Last but not least, thank you, my readers, for letting me tell you this story. As I lob these words into the void, it means everything to me that you're there to catch them. In your hands, their journey is complete.

extras

about the author

Melissa Caruso was born on the summer solstice and went to school in an old mansion with a secret door, but despite this auspicious beginning has yet to develop any known super-powers. Melissa has spent her whole life creating imaginary worlds, and in addition to writing is also an avid LARPer and tabletop gamer.

She graduated with honors in creative writing from Brown University and has an MFA in fiction from the University of Massachusetts Amherst. Melissa's first novel, *The Tethered Mage*, was shortlisted for a Gemmell Morningstar Award for best fantasy debut.

Find out more about Melissa Caruso and other Orbit authors by registering online for the free monthly newsletter at www.orbitbooks.net.

if you enjoyed
THE OBSIDIAN TOWER

look out for

THERE WILL COME
A DARKNESS

by

Katy Rose Pool

THE AGE OF DARKNESS APPROACHES. FIVE LIVES STAND IN ITS WAY. WHO WILL STOP IT . . . OR UNLEASH IT?

For generations, the Seven Prophets guided humanity. Using their visions of the future, they ended wars and united nations – until they disappeared, one hundred years ago.

But they left behind one final, secret prophecy, foretelling an Age of Darkness and the birth of a new Prophet who could be the world's salvation . . . or the cause of its destruction. As a dark new power begins to make war on the magically gifted, five souls are set on a collision course that will determine the fate of their world:

A prince exiled from his kingdom
A ruthless killer known as the Pale Hand
A once-faithful leader torn between his duty and his heart
A reckless gambler with the power to find anything or anyone
And a dying girl on the verge of giving up

One of them – or all of them – could break the world. Will they be saviour or destroyer?

if you enjoyed
THE OBSIDIAN TOWER
look out for
THERE WILL COME
A DARKNESS
by
Katy Rose Pool

1

EPHYRA

IN THE MOONLIT ROOM OVERLOOKING THE CITY OF FAITH, A PRIEST KNELT before Ephyra and begged for his life.

"Please," he said. "I don't deserve to die. Please. I won't touch them anymore, I swear. Have mercy."

Around him, the lavish private room at the Thalassa Gardens taverna lay in disarray. A sumptuous feast spilled from overturned platters and filigreed pitchers. The white marble floor was littered with ripe berries and the smashed remains of a dozen tiny jewel-like bottles. A pool of blood-dark wine slowly spread toward the kneeling priest.

Ephyra crouched down, placing her palm upon the papery skin of his cheek.

"Oh, thank you!" the priest cried, tears springing into his eyes. "Thank you, blessed—"

"I wonder," Ephyra said. "Did your victims ever beg you for mercy? When you were leaving your bruises on their bodies, did they ever cry out in Behezda's name?"

He choked on a breath.

"They didn't, did they? You plied them with your monstrous potion to make them docile so you could hurt them without ever having to see their pain," she said. "But I want you to know that every mark you left on them left a mark on you, too."

"*Please.*"

A breeze rustled in from the open balcony doors behind Ephyra as she tilted the priest's chin toward her. "You've been marked for death. And death has come to collect."

His terror-struck eyes gazed up at Ephyra as she slid her hand to his throat, where she could feel the rapid tap-tap-tap of his pulse. She focused on the rush of blood beneath his flesh and drew the *esha* from his body.

The light drained from the priest's eyes as his lungs sputtered out their last breath. He collapsed to the floor. A handprint, as pale as the moon, glowed against the sallow skin of his throat. Dead, and only a single mark to show for it.

Drawing the dagger from her belt, Ephyra leaned over the corpse. The priest had not been alone when she'd found him. The two girls he'd had with him—hollow-eyed girls, their wrists mottled with green and purple bruises—had fled the moment Ephyra had told them to run, as if they couldn't help but obey.

Ephyra slid the tip of her blade into the flesh of the priest's throat, cutting a line of red through the pale handprint. As dark blood oozed out, she turned the dagger over and opened the compartment in its hilt to extract the vial within. She held it under the flow of his blood. The priest's desperate words had been a lie—he *did* deserve death. But that wasn't why she'd taken his life.

She had taken his life because she needed it.

The door burst open, startling Ephyra from her task. The vial slipped from her hand. She fumbled with it but caught it.

"Don't move!"

Three men spilled into the suite, one holding a crossbow, and the other two with sabers. Sentry. Ephyra wasn't surprised. Thalassa sat at the edge of Elea Square, just within the High City gates. She'd known from staking it out that the Sentry ran their foot patrols through the square every night. But they'd gotten here quicker than she'd expected.

The first Sentry through the door stopped short, staring at the priest's body, stunned. "He's dead!"

Ephyra sealed the vial of blood and hid it back within the dagger's hilt. She drew herself up, touching the black silk that covered the bottom of her face to make sure it was still in place.

"Come quietly," the first Sentry said slowly, "and you don't have to get hurt."

Ephyra's pulse hammered in her throat, but she made her voice calm. Fearless. "Take another step and there will be more than one body in this room."

The Sentry hesitated. "She's bluffing."

"No, she isn't," the one with the crossbow said nervously. He glanced down at the priest's corpse. "Look at the handprint. Just like the ones they found on the bodies in Tarsepolis."

"The Pale Hand," the third Sentry whispered, frozen as he stared at Ephyra.

"That's just street lore," the first Sentry said, but his voice was trembling slightly. "No one is so powerful that they can kill with only the Grace of Blood."

"What are you doing in Pallas Athos?" the third Sentry asked her. He stood with his chest out and his feet apart, as if staring down a beast. "Why have you come here?"

"You call this place the City of Faith," Ephyra said. "But corruption and evil fester behind these white walls. I will mark them the way

I mark my victims, so the rest of the world can see that the City of Faith is the city of the fallen."

This was a lie. Ephyra had not come to the City of Faith to stain it with blood. But only two other people in the world knew the real reason, and one of them was waiting for her.

She moved toward the window. The Sentry tensed, but none tried to go after her.

"You won't get away with killing a priest so easily," the first said. "When we tell the Conclave what you've done—"

"Tell them." She tugged her black hood over her head. "Tell them the Pale Hand came for the priest of Pallas. And tell them to pray that I don't come for them next."

She turned to the balcony, throwing open the satin drapes to the night and the moon that hung like a scythe in the sky.

The Sentry shouted after her, their blustering voices overlapping as Ephyra flew to the edge of the balcony and climbed over the marble balustrade. The world tipped—four stories below, the steps of Thalassa's entrance gleamed like ivory teeth in the moonlight. She gripped the edge of the balustrade and turned. To her left, the roof of the public baths sloped toward her.

Ephyra leapt, launching herself toward it. Squeezing her eyes shut, she tucked her knees and braced for impact. She hit the roof at a roll and waited for her own momentum to slow before picking herself up and racing across it, the voices of the Sentry and the lights of Thalassa fading into the night.

Ephyra moved through the mausoleum like a shadow. The sanctum was still and silent in the predawn darkness as she picked her way through broken marble and other rubble around the tiled scrying pool in the center, the only part of the shrine left unscorched. Above, the caved-in roof gave way to the sky.

The ruins of the mausoleum sat just outside the High City gates, close enough that Ephyra could easily sneak back into the Low City without drawing notice. She didn't know exactly when the mausoleum had been burned down, but it was all but abandoned now, making it the perfect hideout. She slipped through the scorched shrine into the crypt. The stairwell creaked and moaned as she climbed down and wrenched open the rotted wood door to the alcove that had served as her home for the past few weeks. Shedding her mask and hood, she crept inside.

The alcove used to be a storeroom for the acolyte caretakers who had tended to the shrine. Now it was abandoned, left for rats, rot, and for people like Ephyra who didn't mind the other two.

"You're late."

Ephyra peered through the darkened room to the bed that lay in the corner, shadowed by the tattered sheets that hung over it. Her sister's dark eyes peered back at her.

"I know," Ephyra said, folding the mask and hood over the back of the chair.

A book slid from Beru's chest as she sat up, its pages fluttering as it bounced onto the sheets. Her short, curly hair was raked up on one side. "Everything go all right?"

"Fine." No point telling how close her escape had been. It was done now. She forced a smile on her face. "Come on, Beru, you know my days of falling off slyhouse roofs are behind me. I'm better than that now."

When Ephyra had first assumed the mask of the Pale Hand, she hadn't been quite as good at sneaking around and climbing as she was now. Having the Grace of Blood didn't help her sneak into crime dens or scale rich merchants' balconies. She'd had to gain such skills the traditional way, spending countless nights honing her balance, reaction time, and strength, as well as gathering information necessary for specific targets. Beru had joined her, when she was well enough, racing Ephyra to see who could climb a fence faster or leap between rooftops more quietly. They'd spent many nights stealing through the shadows, tailing behind a potential mark to learn vices and habits. After years of training and close calls, Ephyra knew how to get in and out of the dangerous situations she courted as the Pale Hand.

Beru returned her sister's smile weakly.

Ephyra's own smile faded, seeing the pain in Beru's eyes. "Come on," she said softly.

Beru lifted the rough blanket away from her body. Beneath it, she was shivering, her brown skin ashen in the low light. Tired lines had etched themselves into the skin below her bloodshot eyes.

Ephyra frowned, turning to the crate beside Beru's bed, where a shallow bowl rested. She opened the compartment in her dagger's hilt and poured the contents of the vial into the bowl. "We let this go for too long."

"It's fine," Beru hissed through clenched teeth. "I'm fine." She unwrapped the cotton from her left wrist, revealing the black handprint that marred the skin beneath it.

Ephyra pressed her hand into the bowl, coating it with wet blood. Placing her bloody palm over the dark handprint on her sister's skin, she closed her eyes and focused on the blood, guiding the *esha* she'd taken from the priest and directing it into her sister.

The blood Ephyra collected from her victims acted as a conduit to the *esha* she drained from them. If she were a properly trained healer, she would have known the correct patterns of binding that would tether her victims' *esha* to Beru. She wouldn't need to use the binding of blood.

Then again, if Ephyra were properly trained, she wouldn't have been killing in the first place. Healers with the Grace of Blood took an oath that forbid drawing *esha* from another person.

But this was the only way to keep her sister alive.

"There," Ephyra said, pressing a finger into Beru's skin, which was starting to lose that worrying grayish tinge. "All better."

For now, Beru didn't say, but Ephyra could see the words in her sister's eyes. Beru reached over and opened the drawer of the table beside the bed, withdrawing a thin black stylus. With careful, practiced motions, she pressed the stylus against her wrist, drawing a small, straight line there. It joined the thirteen others, permanently etched in alchemical ink.

Fourteen people killed. Fourteen lives cut short so that Beru could live.

It wasn't lost on Ephyra, the way Beru marked her skin each time Ephyra marked another victim. She could see the way the guilt ate at her sister after every death. The people Ephyra killed were far from innocent, but that didn't seem to matter to Beru.

"This could be the last time we have to do this," Ephyra said quietly.

This was the real reason they'd come to Pallas Athos. Somewhere in this city of fallen faith and crumbling temples, there was a person who knew a way to heal Beru for good. It was the only thing Ephyra had hoped for in the last five years.

Beru looked away.

"I brought you something else," Ephyra said, making her voice light. She reached into the little bag that hung at her belt and held out a glass bottle stopper she'd picked off the ground in the priest's room. "I thought you could use it for the bracelet you're making."

Beru took the bottle stopper, turning it over in her hand. It looked like a little jewel.

"You know I'm not going to let anything happen to you," Ephyra said, covering her sister's hand with her own.

"I know." Beru swallowed. "You're always worrying about me. Sometimes I think that's all you do. But, you know, I worry about you, too. Every time you're out there."

Ephyra tapped her finger against Beru's cheek in reproach. "I won't get hurt."

Beru brushed her thumb across the fourteen ink lines on her wrist. "That's not what I mean."

Ephyra drew her hand away. "Go to sleep."

Beru rolled over, and Ephyra climbed into the bed beside her. She lay listening to her sister's even breaths, thinking about the worry that Beru would not give name to. Ephyra worried, too, on nights like tonight, when she felt her victims' pulse slow and then stop, when she pulled the last dregs of life from them. Their eyes went dark, and Ephyra felt a sweet, sated relief, and in equal measure, a deep, inescapable fear—that killing monsters was turning her into one.